DANTE ALIGHIERI

THE DIVINE COMEDY

Translated by Lawrence Grant White

DANTE ALIGHIERI

DANTE ALIGHIERI
The Divine Comedy

THE INFERNO, PURGATORIO, AND PARADISO

A New Translation into English Blank Verse
by LAWRENCE GRANT WHITE

with Illustrations by GUSTAVE DORÉ

NEW YORK: PANTHEON BOOKS
MCMXLVIII

Designed by Richard Ellis

TO

MARGARET WARD CHANLER

"Pero se le mie rime avran difetto, . : :
Di cio si biasmi il debole intelletto
E 'l parlar noſtro che non ha valore
Di ritrar tutto . . ."

DANTE, CONVIVIO, III.

TRANSLATOR'S NOTE

Iɴ *the Divine Comedy Dante describes his imaginary journey through Hell, Purgatory, and Paradise. No other poem in any language has had such a wide appeal: the conception is so lofty, the music so beautiful, and the interest of the narrative so sustained, that its importance has steadily increased. For the last six hundred years learned commentaries have been accumulating; and so, inevitably, have the translations.*

The luckless translator can never recapture the beauty of Dante's music. He must try to convey the meaning, often obscure, as musically as he can in another tongue. In this version the aim has been to tell Dante's story as simply and accurately as possible. Any archaic and unfamiliar constructions that would impede the swift pace of the narrative have been avoided, although the second person singular has been used in the Paradiso—for such is the language of heaven.

As the "terza rima" form of the original is alien to English, blank verse has been chosen, the form used by Milton in Paradise Lost. In his foreword to that poem, he says: "The measure is English heroic verse without rime, as that of Homer in Greek, and of Virgil in Latin—rime being no necessary adjunct or true ornament of poem or good verse, in longer works especially, but the invention of a barbarous age, to set off wretched matter and lame metre; graced indeed since by the use of some famous modern poets, carried away by custom, but much to their own vexation, hindrance, and constraint to express many things otherwise, and for the most part worse, than else they would have expressed them."

It is natural that the scenes so vividly described by Dante should have inspired many artists—such as Botticelli, Flaxman and Blake—to depict them. Most famous of all the illustrations are those of Gustave Doré (1833-1883) whose dramatic portrayals, particularly of the horrors of the Inferno, are unsurpassed. A careful selection, reproduced from the original illustrations, embellish this edition.

The translator has benefited from the fine scholarship of William Warren Vernon's "Readings," and also from Charles Eliot Norton's prose translation. Grateful acknowledgment is due to Mr. Alexander Harvey for his painstaking and salutary criticism.

LAWRENCE GRANT WHITE

St. James, Long Island

CONTENTS: *INFERNO*

CONTENTS: *PURGATORIO*

CONTENTS: *PARADISO*

DANTE ALIGHIERI

THE DIVINE COMEDY

INFERNO

Canto 1 : Dante astray in the Dusky Wood

DANTE ALIGHIERI
THE DIVINE COMEDY

INFERNO
Canto 1

Midway upon the journey of our life
I found that I was in a dusky wood;
For the right path, whence I had strayed, was lost.
Ah me! How hard a thing it is to tell
The wildness of that rough and savage place,
The very thought of which brings back my fear!
So bitter was it, death is little more so:
But that the good I found there may be told,
I will describe the other things I saw.

   How I arrived there, it were hard to tell:
So weary was my mind, so filled with sleep,
I reeled, and wandered from the path of truth.
When I had come before a mountain's base—
The ending of that steep and rugged valley
That lately had so struck my heart with fear—
I raised my eyes, and saw the mountain's shoulder
Already covered by the planet's rays
That safely guide the steps of other men.
Then was my terror somewhat quieted
That through the last night's anguish I had borne
Within the very wellsprings of my heart.
Like one who having battled with the waves,
In safety on the shore, with panting breath
Looks back upon the perils of the deep:
So did my soul, which still in terror fled,
Turn back to contemplate with awe and fear
That pass which man had never left alive.

   After my weary body had been rested,
Again I started up the desert steep,
So that my lower foot was e'er the firmer.
When lo! Close to the bottom of the mount,
A leopardess, light-poised and passing swift,
Her hide all covered o'er with inky spots!
She always stood before me, face to face,
Blocking my path whenever I advanced,
So that I turned and turned again in vain.
   'Twas at the very earliest flush of dawn;
The sun was rising, placed among those stars
Which were surrounding him, when Love Divine
First set those heavenly things upon their course.
The time of day, the soft air of the season
Emboldened me to hope I might prevail
Against that beast with gaily spotted hide—
But not enough to overcome my fear
When I beheld a lion in my path.
He seemed as if he were advancing on me,
His head erect, by rabid hunger driven,
So that the very air did seem afraid!
A she-wolf stood beside him, gaunt and grim,
Whose leanness showed her hunger unappeased,
Though many she had caused to live in woe.
So heavily she bore my spirits down
With terror which her very aspect caused,
That I lost hope of making the ascent.

1

And as a man who glories in his gains,
When comes the time that all he has is lost,
Despairs, his thoughts oppressed by misery:
So I became before that restless beast
Which, coming on against me step by step,
Made me retreat to where the sun is still.

While I was stumbling down to lower ground,
Before my startled eyes appeared a man
Whose voice seemed weak from long-continued
⌊silence;

And when I saw him in that desert place,
«Help, pity me,» I cried, «whate'er you are,
A living man, or spectre from the shades!»

He answered me: «No man am I, though once
A man I was—from Lombard parents sprung
Who both were citizens of Mantua.
Late in the time of Julius I was born,
And lived in Rome while great Augustus reigned,
When false and lying gods still held their sway.
I was a poet, and sang the worthy son
Born to Anchises, who escaped from Troy
After proud Ilion was burned to ashes.
But why do you return to so much woe?
Why not climb upward to that happy mountain,
The origin and cause of every joy?»

«Are you then Virgil—that great fountainhead
Whence such a flood of eloquence has flowed?»
I answered him abashed, with forehead bowed.
«O light and honor of all other poets,
May my long faithful study of your book,
And my great love for it, avail me now!
You are my master, and my very author:
It is from you alone that I have taken
The lofty style for which men honor me.
See yonder beast, from which I turned away:
Protect me from her, O illustrious sage—
My blood is trembling in my veins from fear!»

«Another passage you must seek,» he said,
Perceiving that my eyes were filled with tears,
«If you would safely leave this savage place.
For that wild beast which makes you cry aloud
Suffers no man to pass along her way,
But blocks his passage till he has been slain.

Her nature is so evil and malign
That never is her greedy will appeased:
Food only makes her hungrier than before.
With many another animal she has bred,
And will with many more, until such time
The Hound shall come, to make her die of grief—
That Hound who shall not feed upon the land
Or riches, but on wisdom, love, and valor.
His fatherland shall lie between the Feltres:
The savior, he, of fallen Italy
For whom the maid Camilla died, and Turnus,
Euryalus, and Nixus shed their blood.
Through every city he shall drive her on
Until again she takes her place in hell,
Whence envy sent her forth to plague mankind.
Wherefore I think that it were best for you
To follow me: and I shall be your guide
To lead you hence through that eternal place
Where you shall hear despairing cries of woe,
And see the ancient spirits in their grief
Proclaiming they have died a second death.
Then you shall look on those who are content
To burn in flames, because they hope to join,
Whenever it may be, the blessed throng.
But should you wish to reach the realms of bliss,
For that there'll be a worthier soul than I:
I'll leave you in her care when I depart.
For the great Emperor who rules above
Forbids that I, rebellious to His law,
Approach unto His glorious citadel.
The Lord who ruleth all there sits on high:
There is His city, there His lofty throne.
How happy there is he whom God hath chosen!»

And I to him: «O poet, I beseech you,
By that same God whom you have never known,
That I may flee this wickedness, and worse!
O lead me where you said but now awhile,
So that I may behold St. Peter's gate,
And those you say are so oppressed by grief.»
Then he moved on: I followed in his steps.

2

Canto 1 : The Lion suddenly confronts Dante

CANTO 2

THE day was going, and the dusky air
Unburdened all the creatures of the earth
Of weary toil. I now prepared myself
To face alone the struggle of the journey,
And too, the piteous sights that I must see,
Of which my faithful memory shall tell.

O Muses, O great genius, aid me now!
O memory, that wrote down what I saw,
Here shall your noble character be shown!

I thus began: «O poet, my true guide,
Consider if my courage will suffice
Ere you commit me to such high endeavor.
You tell of how the sire of Silvius,
While yet corruptible, attained the sphere
Eternal, and was there in flesh and blood:
And if the Adversary of All Wrong
Treated him graciously, and bore in mind
His destiny, and who and what he was,
It does not seem unjust, to one of knowledge.
Chosen was he in heaven empyrean
To father Rome and all her mighty realm;
And they were both ordained, if truth be told,
To be established in that holy place
Where now great Peter's follower sits enthroned.
By going there—for which you give him praise—
He learned those things which were to be the cause
Of his own victory, and the papal rule.
The Chosen Vessel went there afterward
To bring back comfort thence unto that faith
Which is the starting of salvation's way.
But I—why should I go? By whose decree?
I am not Paul, nor am I yet Aeneas,
But deemed unworthy by myself and others.
Wherefore, if I allow myself to go,

I fear it would be folly. You are wise,
And understand what I have left unsaid.»
    Like one who wished undone what he had
                                ⌊wished,
Shifting his purpose when his mind is changed,
And thus abandons what he has begun:
Just so was I, upon that dusky slope,
For in my thoughts I dropped that enterprise
Which at the outset sped along so fast.

«If I have well construed what you have said,»
That shade magnanimous replied to me,
«Your soul is now oppressed with cowardice,
Which often is a stumbling block to man,
To turn him backward from a worthy start,
As fancied sights will cause a beast to shy.
So that this fear you have may be dissolved,
I'll tell you why I came, and what I heard
At the first moment that I grieved for you.

«I was among those spirits in suspense;
A blessed lovely woman called to me—
At once I asked her what was her command.
Her eyes were gleaming brighter than a star
When she replied to me in accents mild,
Her voice serene, and like an angel's clear:
'O courteous soul of Mantua, whose fame
Has long endured upon the earth above,
And shall endure as long as time shall move:
A friend of mine—but fortune's enemy—
Is so beset upon the desert slope
That fear has turned him back upon his way.
I am afraid lest he has strayed so far
That I have come too late to succor him,
According to what I have heard in heaven.
Go—with your graceful speech encourage him,
And help him, with whatever he may need
To save him, so that I may be consoled.
Beatrice am I who asks that you should go.
That place I come from, I would seek again.
By agency of love I move and speak;
And when again I go before my Lord,
I oftentimes shall sing your praise to Him.'

«When she was silent I replied to her:
'O lady virtuous, through whom alone

The human race surpasses all contained
Within that heaven of the smallest circles,
So pleasing to myself is your command
That were it done, it still would seem too late:
Nor need your purpose further be disclosed.
But tell me why you have not been afraid
Of coming downward to this lower ring
From that wide sphere you wish to seek again?'

«'Since you desire so earnestly to know,
I'll tell you briefly,' Beatrice replied,
'Why I am not afraid to enter here.
One should be fearful only of those things
Which have the power to harm one's fellow men—
Not of the rest, which give no cause for fear.
By God's own grace, I have been so composed
That by your misery I am untouched,
Nor can I be assailed by yonder flames.
A Lady Most Compassionate, in heaven,
Takes so much pity on this man's sad plight
That she assails the cruel decree on high.
She sought Lucia, and addressed her thus:
«Your faithful one is now in need of you,
And I commend him to your loving care.»

«'Lucia, enemy of cruelty,
Moved, and came to where I chanced to be,
Time-honored Rachel sitting by my side.
Said she: «O Beatrice, true praise of God,
Why not assist this man whose love for you
Is such that he has left the vulgar throng?
Can you not hear the anguish in his cry?
Can you not see the death that threatens him
Above that stream that flows not to the sea?»

«'Never on earth was anyone so swift
To seek his good or shun his ill, as I—
The moment that these words had been
⌊pronounced—
Came hither, downward from my blessed seat,
Relying on the power of your word,
Which honors you, as well as those that hear it.'

«And after she had spoken to me thus,
She wept, and turned on me her radiant eyes,
Whereby she made me still more quick to go:
And so I came to you, as she had wished,

And took you from before the savage beast
That blocked your passage up the mountainside.
Therefore, what troubles you? Why hestitate?
Why is your heart oppressed by cowardice,
Why do you lack in courage and in zeal
When three such blessed women there on high
Now plead your cause before the court of heaven,
And I myself do prophesy such good?»

As flowers bent down and closed by frost of
⌊night,

When brightened later by the morning sun
Stand upright on their stems, with petals wide:
Just so I stiffened my exhausted spirit.
An ardor so benign suffused my heart
That I began to speak like one set free:
«How full of pity, she who succored me!
How kind are you, so swiftly to obey
The words of truth that she addressed to you!
For by your arguments you have disposed
My heart to such an eagerness to go
That to my first intent I have returned.
Lead on! May one sole will inspire us both:
Be you my leader, you my lord and master!»
Thus did I speak; and after he had moved,
I entered on the roadway deep and wild.

CANTO
3

Tʜʀᴏᴜɢʜ ᴍᴇ ʟɪᴇs ᴛʜᴇ ʀᴏᴀᴅ ᴛᴏ ᴛʜᴇ
CITY OF GRIEF.
THROUGH ME LIES THE PATHWAY TO WOE
EVERLASTING.
THROUGH ME LIES THE ROAD TO THE SOULS
THAT ARE LOST.
JUSTICE IMPELLED MY MIGHTY ARCHITECT:
THE POWER DIVINE, AND PRIMAL LOVE AND
WISDOM
SURPASSING ALL, HAVE HERE
CONSTRUCTED ME.

Canto 2 : The Darkening Sky of the First Night

INFERNO: CANTO 3

BEFORE I WAS CREATED, NOTHING WAS
SAVE THINGS ETERNAL. I SHALL LAST
                      FOREVER.
ABANDON HOPE, ALL YE WHO ENTER HERE!

    In characters obscure, above a gate
I saw these words inscribed upon the rock.
«Master,» I said, «their meaning bodes me ill!»

    He answered me like one of understanding:
«Here must all misgiving be cast off;
All cowardice must here be overcome.
For now we have approached unto that place
Of which I spoke, where you shall see those souls
Who mourn the lack of intellect's true light.»

    Then, after he had placed his hand in mine,
With radiant countenance that gave me heart,
He led me onward to the things unknown.

    Here sighs and wails and shrieks of every sort
Reverberated in the starless air,
So that at first it made me weep to hear.
In divers tongues, in accents horrible,
With groans of agony and screams of rage,
In voices weak and shrill, with sounds of blows,
A ceaseless tumult's everlasting roar
Seethed round about that timeless blackened air,
As sand is tossed before the whirlwind's blast.
I asked him, with my head in horror bound:
«O master, tell me what is this I hear,
And who are these so overcome by grief?»

    He answered me: «This miserable lot
Befalls the woe-begotten souls of those
Who lived their lives with neither praise nor
                       ⌊blame.

Commingled with them here, that wretched choir
Of angels stand, who selfishly refused
To keep their faith with God, or to rebel.
Heaven expelled them, not to be less fair;
And yet deep hell refuses to receive them.»

    And I: «O master, what can be the grief,
That makes them thus lament so bitterly?»

    He answered: «I will tell you very briefly.
These have no hope of death; existence here
Is so degraded and obscure, that they
Are envious of any other lot.

The world above has put them out of mind:
Mercy and justice scorn them, both alike.
We won't discuss them. Look, and pass them by.»

    And as I looked, I saw a standard borne
So swiftly round about that it appeared
As if it were disdainful of repose.
Behind it surged so vast a multitude
Of souls, that I should never have believed
That death had overthrown so great a throng.
When I beheld there some that I had known,
I saw, and knew at once, the shade of him
Who basely made the great renunciation.
Forthwith I understood, and felt assured
That I had come among that wretched crew
Which God and all His foes abominate.
These abject cowards who had never lived
Were naked, and were stung incessantly
By monstrous flies and wasps that swarmed about
                       ⌊them,

Making their faces run with streams of blood
That, mingled with their tears, in slimy pools
Lay round their feet, devoured by loathsome
                       ⌊worms.

    And when I turned my eyes to look beyond,
On a great river's bank, I saw a throng,
So that I said: «My goodly master, grant
That I may know who yonder spirits are,
And why it seems, by this dim light, as if
Some reason makes them eager to cross over.»

    And he to me: «These things will be explained
In time, when we shall bring our steps to halt
Upon the dismal shore of Acheron.»

    With eyes downcast in shame, and fearing lest
My speech offend the sage, I held my tongue
Until we came upon the river's brink.

    And lo! Toward us came, upon a bark,
An ancient man whose hair was long and white.
He cried: «Beware, beware, ye guilty souls!
Nor ever hope to see the sky again:
I come to take you to the other bank,
To everlasting gloom and flames and ice.
And you, a living soul that still draws breath,
Begone from those who are already dead!»

5

But when he saw I did not go away,
He said: «Not here, but by another road,
Through other portals, you shall reach the shore:
A lighter bark must carry you across.»

«Charon,» my leader said, «why vex yourself?
It is so willed where there is power to do
That which is willed: and therefore ask no more!»

By this were quieted the hoary cheeks
Of the fell boatman of that dark lagoon,
Whose eyes were ringed about with wheels of
                                    ⌊flame.

But now those souls, those naked, weary souls
Grew pale, and seemed to gnash their teeth in rage
As soon as they had heard those cruel words.
They cursed the name of God, their parents'
                                    ⌊names,

The human race, the time, the place, the seed
That had begotten them, and their descendants.
Then all of them together, with loud cries
Withdrew themselves from that accursed shore
Which waits for every man that fears not God.
The demon Charon, with his eyes of coals,
Beckoned to them and herded them together,
Beating to earth the laggards with his oar.

As when in autumn, leaves forsake a tree
And drop down one by one, until each branch
Sees that its spoils are all returned to earth:
Just so fell Adam's evil seed; so now,
Like falcon swooping downward to its lure,
Each shade, when called, plunged downward from
                                    ⌊the bank.

Thus they departed on the murky stream;
And ere they landed on the other shore
Another throng had gathered in their place.

«My son,» the gracious master said to me,
«All those who perish in the wrath of God
Must come together here from every land,
And all wait eagerly to cross the stream.
For heavenly justice now so spurs them onward
That fear is changed for them into desire.
Here may no worthy spirit ever pass;
And hence, if Charon has complained of you,
Well should you grasp the meaning of his words!»

6

When this was said, the darkened countryside
Shook with a mighty spasm of such force
That thinking of it bathes me still in sweat.
The anguished earth gave forth a blast of wind
That lit the sky with a vermilion glow.
This snatched my senses from me, and I fell
As one who falls when stricken with a swoon.

CANTO 4

A CLAP of thunder broke the bonds of sleep
Within my brain, so that I started up
Like one who has been roused by violence.
With rested eyes, I looked about the scene:
I rose erect, and with attentive gaze
I sought to recognize my whereabouts.
In truth I found that I was on the brink
That rims the gulf of the abyss of woe,
Which echoes with eternal cries of grief.
So deep it was, so cloudy and obscure,
That nothing there could possibly be seen,
However I might peer into its depths.

«Into that sightless world let us descend,»
The poet said, his face as pale as death.
«I shall go first, and you shall come behind.»

Perceiving his pale hue, I questioned him:
«How shall I go, when you, my only hope
Of comfort for my fears, do fear as well?»

He answered me: «The anguish of these people
Who suffer here, has painted on my face
Compassion—which you misread as fear.
Let us be on: our road is long and hard.»

Then he stepped forth, and ushered me within
The topmost ring that girdles the abyss.

But in this ring—as far as one could judge—
There were no cries of woe, but only sighs

Canto 3 : The Doomed Souls embarking to cross the Acheron

INFERNO: CANTO 4

That quivered in the everlasting air.
This murmur came from multitudes of men,
Of women, and of children, who bewailed,
But suffered not. My goodly master said:
«You do not ask me who these spirits are
We see about us. Ere we pass beyond,
I wish to tell you that they have not sinned.
Though they are worthy, this does not suffice,
Because they never have received the joy
Of holy baptism, essence of your faith.
But those who lived before the time of Christ,
Could never worthily adore their God:
And I myself am of this company.
For this defect, and for no other wrong,
Our souls are lost: for this we must endure
A hopeless life of unfulfilled desire.»

My heart was stricken when I understood;
For I knew there were many worthy souls
Eternally suspended there in limbo.
«Tell me, my master, tell me, gracious lord,»
Said I, desiring to be assured
Of that great faith that overcomes all error,
«Has no one yet, by merit of his own,
Or other's help, gone forth from here to heaven?»

Unto my hidden thought he made reply:
«When I was still but new in this estate,
To us came One upon whose noble brow
A great victorious diadem shone forth.
From here he led away the shade of him
Who first was father; Abel's shade, his son's;
Noah's, and Moses', giver of the laws;
The shades of Abraham the patriarch,
Of David; Israel's, his sire's and sons';
And Rachel's, for whose sake He did so much,
And many more. These He beatified.
Moreover, know that previous to that time,
No human spirits ever had been saved.»

We did not halt while he was saying this,
But walked along until we had passed through
That mighty forest of suspended souls.

We had not travelled far from where I swooned
When I beheld a point of flame that cut
A hemisphere of brilliance in the night.

Although we were a little way removed,
We still were near enough to ascertain
That honorable folk were gathered there.
«O you who honor every art and science,
What souls are these? And what their special worth
That keeps them thus from other souls apart?»

He said: «Their honorable fame on earth,
Resounding in their mortal life, has gained them
Grace in heaven, and this distinction here.»

Meanwhile I heard a voice that said to us:
«All honor to the poet sublime whose shade
Had left us, but returns to us again!»

And when the voice was silent, I beheld
Four stately shades that were approaching us
With neither joy nor sorrow in their mien.
My goodly master now began to speak:
«Mark him who with that mighty sword in hand
Comes leading those three others, as their master:
For he is Homer, sovereign lord of poets;
And Horace next him there, the satirist;
Ovid, the third; and Lucan walks behind.
Since each one shares with me the name of poet
Said by the single voice awhile ago,
They honor me—and doing so, do well.»

Thus did my mortal eyes see congregate
The great disciples of that lord of song
Who like an eagle soars above the rest.
And when they had communed awhile together,
They turned to me with courteous regard—
At which my gracious master smiled; and then
They honored me still more, inviting me
To join them, so that I became the sixth
Of that great company of intellects.
Thus we advanced until we reached the light,
And talked of many things: but silence now
Were sweeter than the saying of them then.

We came before a noble citadel
Engirdled seven times by lofty walls;
A lovely river served them as a moat.
This we crossed over, as upon dry land,
And with those sages I passed seven gates
And came upon a meadow, fresh and green.

Spirits were there, with grave majestic eyes,

7

Whose bearing showed their great authority;
They spoke but rarely, and in quiet tones.
Now we went onward from the meadow's edge
To a high open place suffused with light,
From where the company could all be seen.
And there upon that green-enamelled sward
Were shown to me the spirits of the great —
Whom to have seen was glory in itself.

    I saw Electra, with a throng of souls
Among whom Hector and Aeneas were;
Caesar, in armor, with his falcon eye;
I saw Camilla, and Penthesilea,
And King Latinus also, who, apart,
Was sitting by Lavinia, his daughter.
I marked that Brutus who was Tarquin's scourge;
Lucretia, Julia, Marcia, and Cornelia;
And, by himself, the valiant Saladin.

    Then, as I slightly lifted up my brow,
I saw that overlord of all wise men
Among a philosophic family.
Plato was there, and Socrates as well,
Standing above the others, near his side;
Democritus, who thought all due to chance;
Diogenes and Anaxagoras,
Zeno, Empedocles, and Heraclitus.
I saw that pleasant gatherer of herbs,
Dioscorides; and Orpheus, and Linus;
Tullius, and Seneca the moralist;
Euclid the measurer, and Ptolemy,
Hippocrates, and Galen; Avicenna,
Averrhoes, who wrote the Commentary.
All that I saw I cannot well relate:
So lengthy is my theme, that oftentimes
My words are insufficient for the fact.

    Our group of six was now reduced to two.
My leader took me by another road,
Forth from that quiet air to gusty storms:
And I had come to where all light was gone.

CANTO
5

Thus I went downward from the topmost ring
Into the second, where in smaller space
The greater torments bring forth cries of woe.
There Minos stands and snarls, with gnashing
Examines, at the entrance, every sin,   ⌊teeth;
And by his writhings judges and condemns.
I mean that when the soul foredoomed to grief
Comes in his presence, 'tis confessed outright;
And that discerner of transgressions wills
To which infernal pit it shall be plunged,
Coiling his tail around himself, each turn
Denoting a degree of woe. Before him
Stand ever waiting multitudes: each spirit
Passes alone before the judgment seat,
Speaks, hears its fate, and then is hurled below.

    «O you who come to the abode of woe,»
Said Minos as he saw me — then he paused
Even in the act and function of a doom —
«Take heed how you go in, and whom you trust;
Let not the gate deceive you by its width!»
My leader answered him: «Why vex yourself,
Or seek to bar his way, decreed by fate?
It is thus willed where there is power to do
That which is willed: and therefore ask no more.»

    Now I began to hear the cries of grief,
For I was in a place of many groans —
Outcries of pain, that smote me where I stood,
From out a region blind and void of light,
That bellowed like the sea when churned about
By mighty tempests of opposing winds.
The hellish blast with ceaseless fury rages
To sweep along the spirits in its rush,
Molesting them with constant buffetings.
And when they come before the precipice,

Canto 4 : Homer, the Classic Poets

INFERNO: CANTO 5

Cries and lamentations strike the air,
And blasphemies against the Power Divine!
I learned that to such torment are condemned
The sinners of the flesh, who vilely yield
Their reason to their carnal appetite.

    As when in times of cold the starlings fly,
Borne on their wings in large and crowded flocks:
So did that blast convey those wretched souls.
Now up, now down, now round about they
                    ⌊whirled:
No hope of rest could ever comfort them,
Or even a moment's lessening of their pain.

    As cranes proceed with their unearthly cry
Across the heavens in long aerial line:
Thus came a rustling, clangorous company,
A wailing flight of ghosts upon the gale.
Wherefore I asked: «O master, who are those
Whom the tempestuous blackness castigates?»

    «The first of those of whom you would have
                    ⌊news,»
He answered, «was an empress, and held sway
O'er men of many tongues, but was so sunk
In sensual vices, that to lift the blame
From the perversions which she wallowed in,
All licence was permitted by her law.
She is Semiramis, who, history says,
As Ninus' widow sat upon his throne
And ruled the land where now the sultan reigns.
The second, she who slew herself for love,
Unfaithful to the ashes of Sichaeus;
Behind her comes voluptuous Cleopatra.
See Helen there, for whom so many years
Of strife were wasted: next, the great Achilles
Who battled in his final hour with love.
See Paris, Tristan—»These and many more,
More than a thousand shades whom love divorced
From life, he pointed out and named for me.

    And when I heard my master call by name
Those knights and ladies of antiquity,
Pity so smote me that I nearly swooned.
I said to him: «O poet, I would speak
To that sequestered pair that cling together
And seem to float so lightly on the wind.»

He answered me: «Take heed when they
                    ⌊approach
More nearly to us: ask them by that love
Which bears them on, and they will come to you.»

    Now when the wind had wafted them to us,
I raised my voice: «O wearied souls, unless
Forbidden by Another, come, and speak!»
Like doves that with their wings upraised and still
Are borne upon the air by their desire
When longing calls them back to their soft nest:
Just so these two left Dido's company
To come toward us through the fetid air,
So strongly were they drawn by my appeal.

    «O living creature, gracious and benign,
Who through this air as dark as pitch has come
To seek us who have stained the earth with blood—
Were He who rules the universe our friend,
We would beseech Him for your soul's repose
Because you have compassion for our lot.
Of what it pleases you to hear and speak
We will converse with both of you, so long
The bitter blast is lulled as it is now.

    The land where I was born lies on the shore
Where Po, with all his riot retinue
Pours toward the ocean stream in search of peace.
Love, which lies smouldering in each gentle heart,
Inflamed him for the beauty that was mine;
And how 'twas taken from me, shames me still.
Love, that will take for answer only love,
Caught me so fiercely up in his delight
That, as you see, he still is by my side.
Love led us to one death: Caina waits
For him who quenched the flame of both our
                    ⌊lives.»
These were the words that came to us from them.

    When I had understood those injured souls,
I bowed my head, nor ever lifted it
Until the poet said: «What are your thoughts?»

    I answered him, beginning in this manner:
«Alas, what loving thoughts, what fond desires
Have brought them to this lamentable pass!»

    Once more I turned to them and raised my
«Francesca, I am moved to bitter tears   ⌊voice:

9

By pity for the torments you have suffered.
But tell me, in that hour when sighs were sweet,
How did love let you know, or chance discover
The drift of all your fond imaginings?»

And she replied: «There is no greater grief
Than to recall a bygone happiness
In present misery: that your teacher knows.
But if you have so great a wish to learn
The very root whence sprang our sinful love,
I'll tell our tale, like one who speaks and weeps.

«One day, to pass the time, we read the book
Of Launcelot, and how love conquered him.
We were all unsuspecting and alone:
From time to time our eyes would leave the page
And meet to kindle blushes in our cheeks.
But at one point alone we were o'ercome:
When we were reading how those smiling lips
Were kissed by such a lover—Paolo here,
Who nevermore from me shall be divided,
All trembling, held and kissed me on the mouth.
Our Galeot was the book; and he that wrote it,
A Galeot! On that day we read no more.»

While the first spirit told her tale, the other
Wept with a passionate grief that mastered me;
I felt a faintness, as it were of death,
And like a corpse fell headlong to the ground.

CANTO
6

WHEN once again my senses come to me
That left me, when the anguish of those two
So altogether stunned me with compassion,
Whichever way I move or turn or look
My eyes behold, on every side alike,
New torments and tormented souls anew.
To the third circle of eternal rain,

Accursed, cold and heavy, I am come.
Thick hail, dark water, and unending snow
Come pouring down athwart the murky air—
Their quality and cadence never changing—
Upon the putrid earth. A monster fierce,
The direful Cerberus with triple throat,
Barks doglike o'er the people here submerged.
Red are his eyes; his beard befouled and dark,
His belly large, his paws with talons armed;
He claws the spirits, flays and quarters them.
The endless downpour makes them howl like dogs;
Trying with one side to protect the other,
The abject wretches often writhe and turn
In vain attempt to find relief from pain.

When Cerberus took heed of our approach,
He opened wide his jaws with horrid fangs,
And quivering with rage in every limb
Stood thwart our path; and then my noble leader
Stretched forth his hands, and picking up some
He hurled it full within the rabid jaws.   ⌊earth,
Just as a hungry dog that barks for food
Is quieted when first he gnaws his meat,
Thinking and striving but to devour it:
Just so were stilled the jaws of Cerberus,
That demon whose loud, raucous bark so stuns
The spirits, that they wish that they were deaf.
We passed o'er shades beaten to earth by rain:
Our feet were stepping on their hollow forms,
Which were but shadows, though they seemed
All of them were lying on the ground   ⌊like men.
Save one, who painfully arose to sit
As soon as he perceived us passing by.
«O you who through this hell are being led,»
He said to me, «recall me if you can:
For you were born while I still breathed above.»

I answered him: «The anguish in your face
Perchance withdraws you from my memory,
As if I had not looked on you before.
But tell me who you are, and why condemned
To suffer such a penalty, that none
Is worse to bear, although it were a greater.»

«Your city, which of envy is so full
Its brim is overflowing, in tranquil life

Canto 5 : The Souls of Paolo and Francesca

Held me within its walls,» he answered me.
«Your citizens gave me the name Ciacco.
For the pernicious sin of gluttony
I languish as you see in endless rain.
And I am not the only wretched soul:
All these are suffering like punishment
For like offense.» No other word he spoke.

«Ciacco,» I answered him, «your wretchedness
So burdens me that tears start in my eyes.
But if you can, tell what the future holds
For citizens of our divided state.
Tell me if any man be just, and why
So great a discord has afflicted it.»

He said to me: «After long years of strife
Blood will be shed; the faction from without
Will chase the other off with bitter loss.
Within three years the conquerors shall fall,
The conquered rule, by help of one who now
Uncertain, vaccilates between the two.
Long will this faction hold its forehead high,
Keeping the other heavily oppressed
With tears of shame and wrath. Two men are just:
Yet no one heeds them there, for arrogance,
Envy, and avarice are the triple flames
That burn within her citizens' proud hearts.»
Here ended his most lamentable tale.

Said I to him: «I beg you, tell me more:
Grant me the boon, I pray, of further speech.
The worthy Farinata, and Tegghiaio,
Jacopo Rusticucci, Mosca, Arrigo,
And all the other men who strove for good —
Pray tell me where they are, and help me find
Their souls; for greatly I desire to know
If heaven doth soothe or hell embitter them.»

He said: «They are among the blackest souls;
Their crimes have dragged them down to deepest ⌊hell.
If you descend so far, you'll see them there.
But when you seek again the world above,
Bring tidings of me to the others there.
Further I'll tell you not, nor answer more.»

He turned his gaze aside, then looked at me;
Then bowed his head, and in the reeking mud
Fell prone, to join the other sightless souls.

The leader said to me: «He'll wake no more
Until the sound of the angelic trump.
When the avenging doom will be fulfilled,
Each spirit will seek out his dismal tomb,
Resume his mortal shape, and hear his sentence
Reverberating through eternity.»
So we passed on, across the filthy mess
Of spirits mixed with sleet, with lingering steps,
Discoursing somewhat on the future life.

I said to him: «O master, will these torments
After the mighty sentence, be increased,
Or mitigated, or remain unchanged?»

And he replied: «Your science teaches you
That true perfection has the greatest sense
Of pleasure — hence, the greatest sense of pain.
Though these ill-fated souls cannot arrive
At true perfection, yet they will be nearer
After the Judgment Day, than now.» Along
The curving road we went, conversing more
Than I shall now repeat; and so we came
Abreast the point where one descends below.
Here we found Plutus, the archenemy.

CANTO 7

Pape Satan, Pape Satan, aleppe!
We heard the raucous voice of Plutus say.

And then that noble sage who knew all things
Spoke forth to comfort me: «Let not your fear
Disturb you: for whatever power he has,
It cannot stop your going down this cliff.»
He turned around to face those bloated lips
And said: «Be silent, O accursed wolf,
And let your rage consume you from within!
Not without cause we come to the abyss:
Thus it is willed on high, where Michael wrought

Vengeance divine for the adulterous pride.»
　　Even as sails inflated by the wind
Collapse and drop, when snaps the mast in twain:
So fell that cruel monster to the earth.
Now we descended to the fourth abyss,
Down deeper yet into that woeful sack
Stuffed with all evil of the universe.
Justice divine! What hand could pack together
So many torments as I now beheld?
And why are we thus ruined by our sins?

　　Just as the mighty wave above Charybdis
Shatters itself on the opposing tide:
So must these spirits dance and counterdance.
More numerous than elsewhere, I perceived
On both sides of the ring, a screaming crowd
Pushing heavy weights by strength of chest.
They came together with a shock; and there
They wheeled about, shouting to one another:
«Why do you squander?» «Why do you hoard?»
　　　　　　　　And then
Along the gloomy circle they returned
On either hand, shouting their words of shame
Till at the opposite point they met again.
Then each one turned around, when he had
The other joust, along his semicircle.　⌊reached

　　And I, who felt my heart oppressed with grief,
Said: «Master, show me now what men are these.
And were these tonsured people on our left
In holy orders, one and all?» He answered:
«In life, the mind's eye of each one of them
Was so asquint, he could not see to spend
With any sort of measure or restraint.
They clearly shout it forth, when they arrive
At those two points upon the circle's rim
That separate opposing forms of guilt.
These men who have no hair upon their heads
Were clerics—even cardinals and popes,
Among whom avarice grows as it wills.»
　　Said I: «O master, among such as these
I think I ought to recognize a few
Whose lives were blackened by these very sins!»
　　He answered me: «My son, your thoughts are
That senseless life that so polluted them　⌊vain:

Has darkened them beyond all mortal ken.
Forever they must run their double course;
These from their tombs shall rise with tight-
　　　　　　　⌊closed fists,
Those others, with their heads all shorn of hair.
The evil of their hoarding and their spending
Has lost them paradise, and left them here
In scuffles—I shall waste no better word.
Here you can see the short-lived vanity
Of worldly goods—by men consigned to Fortune—
For which the human race forever strives.
But all the gold there is beneath the moon,
Or ever was, would not suffice to give
A moment's rest to one poor weary soul.»
　　«Master,» I said to him, «explain to me
This Fortune that you just alluded to,
Who holds all worldly goods within her grasp.»
　　And he to me: «Creatures, what fools you are!
What monstrous ignorance oppresses you!
I wish that you should clearly understand
What I now say. He whose omniscience
Transcendeth all, the heavens made, and then
Angels to govern them, so that the light
Shines equally on each and every part.
Likewise, for worldly splendors, He ordained
A ministress and guide, whose duty is
To change, when time is ripe, this hollow wealth
From nation unto nation, man to man,
Unprejudiced by human interference.
Therefore one nation rules, another falls,
As Fortune wills; but she remains concealed,
Just as a snake lies hidden in the grass.
Man's knowledge has no shield it can oppose:
She can foresee, judge, and confirm her rule
On earth, as do the other gods in heaven.
Her changes have no truce; necessity
Makes them come swiftly, for they must keep pace
With those who come so often for their turn.
This, then, is she—she who is so reviled
Even by those who most should give her praise,
But wrongly give her blame and foul abuse.
Blessed is she, and so she heeds them not,
But with the angels gladly turns her wheel,

Canto 7 : Virgil shows Dante the Souls of the Wrathful

Blessed in her happiness serene.
   «Let us descend to deeper woe: those stars
Are sinking fast, that when I first set out
Were rising high; we must not tarry long.»
    We cut across the circle to a bank
Above a spring, which bubbled as it ran
Through a deep gully leading further downward.
Blacker than ink was that forbidding stream;
By a rough path we took our way below,
Companioned by the murky river's wave.
And when that dismal stream had reached the foot
Of the malign and dusky precipice,
It spread into a marsh that men call Styx.
And I, who stood intent to gaze and wonder,
Beheld a host of spirits, foul with mud,
All naked, and with hatred in their looks.
They struck each other, not with hands alone,
But with their feet and heads and breasts as well,
And tore each other piecemeal with their teeth.
The goodly master said: «My son, see there
The souls of those whom wrath has overcome;
Also, I wish that you should truly know
That other people lie beneath the water;
Their sighs produce those ripples on the surface
That you can see, whichever way you look.
Sunk deep in loathsome slime, they try to say:
'Sullen were we, in the sun-gladdened air,
Bearing within ourselves the fumes of sloth;
Now we are sullen in this black morass!'
This dreary chant they gurgle in their throats,
Unable as they are to speak it clearly.»
    We walked on, far around the swampy shore
Between the dry bank and the reeking pool,
Our eyes turned on those souls who gulped its
At last we reached a lofty tower's base.   ⌊filth;

CANTO
8

To carry on my tale. Some time before
We had attained the lofty tower's base,
Our eyes were lifted upward to its summit,
On which two flaming torches had been set;
And far away another answered back,
So distant that the eye could scarce discern it.
I turned toward that sea of understanding,
And said: «What mean these lights? And what
        ⌊replies *Lights*

That other signal? Who has set them there?»
   He answered me: «Across the reeking wave,
Already you can see what we await,
Unless the murky vapors hide it from you.»
   No arrow ever sped so swift from bow
To cleave its course athwart the startled air,
As I beheld a little bark come toward us.
It skimmed across the water's dark expanse
Steered by a single oarsman, who cried out:
«Are you arrived at last, O guilty soul?»
   «O Phlegyas, this time you cry in vain,»
My master said. «You'll hold us but the time
You ferry us across the murky pool!»
As one who learns that he has been deceived,
And chafes thereat: so Phlegyas became,
Chafed by the pent-up fury of his rage.
My leader now embarked upon the skiff
And made me follow him; but only then,
With me on board, the boat seemed laden down.
When both my guide and I were in the hull,
The ancient prow moved off, and cut the wave
Deeper than was its wont with empty shades.
    While we were passing o'er the stagnant pool,
Before us rose one caked with mud, who cried:
«What man are you, to come before your time?»

Said I: «Though here, I am not here to stay!
But who are you, in such a filthy state?»

He said: «You see that I am one who weeps.»

I answered him: «In weeping and in woe,
O spirit maledict, remain forever!
I know you well, all muddy though you are!»

The shade stretched forth his hands to grasp
                       ⌊the boat,
At which my watchful master thrust him back,
Saying: «Away there, with the other dogs!»
And then he put his arms around my neck
And kissed my face, and said: «Indignant soul!
May she who bore you be forever blessed!
In life he was both arrogant and cruel;
No good repute adorns his memory;
Hence is his shade so furious here below.
How many those on earth who stalk as kings,
And yet will lie as hogs here in the mire,
Leaving behind them naught but calumny!»

«Master,» said I, «I would be greatly pleased
To see him plunged deep in this hellish broth
Before we have departed from the lake!»

He answered me: «You'll soon be satisfied:
Before the other shore comes into view
You must, perforce, have such a wish fulfilled.»
We had not travelled far, when I beheld
The muddy souls attack him with such rage
That even now I praise and thank God for it.
«At Filippo Argenti!» they cried out;
The frenzied spirit of the Florentine
Bit his own flesh in rage, and gnashed his teeth.

We left him there, so I shall tell no more.
But now a bitter wailing smote my ears,
And I peered forward, seeking out its cause.
The goodly master then explained to me:
«We now approach the citadel of Dis,
Whose garrison is laden down with sin.»

«Master,» I said, «already I discern
Its mosques, all fiery red, as if but now
Just issued from the flames!» He answered me:
«Eternal fire, enkindling them within,
Makes them glow red against the murky gloom
Of this deep hell, as you have just perceived.»

We now arrived within the belt of moats
That girds about the city of despair:
Its walls were iron, so it seemed to me.
But not till we had circled far around
Came we to where the grisly ferryman
Exclaimed to us: «Get out! Here is the entrance!»

Above the gate I saw a host of those
Cast down from heaven, who shouted angrily:
«Who is this man who dares, while still alive,
To journey through the kingdom of the dead?»

At this my noble master made a sign
Of wishing to confer with them apart.
Then they repressed their anger for a while
And cried: «You come alone! Let him be off
Who has been bold enough to enter here:
Let him go back alone—if he can do so!
For you who have escorted him thus far
Across the dark expanse, shall stay behind.»

Imagine, reader, my discomfiture,
Hearing the sound of those accursed words:
For I believed I never would return!
«Beloved leader, who has many times
Protected me from dangers imminent,
And kept me safe—I beg you, do not now
Abandon me in this adversity!
If passage is forbidden, let us now
Retrace our steps together, and at once!»

That noble leader who had brought me there
Replied: «Fear not: for no one can obstruct
Our passage: it is so decreed on high.
Await me here. Comfort your weary soul
And feed it with high hopes till I return;
For I will not forsake you here in hell.»
With this my gentle father went away
And left me in an agonized suspense,
For yes and no had torn my mind in two.
I could not hear what arguments he used;
But soon they turned about and rushed within,
Each striving with the others to be first.
They shut the gates, those enemies of ours,
Right in my master's face. He stayed without
And walked back to my side with measured steps.
With downcast eyes, and deeply troubled brow

Canto 8 : *Phlegyas ferries Dante and Virgil across the Styx*

He murmured, in a voice perturbed with sighs:
«Who has denied me the abode of woe?»
And then to me: «My son, be not alarmed
At my distress, for I shall yet prevail,
No matter who within shall bar our way.
This insolence of theirs is nothing new;
For once before they have made use of it,
At a less secret gate, that's still unlocked:
Above it you saw cut the words of doom.
Even now, within its portal there descends,
Passing alone through circle after circle,
One who has power to force the city gate.»

CANTO 9

THE ashen hue that fear brought to my cheek
When I perceived my leader turning back,
Made him repress at once his flush of shame.
He stopped attentively, like one who listens:
So heavy was the mist, so dark the air,
The eye could see but for a little space.
«In spite of all, our destiny must win,»
He said, «Unless—but no! Our heavenly aid
Is surely pledged. How slowly, though, it comes!»
  I clearly saw how he had covered up
His earlier meaning by the words that followed—
So different from what he said before.
But nonetheless, his speech had frightened me;
For I had misconstrued his first intent,
Ascribing a worse import than he wished.
  «Into this region of the great abyss,
Has any soul descended yet from limbo
Whose only punishment is hope destroyed?»
Thus I inquired of him, and he replied:
«Seldom, indeed, has any one of us
E'er made this journey I now undertake.

In truth, I came here once before myself,
Summoned by fell Erictho, who was wont
To call the spirits back into their flesh.
Soon after I had left my mortal form,
She made me enter in those dreadful walls
To fetch a spirit from the ring of Judas:
No ring so low, and none so dark as it,
Nor farther from the all-encircling heaven.
Full well I know the way: be reassured.
This marsh, that belches forth so foul a stench
Lies 'round about the citadel of woe,
Wherein we cannot enter unassailed.»
  And more he said, which I have not in mind,
Because my eye had drawn my whole attention
To that tall tower with its flaming summit:
And as I gazed, there suddenly uprose
Three hellish Furies, all besmeared with blood,
With women's limbs, and aspect womanly.
About their waists were greenest hydras girt;
For hair, horned serpents in a seething mass
Hissed as they twined about their horrid brows.
Then he, who knew full well these handmaidens
Of her who rules the land of endless tears,
Said: «See the fierce Erinyes: on the left
Megaera rages; there, upon the right
The sad Alecto weeps; Tisiphone
Stands in between.» This said, he spoke no more.
  Each Fury with her talons tore her breast,
And smote herself with such unearthly shrieks,
I pressed the poet close in mortal fear.
«Bring on Medusa! Then he'll soon be stone!»
They cried together o'er the parapet.
«Alas that Theseus escaped our wrath!»
  «Turn around, and keep your eyes tight closed:
For if the Gorgon come, and you behold her,
Never again will you return above!»
So spoke my guide: He turned me round himself;
He did not dare to trust my mortal hands,
But with his own he covered both my eyes.
  O ye who have sound intellects, discern
The truth that lies concealed beneath the veil
Of these strange lines, and read their meaning
⌊clear!

Across the troubled waters now there came
The sound of crashing thunder, full of terror,
That shook the very shores on either side—
As hurricanes, by adverse heats impelled,
Will smite a forest, snapping off the boughs
With fury unrestrained, and beat them down
To bear them off in clouds of whirling dust;
Proudly the wind sweeps on, and from its wrath
The frightened animals and shepherds fly.

He now removed his hands that I might see,
And said to me: «Across the stagnant pool,
There, where the smoke is thickest, turn your
As frogs before their foe the serpent flee, ⌊eyes.»
Scattering through the water, till each one
Hides for protection underneath the bank:
Thus I beheld some thousands of lost souls
Flee before one who walked across the Styx
Dry-shod, where we had just been ferried over.
He slowly waved the murky air aside
And ever moved his hand before his face,
Seeming thereby to suffer weariness.
Certain was I that he was sent from heaven.
I turned toward my master, but he signed
For me to hold my tongue and bow my head.

How full of scorn that messenger appeared!
He came before the gates, and with a wand
He opened them, as though their bars were
⌊naught.

«O outcasts from the skies, O race despised,»
He said, while still astride that threshold grim,
«Whence comes this insolence that you display?
Why do you pit yourselves against that Will
Which cannot be opposed, and oftentimes
When thwarted has increased your sufferings?
Of what avail to butt against the Fates?
Your Cerberus, as you can well recall,
Still has no hide upon his throat and chin!»
Then he returned along the miry way
Speaking no word to us—like one
Whose mind is burdened down with graver cares
Than those of him who chances to be by.

Now, reassured by that divine pronouncement,
We took our way toward the land of woe.

16

We entered through the portal unopposed;
And I, who was most curious to see
What punishments the fortress might contain,
Gazed round about me as I stepped within.
On either side I saw a wide expanse
With anguish filled, and torments horrible.
Even as at Arles, where rests the Rhone awhile,
Or as at Pola, on Quarnaro's gulf
That shelters Italy, and bathes its shores,
The tombs diversify the countryside:
So here the tombs were everywhere about,
Save that they were more bitter to behold.
For round about those many monuments
Flames were scattered, so that they were heated
Brighter than iron e'er was made to glow.
The covers everywhere were lifted off,
And from each tomb there rose such piteous
As only souls in torment could produce. ⌊groans
I asked my master: «Tell me, who are these
Who, buried in these sepulchres, proclaim
Their anguish with such piteous laments?»

He answered: «The archheretics lie here,
With all their followers, of every sect;
The graves are crowded more than one would
⌊think.

Like is entombed with like; the monuments
Are heated each in varying degree.»
He turned off to the right, so that we passed
Between the fiery torments and the walls.

CANTO
10

By a secluded path that wound its way
Between the torments and the city wall,
My master goes; I follow at his heels.
«Wisdom incarnate, guiding me across

Canto 9 : Megaera, Tisiphone and Alecto

These rounds of wickedness,» I said to him,
«Speak, if you will, and satisfy my wish.
The people lying in these sepulchres—
Can they be seen? The lids are off already,
With no one there to guard them.» He replied:
«All will be sealed, when from Jehoshaphat
Their inmates shall return, and bring with them
Their mortal flesh which they have left behind.
Here Epicurus lies, and round about him
His many followers, who all believed
Their souls together with their bodies died.
And as for the request that you just made,
You soon will have your wish fulfilled—and too
That other wish you have kept hidden from me.»

«Good leader, I but keep my heart concealed
Lest I may say too much; at other times
You have disposed me so,» I answered him.

«O living Tuscan, who with modest speech
Are passing through this citadel of flames,
Be willing, pray, to tarry here a while.
Your tongue reveals you as a citizen
Of my own fatherland—on which, they say,
I may have wrought great harm while I was
⌊living»—

This sound came suddenly from out a tomb,
So that in fear I drew me somewhat closer
Unto my leader's side; whereon he said:
«Turn, turn around: what are you doing here?
See Farinata yonder, who has risen
To show his body from the girdle upward.»

Already I had fixed my eyes on his,
While he was rising, breast and brow erect,
As if in lofty scorn of hell's domain.
The deft and ready hands of my dear leader
Pushed me between the sepulchres to him.
He said: «Now let your words be well considered!»

When I had come before his flaming tomb,
He eyed me for a while; and then with scorn,
He asked: «Who were your ancestors?» And I,
Wishing to heed my master's admonition,
Concealed them not, but told them one and all.
He raised his eyebrows somewhat; then he said:
«To me, my fathers, and my party, all

Were violently opposed, so that I twice
Drove them to exile.» I replied to him:
«If they were driven forth, they soon returned
From every side, not only once, but twice;
Your faction never rightly learned that art!»

Above the opening of the sepulchre
There rose another spirit by his side,
Disclosing but his face; I think he knelt.
He looked around me, showing that he sought
Another by my side; but when he saw
His hope was vain, he wept, and said to me:
«If by your lofty genius you have come
To journey through this prison, tell me, pray,
Where is my son, and why is he not with you?»

I answered him: «I come not by myself:
He who awaits me yonder, is my guide.
Perchance your Guido held him in disdain.»

His words, his mode of punishment as well,
Already had revealed his name to me;
Therefore I answered him in full detail.
He quickly rose and cried: «*Held*, did you say?
He lives no more? No longer do his eyes
Behold the sweet and blessed light of day?»
When he perceived that there was some delay
Before I answered him, upon his back
He fell forthwith, and showed himself no more.

That other noble shade, at whose request
I had remained, changed not his countenance
Nor turned aside. Continuing our talk,
He said: «If it be true the Ghibellines
Have learned that art amiss, the news torments
More than all the torments of these flames. ⌊me,
But ere the face of her who reigneth here
Is fifty times rekindled, you shall know
How heavy is that art of which you speak!
But as you hope e'er to return above,
Tell me, why is that people so relentless
In every law they pass against my party?»

I answered him: «The rout and massacre
That dyed the Arbia with blood, have caused
Such orisons as these within our church!»

At that he sadly shook his head and sighed.
«It was not I alone who fought you then,»

He said, «and surely, not without good cause.
But once I was alone; when everyone
Agreed to sweep away your city, Florence,
'Twas I defended her, before the world.»

I questioned him: «Even as you may hope
Your seed may rest within that city's walls,
Solve me this riddle that perplexes me:
You seem to see the future, and foretell
What will occur—yet do not seem to know
Events now current in the world above.»

«We view like one who has imperfect sight,»
He said, «such things as are remote from us.
This much the Lord of All vouchsafes us here.
When they draw nigh, our vision is impaired:
We have no knowledge of your present state,
Unless perchance we learn of it from others.
Upon that day when, at the angel's trump,
The portals of the future will be closed,
Know that our knowledge will have ceased to be.»

Distressed by my discourtesy, I said:
«Pray tell your neighbor who fell back just now,
His son is still alive; and let him know
That when I made no answer to his question,
I was already thinking in that error
Which you resolved for me a while ago.»

My master was already calling me,
So that I begged the spirit in all haste
To tell me who was with him. He replied:
«With many a thousand others I lie here.
The second Frederick, and the cardinal
Are here within: no others will I name.»
He dropped from sight, and I turned back my   ⌊steps
Toward the poet of antiquity,
Pondering on that hostile prophecy.
And as he walked ahead of me he said:
«Why are you so distracted?» Whereupon
I answered him his question straightaway.

«What you have heard against you,» said the   ⌊sage,

«Remember well; and also hearken well
To what I say to you.» He raised his finger:
«When you shall stand before the radiance
Of her whose lovely eyes perceive all things,

From her you'll learn the journey of your life.»
Quitting the wall, we took a left-hand path
Across a valley of revolting stench
That smote our nostrils even on the heights,
And toward the centre downward took our way.

CANTO
11

UPON the edge of a high precipice
Formed by a circle of huge broken rocks,
We came upon a throng in greater torment.
And here the nauseating stench that rose
From out the deep abyss, forced us to rest
Behind the lid of a large monument,
On which I noticed this inscription carved:
**I HOLD POPE ANASTASIUS WHOM PHOTINUS
LURED FROM THE RIGHT PATH.** My master
⌊said:

«We now must go down slowly, that our senses
May get accustomed to this sickening blast;
Then we need fear no more.» I said to him:
«Pray find some compensation while we wait,
So that no time be lost.» And he exclaimed:
«Lo! I am thinking of that very thing!

«My son, within the ring formed by these rocks
Three lesser circles lie,» he said to me,
«Like those we left, each lower than the last.
They all are filled with spirits maledict;
I'll tell you how and why they are confined,
So when you see them you will understand.
Of every vice that moves the heavens to wrath
The end is wrong; and therefore every end
By violence or fraud does harm to others.
Fraud is a vice peculiar to mankind;
Hence it displeases God the more, and thus
The fraudulent are placed in greater woe.

Canto 10 : Farinata degli Uberti addresses Dante

INFERNO: CANTO 11

In the first circle are the violent;
But as their vice is threefold, so the ring
Is likewise built in three concentric rounds.
Against their God, themselves, or fellow men
Can violence be wrought—against their persons
Or their property, as you shall hear.
Murder by violence, and painful wounds,
Are wrought against one's neighbor; on his goods
Are wrought destruction, arson, usury.
Hence murderers, and those who wrongly struck,
Spoilers and robbers, all in separate groups
Are tortured in the first of these three rounds.
Man can lay violent hand upon himself
And on his property: the second round
Confines, in vain repentance, all of those
Who took their own lives from the world above,
And those who squandered all their property—
Who weep for that which should be cause for joy.
Violence is wrought against the Deity
By blasphemy, or by denying Him,
Or by despising nature and His gifts.
Hence in the lowest and the smallest round
Are found both Sodom and Cahors, and all
Who speak with scorn of God within their hearts.

«Now fraud, by which men's consciences are
Is of two kinds, and can be wrought upon ⌞stung,
Those who have trusted, or the opposite.
The latter kind seems only to destroy
Affection's link, that is by nature forged.
Within the second circle are confined
Hypocrisy and flattery, and those
Who practise witchcraft, sorcery, and theft,
Falsehood and Simony, and suchlike filth.
The second kind of fraud kills both that love
Which nature forms, and added love as well
That springs from special confidence and trust.
Hence in the smallest ring, where Lucifer
Is seated on the centre of the world,
All traitors are eternally consumed.»

«Master,» said I, «your argument proceeds
Most clearly, and distinguishes full well
The great abyss, and those contained within it.
But tell me why those in the reeking swamp,

Those others in the wind and in the rain,
And those who always meet with bitter speech,
Are not within the flaming citadel
For punishment—since God holds them in wrath?
If not, why are they in such sorry plight?»

He said to me: «Why goes your mind astray
So far beyond its usual boundaries,
Or has your memory forsaken you?
Do you not recollect those words in which
Your *Ethics* treats of those three dispositions—
Those dispositions never willed by heaven—
Incontinence, bestiality, and vice?
And how incontinence the least of all
Offends our God, incurring lesser blame?
If you can rightly understand my words,
And well remember who those spirits are
Who suffer punishment outside these walls
Above us there, then you will comprehend
Their separation from these guilty souls,
And why the heavenly vengeance strikes them
«O sun, that clarifies all faulty vision, ⌞less.»
You so content me when you solve my doubts
That I like doubts themselves as much as
                                    ⌞knowledge.

Turn back again,» I asked, «to where you said
That usury offends the Power Divine,
And pray explain to me this knotty point.»
«Philosophy,» my master answered me,
«To him who understands it, demonstrates
How nature takes her course, not only from
Wisdom divine, but from its art as well.
And if you read with care your book of physics,
After the first few pages, you will find
That art, as best it can, doth follow nature,
As pupil follows master; industry
Or art is, so to speak, grandchild to God.
From these two sources (if you call to mind
That passage in the Book of Genesis)
Mankind must take its sustenance and progress.
The moneylender takes another course,
Despising nature and her follower,
Because he sets his hope for gain elsewhere.
But follow me, for now we must proceed.

19

The Fish are quivering on the dim horizon,
And all the Wain is lying over Caurus;
Long is our pathway to the precipice!»

CANTO
12

FORBIDDING was that rugged alpine steep
On which we came, to pass down from the brink,
And horrible besides, from what was there.
As in that avalanche which struck the bank
Of Adige, upon this side of Trent—
Or from an earthquake or from sheer collapse—
Where, from the mountain top whence it began
Down to the plain, so shattered are the rocks,
A difficult descent is possible:
So was our passage down to the abyss.

Upon the summit of the rugged slope
There lay outstretched that infamy of Crete
Conceived by guile within a wooden cow;
And when he saw us come, he bit himself,
Like one whom frenzy has deprived of reason.
My sage cried out to him: «Do you believe
The prince of Athens has come here before you,
Who in the world above put you to death?
Monster, begone! For this man comes not here
Directed by your sister's magic arts,
But passes by to view your punishments.»

Just as a bull, when stricken unto death,
Will break his halter, and will toss about
From side to side, unable to go on:
Thus did I see the Minotaur behave.
«Run to the passage,» Virgil cried to me,
«Get down the cliff while he is still enraged!»

Accordingly we downward took our way
Among those scattered broken stones, which ⌊moved
Beneath the novel burden of my feet.

I still was deep in thought. He said: «Perchance
You wonder at this avalanche of rock,
Guarded by that beast I just subdued.
I'd have you know that at that former time
I took this pathway to the nether hell,
The precipice had not yet fallen down.
But certainly, I think, not long before
He came who carried off with him from Dis
So great a booty from the topmost ring,
This loathsome valley shook in all its bounds—
So that I thought the universe entire
Thrilled with a love divine, through which, some ⌊say,
The world has often been reduced to chaos.
At that time, here and in another place
The ancient rocks were overthrown like this.
But fix your eyes below: for near at hand
There runs that stream of blood, wherein are
⌊steeped

Those who have sinned by violence to others.»
O blind cupidity, both mad and guilty,
That in our brief life spurs us on to evil,
To keep us here throughout eternity!

I saw an ample moat, curved like a bow,
So formed that it encircled all the plain,
Just as my noble escort had described.
Between it and the bottom of the cliff
Were centaurs galloping in single file,
Armed with their arrows, as they used to hunt.
On seeing us approach, they all stopped short;
Then three of them departed from the band
With bows in hand and arrows picked with care,
And from a distance, one of them cried out:
«What torments seek you, coming down the cliff?
Speak out from there, or else I'll draw my bow!»

My master said: «We will make our answer
To Chiron there, as soon as we approach;
Your headstrong will has always cost you dear!»
He nudged me then and said: «That's Nessus
Who for the lovely Deianira died ⌊there,
And with his very blood avenged himself.
He in the centre, looking at his chest,
Is Chiron, tutor to the great Achilles;
That other Pholus, ever filled with rage.

Canto 12 : The Minotaur on the Shattered Cliff

Around the moat they go in many thousands,
Shooting at any soul that lifts itself
Further from out the blood than is allowed.»

    Nearer to those fleet monsters we approached;
And Chiron drew a shaft, and with its notch
Combed back his beard on either side his jaws.
When he had thus uncovered his huge mouth,
He said to his companions: «Have you seen
That he who goes behind moves what he touches?
Not so the feet of shades are wont to do!»

    And my good leader, who was standing now
Beside his breast, where man and beast are joined,
Replied: «He is indeed alive; and thus,
Alone, I show him through this dismal vale.
Necessity doth bring him, not desire.
A blessed one withdrew from chanting hymns,
Entrusting me with this unwonted task.
He is no thief—nor I a robber's shade.
But by that Power through which I take my way
Along so wild and difficult a road,
Lend us one of your fellows standing by,
That he may show us where there is a ford,
And carry on his croup this man beside me,
Who is no spirit that can walk on air.»

    Chiron, on hearing this, turned to his right
And said to Nessus: «Go back, guide them on,
And turn aside what other bands you meet!»

    We with our trusty escort moved along
The margin of the boiling crimson flood
From which the parboiled sinners cried in pain;
Some I beheld immersed up to their brows.
And the great centaur said: «All tyrants these,
Who laid their hold on plunder and on blood;
Now they bewail their cruel punishments.
Here's Alexander; Dionysius there,
Whose reign brought years of woe to Sicily.
He with the raven locks is Azzolino;
That other one beside him, who is fair,
Opizzo da Este, whom, if truth be told,
His stepson murdered in the world above.»

    I turned toward the poet, who was saying:
«You mount in front, and I shall ride behind you.»

    A little further on, the centaur stopped

Above a multitude, who, to their necks,
Stood out above the boiling stream of blood.
He pointed out to us a shade apart,   ⌊pierced
And said: «That man, in God's own bosom
The heart now venerated on the Thames.»

    I next saw people with their heads and breasts
Exposed above the surface of the river;
Of these I recognized a goodly throng.
Thus more and more the shallowness increased
Until the victims' feet alone were boiled;
And here we made our passage of the moat.
«The boiling stream is getting shallower
As you can see from here,» he said to me.
«Believe me when I say the river's bed
Slopes downward there upon the other side,
Deepening more and more until it joins
That part where tyranny must cry in anguish.
Justice divine keeps there in endless torment
Attila, who was a scourge on earth,
Pyrrhus and Sextus, and for evermore
By torture of the boiling flood, draws tears
From two Rinieri, Pazzo and Corneto,
Who on the highways wrought such violence.»
Then he turned back, and crossed the ford again.

CANTO 13

Nessus had not yet reached the other bank
Before we entered in a tangled wood
Unmarked by any sign of path or road.
The foliage was not green, but dingy black;
Not smooth the branches, but entwined and
                         ⌊gnarled;
There were no fruits, but venom-laden thorns:
Not so rough or tangled are the wilds
Frequented by those savage beasts who shun

The fields between Cecina and Corneto.
Here the loathsome Harpies make their nests
Who drove the Trojans from the Strophades
By croaking prophecies of doom to come.
Broad wings they have, and human necks and
⌊faces,

Claws on their feet, and feathered bellies huge;
From the strange trees they utter cries of woe.

My noble master now began to speak:
Before you enter further, know that you
Are in the second round, and still will be
Until you reach the dreadful waste of sand.
Therefore, look well about, for you shall see
Such things as might discredit aught I say.»

Loud wails smote on my ears from every side,
Yet no one could I see to utter them,
So that I stood bewildered in my tracks.
Perchance my master thought that I believed
Those many voices issued through the trunks
From people hiding there because of us.
Wherefore he said: «If you break off a twig
From any of these trees, then will those thoughts
You have in mind be altogether changed.»

Forthwith I stretched my hand a little way
To pluck a branch of thorn from its great bush.
Its trunk cried out: «Why do you break me thus?»
And after it was darkened o'er with blood
It cried again: «Why do you mangle me?
Have you no sort of pity in your soul?
Men were we once, but now are changed to trees.
Your hand should have been more compassionate,
In sooth, if we were only souls of serpents!»

As a green firebrand, burning at one end
Will bubble at the other, and spit out
The hissing air escaping from within:
So from the broken twig there issued forth
Both words and blood together; thereupon
I let it fall, and stood as one afraid.

«O wounded soul,» my sage replied, «could he
But have believed this marvel possible
That he had read of only in my rhyme,
Then would he not have lifted up his hand
Against you; but the wonder of the thing

Caused me to urge an act that I regret.
But tell him who you were: to make amends,
He may refresh the memory of your name
Up in the world above, when he returns.»

The trunk replied: «So gentle is your speech
I cannot hold my tongue; but be not vexed
Should I be tempted to discourse at length.
I am he whose hand held both the keys
Of Frederick's heart; so softly did I turn
In locking and unlocking, I was able
To keep most men excluded from his trust.
So faithful was I to my glorious task
I sacrificed my sleep, and all my strength.
That harlot, common bane and vice of courts,
Who never took her eyes from Caesar's house,
Did so inflame the minds of all against me,
And they in turn did so inflame Augustus,
That all the happy honors I had gained
Were turned instead to woe and bitterness.
My spirit, in a shameful fit of temper,
Hoping in death to find escape from shame,
Made me, the just, unto myself unjust.
By the new roots of this strange tree I swear
That never did I break my faith with him,
My lord, who was deserving of all praise.
If either of you should return above,
Let him attempt to raise my reputation,
That now lies stricken down by blows of envy.»

He paused awhile. The poet said to me:
«Since he is silent, do not hesitate,
But speak, and ask him further what you will.»

I answered him: «Rather do you again
Ask him what you think that I should know.
I cannot—so has pity struck my heart!»

Then he began anew: «Imprisoned soul,
That this man may do freely what you ask,
So may it please you further to explain
How souls are bound within these twisted trunks,
And also to inform us, if you can,
If any shade can ever be released.»

The trunk blew heavily awhile, and then
The wind transformed itself into these words:
«Briefly it shall be told, as you request.

Canto 13 : *Harpies in the Forest of the Suicides*

When the maddened soul forsakes its body
From which it has removed itself by force,
Minos consigns it to the seventh ring.
It falls into the wood, without design,
Dropping wherever chance may hurl it down.
There, like a grain of seed, it germinates.
It grows into a sapling, then a tree;
And now the Harpies feeding on its leaves
Give pain, and also for that pain an outlet.
Like other spirits, we shall seek our flesh,
But none of us may put it on again,
For none deserves what he has cast away.
Our bodies we shall drag here through the wood;
They will be hanged, each body from the tree
Belonging to the shade that wrought it ill.»

    And while we stood attentive by the trunk,
Thinking that it might wish to tell us more,
We both were startled by a sudden noise—
Like one who, waiting in the silent wood,
Glimpses a boar come crashing toward his post,
And hears the animals and snapping twigs.
When lo! Upon the left there now approached
Two naked, bleeding men, who fled so fast
That they broke everything that barred their way.
The foremost cried: «O death, come quickly now!»

    The other one, who feared himself too slow:
«Lano, not so nimble were your legs
When you were in the skirmish on the Toppo!»
And then, perhaps because his breath was spent,
He hid himself within a near-by bush.

    Behind them, the entire wood was filled
With black-haired bitches, ravenous and swift
As greyhounds slipped to freedom from the leash.
On him who cowered there they set their teeth
Rending him piecemeal with their cruel fangs,
Then bore away his torn and suffering limbs.

    My guide now took me by the hand, and led me
Beside the bush, which through its bleeding
                                    ⌊wounds
Was uttering anguished cries, though all in vain.
«O Jacomo,» it said, «da Sant' Andrea—
What do you gain, to make a screen of me?
What blame have I for all your guilty life?»

    My master stood beside the bush, and said:
«Who were you, who through so many wounds
Blow forth such words of suffering, and blood?»

    And he: «O souls that come to gaze upon
The havoc that has torn my branches from me,
Gather them, I pray, and lay them down
Most gently at the foot of this sad bush.
I once lived in that city which exchanged
Its earlier patron for the Baptist: hence
He with his arts of war will make her grieve.
And were it not that on the Arno's bridge
Some semblance of the Warrior still remains,
Those citizens who afterward rebuilt it
Upon the ashes left by Attila,
Had done their labors all to no avail!
I made a gibbet of my palaces.»

CANTO 14

Because affection for my native town
So moved me, I collected all the twigs
And gave them back to the exhausted shade.
We went on to the boundary that divides
The third round from the second—whence are
The horrible contrivances of justice.   ⌊seen
Well to describe the strange things we beheld,
I say that we arrived before a plain
Which from its soil repels all growing things.
The dismal forest girds it round about,
As it is by the fosse itself enclosed;
We halted here, upon the very brink.
The ground was of a deep and arid sand,
Of the same fashion as that sand they say
The feet of Cato trod in ancient times.

    Vengeance of God! what dread must thou
                                    ⌊inspire

In everyone who now shall read and learn
Of that which was revealed before my eyes!

 For I saw multitudes of naked souls
Who all were weeping piteously, and seemed
Tormented all in varying degrees.
While some were lying supine on the ground,
Others were sitting huddled in a heap,
Or running round about incessantly.
More numerous were those who ran about;
The fewer, those who in their torment lay,
Although they cried the louder in their pain.

 Over that sandy waste fell slowly down
Broad flakes of fire, falling measuredly
Like snow upon the Alps in quiet air.
Even as those flames which Alexander saw
Fall down unbrokenly upon his host
From out the torrid skies of India,
So that he bade his men to stamp the earth,
The better to put out the burning vapor
Before it spread into a sheet of flame:
Just so th' eternal heat was falling down,
From which the sand, like tinder under steel,
Burst into flame, the torment to redouble.
Without a moment's rest the slapping hands
Danced frantically on, now here, now there,
To brush away the torture of the flames.

 «O master,» I began, «who overcomes
All things, except that evil company
Who came against us at the gate of Dis—
Who is that mighty one who does not seem
To heed the flames, but lies so stern and scornful,
As if the rain of fire did not assail him?»

 And that same shade, perceiving that I asked
About him from my leader, shouted out:
«Such as I was alive, so am I dead:
Though Jove should tire out his armorer,
From whom he seized in wrath the thunderbolt
With which I finally was stricken down—
Or even if he should tire out those others
Who work in Mongibello's blacksmith shop,
And he should cry, 'Help, help, good Vulcan, help!'
(As once he did on Phlegra's field) and launch
His thunderbolts at me with all his might,—

Not even then could he have his revenge!»
 My leader then spoke out more forcefully
Than I had ever heard him speak before:
«O Capaneus, as your arrogance
Is yet unquenched, your punishment is greater:
No torment other than your own mad rage
Could ever pain enough to match your fury!»
He now turned round to me, with gentler mien,
And said: «One of the seven kings was he
Who once invested Thebes. He scorned his God,
And it would seem, esteems him lightly still;
But, as I said, his evil passions are
The ornaments most fitting for his breast.
Now follow after me, and take good care:
Set not your feet upon the red-hot sand,
But keep them always close beside the wood.»

 We came in silence to a place at which
A rivulet flows outward from the forest,
So red, that even now it makes me shudder.
As from the Bulicame gushes forth
That stream the sinful women later use,
So ran this rivulet upon the sand.
Its bottom and its sloping inner banks
Were made of stone, its outer sides as well:
Hence I perceived the passage must be there.

 «Of all the things that I have shown to you
Since we passed through the portals of that gate
Of which the threshold is denied to none,
Nothing has been discovered to your eyes
So worthy of remark as this red stream
That quenches all the flakes of fire above it.»

 Thus spoke my noble leader; whereupon
I begged him to bestow on me the food
For which he had aroused my appetite.
«Surrounded by the sea,» he said, «there lies
A wasted land called Crete, under whose king
The world, in olden time, lived innocent.
A mountain rises there, that once was decked
With laughing rills and verdure, but is now
Deserted and a waste: men call it Ida.
Rhea once chose this mountain as a cradle
To hide her son, and made it clangorous,
The better to conceal him when he cried.

Canto 14 : The Violent, tortured in the Rain of Fire

Within the mount there stands an ancient man
Erect and huge, who keeps his shoulders turned
On Damietta, while he looks on Rome
As in a glass. His head is finest gold,
His arms and breast of purest silver formed;
Thence to the fork, his body is of brass.
From that point downward he is made of iron,
Save for his right foot, which is formed of clay:
He seems to stand on this, more than the other.
And every part except the gold is riven
By a mighty cleft, distilling tears.
They, when collected, perforate that cavern
And dropping to this vale, from rock to rock,
Form Styx and Acheron and Phlegethon.
The last runs downward through this narrow
⌊channel

Until it meets the end of all descent;
Cocytus there is formed. Upon that lake
You soon will gaze; so here I say no more.»

Said I to him: «If, then, this present stream
Springs from a source up in our world above,
Why only on this rim has it appeared?»

And he replied to me: «You know this place
Is circular; and though you have come far,
And ever turning left in your descent,
You have not yet traversed its round in full.
Therefore, if any strange, new thing appear
It need not bring amazement to your face.»

And I: «My master, where is Lethe found
Of which you did not speak, and Phlegethon,
Which, as you say, is of this rain composed?»

«You give me joy in everything you ask,»
He answered, «but the boiling crimson flood
Might well have showed the answer to your
⌊question.

And Lethe you shall see—not here in hell,
But where the spirits go to wash themselves
After the expiation of their sins.»
And then he said: «We now must leave the wood.
Mind that you follow closely at my heels:
The margins make a pathway through the fire,
For over them all flame is quenched at once.»

CANTO
15

ONE of the stony margins bears us on,
And over it the stream creates a mist
That shields the water and the dykes from fire.
Even as the Flemings, from Wissant to Bruges,
Fearing the flood that presses on their flank,
Erect their dykes to hold the sea in check—
Or as the Paduans, along the Brenta,
Likewise protect their castles and their towns
Ere Chiarentana feel the summer heat—
In like formation were these margins built,
Although their architect, who'er he was,
Had made them not so lofty, nor so wide.

When we had walked so far beyond the wood
That even had I turned to look behind
I could not have discerned its whereabouts,
We came upon a company of shades
Who marched beside the bank; and every one
Peered at us earnestly, as men are wont
To gaze at one another in the moonlight,
And puckered up their brows at us, the way
A tailor will before his needle's eye.

While we were stared at by this company
I soon was recognized by one of them,
Who seized my gown and cried: «What marvel
⌊this?»

And I, when he stretched forth his arm to me,
Peered so intently at his crusted face
That even the scorching of his countenance
Could not prevent my recognizing him;
And reaching down my hand toward his head
I answered: «Ser Brunetto, you are here?»

And he: «My son, pray do not be annoyed—
Brunetto Latini will turn back to walk
With you a way, and let the troop file on.»

I said to him: «As far as is allowed.
And if you want me to sit down with you,
I'll do so, if my master will permit.»

«My son,» said he, «if any in this throng
Should stop, he then must lie a hundred years
Without relief from turning, in the fire.
Therefore move onward; I will come behind
And shortly will rejoin my company,
Who weep in their parade of endless woe.»

I did not dare to step down from the dyke
To walk with him below, but kept my head
Inclined, as if to do him reverence.

He said to me: «What fortune, or what fate,
Has brought you here below before your time,
And who is he that guides you on your way?»

«When I was in the tranquil life on earth,»
I answered him, «I wandered in a vale,
Before I had attained to man's full age;
But yesternoon I turned my back upon it.
This man appeared when I was losing ground,
And by this path now leads me to my home.»

And he: «As long as you are guided by your
You cannot fail to reach the glorious haven, ⌞star,
If I have judged you well in life on earth.
Had I not died so early in my life—
Seeing that heaven is so benign to you—
I might have given you comfort in your work.
But that ungrateful people and malign
Who came down from Fiesole of old—
And still retain its granite in their hearts—
Will, for your good deeds, become your foes.
But it is just: for it is not befitting
The fig should bear among the sour sorb trees!
Their bad repute has long proclaimed them
An envious, arrogant, and greedy race! ⌞blind—
See that you cleanse yourself of their bad ways.
Your future holds such honor in its store,
The factions both will hunger after you,
But far will be the herbage from the goat!
Let the beasts of Fiesole make fodder
Of their own selves: let them not touch the plant
That grows upon their dunghill, and contains
The sacred seed of those brave men of Rome

Who stayed there, even when it had become
The nest of so much wickedness and vice.»

«Were all my wish fulfilled,» I answered him,
«You would not yet have quit the human race:
For in my memory is firmly fixed—
It strikes me now, down to my very heart—
Your aspect, ever kind and fatherly,
When, in the world, for hour and hour on end
You used to teach of man's eternal goal.
How much I prize it, must be evident
In what I write, as long as I draw breath.
That which you tell me of my fate to come
I shall note down, and save with other texts
To show to one who knows, if I can reach her.
But this one thing I wish to show you plain,
Provided that my conscience chide me not:
I am prepared for Fortune, as she lists.
Such earnest money is not new to me;
Therefore let Fortune spin her wheel about
Or churl strike with his mattock where he wills!»

My master now turned backward on his right,
And after he had eyed me for a while
He said to me: «He listens well who notes.»

Yet notwithstanding this, I walked ahead
And talked with Ser Brunetto, asking him
To name me the most famous of his fellows.
And he to me: «'Tis well to speak of some;
Of others it were better to say nothing,
For time would not suffice for so much talk.
Know then, in brief, that they were clerics all—
Scholars of great renown, who on the earth
Were all polluted with the selfsame sin.
Priscian goes there with that degraded throng,
And with him is Francesco of Accorso.
If you have any wish to see such scurf,
Behold him there, who by the Servants' Servant
Was moved from Arno to the Bacchiglione,
Where at his death he left his sin-stained flesh.
More would I say, but progress and discourse
Are both cut short; for I behold afar
A new smoke rising yonder from the sand.
People approach with whom I may not be.
Into your care I recommend my *Treasure*

Canto 15 : Brunetto Latini accosts Dante

In which my name lives on. I ask no more.»

Then he turned back, and ran like one of those
Who at Verona race for the green cloth
Across the plain; and as he ran, he seemed
The one who wins, and not the one who loses!

CANTO
16

I NOW had come to where I heard the roar
Of water falling to the other circle,
That sounded like the droning of a hive —
When suddenly three running shades broke forth
From out a company that passed us by
Beneath the bitter downpour of the flames.
They came toward us, shouting as they ran:
«Halt, you who by your cloak appear to be
A citizen of our corrupted land!»

'Ah me! What scars I saw upon their limbs,
Both new and old, burnt deeply by the flames!
It grieves me still when I but think of it.
My teacher paused, attentive to their cries.
Turning his face to me, he said: «Now wait —
Because to these we ought to be polite.
And were it not for all these fiery darts
That rain down here about us, I should say
That haste were more befitting you than them.»

We stopped, and they repeated their refrain;
And when they had come up with us, all three
Made of themselves a wheel, and whirled about.
Like champions stripped and oiled, who watch
⌊each grip
And vantage point before a blow or thrust:
So, as they wheeled, each sinner turned his face
Upon me, in such manner that his neck
Seemed always to be turning round and round
In opposite direction to his feet.

«Ah, though the misery of this waste of sand
And our charred aspect,» one of them began,
«Should make you scornful of us and our prayers,
Let our renown incline your mind to tell
Who you may be, that in security
Thus move with living feet through hell's domain.
This man, upon whose heels I press so close,
Albeit he goes naked now and scorched,
Was yet of higher rank than one might think:
For he was grandson to the good Guaralda.
His name was Guido Guerra, and in life
He shone in wisdom and in valorous deeds.
That other, treading on the sand behind me,
Tegghiaio Aldobrandi, whose advice
Should have been welcome in the world above.
And I, placed with them both in torment here,
Jacopo Rusticucci; and in truth
My savage wife is cause of all my sins.»

Had I been sheltered from the rain of fire,
I should have thrown myself into their midst,
And I believe my teacher would have let me;
But as I should have burned and baked myself,
My prudence overcame the good intention
That made me eager to embrace them all.
I said to them: «It was not scorn, but grief
Which your sad fortune fixed in me so deeply
That it shall not be easily forgotten,
When first I learned, from this my master's words,
That some such honorable folk as you
Were coming forward to converse with us.
I am your countryman — and ever have
With true affection told and listened to
Reports of your good deeds and honored names.
I leave the gall and go to seek the fruit
That has been promised by my trusty guide;
But first I must go down into the centre.»

«Long may your soul direct your limbs above,»
He answered, «and your fame shine after you:
By these high hopes, I beg you to reply
If courtesy and valor still are found
Within our city as they used to be,
Or have they gone entirely out of it?
Guglielmo Borsiere, who has been

But some brief while in torment with us here
And runs across there, tells us grievous news.»
  «The upstart people, and their sudden gains,
O Florence, have engendered in your midst
Such pride and discord, that you weep aloud!»
Thus I cried out to them, with head held high.
The three, who understood this for an answer,
Gazed one upon the other, knowingly.
«Take care!» they all replied, «Another time
Should you speak thus to satisfy another,
It well may cost you more! We beg of you,
If ever you escape from these dark places
To look again upon the stars of heaven —
When you may wish to say, 'I once was there!'
See that you speak of us to other men.»

  They then broke up the wheel and ran away,
Winged on their nimble legs, and disappeared.
Not even one amen could have been said
As quickly as they vanished; thereupon
My master thought it fitting to depart.

  I followed him, and we had not gone far
Before the water's roaring was so near
That had we spoken, we could scarce have heard.
And even as that stream which takes its course
At first from Monte Viso to the eastward
Upon the left-hand slope of Appenine
(And higher up is Acquacheta called
Before it rushes to its lower bed
And takes another name beyond Forlì),
Leaving the mountain crag of Benedict,
From which a thousand streamlets might have
                              ⌊fallen,

Drops thundering downward in a single leap:
Just so, downpouring from a lofty cliff,
We heard that crimson cataract resound,
So loud that it would soon have made us deaf.
  Around my waist was tied a knotted cord
With which I had intended, at one time,
To noose the leopard with the spotted hide;
And after I had quite unfastened it
As my good leader had commanded me,
I coiled it up and handed it to him.
He took it from me, turning to the right,

And cast it out some distance from the brink
Straight down into that bottomless abyss.
«Now certainly,» I said unto myself,
«Some strange new thing will answer this odd
For he is peering downward so intently.» ⌊signal,

  Ah me! How very cautious one must be
With those who look not at the deed alone,
But also have the power to read one's thoughts!
For then he said: «There shortly will come up
What I await; and what your fancy paints
Will forthwith be presented to your eyes.»
  Before a truth that wears the guise of
                              ⌊falsehood,

A man must close his lips as best he can,
Because, though blameless, he may be ashamed.
But reader, here I cannot hold my peace:
And by the verses of this comedy
I swear to you — so may their fame endure —
That through that dark and heavy air I saw
Come swimming upward a most gruesome shape
That well might frighten any steadfast heart —
Like one returning who has dived to clear
An anchor that has fouled upon a rock,
Or something else deep hidden in the sea,
And rises, breast erect and feet drawn in.

CANTO
17

Look on that monster with the pointed tail
Who passes mountain walls and shatters
                              ⌊weapons —
Look on this thing whose venom fills the world!»
Thus did my noble leader speak to me,
And beckoned him to come up to the bank
Beside the rim of rock that we had passed.

Canto 17 : The Descent of the Abyss on Geryon's Back

And then that loathsome counterfeit of fraud
Approached, and landed with his head and chest,
But did not draw his tail up on the brink.
He had the features of an honest man,
So mild an aspect bore he from without,
But all the rest was fashioned like a serpent.
Two paws he had, all shaggy to the armpits;
His back and breast and both his scaly sides
Were patterned with a mass of coils and bucklers.
Nor Turk nor Tartar ever made a cloth
So rich in varied color and design,
Nor were such stuffs laid on Arachne's loom.

As skiffs will sometimes lie along a bank,
Partly ashore and partly in the wave,
Or as the beaver, 'mongst the greedy Germans,
Will take his stand while waiting for his prey:
Just so that direful beast had come to rest
Upon the stony rim that girds the sand.
All of his tail was writhing in the void,
And twirled about on high the poisoned fork,
Shaped like a scorpion, that armed its point.

My leader said: «We now must bend our course
And go to meet that monster of ill omen
Who crouches over there upon the bank.»

Accordingly we went down to the right,
And walked some paces on the very brink,
Avoiding thus the sand and flakes of fire.

When we had come beside him, I perceived
A little way beyond, upon the sand,
Some people sitting close beside the void.
My master said to me: «That you may gain
A fuller understanding of this round,
Go forward now, and look at their condition.
But let your talk with them be brief. And I,
Till you return, will parley with this beast,
That he may lend his brawny shoulders to us.»

Thus once again I wandered on alone,
Upon that seventh circle's very rim,
To where those grieving folk were sitting down.
Their grief was gushing outward from their eyes;
Now here, now there, they vainly moved their ⌊hands
To stay the scorching vapors or the sand,
As dogs will do in summer, with their paws

And with their muzzles, when they have been
By fleas or gnats or gadflies in the heat. ⌊bitten
When I looked on the faces of those shades
Who sat beneath the grievous rain of fire,
I recognized them not; but I remarked
Hung from the neck of each of them, a pouch
On which were blazoned color and device:
Therewith, it seemed, their wretched eyes are fed.
And as I looked among them, I beheld
Upon a yellow purse, a blue design
That had the face and bearing of a lion.
Then, as I looked beyond, I saw another
As red as blood, charged with a silver goose
That gleamed, beneath the flames, as white as
⌊butter.

A shade who had a little white sack bearing
Azure, a gravid cow, accosted me:
«What are you doing in this ditch of woe?
Now get you gone, since you are still alive!
Know that Vitaliano, who's my neighbor,
Will sit here presently upon my left.
A Paduan, I am with these Florentines.
Often they deafen me, when they cry out,
'Make room for him, that sovereign cavalier,
Whose pouch will bear three eagles' beaks
⌊displayed!'»

He twisted up his mouth, and like an ox
That licks its nose, stuck out his loathsome tongue.

And I, afraid that longer stay might vex
Him who admonished me to stay but little,
Turned back again, and left those weary souls.
I found my leader, who already sat
Upon the croup of that fierce animal.
He said to me: «Be brave—call on your strength,
For now we must descend such stairs as these!
You mount in front, for I would be between,
So that the monster's tail do you no harm.»

Like one who shivers in the quartan's grasp,
So that his nails already have turned pale,
And the mere sight of shade will make him
⌊tremble:
So I became when he had said those words.
But his reproofs aroused in me that shame

29

Which makes a servant bold before his lord;
And on those unclean shoulders I sat down.
I wished to say, «Dear master, hold me tight!»
But found my voice came not as I desired;
And he who once before had succored me
In time of dread, as soon as I had mounted
Clasped me tight in his sustaining arms,
Saying: «Move on now, Geryon—take care
That your descent be slow, your circles wide:
Think of the novel burden that you carry!»

Just as a little bark will leave its berth,
So backward, ever backward, he withdrew;
But when he felt that he was clear and free,
There where his breast had been he turned his tail,
And moved it all extended, like an eel,
While with his paws he gathered in the air.
Never was greater fear, I think, than mine
When I saw round about on every side
Nothing but air, nor sight of anything
Except the scaly members of the beast—
Not when Phaethon dropped the heavenly reins
So that the sky, as still appears, caught fire,
Nor when the hapless Icarus perceived
His loins unfeathering from the melting wax,
So that his father cried: «Ill goes your way!»

The beast swam slowly, ever slowly downward,
And wheeled about—though I should ne'er have
⌊known

But for the wind below and from the side.
Upon the right I heard the cataract
Falling beneath us with a dreadful roar,
So that I craned my neck and peered below.
Now I became more fearful of the pit,
As I perceived its flames and heard the cries
That set me trembling, and I crouched in dread;
For now I saw what I had not perceived,
Our wheeling and descent; and torments horrible
Were drawing near to us on every side.

Just as a falcon, long upon the wing
Without perceiving either bird or lure,
Will make the falconer cry, «Alas! She stoops!»
Descending weary whence she rose so fast,
Wheeling a hundred times, and settling down

Far from her master, sullen and disdainful:
So Geryon set us down upon the ground
At the abutment of the rocky cliff.
And when he felt unburdened of his load
He fled, as flies an arrow from its cord.

CANTO
18

A PLACE there is in hell called Malebolge,
Which with the precipice surrounding it
Is all composed of iron-colored stone.
Right in the centre of this field malign
There yawns a mighty crater, broad and deep:
Its structure I will tell of, in its place.
That space is circular which thus remains
Between the crater and the precipice;
Into ten valleys is its bed divided.

As when for the protection of the walls
Ring upon ring of moats surround a castle,
Making a pattern on the countryside,
Just so was the appearance of these valleys.
And as such fortresses have narrow bridges
To join their portals to the outer bank,
So, springing from the cliff, were bridges here,
That struck across the ramparts and the valleys,
Converging toward the pit which cut them short.
'Twas here we found ourselves when Geryon
Had shaken us from off his back. The poet
Held to the left, and I moved on behind.

Upon the right, new torments I beheld—
New miseries, new hosts of scourging fiends,
With which the first division was close packed.
All naked were the sinners at the bottom;
The nearer half came toward us as they walked,
The rest went with us, at a swifter pace—
Just as the Romans, for the multitude
Thronging the bridge, the year of jubilee,

Canto 18 : Virgil shows Dante the Shade of Thaïs

Devised a method for the folk to pass,
So that all those upon the hither side
Faced toward the castle, going to St. Peter's,
While those beyond the barrier faced the mount.

On every hand along the dreary vale
Horned demons I beheld, each with a scourge,
Who cruelly flogged the people from behind.
How nimbly did they make them lift their heels
At the first stroke! Indeed, there were not those
Who waited for the second and the third!
And as I walked along, one met my gaze,
So that I said at once: «It seems to me
That I have seen this person's face before!»

Therefore I slowed my pace to see him closely,
And my kind leader paused with me awhile,
Consenting that I should retrace my steps.
At that, the scourged one sought to hide himself
By bowing down his head; but all in vain,
For I cried out: «O you with downcast eyes,
Unless the features that you bear are false,
You are Venedico Caccianimico!
But what has brought you to such bitter
⌊torment?»

And he to me: «Unwillingly I'll tell;
But your plain speech, which brings back to my
⌊mind

The world I left, constrains me to speak forth.
That man was I, who led Ghisolabella
To yield herself to the marchese's will—
No matter how the shameful tale be told.
And I am not the only Bolognese
Who's weeping here: so full of them this place,
That not so many tongues were ever taught
'Twixt Reno and Savena to say *sipa*.
And if you seek for proof or evidence,
You only need recall our greedy hearts.»

As he was saying this, a demon came
And smote him with his scourge, and said to him:
«Pander, begone! No women here for profit!»
Whereat I left, to join my kindly guide.

We walked but little onward ere we reached
A rocky bridgeway jutting from the bank.
This we ascended, taking easy steps;

And turning to the right along its ridge,
We left the huge encircling wall of cliffs.

When we had come to where the bridge below
Was open to give passage to the scourged,
My leader said: «Take hold, and let your eyes
Rest on these other spirits born for evil,
Whose faces you have not as yet beheld
Because their way has been the same as ours.»

And from the ancient bridge we viewed the file
That came toward us on the inner side;
And these were likewise driven by the scourge.

My goodly master, of his own accord,
Addressed me: «See that mighty one who comes,
And seems, for all his pain, to shed no tear:
What kingly bearing doth he still retain!
Jason is he, whose prowess and whose wiles
Deprived the Colchians of their cherished ram.
He passed the isle of Lemnos on his voyage,
After its women, merciless and bold,
Had put to death all men who had remained;
And with false tokens and with honeyed words
He there deceived the fair Hypsipyle—
Who had herself deceived the other women—
And then forsook her, pregnant and forlorn.
Such guilt condemns him to such punishment,
And likewise is Medea here avenged.
With him are all deceivers of like sort:
Let this suffice for knowledge of this valley
And of the spirits held within its fangs.»

Already had we come to where the pathway
Crosses the second rampart, where it formed
A new abutment for another arch.
From here we heard the muffled sound of moans
From people in the valley next beyond,
Who puffed with mouth and nose, and struck
⌊themselves.

The banks were covered with a crust of mould,
Deposited by vapors from beneath,
That sore offended both the eyes and nose.
The bottom was so hollowed out below,
Naught could be seen, save from the vantage point
Above the arch that overhangs it most.
Thither we came; and thence I now could see

Below us in the fosse, some folk immersed
In filth: it seemed to come from human privies.
And while I peered into the depths beneath,
I saw a man whose head was so befouled
One could not tell if he were clerk or layman.
He snarled at me: «Now why are you so eager
To look at me instead of at the rest?»

And I replied: «Because, as I recall,
I once before have seen you, with dry hair.
You are Alessio Interminei of Lucca:
Therefore I seek you out among the others.»

And as he answered me he struck his pate:
«Here I am submerged by flatteries,
With which my tongue was never satisfied!»

My leader said to me: «Now stretch your neck
A little further forward, so that you
Can look upon the loathsome countenance
Of that dishevelled baggage over there,
Who tears her flesh away with dung-filled nails,
And now sits down, and now stands up again.
Thais is she, the harlot, who replied
Unto her lover, when he asked of her,
'Have I your gratitude?' 'Nay, rather say,
«My heart's desire!» Now we have seen enough.»

CANTO
19

O SIMON MAGUS, and your wicked tribe!
Rapacious brutes, who take the things of God
That ought to be the brides of righteousness,
And then make them debauch themselves for gold!
Now it is meet the trumpet sound for you,
Because in this third valley you abide!

Already had we reached the next division,
By climbing to that portion of the bridge
Which overhangs the middle of the fosse.
Wisdom Divine! How mighty is that art

Thou dost display in heaven, earth, and hell!
How just the manner of thy punishments!
I saw the dark grey rock on every side,
And on the bottom, pierced with many holes
All of one size, and each was circular.
They seemed to me no greater, nor less wide
Than those which in my beautiful St. John's
Are fashioned as a place for our baptizers.
One of these holes, not many years ago,
I broke, to rescue one who was caught fast:
And by this seal let men be undeceived!

Beyond the mouth of each of them stuck forth
A sinner's feet and legs up to his calves,
While all the rest of him remained within.
All of them had both their soles on fire,
From which their joints were writhing with such
⌊force

They would have broken any ropes or withes.
As upon oily things the flame is wont
To flicker on the outer part alone,
So did it here, between their heels and toes.

«Master,» said I, «who thus torments himself
By struggling more than his companions here—
He whom, it seems, a ruddier flame is licking?»

He answered me: «If I but take you down
By yonder cliff that slopes more easily,
Then he himself can tell you of his crimes.»

And I: «What pleases you is my desire.
You are my lord, whose will is ever mine:
You even know my thoughts which are unsaid.»

On the fourth parapet we had arrived;
We turned upon our left, and then went on
Down to the narrow bottom pierced with holes.
My goodly master did not set me down
From off his hip, until we reached the pit
Of him whose shanks were writhing in such pain.

«O wretched soul,» said I, «whoe'er you are
That like a planted post keeps down below
Your upper part—speak to me, if you can!»
I stood just like the friar who confesses
The treacherous assassin in the hole,
Who, bound, recalls him, thus to put off death.

He cried to me: «Are you already there,

Canto 19 : Dante addresses Pope Nicholas III

INFERNO: CANTO 19

Already, Boniface, upon your feet?
The screed of fate is false by many years!
Have you so soon been glutted with that wealth
For which you did not fear, by base deceit,
To wed the Lady fair, and outrage her?»

    I thereupon became like one ashamed
From understanding not what is replied,
And then himself does not know what to answer.
But Virgil said: «Tell him at once and say,
'I am not he, I am not he you think.' »

      And I made answer as I had been told.

      Thereat the spirit twitched his feet amain.
He sighed, and with a voice that spoke through
                ⌊tears,

Replied: «What, then, do you require of me?
If you have such desire to know my name
That you have crossed the bank for this alone,
Know that I once was vested in the mantle,
And truly was a scion of the she-bear;
So greedy that the bear cubs should advance,
I pocketed wealth there, and here myself.
Beneath my head, dragged downward through
                ⌊the cracks,

Lie pressed between opposing walls of rock
Those who preceded me in simony;
And down there likewise I myself shall drop
As soon as he for whom I just mistook you,
When first I questioned you, shall here arrive.
But longer is the time I have remained
Inverted as you see, here in this pit,
Than he will stay inside with burning feet:
For after him will come from out the west
One of yet fouler deeds—a lawless pastor
Who fittingly will cover him and me.
Another Jason he, of Maccabees;
As Jason's king was pliant to his wishes,
So unto his will be the King of France.»

    I know not if I was not here unwise
In that I simply answered in this strain:
«Pray tell me now, just what amount of treasure
Our Lord required in payment from St. Peter
Before he gave the keys into his hands?
Forsooth, he but demanded, 'Follow me.'

Nor Peter, nor the rest, received from Matthew
Silver or gold, when he had won by lot
The post that guilty soul had forfeited.
Here then remain, for you are rightly punished;
And take good care of that ill-gotten gold
Which made you dare to cross the will of Charles.
And were it not that even now I shrink
Because of reverence for the mighty keys
That you once held while in your life above,
The language that I use would be much harsher,
Because your avarice afflicts the world,
And trampling down the good, exalts the bad.
Shepherds like you the evangelist had in mind
When he saw her that sitteth on the waters
Committing fornication with the kings—
That woman who was born with seven heads,
And with ten horns imposed her government
So long the way of virtue pleased her husband.
You have set up a god of gold and silver:
How do you differ from idolaters,
Save that they worship one, and you a hundred?
Ah Constantine! How evil was the seed
Sown not by your conversion, but by the dower
The first rich father once received from you!»

    While I was opening my mind to him,
Either from rage, or from the pangs of conscience,
He kicked out violently with both feet.
My leader, I believe, was pleased thereby:
For with a happy countenance he heard
The voice of truth resounding in those words.
And then he caught me up in both his arms,
And when he held me fast upon his breast,
He mounted by the way that we had come;
Nor did he weary of his close embrace
Until he carried me atop the arch
Joining the fourth escarpment to the fifth.
Once there, he gently set his burden down—
Gently, by reason of the rugged cliff,
Almost too steep for goats to walk upon.
From there I saw another spacious valley.

CANTO
20

OF a new punishment I now must sing,
To furnish matter for the twentieth canto
Of this first lay, which tells of those submerged.

I now had reached a point whence I could see
The great abyss that opened out below,
Eternally bedewed by tears of anguish.
People I saw who ever circled round
That great expanse, in silence and in weeping,
Dragging their steps, as litanies are paced.
And when my eyes were lowered, I perceived
That each one seemed to be most strangely twisted
Between the chin and where the chest begins.
The face of every one turned to his back;
So ever backward they were forced to walk,
Unable as they were to look ahead.
Perhaps, because of some paralysis,
Ere now, some people may have been so twisted:
I've seen it not—nor think that it can be.

Reader, as God may grant you gather fruit
From reading this, take counsel with yourself:
How could I stop my tears from streaming down
When I beheld so near, our human frame
So turned about, the weeping from the eyes
Ran down to bathe the cleft between the
⌊buttocks?

Of course I wept—and as I wept, I leaned
Against a rock projecting from the cliff.
My master said: «Are you, as well, a fool?
Piety thrives here when pity dies.
Who is more blameable than he who weeps
When he beholds the judgement of the Lord?
Lift up your head, and see the man for whom
The earth once yawned before the Thebans' eyes,
So that they cried: 'O Amphiaraus,

Where are you falling? Why do you leave the
And ever down he fell, until he came ⌊war?'
To Minos, who lays hold on all who come.
See how he now has shoulders for a breast:
Because he sought to look too far ahead,
He now looks back, and treads a backward path.

«See there Tiresias, who changed his semblance:
No longer man, a woman he became,
And all his members likewise were transformed.
Later, he was forced again to strike
The intertwining serpents with his wand
Before he could resume his manly plumes.

«That man whose back is close behind his belly
Is Aruns, who once dwelt on Luni's mount,
Near where Carrara's toilers work below;
And from his cave among the snow-white marbles
He could observe the galaxy of stars,
And glimpse the azure of the ocean wave.

«She there—whose loosened tresses now conceal
Her breasts, as yet still hidden from your sight,
And on the other side has hairy skin—
Was Manto, wanderer through many lands,
Who brought her steps to halt where I was born:
Of which it pleases me that you shall hear.

«After her father had forsaken life
And Bacchus' city had become enslaved,
She roamed about the world for many years.
Above, in Italy, there is a lake
Below that alp that shuts in Germany
Above the Tyrol: Benaco is its name.
And there, between Camonica and Garda,
A thousand freshets bathe Mount Apennine
And tumble downward to that lake for rest.
Amid the lake's expanse there is a spot
Where Brescia's bishop, Trent's, Verona's too,
Might each give benediction if he passed.
Now where the lake's encircling shore lies lowest,
Peschiera stands, a fortress fair and strong,
To front the Brescians and the Bergamese;
And there perforce the water overflows
That cannot linger in Benaco's bosom,
Making a river through the pastures green.
From where this river first starts on its course

Down to Giverno, where it joins the Po,
'Tis not Benaco called, but Mincio.
It flows but little ere it meets a plain
Upon which it extends to form a swamp
That in the heat is often pestilential.
  «When passing by this spot, that evil witch
Espied some ground amid the reeking fen,
Untilled, and uninhabited as well.
There, to avoid mankind's companionship,
She settled, with her slaves, and plied her arts,
And dying, left behind her empty clay.
Later, the men who lived in the surroundings
Assembled at this spot, whose strong defence
Lay in the marsh that girds it on all sides.
Over her dead bones they built their city;
And after her who first had found the spot
They called it by the name of Mantua.
It was more populous in olden times,
Ere the stupidity of Casalodi
Was caught by Pinamonte's stratagem.
Therefore I warn you: should you hear perchance
A different story of my native place,
Let no man's falsehood ever cheat the truth.»
  «Master, your reasonings appear to me
So certain, and they so constrain my faith,
That others seem to me like burnt-out embers.
But tell me of these people passing by,
If you should notice any worth remark:
That is the theme to which my mind reverts.»
    He answered: «Yonder man, who from his
                                    ⌊cheek
Stretches his beard across his dusky shoulders,
An augur was, when Greece was so bereft
Of men, the cradles too were nearly empty.
With Calchas, he it was who named the time
When the first cable should be cut at Aulis.
Eurypylus his name: of him doth sing
Some passage in my lofty tragedy —
As you must know, who know the whole so well.
That other one, so spare about the loins,
Is Michael Scott, who, verily, knew well
The canny tricks of magical deceit.
Guido Bonatti see: and mark Asdente,

Who wishes now that he had kept his mind
On leather and his thread — alas, too late!
And see the wretched women who forsook
The needle, spool, and distaff, to become
Foul witches who wrought spells with herbs and
                                    ⌊wax.
But now come on: Cain with his bundled thorns
Bestrides the confines of the hemispheres,
And touches on the wave below Seville.
Already yesternight the moon was full,
As you should well recall — for oftentimes
In the deep wood it served you far from ill.»
Thus he instructed me, as we walked on.

CANTO 21

WHILE we were talking thus of other matters
Of which my comedy cares not to sing,
We passed from bridge to bridge, and reached the
                                    ⌊summit;
And here we stopped, to see the next division
Of Malebolge, filled with vain laments:
I saw that it was marvellously dark.
    As in the arsenal of the Venetians,
In wintertime, the workmen boil their pitch,
To serve as caulking for the gaping seams
Of craft in which they dare not put to sea —
Instead, perchance, one builds his ship anew,
Another caulks an ancient vessel's sides,
One hammers at the prow or at the stern,
One makes his oars, another twists his rope,
Or mends his mainsail or his mizzen sail —
So, not by fire, but by the will divine,
There bubbled in those depths a mass of pitch
That smeared the valley's bank on every side.
I saw it; but no more could I discern

Than bubbles rising in the boiling mass;
It seemed to heave, and then subside again.

While I was gazing fixedly below,
My leader, crying out, «Take care, take care!»
Dragged me from where I stood close to his side.
I turned around like one who longs to look
At unseen danger that he would avoid,
Yet by his sudden fear is all unmanned,
And looking backward, cannot wait to see it.
I saw a jet-black demon there behind us
Come running down the causeway's rocky path.
Ah me, how fierce he was to look upon!
Yet in his actions he was fiercer still.
His wings were spread, his feet were light and free;
His pointed shoulder, which was square and high,
Was burdened with the haunches of a sinner;
His talons gripped the tendons, near the feet.
And from our bridge he cried: «O Malebranche,
Here's an elder of St. Zita for you!
Thrust him beneath, while I go back for more,
Back to that city that's so full of them.
There all are barrators—except Bonturo!
There every no for coin is changed to yes.»

He hurled him down, and off above the ridge
He quickly sped—and never in such haste
Did unleashed mastiff chase a thief in flight.
The other sank, and rose again hunched up;
Demons in cover at the bridge cried out:
«The *Santo Volto* has no business here—
The swimming here's not like that in the Serchio!
Therefore unless you wish to feel our hooks,
Keep down beneath the surface of the tar!»
They caught him with at least a hundred prongs,
And shouted: «Dance away beneath the pitch,
And carry on your trade, if you can do so!»

Not otherwise will cooks direct their scullions
To poke the meat with forks down in the cauldron,
Whenever pieces float upon the top.
My master said to me: «Don't let them see you;
Crouch down behind a rock, and hide yourself
With any sort of screen that you can find.
No matter what offense be offered me,
Fear not: I have good knowledge of these things,

For once before I've been in such a wrangle!»
He crossed the bridge; and when he had
Upon the margin of the sixth escarpment, ⌐arrived
Full need had he for an undaunted front.
For with that rage and sudden violence
With which a dog will set upon a beggar
Who quickly asks his alms from where he stands,
Those demons rushed from underneath the bridge
And levelled all their grapples at my master.
But he cried out: «Let none of you do ill!
Before a hook of yours shall touch my skin,
Let one of you step forth and hear my words,
And then consider if he'll grapple me!»

They all exclaimed: «Let Malacoda go!»
Then one of them advanced. The rest stood still
While he approached and said: «To what avail?»

«Do you believe,» my master answered him,
«O Malacoda, that you see me come
As far as this, secure from your assaults,
Except by will divine, and fate's decree?
Let us pass by; for it is willed in heaven
That I should lead another by this way.»

At this, his arrogance was so abased
He dropped his hook, and said to his companions:
«He must not be molested for the moment.»

My leader said to me: «You who I know
Are crouching there behind the shattered bridge,
Return to me, in all security.»

At that I rose and quickly came to him.
The demons all sprang forward, and I feared
That they might fail to keep their promises:
In just this way I saw some infantry,
When marching from Caprona under truce,
Show fear among a host of enemies.
I drew my body close beside my leader's,
And never turned my eyes away from those
Whose evil looks were far from reassuring.
They now inclined their grapples, and cried out
To one another: «Shall I prod his rump?»
And answered: «Yes, just nick it into him!»

At this the demon who was talking then
With my good leader, quickly turned and said:
«Be quiet, oh be quiet, Scarmiglione!»

Canto 21 : The Demons threaten Virgil

And then to us: «No farther can you go
Along this bridge: for yonder underneath,
The sixth arch lies in pieces at the bottom.
But if you still desire to pass beyond,
Then take your way along this precipice;
Another bridge lies near, that you can cross.
Yesterday—five hours beyond this time—
Twelve hundred years and sixty-six besides
Were finished since the way was broken here.
In that direction I must send some demons
To see if any sinners air themselves;
You can go with them, for they will not harm you.
Come forward Alichino, Calcabrina,»
He ordered them, «and you, Cagnazzo, too;
Let Barbariccia command the ten.
Come hither Libicocco, Draghignazzo,
Ciriatto with the tusks, and Grafficane,
And Farfarello, and mad Rubicante.
Go, and search the boiling pitch; and see
That these are unmolested, till you reach
The next unbroken bridge that spans the valley.»

  «Alas, my master! What is this I see?
I beg you,» said I, «let us go alone;
If you but know the way, I ask it not.
If you are as observant as your wont,
You must have noticed how they grind their teeth
And threaten us with mischief as they scowl!»

  And he to me: «I will not have you fear.
Let them all grind their teeth as they may wish;
'Tis at the boiling sinner, not at us.»

  They wheeled around upon the left-hand bank;
But first had each of them stuck out his tongue
Between his teeth, as signal to their leader,
And he had made a trumpet of his rump.

CANTO
22

ERE now have I seen horsemen breaking camp,
Preparing battle, mustering their men,
Or in retreat when fleeing for their safety:
Scouts I have seen, O people of Arezzo,
And pillagers, upon your countryside:
Tournaments fought, and jousts run in the lists,
At times to sound of trumpets or of bells,
With drums, or signals from a castle tower,
Alike with native and with foreign usage:
But never yet, to such a bugle call
Have I seen foot or horsemen starting forth,
Or ship set sail to such a signal gun!

  With the ten demons on our way we went.
Bad company, indeed! But, as they say,
«To church with saints, and to the inn with
⌊gluttons.»

I gave my whole attention to the pitch,
To notice every detail in its depths,
And of the people who were boiling there.

  As dolphins, by the arching of their backs,
Warn mariners that they must shorten sail
And thus secure the safety of their ship:
So, every now and then, to ease his torment
A sinner here or there would show his back
And quick as lightning dive below again.
Just as in a moat, along the bank,
Frogs will lie still, with snouts alone exposed,
So that their legs and bodies are concealed:
Just so on every side the sinners lay.
As soon as Barbariccia drew near
They ducked again beneath the boiling pitch.
I saw—and even now it makes me shudder—
One stay too long, as oft it will befall
One frog remains, while others dart away;

And Grafficane, who was nearest him,
Hooked him by his tarry, matted locks
And dragged him like an otter up the bank.
Already I knew each of them by name,
For I had marked them well when they were
⌊chosen,

And later when they called to one another.
«O Rubicante,» yelled in unison
Those fiends accurst, «see that you plant your
⌊claws

Deep in his back, so you can flay him well!»
And I to him: «My master, try to learn
The name of that ill-fated being there
Who fell into the clutches of his foes.»
My kindly leader now went up beside him
And asked him whence he came, and he replied:
«Navarre was where I saw the light of day.
My mother placed me in a lord's employ,
For she had borne me to a ribald man,
Destroyer of himself and of his goods.
Later I was at good King Thibault's court,
And there I took my money where I could—
For which I pay full reckoning in this heat!»

Then Ciriatto—from whose mouth stuck forth
On either side great tusks just like a boar's—
Made him feel how one of them could rip.
The mouse had fallen among hungry cats!
But Barbariccia clasped him in his arms
And said: «Away there, while I hold him tight!»
Turning his face toward my goodly master,
«Ask on,» he said, «if you desire to learn
Still further, ere the others rend him piecemeal.»

My leader spoke: «Tell me about the others;
Do you know anyone beneath the pitch
Who is Italian?» «Not long since,» he said,
«I parted from a neighbor to those regions.
Would I were with him now beneath the pitch,
So that I need not fear these claws and hooks!»

Said Libicocco: «We have borne enough!»
And with his grapple caught him by the arm,
Rending his flesh and tearing off a sinew.

Draghinazzo too would have laid hold
Upon the sinner's legs, had not their leader

Turned round upon them with a threatening
⌊glance.

Now that their anger was appeased somewhat,
My gentle leader asked the hapless shade,
Who still was gazing sadly at his wound:
«Who was that man from whom, you said just
⌊now,
You parted lucklessly to come to shore?»

«That was Fra Gomita,» he replied,
«He of Gallura—vessel of all guile,
Who held his master's foes within his grasp,
So treating them that each of them is grateful.
Money he took, and let them freely go,
As he himself relates. In other trusts
He also was a sovereign barrator.
Here in his company is Michael Zanche
Of Logodoro; never do their tongues
Grow weary talking of Sardinia.
Ah me! Look how that fellow gloats on me!
I would say more, if I were not afraid
His ugly claws would sink into my skin!»

Now the grand marshal turned to Farfarello,
Whose leering eyes were turned upon his prey,
Saying: «You bird of evil, stand aside!»

«In case you wish,» the frightened shade
⌊continued,

«To see or talk with Tuscans or with Lombards,
I'll cause a few to come above the pitch.
But let the Malebranche stand aside,
So that the spirits may not fear their vengeance:
And I, while seated on this very spot,
For one that here I am, will call forth seven
If I but whistle—as we often do
When one of us comes up above the surface.»

At this Cagnazzo lifted up his muzzle,
Wagging his head, and said: «It's just a trick
He has contrived, for jumping in again!»

But he, who had his share of craftiness:
«Too full of tricks indeed am I,
When I but serve to aggravate our woe!»

Alichino could keep still no more,
But said to him, opposing all the others:
«If you leap down, I will be after you—
Not on my feet, but swooping on my wings!

Canto 22 : Ciampolo escaping from the Demon Alichino

Let's leave this cliff, and go behind the bank:
Then we can see if you outwit us all!»

    O reader, hear about new kinds of sport!
For all of them now turned their eyes aside,
He first who formerly was most reluctant.
He of Navarre, choosing his moment well,
Stood firmly on the ground, and in a trice
Leaped down, and thus escaped their evil purpose.
At this all of the fiends were mad with rage,
But most of all, the one who caused the blunder.
He started forward, yelling: «You are caught!»

    But little it availed him, for his wings
Were fast outstripped by fear. The one dived in,
The other, as he flew, rose up again,
Just like a duck who dives beneath the water
To seek a refuge from the falcon's claws,
And then soars up again, discomfited.
Calcabrina, furious at the trick,
Kept close behind him on the wing, well pleased
At the excuse it offered for a quarrel.
The moment that the shade had disappeared,
He swiftly turned his talons on his comrade
And grappled with him, close above the pitch;
But Alichino like a sparrow hawk
Fastened his claws on him—so they both fell
Into the middle of the boiling flood.
The scalding heat drove them apart at once;
But their attempts to rise were all in vain,
For both of them had wings stuck fast with pitch.
Now Barbariccia, with his howling crew,
Made four of them fly to the other shore
With all their hooks; and speedily enough
On either hand, each one took up his post.
They thrust their grapples toward the sticky pair
Who were already scalded through their skins;
And there, in such a sorry plight, we left them.

CANTO
23

Silent, alone and unaccompanied
We went our way, he first and I behind,
As Friars Minor go upon the road.
The brawl that I had seen reminded me
Of Aesop's fable, where he tells the tale
About the frog and the unlucky mouse.
At once and *now* are no more nearly like
Than one is to the other, for they match
From first to last—as a keen mind can see.
As one idea will blossom from another,
So, out of that, another thought arose,
Which served but to intensify my fear.
I reasoned thus: «These fiends, by our intent,
Are made ridiculous; and so much so,
I think they must be greatly vexed thereby.
If wrath be added to their evil will,
They will come after us more ruthlessly
Than ever hound pursued a hunted beast.»
Already I could feel my hair on end
From terror, and I looked back anxiously.
And then I said: «Master, unless at once
We both conceal ourselves, I greatly fear
The Malebranche. There they are behind us:
They seem so near, I think that I can hear them!»

    And he: «Though I were made of silvered ⌊glass,
No faster could I catch your outer image
Than I receive that other from within.
Your thoughts just now were mingled with my ⌊own,
Alike in action and in show of fear,
So that of both I have made one resolve.
If it be true that yonder cliff provides
A pathway sloping downward to the valley,
We can escape from that pursuit you fear!»

    Ere he had finished telling me his plan

I saw them, not far off, with wings outspread
Coming upon us, eager to attack.
My leader instantly laid hold of me,
Just as a mother, wakened by a noise,
And seeing how the flames are near at hand,
Will snatch her child and run, nor think to ⌊pause
Not long enough to slip into her shift —
Having more care for him than for herself.

    Down from the summit of that rocky cliff
He slid upon his back, along the bank
That closes in the valley next below.
Never ran water faster through a sluice,
Rushing on headlong till it strikes the paddles
To turn a mill wheel on the waterside,
Than my good master glided down that cliff,
Bearing me tenderly upon his breast,
More as his son than as a fellow traveller.
Scarcely were his feet upon the ground
Before the demons reached the cliff above us.
But down below we had no need to fear:
For Providence, which designated them
To minister within the fifth enclosure,
Witheld from them the power of leaving it.

    Below we found a painted multitude,
Who slowly moved about with dragging steps,
Weeping and sad, and wretched to behold.
They wore great mantles, with low-hanging hoods
That hid their eyes, and fashioned with that cut
Which Cluny's monks adopted for their habit.
Their outer surface was of dazzling gold;
Within, they were composed of lead so heavy
That Frederick's might seem as straw beside ⌊them.
O mantle, heavy through eternity!
And now we turned again toward the left
And walked beside them, hearkening to their ⌊groans;

But those poor weary souls moved on so slowly
By reason of their load, that at each step
We found ourselves in different company.
I asked my leader: «Pray, among this crowd,
Find someone who is known by name or deed:
Look at them closely as you walk along.»

    A shade behind us, hearing Tuscan speech,

Cried out: «Delay your steps, O you who speed
So swiftly through the dusky air: perchance
You may obtain from me what you desire.»

    My noble leader turned to me and said:
«Wait here; and then walk onward at his pace.»
I stopped, and saw two souls whose faces ⌊showed

That they were eager to come up with me,
Though hindered by their load and crowded path.
When they caught up with us, with eyes askance
They gazed upon me long, without a word;
Then one turned to the other, and remarked:
«He seems alive, that one who moves his throat:
If they be dead, then by what privilege
Are they not burdened by the heavy stole?»
And then to me: «O Tuscan who have come
Among this crowd of wretched hypocrites,
Do not disdain to tell us who you are.»

    «Within the mighty city on the Arno
I first saw light,» I said, «and there grew up;
And I have come here in my mortal body.
But who are you, whose woe, as I can see,
Is coursing down your cheeks in bitter tears, —
And what your punishment that glitters so?»

    A shade replied to me: «These orange cloaks
Are made of lead — so heavy, that their weight
Causes the scales to creak beneath their load.
We once were Jovial Friars from Bologna —
I, Catalano; Loderingo, he.
Together we were chosen by your city —
As one alone is usually chosen —
To keep the peace; and how we wrought our will
Can still be ascertained at the Gardigno!»

    I started to remark: «O friars, your wicked» —
But said no more, because upon the ground
I saw a spirit crucified with stakes.
When he had seen me, he commenced to writhe,
Breathing amain and sighing in his beard.
This Friar Catalano saw, and said:
«That soul transfixed, that you are gazing on,
Counselled the Pharisees that it were wise
To put one man to torture for the people.
Across this path he lies in nakedness,

Canto 23 : The Hypocrites address Dante

As you now see; he is the first to feel
The weight of every hypocrite that passes.
And in like manner is his kinsman here
In torment with the other councillors
Who sowed such seeds of evil for the Jews.»

I saw that Virgil gazed in awe at him
Who was so ignominiously stretched
Upon a cross, in endless banishment.

A short while later he addressed the friar:
«Let it not displease you, if allowed,
To tell us if there lies, upon the right,
An opening through which we both may leave
Without constraining any of the demons
To come and extricate us from this depth.»

And he replied: «Much nearer than you think,
Starting from the great encircling wall
There is a bridgeway crossing all these valleys,
Save that in this one it is broken down
And spans it not; but you can clamber up
Along the ruins, on the side and bottom.»

My leader stood awhile with head inclined,
And said: «I think he gave us bad advice
Who yonder hooks the sinners in the pitch!»

The friar then: «I once heard, at Bologna,
The devil's vices told: with other things,
That he's a liar, and of lies the father!»

My leader walked away with mighty strides,
Somewhat disturbed, with anger in his mien;
And I as well left all those laden souls,
Behind the prints of his beloved feet.

CANTO 24

WHEN in that earliest season of the year
The sun beneath Aquarius warms his locks,
And the long nights are moving toward the south,
And when the hoarfrost copies on the ground

The image of the snow, her whiter sister
(Although it stays there but a little time),
The husbandman, his fodder running low,
Arises and looks forth, and sees the plain
All glistening white: at this he smites his thigh,
Turns back into the house and sulks about
Like a poor wretch who knows not what to do,
And then comes out again, regaining hope
At seeing that the countryside has changed
In but a little while. He takes his crook
And drives his flocks of sheep forth to their
⌊pasture.

Just so the master made me stand in fear
When I perceived his aspect so disturbed;
And just as quickly was the wound relieved.
For as we came upon the ruined bridge,
My leader turned to me with that sweet look
Which I had noticed at the mountain's base.

When he had taken counsel with himself,
He looked about the ruins carefully,
Opened his arms, and clasped me to his breast.
Just as a thoughtful workman, as he toils,
Will think ahead of what must yet be done:
Just so, while lifting me toward the crest
Of one great rock, he scanned another crag,
Saying: «That is the next for you to climb—
But first try if its strength will bear your weight.»

No pathway this for one who wears a cloak!
Though he was light, and helped me all he could,
We hardly made our way from rock to rock:
And were it not that on the inner side
The cliff was shorter than upon the outer,
I must have been o'ercome: for him, I know not.
But as the whole of Malebolge slopes
Down to the opening of the lowest pit,
Each valley is so placed that of necessity
One rampart rises higher than the other.
At last, however, we had reached the point
Where the last stone was broken from the cliff.
The breath was so exhausted from my lungs
When I was up, that I could go no farther;
So I sat down as soon as I was there.
«Now we have come where you must cast off sloth,

My master said, «for neither upon down
Nor under coverlets, men come to fame;
Without which, he who runs his course of life
Leaves of himself on earth the selfsame trace
That smoke leaves in the air, or foam on water.
Therefore rise up, and conquer your fatigue
With that same spirit that wins every fight,
Unless the heavy body weighs it down.
A longer stair than this must yet be climbed,
And to have mastered this, is not enough;
If you have understood me, act at once!»

Then I stood up, finding I had more breath
Than I myself believed, and answered him:
«Lead on, for I am staunch and fearless now.»

We took our way aloft upon the ridge
Of jagged rocks: it was more difficult
And even steeper than the one before.
I went on speaking, lest I might seem faint.
From out the other depth there came a voice
That could not sound distinctly what it spoke.
I know not what it said, although by then
I stood upon the arch that crossed above:
But he who made those sounds seemed moved
⌊to anger.

I had bent downward, but my mortal eyes
Were powerless to reach into the bottom,
So that I said: «My master, pray contrive
To leave this side, and mount the other rampart:
For, as I hear but cannot understand,
So, when I look below, I cannot see.»

«No other answer will I give to you,»
He said, «than by performance: your request
Is worthy to be carried out in silence.»

We clambered down the bridgeway at its head,
Just at its junction with the eighth enclosure;
And then the valley was disclosed to me.
Within I saw a loathsome swarm of snakes,
So strange and horrible to look upon
That even now it makes my blood run cold.
No more can Libya vaunt her burning sands:
For though she bring forth chelydri and jaculi,
Amphisbaena, phareae, and cenchri—
Never, in all of Ethiopia

Nor in that region over the Red Sea,
Could she display so many fearful pests!
And there, among this dreadful seething mass
The naked souls were running horror-struck,
Deprived of lurking hole or heliotrope.
Their hands were bound behind their backs with
⌊snakes

That thrust their heads and tails out through
⌊their loins,

So that they coiled and writhed in knots before
⌊them.

And lo! At one who stood upon our side
A serpent darted, and transfixed his flesh
Just where his neck was to the shoulders joined.
Never was *O* or *I* so quickly penned
As he took fire and burned: and as he fell
He met his fate by turning into ashes.
While he was lying thus upon the ground,
The ashes reunited of themselves
And instantly resumed his spirit's form.
So, by the poets it has oft been told,
The Phoenix dies and comes to life again
When it approaches its five-hundredth year.
During its life, it eats not grass nor grain,
But tears of frankincense and of amomum:
And nard and myrrh are its last swathing bands.

As a man who falls, yet knows not why—
Either from evil force that drags him down,
Or some constriction that may seize upon him—
Will slowly rise and turn his gaze about him,
Bewildered by the pain he has endured,
And as he looks around will breathe a sigh:
Such was the sinner after he had risen.
O Power Divine! How stern are Thy decrees,
When Thou dost rain down such avenging strokes!

My goodly leader asked him who he was.
He answered: «I fell down from Tuscany
To this vile gullet, but a while ago.
I led a brutish, not a human life,
Mule that I was: I'm Vanni Fucci—beast;
Pistoia was a fitting stable for me!»

I begged my leader: «Tell him not to leave,
And ask what crime has thrust him here below—

Canto 24 : The Thieves tortured by Serpents

Him, whom I knew as man of blood and wrath.»
   The sinner, who had heard, made no pretence,
But turning toward me, gave me his attention
And reddened with an ignominious shame,
Saying: «It grieves me more, thus to be found
In misery, which you are here to see,
Than when I left that other life above.
I cannot well refuse what you have asked:
Here am I consigned, because I stole
The ornaments from out the sacristy;
The blame was falsely placed upon another.
But so that you may not exult at this—
In case you ever leave this darksome place,—
Open your ears, and listen to my words:
Pistoia first will rid herself of Neri;
Then Florence will renew her government.
Mars will call forth a bolt from Val di Magra,
Which will be swathed about in turbid clouds;
Amid the bitter ragings of a tempest
There will be battle on the Pescian plain:
Then suddenly the mist will burst asunder,
And every single Bianco will be wounded.
This I have told in order to distress you.»

CANTO
25

WHEN he had said these words, the thief
              ⌊upraised
His hands with obscene signs, and cried aloud:
«Take that, O God! At Thee I make the figs!»
From that time forth the serpents were my friends;
For one of them now coiled about his throat
As if to say: «I'll let you say no more!»
Another round his arms bound him so fast
And clinched itself so perfectly in front,
That not a jog or motion could he make.

Pistoia, ah Pistoia! It were meet
That thou decree the burning of thy city,
Because thou dost surpass thy seed in evil!
In all the dark circumference of hell,
No soul so arrogant to God I saw,
Not even he who fell from Thebes of old.
   He fled, so that he spoke no other word:
Then I beheld a centaur, full of rage,
Who came and cried: «Where is that hardened
              ⌊sinner?»
   I do not think there are in the Maremma
As many serpents as were on his croup,
As far as where our human shape begins;
And on his shoulders, close behind his nape,
There lay a dragon with its wings outspread,
That sets afire everything it meets.
My goodly master told me: «That is Cacus,
Who in the shadow of Mount Aventine
Made many and many a time a lake of blood.
He does not tread the same path as his brethren,
By reason of the most deceitful theft
He made of the great herd that grazed beside him.
His crooked deeds were ended once for all
Beneath the club of Hercules, who dealt
A hundred blows, perchance—he felt but ten.»
   While this was being said, he sped away;
And down below, three spirits came toward us,
But neither he nor I had noticed them
Until they shouted at us: «Who are you?»
When they drew near, our talk was broken off,
And our attention turned itself upon them.
I did not know them; but it so befell,
As oftentimes will happen by some chance,
That one was called upon to name another,
Saying: «Where do you think Cianfa stopped?»
And I, so that my leader might give heed,
Put up my forefinger from chin to nose.
   If, reader, you are slow to credit me
In what I shall relate, it is not strange:
For I myself, who saw, could scarce believe it.
   While I was gazing fixedly at them,
Behold, a serpent with six legs, who darts
Upon the breast of one, and holds him fast.

Now with its middle feet it clasps his belly,
And with its forefeet fastens on his arms,
Fixing its horrid fangs in both his cheeks.
The hinder feet it puts around his thighs,
And sticks its tail between them, till it reaches,
Extended upward, to his loins behind.
Never did ivy clasp a tree so tightly
As this foul reptile twined itself around
The members of that most unhappy shade.
They clove each to the other, as it were
They had been melted wax, and mixed their colors,
So neither seemed what it had been before—
In just this way the brownish margin creeps
Before the flame upon a burning paper:
Not black as yet, but still no longer white.

The other two were looking on, and cried:
«Alas! How you are changing, Agnolo!
Behold! You look like neither two nor one!»

By now the heads of both were fused together,
And there appeared two faces intermingled
And lost within a single countenance.
From the four limbs, two arms then took their
⌊shape;

Thighs joined with legs; the belly and the chest
Became such members eye has never seen.
In each the former aspect was erased;
Two, and yet none, the monstrous shape appeared,
And thus transformed, went slowly off the scene.

Oft, in the fiercest heat of the dog days
A lizard will leap forth from hedge to hedge,
Flitting like lightning, if it cross a road:
Just so a little serpent now appeared,
All black and livid like a peppercorn,
That darted at the bellies of those two.
On one of them it first transfixed that part
From which our nourishment is earliest drawn,
And then fell down, extended at his feet.
He that was pierced said naught, but gazed at it:
Unmoved, he stood and yawned, as if he were
Assailed by fever or by drowsiness.
He eyed the snake, the serpent stared at him:
One from his wound, the other from his mouth
Emitted clouds of smoke, which soon commingled.

Let Lucan now be silent, where he tells
The woes of poor Sabellus and Nassidius,
And hearken to what I shall now relate!
Ovid, speak not of Cadmus, Arethusa:
I grudge it not, that in your verse you change
One to a snake, the other to a fountain;
For never have you altered, face to face,
Two natures in such wise that both their forms
Were ready to exchange their substances!

They each became the other in this manner:
The serpent clove his tail into a fork,
The other's feet became a serpent's tail;
And legs so stuck themselves upon the thighs
That in a little while their place of juncture
Left not a trace that any eye could see.
Slowly the forked tail now assumed the shape
That in the other one was disappearing:
Its skin was softening, while the other's hardened.
I saw the arms retreat into the armpits;
And then the reptile's feet, which had been short,
Grew longer, while the other's arms were
⌊shortening.

Later the hinder feet, entwined together,
Became that member which a man conceals;
While from the wretched shade's, two feet grew
⌊out.

Meanwhile the smoke veils both in changing
And generates on one a growth of hair ⌊hues,
And from the other takes his hair away.
The former rose, the latter fell to earth;
But neither turned away his glaring eyes,
Beneath which each was changing his appearance.
He that was upright narrowed in his face
Toward the temples; from the ampler flesh
The ears grew outward from the naked cheeks.
That flesh which ran not back but was retained
From that excess, formed in the face a nose,
And lips were made, as thick as were required.

He on the ground thrust forth his sharpened
And pulled his ears right back into his head, ⌊face
Just as a snail will draw its horns inside.
His tongue, which formerly was undivided
And capable of speech, now clove in two.

Canto 25 : Agnello changing into a Serpent

The other's cleft healed up; the smoke dispersed.
The soul that had become a reptile fled
Hissing along the valley; and behind him
The other followed, spitting as he talked.
His new-formed shoulders he now turned about,
And to the other said: «I wish Buoso
To run, like me, along upon his belly!»

    Thus did I see the seventh circle's cargo
Change and rechange; and if my pen has
Pray let the novelty be my excuse. ⌊wandered,
And even if my eyes were somewhat blurred,
My mind confused, those two could not take flight
So secretly, that I could not perceive
That one of them was Puccio Sciancato:
And he it was, alone of all the three
That first appeared, who had not been
                      ⌊transformed.
The third was he for whom you, Gaville, mourn.

CANTO 26

Exult, O Florence, since thou art so great
That thou hast wings widespread o'er sea and land,
And even through hell itself thy name extends!
Among the thieves, five of thy citizens
I found, of such importance that I blush;
Nor dost thou gain in honor from the fact!
But if one dreams the truth before the dawn,
Thou soon shalt know what Prato and the rest
So eagerly desire now for thee.
Had it occurred, 'twould not have been too soon!
Would that it had, since surely it must come:
For as I grow in years, I'll grieve the more.

    We left, and now my kindly guide went up
That selfsame stairway whose projecting rocks
Had given us passage, drawing me behind him.
As we pursued our way among the stones

And rugged fragments of the shattered bridge,
The foot moved not without the hand for aid.
Compassion smote me: even now I grieve
When I remember what I saw before me.
Beyond my wont I now must curb my genius
Ere it outrun the guiding hand of virtue:
So, if a lucky star, or something better
Hath favored me, I may not wreck my fortune.

    When he who lights the world least hides his
                                ⌊face—
Just when mosquitoes take the place of flies—
The husbandman, reclining on the hill,
Will watch the countless fireflies in the valley,
Down where perchance he tends his vines and
                                ⌊ploughs.
With just so many flames was glittering
That eighth great valley, as I soon perceived
When I had come to where its depth appeared.

    As he who wrought his vengeance by the bears
Beheld Elijah's chariot at their parting—
The horses rising straight up into heaven
Too swiftly for his eyes to follow them,
So that he could see nothing but the flame
As a light cloud go soaring through the skies—
Just so each flame was moving in the chasm.
But none of them disclosed to us its booty—
For every flame had snatched a sinner's soul.

    While I was standing on the bridge to look,
So straight, that if I had not grasped a rock
I would have fallen at the slightest push,
My leader, who perceived me so absorbed
Remarked: «Within these flames the spirits dwell:
Each one is swathed by that in which it burns.»

    «O my Master,» I replied to him,
«From hearing you, I now feel more assured.
Already had I thought it might be so,
And longed to ask of you: 'Who is that flame
Divided at the top, as if it rose
From the twin pyre of Eteocles?'»

    He answered me: «Within it are tormented
Diomed and Ulysses: thus they go,
Joined here in punishment, as once in wrath.
Within their flame they constantly lament

That trick by which the horse passed through the⌐
⌊gate

Whence issued forth the Romans' noble seed.
Therein they rue the artifice by which
Deidamia, in death, still mourns Achilles:
Therein is the Palladium atoned for.»
  «If they can speak within those sheets of
⌊flame,»

I said, «my goodly master, I entreat you,
And ask of you again a thousandfold,
That you will not forbid that I may wait
Until that two-horned flame shall pass this way:
See how I bend toward it with desire!»
  «Your prayer is worthy of much commenda-
⌊tion,»

Said he to me, «and therefore I will grant it:
But take heed that your tongue restrain itself.
Let me be spokesman, for I understand
What you desire; and, since they are Greeks,
They might perchance be scornful of your words.»
  And later, when the flame had reached such
⌊point

That time and place seemed fitting to my leader,
I heard that he was speaking to it thus:
«O you, who in a single flame are two,
If when alive I well deserved of you,
If I was ever worthy of your praise
When in the world I wrote my lofty verses,
Move not away: let one of you relate
How, being lost, he went away to die.»

  The greater portion of that ancient flame
Began to writhe, and murmur as it writhed,
As will a fire when beaten by the wind.
Then, waving its extremity about
As though it were the flame's own tongue that
⌊spoke,

From out its depth it sent a voice that said:
«When I escaped from Circe, near Gaeta,
Where she had kept me hidden for a year—
Before Aeneas had so named the place—
Neither the tenderness I bore my son,
Nor filial piety, nor yet that love
Which should have gladdened my Penelope,

Sufficed to overcome my eager wish
To gain experience of the world, and learn
The vices and the virtues of mankind.
So I put forth upon the open sea
With but a single ship, and that small band
By whom I never yet had been deserted.
I saw the coasts on either hand, as far
As Spain, Morocco, and Sardinia,
And other islands lying in that sea.
I and my men were old and broken down
When we arrived before that narrow strait
Where Hercules of old set up his marks,
As signs that man should never venture farther.
Upon the right I left Seville behind,
And on my other hand passed by Ceuta.
  « 'Brothers,' I said, 'who now have reached the
⌊West

By conquering a hundred thousand dangers,
Deny not to that little span of life—
The brief allotment of your waking hours
That yet remains to you—experience
Of that unpeopled world behind the sunset.
Consider from what noble seed you spring:
You were created not to live like beasts,
But for pursuit of virtue and of knowledge!'
  «So eager to set out I made my men
By this short speech, that after it was spoken
I would have tried in vain to hold them back.
When we had turned our poop toward the dawn,
Winged by our oars for our insensate flight,
We worked our vessel more and more to port.
At night I now could see the strange new stars
That guard the other pole—and ours so low
It did not rise above the ocean floor.
Five times the light beneath the moon was kindled
And then put out as many times again,
While we coursed o'er the highways of the deep,
When there appeared to us a murky cliff.
It loomed afar and seemed exceeding high—
Higher than any I had seen before.
Our sudden joy to weeping soon was turned;
For from this land, a whirlwind now uprose
And smote upon the forepart of our ship.

46

Canto 26 : *The Flaming Spirits of the evil Counsellors*

Three times it whirled us round with all the
⌊waters:

The fourth, it made the poop rise in the air,
The prow go down—as was Another's will—
Until the ocean had closed over us.»

CANTO
27

Erect and still the flame had now become
Because it spoke no more. It moved away
With the permission of the gentle poet,
When yet another, coming on behind it,
Caused us to turn our eyes toward its top,
Whence a confusing sound was coming forth.

As that Sicilian bull—which first resounded,
And properly, with anguished cries from him
Who with his file had fashioned it in brass—
Bellowed so truly with the victim's voice
That notwithstanding it was made of metal,
It yet appeared transfixed with agony:
Just so it was these melancholy words,
Because they had no outlet from the flame,
Were turned into the murmur of a fire.
But after they had found their way aloft,
Up to the point that quivered with the motion
The tongue had given them in passing through,
We heard it say: «O you whom I address,
And who a while ago were speaking Lombard,
Saying, 'Now get you gone: I ask no further'—
Although perhaps I come a little late,
Pray have the courtesy to pause and speak:
You see that I am willing, though I burn!
If you have just dropped down to this blind world
From that fair land of Italy, whence I
Have brought below the burden of my guilt,
Say if the Romagnoles have peace or war;
For I came from the hills between Urbino

And those from which the Tiber takes its source.»
I still was listening, and was bending down,
When my good leader touched me on the side
Saying: «Speak out, for he is an Italian!»
And I, who had my answer all prepared,
Began to speak to him without delay:
«O wretched soul enshrouded in a flame,
Romagna is not now—nor ever was—
Without war in her tyrants' wicked hearts;
But open strife was absent when I left.
Ravenna stands, as she has stood for years.
Polenta's eagle broods above her still,
With Cervia in the shadow of his wings.
That city which withstood the long-drawn siege
And of the Frenchmen made a gory pile,
Again lies underneath the paws of green.
The mastiffs of Verucchio, old and young,
Who wrought of old their evil on Montagna
Make gimlets of their teeth, when so they wish.
The cities of Lamone and Santerno
Lie 'neath the lion cub on field of white,
Who changes sides from summertime to winter.
That town whose flank is washed by Savio's
⌊stream,

Even as it lies between the hill and plain,
So does it live 'twixt tyranny and freedom.
Now, I beseech you, tell us who you are,
And be not more unyielding than your neighbor—
So may your name preserve its good repute!»
After the flame had roared a little while
In its peculiar way, it moved its point
Hither and yon, as it spoke forth these words:
«If I believed my answer were addressed
To one who might return to earth above,
No further quiverings would move this flame.
But inasmuch as no one has returned
From out this depth—if I have heard aright—
Free from all fear of infamy, I'll make reply.
«I first bore arms, and then a friar's cord,
Trusting, thus girt about, to make amends:
And haply would my trust have been fulfilled
But for the mighty priest—whom ill befall!—
Who put me back into my wicked ways:

Just how and why I will relate to you.

«While I still kept the form of bones and flesh
My mother gave to me, my mortal deeds
Were those not of the lion, but the fox.
The subtle wiles, the devious hidden ways,
I knew them all, and so applied their art
That to the ends of earth my fame went forth.
When I perceived that I had reached the age
When every man of prudence takes in sail
And gathers in his tackle for the storm,
What I once revelled in now caused me shame:
In penance I confessed, surrendering all.
Ah, hapless me—for still I was not saved!

«The prince of all the modern Pharisees
Was waging war, near to the Lateran.
He was not fighting Saracens or Jews,
But every foeman was a Christian soldier,
And none of them had gone to conquer Acre
Nor yet to traffic in the sultan's land.
He recked not in himself his holy orders
Nor his exalted office—nor, in me,
That cord which used to make its wearers lean.
But just as Constantine besought Sylvester
To cure his leprosy within Soracte,
So he besought me, as I was a doctor,
To cure him of the fever of his pride.
He asked my counsel: and I answered not,
Because his words seemed like a drunken man's.
Then he insisted: 'Let your heart not fail:
From now on, I absolve you. Teach me, then,
To hurl down Palestrina in the dust.
To lock and unlock heaven I have the power,
As well you know; I hold a pair of keys
That were not cherished by my predecessor.'

«His weighty arguments so urged me on
That silence seemed no longer to be wise.
'Father,' I said, 'since you will wash me clean
From any sin that I may now commit:
Long promises, which are but shortly kept
Will make you triumph on the mighty seat.'
St. Francis came for me when I was dead;
But one of the black cherubim demurred,
Saying: 'You shall not take him: cheat me not!

For down among my minions he must come,
Because he gave such fraudulent advice.
Since then I have been clutching at his hair.
He who repents not, cannot be absolved:
No more can he repent and act at once,
Because the contradiction won't permit it!'
Alas for me! How violently I shuddered
When he laid hold on me and said: 'Perhaps
You did not think that I was a logician!'

«He bore me down to Minos, who had wound
His tail eight times around his stubborn back.
And after he had bitten it in rage,
He said: 'This is a sinner for the fire!'
And so I am consigned here where you see me:
And going thus attired, weep my shame.»

Now when he had completed his sad tale
The flame, in anguish, sped away from us,
Twisting and flapping its sharp horn amain.
Onward we went, my noble guide and I
Upon the bridgeway, to that other arch
Which spans the valley holding those in torment
Who, sowing discord, reap a crop of guilt.

CANTO
28

Who, even in words unbound by rules of verse,
Could possibly describe—tell how he might—
The waste of blood and wounds I now beheld?
Assuredly would every tongue fall short,
By reason of our speech and intellect,
Which serve but little to describe so much.
If all the people were again assembled
Who wept upon Apulia's stormy plain
The blood shed by the warriors of Troy;
And with them those who fell in that long war
Which made a spoil of rings heaped to the skies,

Canto 28 : The Mutilated Shade of Mahomet

As Livy writes, who wanders not from truth;
And also those who suffered painful wounds
Opposing Robert Guiscard; and that host
Whose bones are still picked up at Ceperano,
Where each Apulian proved to be a traitor;
And those as well who died at Tagliacozzo,
Where old, unarmed Alardo's guile prevailed:
And even if one should show his limb pierced
⌊through,
Another, limbs lopped off—the sight would be
As naught compared to this ninth valley's woe.

No cask without an end stave or a head
E'er gaped so wide as one shade I beheld,
Cloven from chin to where the wind is voided.
Between his legs his entrails hung in coils;
The vitals were exposed to view, and too
That sorry paunch which changes food to filth.
While I stood all absorbed in watching him
He looked at me and stretched his breast apart,
Saying: «Behold, how I now split myself!
Behold, how mutilated is Mahomet!
In front of me the weeping Ali goes,
His face cleft through from forelock to the chin;
And all the others that you see about
Fomenters were of discord and of schism:
And that is why they are so gashed asunder.

«A demon stands behind here, unrelenting,
Who tricks us cruelly; for every one
Must taste again the keenness of his blade
When he has trod the path of anguish round;
And all the wounds are healed and well again
Ere one of us may pass once more before him.
But who are you, thus musing on the bridge—
Perhaps in order to delay the fate
Adjudged you by your own self-accusation?»

«Neither has death yet overtaken him,»
My master said, «nor crime led him to torment:
It is my duty, who am dead, to lead him
Through hell's domain, from circle unto circle,
To gain experience. This is the truth,
Even as I am speaking here to you.»

On hearing this, more than a hundred shades,
Down in that ditch, stopped short to look at me,

Forgetting all their torment in their wonder.
«You who perhaps will shortly see the sun,
Tell Fra Dolcino to provide himself,
Unless he wants to follow me here quickly,
With victuals, so that any stress of snow
May not bring victory to the Novarese,
Which otherwise 'twere hard for them to gain.»
Mahomet said these words to me, as he
Already raised one foot to go his way:
Then, as he left, he put it to the ground.

Another shade, his throat pierced through and
⌊through,
His nose cut off from just below the eyebrows,
While but a single ear remained to him,
Pausing to marvel at us with the rest—
Before the others, opened up his windpipe,
Which all without was crimson with his blood:
«You who have come here uncondemned by guilt,
And whom I saw above in Italy—
Unless too great a likeness has deceived me—
Remember, pray, Pier da Medicina,
If ever you should see the smiling plain
That from Vercelli slopes to Marcabò.
I beg you, tell the two best men of Fano—
To Messer Guido, and to Angiolello—
That if our foresight here be not untrue,
From out their ship they'll be cast overboard
And drowned, near La Cattolica, because
An evil tyrant shall have played them false.
Between the isles of Cyprus and Majorca
Neptune hath ne'er beheld so foul a crime
Committed by a pirate or a Greek!
The traitor who has but a single eye
And rules that city which my comrade here
Wishes that he had never even seen,
Will make them come before him to a parley,
And will so treat them that they'll have no use
For vows or prayers against Focara's wind!»
And I to him: «Pray tell me and declare,
That I may carry news of you above,
Who is that tyrant with the single eye?»

Thereat he laid his hand upon the jaw
Of a companion, prying wide his mouth,

And cried: «This one is he, and he is mute.
Banished from Rome, he settled Caesar's mind,
Affirming that a man who's well prepared
Can never gain advantage by delay.»

Oh, what a sorry sight was Curio,
His tongue cut from his throat—who once had been
So bold in speech up in the world above! ⌊been

And one of them who had both hands lopped off,
Lifting his mangled stumps in that dark air ⌊off,
So that the streaming blood befouled his face,
Cried out: «You shall remember Mosca too,
Who said, alas, 'A thing once done, is done,'
And sowed such evil for the Tuscan people.»

«And death to your own race,» I quickly added.
On hearing this he went upon his way,
Woe piled on woe, like one in mad distress.

But I remained, still gazing at the crowd,
And saw a thing—that without further proof
I scarce would have the courage to relate.
My conscience, however, reassures me—
That good companion which makes men so bold
Under the breast-plate of its purity.
I surely saw—and seem to see it still—
A trunk without its head, that walked along
Even as others in that wretched crowd.
The severed head he dangled by its hair,
Holding it like a lantern in his hand.
It gazed at us and cried: «Alas for me!»
Of his own self he made himself a lamp,
So two in one, and one in two they were:
How that can be, He knows Who so ordains.

When he had come to just beneath the bridge,
He bore the head aloft upon his arm
So as to bring his words the nearer to us,
And said: «Behold this grievous torment, you
Who look upon the dead while still alive,
And see if any torment could be greater.
And so that you may carry news of me,
Bertrand de Born am I, the man who gave
Such evil counsel to the youthful king.
Father and son I set against each other:
Ahitophel himself sowed no more discord
For Absalom and David with his plots.

Because I parted persons so united,
Alas, my brain is parted from its source,
Which once was in this mutilated trunk:
And thus is retribution shown in me.»

CANTO
29

THE countless multitude and their strange wounds ⌊wounds

Had caused my eyes to be so drunk with tears
That they had rather linger there to weep.
But Virgil said: «Why do you naught but stare?
Why are your eyes fixed only there below
Upon those sad and mutilated shades?
You did not do so in the other valleys.
Consider—if you seek to number them—
The valley curves eleven miles each way.
Already is the moon beneath our feet,
And our allotted time is running short,
While other sights remain as yet unseen.»

«Had you but given heed,» I answered him,
«Unto the reason for my gaze, perhaps
You also might have granted my delay.»
Meanwhile my leader travelled on ahead,
And I, behind him, pondered my reply,
And added: «Down within that darksome pit
Upon which I was gazing so intently,
I think a spirit of my kin bemoans
The crime that has such fearful retribution.»

My goodly master: «Do not let your thoughts
Henceforward be distraught on his behalf:
Attend to other things, and leave him there.
For I beheld him, at the bridge's foot,
Signal you out and point at you in wrath:
Geri del Bello was his name, I heard.
Just then your thoughts were utterly absorbed

Canto 28 : The Severed Head of Bertrand de Born speaks

By him who once held sway in Altaforte;
You did not look that way till he was gone.»

«O leader mine,» I said, «his violent death
That still is unavenged by anyone
Of those who were dishonored by the crime,
Make him indignant. For this cause, I think,
He passed me by and spoke no word to me;
And so he makes me pity him the more.»

Thus we conversed until we reached a point
Where from the bridge the next fosse could be
Down to the bottom, were it not so dark. ⌊seen

When we had come above the last enclosure
Of Malebolge, so that its foul fiends
Had now become apparent to our view,
Groans and laments, the arrows of a woe
That dipped its darts in pain, struck on my ears,
So that I had to place my hands upon them.
If from the hospitals of Valdichiana
Maremma, and Sardinia, all the sick
Were heaped on one another in a ditch,
'Twould scarce have matched the suffering I
And from the valley such a stench arose ⌊beheld;
As oftentimes will come from putrid limbs.

To the last rampart we had now descended
From the long bridge, still bearing to the left:
Now I could see the bottom more distinctly
Where that unerring Justice, minister
Of the Omnipotent, doth penalize
The falsifiers she has there condemned.
No greater sorrow was it to behold
Aegina's people stricken with disease—
When all the air gave forth so foul a stench
That animals down to the smallest worm
Were killed: and afterward, the ancient races
(Or so the poets at least have written it)
Were re-established from the seed of ants—
Than when I saw, within that dismal valley,
The spirits suffering in divers heaps.
Some on their bellies lay, and some upon
The shoulders of a fellow; others crawled
Upon the ground, along the dreary path.

We walked on step by step, and spoke no word,
But saw and hearkened to the sickly shades

Who were unable to lift up their forms.
I noted two who leaned against each other—
As stewpans are propped up while they are
⌊warming—
Spotted from head to foot with loathsome scabs.
I never saw a currycomb so plied
By stableboy for whom his master waits,
Or one aroused at night against his will,
As each one ceaselessly applied his nails
To tear his flesh, by reason of the frenzy
Caused by the itch, which has no other salve.
Their nails tore off the scabs the selfsame way
A knife will clean the scales from off a bream,
Or other fish with even larger scales.
«O you whose fingers scratch your flesh away,»
My loving master said to one of these,
«And who at times are using them as pincers,
Tell us if an Italian can be found
Among those who are here: so may your nails
Perform your bidding through eternity!»

«Italians are we both, whom you behold
Disfigured here,» one answered him in tears.
«But who are you that asks for news of us?»

My leader: «I am one who goes below
From ring to ring with this still-living man.
It is my mission here to show him hell.»

Then was that mortal prop asunder split,
And each of them turned toward us all atremble,
As well as others who had overheard.
The goodly master now drew close beside me
And said: «Speak freely to them as you will.»
And I began, as he had wished it so:

«So may your memory not fade away
From human cognizance up in the world,
But so that it may live for many suns:
Inform me who you are, and of what race.
Let not your sad, revolting punishment
Prevent you from disclosing both your names.»

«I was from Arezzo,» answered one,
«And Albero of Siena had me burned:
But what I died from, does not bring me here.
The truth is that when speaking once in jest,
I told him I could raise myself in flight;

And he, who had desire, but little wit,
Ordained that I should school him in that art.
Because I failed to make him Daedalus,
He had his father burn me up alive.
But to this lowest pocket of the ten
Minos, who cannot err, committed me
Because I practised as an alchemist.»

　　I said unto the poet: «Was there ever
So vain a people as the Sienese?
Even the French are not so vain by half!»

　　Whereat the other leper, who had heard,
Answered my words: «Excepting always Stricca,
Who well knew how to keep expenses down!
And Niccolò, who was the first to learn
To burn the clove in sheer extravagance
In that rich garden where such seed takes root—
Excepting also that brave company
That Caccia squandered all his lands upon,
When Abbagliato so displayed his wisdom.
But so that you may know who thus supports you
Against the Sienese, fix well your eyes,
So that my face may give the right response.
Then you will see I am Capocchio's shade,
Who made false metals once by alchemy;
And you should recollect, if I mistake not,
How as an ape to nature I excelled.»

CANTO
30

WHEN Juno, on account of Semele,
Was angered at the royal blood of Thebes,
And showed her jealousy more times than one:
When Athamas was stricken with such madness
That when he saw his wife come on her way
Burdened on either hand with their two sons,
And cried, «Spread out the nets, that I may catch

The lioness and her cubs as they pass by!»
And then relentlessly stretched forth his hands,
Seizing his infant (who was named Learchus),
Whirled him around and dashed him on a rock,
And she, with her young son, then drowned
Or as, again, when fortune had abased ⌊herself:
The Trojan's dauntless pride, so that their king
Together with his kingdom was destroyed,
And Hecuba, in sad captivity,
Cast weeping eyes on dead Polyxena,
After, upon the seashore, she had found
The body of her own son Polydorus—
To such degree did grief unhinge her mind,
She barked in senseless fury like a dog:
Rage so merciless was never seen,
Either at Thebes or Troy—nor yet again
When beasts, or human limbs, are gashed with
⌊wounds—

As that I saw, in two pale naked shades
Who, biting, ran about in that strange way
A boar will do, when loosened from his pen.
One, seizing on Capocchio, fixed his teeth
So firmly in his neck, he dragged him down,
Making his belly scrape along the bottom.

　　He of Arezzo, who stood trembling by,
Said to me: «That mad soul is Gianni Schicchi
Who mangles others in his frenzied rage.»

　　«Oh,» I replied, «so may that other spirit
Never attack you! Pray do not disdain
To tell us who it is, ere it departs.»

　　And he to me: «That is the ancient shade
Of the abandoned Myrrha, who became
Her father's mistress in unhallowed love.
'Twas by deceit she came to sin with him,
Assuming for the nonce another's form—
Even as that other frenzied shade once dared,
That he might gain the fairest of the stud,
To counterfeit the person of Donati,
Making a will in proper legal form.»

　　When they had passed along—that raging pair
Upon whom I had kept my eyes directed—
I looked among the other wretched shades.
One I beheld who would have seemed a lute,

Canto 29 : Virgil reproves Dante's Curiosity

If only he had had his groin cut off
Just at that part of him where men are forked.
The heavy dropsy, which so disproportions
The members putrifying with its humor
That face and belly do not correspond,
Compelled this shade to keep his limbs apart—
Just like a hectic patient, who, from thirst,
Curls one lip toward his chin, the other upward.

«O you,» said he, «who without punishment
Are in this world of woe—I know not why—
Behold, and then attentively consider
Master Adamo's most unhappy lot.
Alive, I had enough of what I wanted:
And now, alas! I crave a drop of water.
The little brooks that from the verdant slopes
Of Casentino flow into the Arno,
Keeping their channels always fresh and moist,
Seem e'er before me—not without good purpose!
Because their image dries me up far more
Than this disease that makes my face so thin.
Inexorable justice, which pursues me,
Uses the very place where I have sinned
To set my sighs the more upon the wing.
That is Romena, where I falsified
Alloys that bear the saintly Baptist's seal;
For this on earth I suffered at the stake.
But if I could see here the wretched souls
Of Guido, Alessandro, or their brother,
I would not miss the sight of Fonte Branda!
Already one of them is here within,
If true reports the raging spirits bear:
But what avails it me, whose limbs are tied?
If I were only lighter by enough
To move an inch within a hundred years,
Already would I be upon my way,
Seeking him out from this disfigured crowd,
Although it circles round eleven miles
And is not less than half a mile across.
Because of them I am among this tribe:
They urged me on to counterfeit those florins
Which had at least three carats of alloy.»

And I to him: «Who are that wretched pair
Who lie so close together on your right,
And smoke like hands when they are wet in
⌊winter?»

«I found them here when I fell in this ditch,»
He answered me. «Since then they have not
Nor will they do so, for eternity. ⌊turned,
The first is she who falsely spoke of Joseph;
The other Sinon, lying Greek at Troy.
From burning fever they emit that stench.»

And one of them, who took offence, perhaps,
At being named so meanly, with his fist
Smote Master Adam on his hardened belly,
Making a hollow noise just like a drum;
And Master Adam struck him on the face,
Using his arm, which did not seem less hard,
And said to him: «Although I be denied
The power to move, because my limbs are heavy,
I have an arm still free for such a need!»

He answered him: «Once it was not so ready
When you were standing there before the fire:
But more so, when you used to make false coins!»

And then the dropsied one: «You speak the
But you were surely not so good a witness ⌊truth:
When you were asked about the truth at Troy!»

«If I spoke falsely, you made money false!»
Said Sinon. «I am here for one offence:
But you, for more than any other sinner.»

«Perjurer, do not forget the horse!»
He with the swollen belly answered back, ⌈it!»
«And may you rue that all the world doth know
«And may you rue the thirst,» the Greek
⌊retorted,

«With which your tongue now cracks, and that
⌊foul water

Which rears your belly up before your eyes!»

The coiner then: «Thus does your mouth gape
To its own ill again! And if I thirst ⌊wide
And humor stuffs my skin, you burn in torment
With aching head; and you would not require
So very many words of invitation
To lick, I think, the mirror of Narcissus!»

In listening to them I was absorbed,
When my good master said to me: «Take heed!
It lacks but little that I quarrel with you!»

And when I heard him speak to me in wrath,
I turned toward him, covered with such shame
That even now it circles through my memory.
And like a man who dreams of adverse fortune,
And who, while dreaming, hopes it is a dream,
Thus wishing that which is as though it were not:
So I became, who, though I could not speak,
Wished to excuse myself, and all the while
Was doing so, although I knew it not.
«Less shame,» my master said, «would wash away
A greater fault than yours has been, my son:
Therefore be unburdened of your sorrow.
Remember I am always by your side,
If chance should once again conduct your steps
Where men may wrangle in disputes like these;
To wish to hear them is a base desire.»

CANTO
31

THE selfsame tongue that wounded me at first,
Bringing the blush of shame to both my cheeks,
Supplied me with the healing remedy.
Thus, I have heard, the javelin of Achilles
And of his father, had the magic gift
To wound for ill, and then to heal for good.

Turning our backs upon that vale of woe,
We climbed the rocky bank surrounding it,
And spoke no word as we were moving on.
Here it was less than night, and less than day,
So that I saw for but a little space;
But I could hear the sounding of a horn
Whose blast was louder than a crash of thunder,
So that I fixed my eyes upon the spot
From where it seemed to come, seeking its source.
After that direful rout when Charlemagne
Had lost his mighty host of paladins,

Even Roland's blast was not so frightening.
I kept my head turned as it was before
And saw what seemed to be some lofty towers,
So that I asked: «What town is this, my master?»

And he to me: «Because you try to look
Across the darkness from too far away,
Imagination leads astray your senses:
For plainly you shall see, when you approach,
How your perception was deceived by distance.
Therefore go on, and speed your lagging steps!»

Now by the hand he took me tenderly
And said: «Before we travel any farther—
So that the fact may seem less strange to you—
Know that those are not towers which you see,
But giants; and that from the navel downward
They stand within the pit, against its bank.»

As when a mist is clearing, and the eye
By slow degrees will realize the form
Of what the vapor in the air conceals:
Just so, as I peered through the murky air
While I drew ever nearer to the bank,
My fear increased, although my error fled.
For, as upon the circuit of its walls
Montereggione has its crown of towers,
So towered, with half their frames, those fearful
⌊giants
Whom Jove still threatens with his thunderbolts,
Above the rampart that surrounds the pit.

Already I could see the face of one—
His head and shoulders, portions of his belly,
And both his arms, which hung along his sides.
Nature, forsooth, when she left off the art
Of making creatures formed like these, did well,
Depriving Mars of such fell instruments!
If she does not regret that she made whales
And elephants as well, she will be deemed
More just and more discerning by the wise.
For when the mental faculty is joined
To evil will and power of execution,
Mankind has no defence to offer them.
His face appeared to me as long and broad
As that Pine Cone in Rome, before St. Peter's:
And all his other bones were in proportion,

Canto 31 : The Giant Antaeus lowering Dante and Virgil

So that the bank, which from his middle
⌊downward

Served as an apron, left so much exposed
That three tall Frisians would have tried in vain
To reach his hair, the one atop the other:
For I could see full thirty palms of him,
Downward from where a man will clasp his cloak.

Rafel mai amech zabi almi—
Thus the brutish mouth began to bellow,
Unfit to utter any gentler sounds.

My leader now addressed him: «Stupid soul,
Take up your horn, and vent yourself with that,
When you are seized by fits of rage or passion!
Search on your neck, and you will find the cord
That holds it fastened, O demented spirit!
There it is, hanging on your breast!»
And then to me: «Himself he doth accuse:
For he is Nimrod, by whose vile design
The world speaks other than a single language.
Let us not waste our speech, but pass him by,
For every language is the same to him—
As his, which no one knows, is to all others.»

We walked on farther, turning to our left.
A crossbow shot away, we found the next—
A giant larger still, and more ferocious.
I cannot say whose was the master hand
That tied him; but he had his dexter arm
Close bound behind his back. The other one
In front was shackled by a chain that bound him
From the neck downward, so that we could see
It made five turns around his upper body.
«This proud one wished to make a trial of
With Jupiter himself,» my master said, ⌊strength
«Wherefore he merits here his punishment.
His name is Ephialtes: great the deeds
He wrought when giants terrorized the gods.
Those arms he plied so well, will move no more!»

And I to him: «Would that my eyes might see,
If ever opportunity presents,
The terrible Briareus as well.»

And he replied: «Hard by, you soon shall see
Antaeus, who can speak and is unbound.
'Tis he will bear us down into the pit;

But he whom you would see is far beyond,
Held fast in chains, and made like this one here,
Save that he has a more ferocious mien.»

Never did earthquake with a mighty heave
Rock a massive tower so violently
As Ephialtes quickly shook himself.
Then I feared death, more than I did before:
For that, in truth, my fear would have sufficed,
Had I not seen the chains that held him down!

We then proceeded farther, till we came
Before Antaeus, who, without his head,
Stood forth a good five ells above the pit.
«O you, who took as spoil a thousand lions
In that same fateful valley, which, in time,
Made Scipio an heir to deathless glory
When Hannibal's great hosts were put to rout,
And who, had you but joined your brethren
In war on high, as many still believe,
Would have made the sons of earth victorious:
Set us below—do not refuse us—where
Cocytus lies forever locked in ice;
Else must we go to Tityus, or Typhon.
This man can give you what is longed for here.
Therefore bend down; curl not your lip in scorn,
For he can yet restore your fame above.
Alive is he, and long life he expects,
Unless Grace summon him before his time.»
The master thus; the other then stretched out
Those hands whose clutches Hercules had felt
In times of old, and took my master up.
And Virgil, when he felt the giant's grasp
Said: «Come here as well, so I may take you!»
And of himself and me he made one bundle.

As Carisenda's tower often seems,
Under the leaning side, as though it hangs
The other way, when shadowed by a cloud:
So seemed Antaeus to me as I watched
To see him stoop; and then I could have wished
To make the journey by another road!
But in that depth he lightly set us down
Where Lucifer and Judas are engulfed;
Nor made he long delay while thus bent over,
But reared him upward, like a vessel's mast.

CANTO
32

IF I had measures harsh and dissonant,
Appropriate to describe that dismal pit
On which the other circles all converge,
I would press out the juice of my conception
More fully still: but since I have them not,
'Tis with some fear I bring myself to speak.
The utmost depth of all the universe
Is not a theme befitting childish tongues,
Nor one that can be taken up in jest.
Let those nine handmaids help me with my verse
Who aided Amphion to wall in Thebes,
So that the tale may not belie the fact.
O ye, condemned to utmost misery,
Where words can scarce suffice to tell your woe,
Better had ye been sheep or goats than men!

When we were down within that darksome pit
Where stood the giant's feet—down lower still—
While I was gazing at the lofty cliff
I heard a voice cry out: «Walk carefully!
Take care you do not trample with your feet
Upon your miserable brothers' heads.»

Whereat I turned around and saw before me,
Beneath my feet, a lake that from the cold
Seemed to be made of glass instead of water.
Never did Danube form so thick a veil
In winter o'er its stream in Austria,
Nor yet the Don beneath the arctic sky,
As there was here: for even if Tambernic
Or Pietrapana's mount should fall upon it,
'Twould not have creaked—not even at the edge!

And as the frog sits with his muzzle out
That he may croak, while peasant women dream
Of many happy gleanings of the harvest:
Just so those wailing shades within the ice

Were livid, to the place where shame appears,
With chattering teeth that sounded like a stork.
And every spirit kept his face bent down;
Their mouths betrayed the cold, and from their
⌊eyes
The sadness of their hearts pressed bitter tears.

When I had gazed about me for a while,
I looked toward my feet, and saw two shades
Pressed close, so that their hair was intertwined.
«Tell me, O you who breast to breast are clasped,»
Said I, «What are your names?» They raised their
⌊necks,

And after they had turned their faces to me,
Their eyes, whose moisture had been pent within,
Gushed tears beyond their lids, so that the cold
Soon froze them up, and locked them in again.
Never did nail fix plank to plank more firmly!
And thereupon such fury overcame them,
They butted at each other like two goats.
Then one, who from the cold had lost both ears,
And like the others had his head inclined,
Cried out: «Why do you gaze upon us so?
If you would know who these two fellows are,
The valley where Bisenzio flows down
Belonged to them, and to their father Albert.
They issued from one body. If you seek
Through all Caina, you will never find
A shade more worthy to be fixed in ice:
Not he whose breast and shadow both were cleft
By Arthur's hand, all in the selfsame blow;
Nor yet Focaccia; nor this one here,
Beyond whose head I can no farther see.
Sasso Mascheroni was his name;
If you are Tuscan, you will know it well.
And so you may not make me speak still more,
Know that I was Camicion de' Pazzi;
Carlino I await, to plead my cause.»

And after this I saw a thousand faces
Made doglike by the cold, whereat I shuddered—
And will at frozen ponds, forever more.
Now while we were advancing toward the centre,
At which all sin and gravity unite,
And I was shivering in the eternal cold—

Whether from will, or destiny, or chance,
I know not—as I stepped among the heads
I struck my foot hard on the face of one.
Weeping, he cried aloud: «Why do you kick me?
Unless you come here to increase the vengeance
Of Mont' Aperti—why do you molest me?»

And I: «My master, pray await me here,
That I may clear a doubt respecting him;
Then you can make me hasten as you will.»

My leader stopped; and now I said to him
Who still continued bitterly to curse:
«What man were you, who curse at others so?»

«And who are you,» he answered, «that now
⌊walks

Through Antenora, kicking cheeks of others,
With blows too strong for even a living man?»

«I am alive,» I answered, «and perhaps
If you are seeking for renown, 'twould please you
That I inscribe your name among my notes.»

And he to me: «The opposite I wish!
Take yourself hence, and bother me no more:
Ill have you learned to flatter in this pit!»

Then I laid hold upon him by his nape
And said: «Now must you name yourself indeed,
Or not a hair shall stay upon your head!»

Whereat he answered: «Tear it, if you will:
I'll not say who I am, or show it you,
Even if you beat my head a thousand times!»

His hair was wound already in my hand,
And many a tuft of it was torn away.
While he was howling, with his eyes cast down,
Another shade cried out: «What ails you, Bocca?
'Tis not enough to clatter with your jaws,
But you must bark as well! What devil's at you?»

«Now,» I remarked, «I do not need your speech,
Traitor accurst! For even in spite of you
I'll bear true tidings of you to the world.»

«Begone,» he answered, «tell what tales you
But be not silent, if you should return,   ⌊will!
Regarding him whose tongue was now so ready.
Here he bewails the silver of the French.
'I saw,' you will relate, 'him of Duera
Down where the sinners stand within the ice.'

Should you be asked what others too are there,
Here by my side is he of Beccheria,
Whose gullet by the Florentines was slit;
Gian' de' Soldanieri's there, I think,
With Ganellone too, and Tribaldello,
Who, while all slept, unbarred Faenza's gates.»

We had already left him, when I saw
Two frozen in one hole, so close together
That one was to the other like a hat.
And even as bread for hunger is devoured,
So did the upper one gnaw at his fellow,
Just where the head is fastened to the nape.
Not otherwise did Tydeus eat away
The temples, in his rage, of Melanippus,
Than this one gnawed his neighbor's skull and
«O you, that by so bestial a sign   ⌊brain.
Are showing hate against him you devour,
Pray tell me why,» said I, «with this condition:
That if you have a just complaint against him,
I, knowing who you are, and what his crime,
May thus requite you in the world above—
Unless the fountain of my speech run dry.»

CANTO
33

Now from his savage meal he raised his mouth,
And wiped it on the hair of that same head
The back of which he had been fiercely gnawing.
And then: «You wish me to renew,» he said,
«That grief incurable, which breaks my heart
Even at the thought, before I speak of it.
But if my words may later be the seed
Of infamy for him whose head I gnaw,
Then you shall see me speak and weep together.
I know not who you are, nor by what means
You have come here: but it would seem to me

That you are Florentine, to hear your speech.
Know, then, that I was once Count Ugolino;
This was the Archbishop Ruggieri.
Now I will tell why I am here beside him.
How, by the workings of his wicked schemes,
I, trusting him implicitly, was seized
And murdered afterward, I need not tell.
But what you never can have heard about—
How cruel was my death—you now will hear,
And you can judge if he has done me wrong.

«A narrow loophole in that dungeon's side
(Called Tower of Hunger now, because of me,
And wherein others yet must be imprisoned)
Had shown me through its opening many moons;
And then one night I had an evil dream
That tore the future's veil aside for me.
This man appeared as master of the hunt,
Chasing a wolf and cubs toward that mountain
Which blocks the view of Lucca from the Pisans.
With hounds well trained and eager for the chase,
He had sent out before him the Gualandi,
And with them the Sismondi and Lanfranchi.
After a short pursuit, the sire and cubs
Seemed spent to me: and then I thought I saw
Their flanks rent open by the hounds' sharp fangs.

«When I awoke before the morrow's dawn,
I heard my sons, who shared my prison house,
Moan in their sleep and beg a crust of bread.
And you indeed are cruel, unless you grieve
To hear of what my heart foreboded then:
And if you weep not, what can start your tears?
They now had wakened, and the hour approached
At which they used to bring our food to us,
And all of us were troubled by our dreams,
When from below I heard them nailing fast
The doorway of that tower of infamy.
At this I gazed upon my sons in silence.
I did not weep, for I was turned to stone;
But they were weeping, and my little Anselm
Said: 'Father, how you stare! Oh, what is wrong?'
And still I shed no tear, nor made reply
For all that day, nor through the following night,
Until the next sun dawned upon the world.

«When a faint ray had pierced that woeful ⌊prison,
And from the faces of the four about me
I could deduce the aspect of my own,
In anguish of despair, I bit my hands;
And they, believing that my wanton act
Was caused by hunger, rose and stood before me.
'Father, it will give us far less pain,'
They said, 'if you will eat of us.
This wretched flesh you gave us: therefore, take it.
I calmed myself, to stay their misery;
For that day and the next we spoke no word.
Unfeeling earth! Why didst thou not gape open?
When the fourth day broke on our wretchedness,
My Gaddo, falling outstretched at my feet,
Said: 'Father mine, why can't you give me aid?'
Then he expired: and as you see me here,
So did I see those other three sink down
Between the fifth and sixth days, one by one;
Then, though already blind, I felt them over,
And for two days called their names, though ⌊dead,
Until my grief was overcome by hunger.»
When he had spoken thus, with eyes askance,
He seized again the miserable skull,
With teeth as strong as dog's upon a bone.

Ah Pisa! Foul disgrace of all the people
In that fair countryside where *si* is spoken—
Because thy neighbors shirk thy punishment,
Let, then, Capraia and Gorgona move
To form a dam across the Arno's mouth,
So that thy wicked populace may drown!
For though Count Ugolino was reputed
To have betrayed thee in thy fortresses,
His sons should never have been put to torment.
Thou modern Thebes! Their tender age alone
Made guiltless Ugoccione and Brigata,
And those two others mentioned in my song.

We passed beyond, to where another crowd
Are firmly held in ice—not downward bent,
But all upon their backs, with heads upturned.
Their very weeping hinders them from weeping;
And grief, which finds a barrier in their eyes,
Is turned within to swell their agony:
For their first tears congeal to form a block

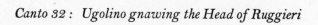
Canto 32 : Ugolino gnawing the Head of Ruggieri

Which, like a crystal vizor, tightly seals
The cavities that lie beneath their brows.

Although, by reason of the bitter cold,
As in a callus, every trace of feeling
Had gone away entirely from my face,
It seemed to me that I could feel a wind.
I said: «My master, what can make this draught?
Is not all wind extinguished here below?»

«Your eyes shall soon behold,» he answered me,
«The cause that moves the blast down from above,
And give to you the answer that you seek.»

One of the wretches frozen in the ice
Cried out to us: «O souls so pitiless
That fate has sent you to this utmost ring,
Pray take these solid veils from off my face
So that my heartfelt grief may have a vent—
Short-lived, for soon my tears will freeze again!»

And I to him: «If you would have my aid,
Then tell me who you are; and if I fail you,
May I go to the bottom of this ice!»

He answered: «I am Frate Alberigo:
He of the evil garden's fruits am I,
And here I get a date back for my fig!»
«Oh,» I exclaimed. «Are you already dead?»

And he to me: «I have no knowledge here
Of how my body walks the world above.
So favored is this place of Ptolomea,
That oftentimes a soul descends to us
Before its thread is cut by Atropos.
But so that you may be compassionate
And take the frozen tears from off my face,
Know that as soon as any soul betrays
As I did, then forthwith a demon takes
Its body from it, ruling it thereafter
Until its time has run its destined course:
The soul falls headlong to this pit of ice.
Perhaps the body still remains above
That once belonged to him behind me here—
And you must know him, if you came here lately.
He is Ser Branca d'Oria; and he
Has been imprisoned here these many years.»

«I think,» I said, «that you are mocking me;
For Branca d'Oria is not yet dead,

But eats and sleeps and drinks and wears his
⌊clothes.»

«Above, within the Malebranche's ditch—
There where the tough pitch forever boils—
Michael Zanche had not yet arrived
When this man left a demon in his stead
Within his body, and a relative's,
Who did that act of treachery with him.
But now stretch forth your hand and break the
That seals my eyes!» I did not open them: ⌊crust
It was but courtesy to treat him thus!

O Genoese! Ye people who are strange
To all morality, and filled with vice—
Why is the world still burdened with your souls?
For with the vilest sinner of Romagna,
I found a son of yours as bad as he:
His soul already plunged deep in Cocytus
While yet his body walks the world above!

CANTO 34

Vexilla regis prodeunt inferni
Toward us; therefore look in front of you,»
My master said, «and see him if you can.»

And then, just as a turning windmill looks,
Seen from afar, when dusk fades into night,
Or through the vapor of a thick miasma,
I thought I saw an engine such as that.
To shun the wind, I drew behind my leader,
For other shelter in that place was none.
Now I had come—I write it down with fear—
To where the shades were wholly covered up,
And, like a mote in glass, showed through the ice.
Some of them are recumbent, others stand—
One on his feet erect, one on his head;
One like a bow, his feet arched to his face.

After we had sufficiently advanced,
My loving master pointed out to me
That creature who once bore the semblance fair.
Stepping aside he made me halt, and said:
«Look upon Dis: and also on this place
Where you must arm yourself with all your
                                    ⌊courage!»

How frozen and how faint I now became,
Ask me not, reader, for all language here
Would not make words enough for me to tell.
I did not die, nor yet remain alive:
If genius flowers in you, now imagine
What I became, deprived of life and death!

The emperor of all the realms of woe
From his midbreast emerged above the ice.
Better with giants I myself compare
Than do the giants with his mighty arms.
Now mark how vast must be the whole of him
To be in scale with parts of such proportions!
If he was once as fair as now he's foul,
Yet lifted up his brows against his Maker,
Well should all tribulation come from him:
And what a monster he appeared to me
When I perceived three faces on his head!
The one in front was of a crimson hue,
And to it were the other two attached
Above the very middle of each shoulder;
There where the crest is borne, all three were
                                    ⌊joined.

The right-hand one was of a yellowish white,
While that upon the left was just as black
As any Ethiopian's on the Nile.
Beneath each face there sprang forth two great
Of size befitting such a monstrous bird: ⌊wings
Sails so immense were never known at sea.
They bore no feathers—rather, they were made
Like wings of bats; and he was flapping them
To make three separate blasts of icy wind,
Enough to freeze the confines of Cocytus.
With all six eyes he wept, and from three chins
The tears and bloody foam were trickling down.
In every horrid mouth he crunched a sinner,
As stalks of flax are broken by a heckle:

He thus kept three of them in constant torment.
For him in front, the biting was as naught
Beside the clawing; for, from time to time,
His back was left entirely stripped of skin.

«That soul up there who suffers greatest pain,»
My master said, «is Judas, the archtraitor,
Who has his head within, and kicks outside.
Those other two whose heads are dangling down
Are Brutus, hanging from the coal-black jaws—
See how he writhes, and utters not a word!—
Cassius the other, who is large of limb.
But night comes on again, and we must go—
For we have seen the whole extent of hell.»

At his command, I clasped him round the
He took advantage of the time and place, ⌊neck.
And when the wings were opened wide enough,
He laid firm hold upon the shaggy flanks.
From shag to shag he now went slowly down,
Between the matted hair and crusts of ice.
When we had reached that point just where the
                                    ⌊thigh

Doth turn upon the thickness of the haunch,
My leader, with fatigue and labored breath
Brought 'round his head to where his legs had
                                    ⌊been,

And grasped the hair like one who clambers up,
So that I thought our way lay back to hell.
«Hold fast! For it is by such stairs as these,»
My master said to me with panting breath,
«We must depart from such great wickedness!»

Now through a rocky cleft he issued forth,
And made me seat myself upon its edge;
He then walked carefully up to my side.
I raised my eyes, believing I should look
On Lucifer as I had seen him last:
But lo! I saw his legs were uppermost.
And if, indeed, I then became perplexed,
Let me be judged in ignorance by those
Who fail to see what point it was I passed!

«Rise to your feet,» the master said to me,
«Long is the way, and difficult the road:
The sun returns already to mid-tierce.»

It was no palace hallway where we were,

Canto 34 : Lucifer, King of Hell

INFERNO: CANTO 34

But rather a vast dungeon in the rock;
Uneven was its floor, and dim the light.
«Before I turn my steps from the abyss,
Dear master,» I said now that I had risen,
«Say a few words to lead me from my error.
Where is the ice? And how is Lucifer
Thus fastened upside down? How has the sun
So quickly moved from evening into morn?»

And he replied: «You still must think yourself
Beyond the centre, where I grasped the hide
Of that fell worm who perforates the world.
You were upon that side when I went down;
But when I turned around, we passed the point
To which all weights are drawn from everywhere.
Now you have come beneath the hemisphere
Facing the region where dry land prevails,
Below whose culminating point was slain
The Man who lived and died without one sin.
Your feet now rest upon the little sphere
That forms the other aspect of Giudecca.
Here it is morn when there the evening falls;

And he whose hair has served us for a ladder
Still remains fixed as he was fixed before.
It was upon this side he fell from heaven:
The earth, which first projected outward here,
For dread of him, made of the sea a veil,
Retreating to your hemisphere. Perhaps
The land where we now are, in fear of him
Rushed upward too, and left this vacant space.»

A place as distant from Beelzebub
As his whole tomb's extent, lies there below.
It is not known by sight, but by the sound
Of a small rivulet that there descends
Along the hollow of a rock, carved out
By its long, twisting course and slight incline.
Upon this secret path my guide and I
Now trod, to seek again the world of light;
And caring not for rest, we mounted upward,
He first and I behind, until I saw
Some of those lovely gems that heaven wears,
Through a round opening far above our heads:
Thence we came forth, again to see the stars.

DANTE ALIGHIERI

THE DIVINE COMEDY

PURGATORIO

Canto 1 : Dante kneeling before Statius

DANTE ALIGHIERI
THE DIVINE COMEDY

PURGATORIO
Canto 1

To run o'er better seas, my talent's bark
Now hoists her sails, for she has left behind
The cruel waters of the ocean deep;
And now my song is of the second kingdom,
Wherein the human soul is cleansed of sin
And rendered worthy to ascend to heaven.

O sacred Muses! Here dead poesy
Must rise again, since I am wholly yours:
And let Calliope arise as well
To amplify my song with harmonies
Like those which smote the wretched magpies' ears
With such a blow that they despaired of pardon.

Blue as a sapphire from the Orient,
The aspect of the sky shone forth serene
From zenith to the rim of the horizon,
So that my eyes were filled again with joy
As soon as I had left that deathly air
Which had so sore oppressed my sight and spirit.
The lovely planet that incites to love
Made all the eastern sky to smile, and cast
A veil upon the Fishes in her train.
I turned me to the right, and set my thoughts
Upon the other pole. I saw four stars
That none but Eden's folk had ever seen:
The very skies took glory in their light.
Widowed art thou, O northern hemisphere,
Deprived forever of the sight of them!

When I had ceased from gazing on their wonder,
I turned myself to face the other pole
From whence the Wain by now had disappeared.
I saw, hard by, a solitary shade,
In aspect worthy of more reverence
Than any son should show toward his father.
His beard was long, of thick and hoary hair
That matched his locks, which in a double fold
Of silvery white fell downward o'er his breast.
The rays that shone from those four holy stars
Adorned his face with such a brilliant light,
I saw him clearly, as beneath the sun.
«Who are you, that counter to the stream
Have fled from the eternal prison house?»
He said, and shook his venerable plumes.
«Who guided you, and lit you on your way
As you came forth from out the darksome night
That ever blackens o'er the vale of hell?
And are the laws of Hades thus transgressed,
Or doth a newer law prevail in heaven,
That lets you come, though damned, to these my
⌊rocks?»

My leader thereupon took hold of me,
And by his words and pressure of his hands
Constrained my knees and brow to reverence.
He answered him: «I came not of myself;
From heaven came down a lady, by whose prayers

I helped this man, and keep him company.
But since it is your wish to understand
More fully our condition, in all truth
My will is powerless to say you nay.
This man has yet to see his final hour —
But, through his folly, came so near to it
That he had little time to turn him back.
Even as I have said, I was sent forth
To rescue him; nor was there other road
Than this along which I have set myself.
The wicked people I have shown to him;
I now desire that he should look on those
Who purge themselves of sin here in your care.
How I have brought him here, 'twere long to tell:
From heaven a power descends that gives me aid
To lead him so that he can see and hear you.
I beg you, look with favor on his coming:
He goes in search of liberty — whose worth
One who has died for her can well appraise.
You know; and for her sake your death was sweet
In Utica, where you have left the vesture
That on the Day of Days will gleam so bright.
The eternal laws are not transgressed by us:
For this man lives, and Minos binds me not,
Because I dwell within that upper ring
Where your chaste Marcia's eyes still beg of you,
O sacred shade, to hold her for your own.
For her love, then, incline to our desire,
And grant us passage through your sevenfold
I will report this grace from you to her,   ⌊realm.
If you should deign to be remembered there.»
    «So pleasing to my eyes was Marcia
When I was on the earth,» he made reply,
«That anything she asked of me, I did.
Now that she dwells beyond the evil stream,
No longer can she move me — by that law
Which was established when I issued forth.
But if a heavenly lady guides your steps —
As you have said — discard all flattery:
Enough that you should ask me in her name.
Go, therefore, and take heed you gird this man
With a smooth reed, and that you wash his face,
So that all foulness may be cleansed from it:

For 'twere not meet that he should go before
The ministrant that is of paradise,
With eye bedimmed by any grimy cloud.
This little islet, at its lowest point —
Down yonder where the wave beats on its shore —
Bears rushes growing in its soft, wet ooze.
No plant of other kind, with leaves and boughs,
Or with a hardened growth, can flourish there,
Because it yields not to the wave's assault.
Let your return be by another road;
The sun, that rises now, will show a way
To climb the mountain by an easier path.»
    On saying this, he left; and I arose
In silence, fixing all my faculties
Upon my leader, drawing close to him.
«Son, follow in my steps,» he said to me.
«Let us turn back; for from this place, the plain
Slopes to its lowest confines by the shore.»
    The dawn was vanquishing the morning mist,
Which fled before it, so that from afar
I now descried the trembling of the sea.
Along the solitary plain we walked
Like one who seeks the road that he has lost,
And, till he finds it, seems to walk in vain.
When we had come to where the dew made strife
Against the thirsty sun — because it lay
Where it was cool, and therefore lingered long —
My gentle master softly laid his hands
Outspread upon the dewy grass; and I
Who understood the meaning of his act,
Toward him turned my cheeks bestained with
                                        ⌊tears;

And there forthwith he brought to light on me
That hue which hell had hidden with its grime.
    We went on downward to that desert shore
Which never saw its waters sailed upon
By any who had e'er returned from there;
And here he bound me as the other wished.
Wonder of wonders! For when he had plucked
The humble plant, another grew again,
Asudden, where the first was rooted out.

Canto 1 : Dante bows before the Angel Pilot

CANTO
2

THE sun had now progressed to that horizon
Whose great meridian, at its highest point,
Extends its arch above Jerusalem;
And night, which courses opposite to him,
Was issuing from the Ganges with the Scales,
Which drop from her when she exceeds the day.
From where I stood, the white and rosy cheeks
Of lovely dawn took on a deeper hue,
And then, in time, assumed an orange tint.

We still were walking by the water's edge
Like folk whose mind is fixed upon the road,
So that their thoughts outrun their lagging flesh;
And lo! As when, upon approach of dawn,
The ruddy glow of Mars shines through the mists
Of western skies, above the ocean floor:
Just so I saw—and hope to see again!—
A brightness come so swiftly o'er the sea
That never was there flight to match its speed.
And after I had turned my eyes aside
While I was questioning my gentle leader,
Again I saw it, larger, brighter still.
Upon each side of it appeared to me
I know not what, of white; and from below
Another issued forth, like unto it.
And still my master did not speak a word
Until those first white portents showed as wings;
But when he clearly recognized the pilot,
He cried: «Make haste, and humbly bend your
⌊knee!

Behold God's angel! Fold your hands in prayer;
Henceforth you'll see such ministrants as this!
See how he scorns all human instruments
And has no need of oars, or other sail
Than his own wings, between such distant shores;
See how he raises them against the sky,

Beating the air with his eternal pinions,
Which change not year by year like mortal
⌊plumes!»
Then, as the bird divine came nearer to us,
Brighter and brighter yet his radiance grew,
More dazzling than my mortal eye could bear.
I bowed my head; and he approached the shore
Upon a little vessel swift and light—
So light, it skimmed the surface of the wave.
Upon the stern the heavenly pilot stood:
Merely to tell of him were blessedness!
A hundred souls or more sat in the bark;
In exitu Israel de Aegypto
They sang together with a single voice,
And all the psalm that after this is written.
He made to them the sign of holy rood,
Whereon they all sprang out upon the beach;
And he departed, swift as he had come.

Those who remained seemed strangers to the
⌊place
And marvelled greatly as they gazed about,
Like one who tries to fathom something new.
On every side the sun, whose arrows bright
Had hunted Capricornus from midheaven,
Was darting forth the radiance of day;
And these new people lifted up their brows
In our direction, saying: «If you know it,
Show us, pray, the way to climb the mount.»

And Virgil answered: «You believe, perhaps,
That we have had experience of this place;
But we are pilgrims, even as yourselves.
Not long before you came had we arrived,
But by another road, so rough and hard
That this ascent will seem like play to us.»

The spirits, who were now aware of me,
Had noticed by my breathing that I lived,
And turned as pale as death in wonderment.
Just as on one who bears the olive branch
The folk will press and strive to hear the news,
Unheeding if they crowd upon their neighbors:
So all those spirits of the fortunate
Gazed on my face, as if they had forgotten
Their need to go and beautify themselves.

I saw that one of them was coming forth
To clasp me in his arms—so eagerly
That I myself was moved to do the like.
O empty shades, save in your outward aspect!
Three times I clasped my hands behind his back,
And every time did but my breast enfold.
I think my face was painted with amazement;
Whereat the spirit smiled and drew away,
And I went after him, a space behind.
Gently he bade me to come back, and tarry;
But then I recognized him—so I asked
That he should stay a while to speak with me.
He answered: «As I loved you when alive,
So, as an empty shade, I love you still:
Therefore I stay. But wherefore are you going?»

«O my Casella, I but make this journey
So that I may return again,» I said,
«But how have you been robbed of so much time?»

And he replied: «No wrong was done to me
If he, who takes but whom and when he wills,
Has many times refused me passage here:
For by a just will is his own determined.
Yet for the past three months he has embarked,
Full willingly, all those who wish to come:
So I, who had been wafted to the shore
Where Tiber's waters mingle with the salt,
Was graciously accepted by him there.
And to that river's mouth he now takes wing;
For there it is that all are brought together
Who have not fallen down to Acheron.»

And I to him: «If no new law deprives you
Of use and memory of those songs of love
With which you used to quiet all my longings:
Pray, with them give comfort to my soul,
Which, since it yet is burdened with its body,
Is now so sore fatigued by coming here.»

«Love, which pleads its cause within my mind,»
He sang for me so sweetly, that even now
The lilting melody still sounds within me.
My master, that great multitude, and I
Were all so captivated with delight
That every other thought had left our minds.
We one and all stood still, intent upon

His song. But lo! The venerable shade
Cried out: «What holds you here, you laggard
⌊souls?

What negligence is this? Why do you halt?
Speed to the mount, that you may rid yourselves
Of earthly dross, which veils the sight of God!»

And just as doves that wander tranquilly,
Without their customary show of pride,
In search of grain or darnel in the fields,
If aught appear to give them cause for fright
Will, of a sudden, let their food alone
Because a greater care has come to them:
So did I see that freshly gathered flock
Forsake the song, and turn toward the hill
Like one who wanders onward aimlessly:
Nor was our own departure far behind.

CANTO 3

ALTHOUGH the spirits, in their sudden flight,
Had scattered on the plain as they turned back
Toward that mount where reason makes us pure,
I now drew close beside my faithful comrade—
For how could I go on without his aid?
Who could have led me to the mountain-top?
He seemed to be abashed with self-reproach:
O conscience! Stainless, upright as thou art,
How bitterly the slightest fault doth sting thee!

Now that his feet no longer moved with haste—
Which steals the dignity from every act—
My thoughts, which hitherto had been restrained,
Loosened their bonds; and eager to know more,
I set my face toward that mountain-steep
Which soars most loftily above the wave.
The sun, that from behind was flaming red,
Traced upon the ground in front of me

Canto 3 : The Company of Souls upon the Cliff

My figure, where my body stopped its rays:
And when I saw the shadow on the earth
In front of me alone, I turned aside,
Fearing my leader had abandoned me.
But my consoler, turning wholly round,
Said to me: «Why are you still distrustful?
Do you not know that I am here to guide you?
It is already evening in that place
Where rests the body which could cast my
        ⌊shadow—
In Naples, though 'twas once in Brindisi.
And if I cast no shade before me now,
Marvel no more than at the heavenly spheres,
Where one does not obstruct another's radiance.
The will of God, whose ways are not revealed,
Ordains that forms like mine are capable
Of suffering torments, both of heat and cold.
And mad is he, who thinks our mortal mind
Can compass the interminable path
One Substance in Three Persons strides upon!
Mankind, remain contented with the *quia*:
Had everything been manifest to you,
No need had been for Mary to bear child;
And ye have seen such intellects sublime
Desiring fruitlessly—so that their failure
Became their sorrow through eternity!
I speak of Aristotle, and of Plato,
And many others»—here he bowed his head,
And said no more, but seemed to be disturbed.

  Meanwhile, we had come near the mountain's
And here we found the rocky crag so steep ⌊base;
That nimble feet could be of no avail.
The roughest, least frequented mountain path
That lies between Lerici and Turbia
Would seem an easy stair compared with it!
«Who knows which side presents a gentle slope,»
My master said, and halted as he spoke,
«So one may climb without the aid of wings?»

  And while he kept his eyes upon the ground
Pondering in his mind about the road,
And I was looking upward at the cliff,
Upon my left appeared a crowd of souls.
Although they moved their feet in our direction,

They seemed not to advance, so slow their pace.
«O master, raise your eyes,» said I, «Behold!
Yonder are people who can give us counsel,
If you cannot obtain it from yourself.»

  He looked at them, and said with happier mien:
«Let us approach them, for their pace is slow:
And you, beloved son, keep up your hopes!»

  That crowd was still as far away from us—
I mean, when we had walked a thousand steps—
As one who throws with skill can cast a stone,
When all of them pressed close the solid walls
Formed by the cliff, and stood there still and
As one who goes in doubt will hesitate. ⌊silent,
«O you of the elect, whose ends were good,»
Began Virgilius, «by that peace of God
Which, I am confident, you all will gain—
Pray tell us where the mountain so inclines
That one may climb the slope. Time that is lost
Displeases him the most who knows its worth!»

  As sheep will come out sometimes from the fold
By ones and twos and threes, while others stand
Timid, with eyes and muzzles on the ground—
And what the foremost does, the others do,
Huddling close beside him when he stops,
Silly and still, nor know the reason why:
Just so I saw the leader of that flock
Of happy spirits now begin to move,
With modest countenance and sober gait.

  When those in front observed that on my right
The sun's rays were obscured, so that I cast
A shadow from my body on the rock,
They halted short, and drew somewhat aback;
And all the others coming up behind
Did likewise, without knowing why they did so.
«Without your asking, I avow to you
That you behold the body of a man,
Whereby the light is parted on the ground.
Stand not to marvel at it: but believe
That not without the power that comes from
        ⌊heaven

He ventures to ascend this mountainside.»
  Thus spoke the master; and that worthy
        ⌊throng

Said: «Turn about, pass on in front of us,»
While making backward motions with their hands.
One said to me: «Whoever you may be,
Pray turn your face toward me as you walk,
And think if you once knew me in the world.»

  I turned around to him, and eyed him closely:
Fair and blond was he, of gentle aspect,
But had an eyebrow severed by a wound.
After I denied, with reverence,
That I had ever seen him, he exclaimed:
«Behold!» and showed a wound above his breast.
He added, with a smile: «In me you see
Manfred, grandson to the Empress Constance:
Wherefore I beg you, if you should return,
To seek my lovely daughter, who has borne
The kings of Aragon and Sicily;
And tell the truth, if other tale be rife.

  «After my body had been torn apart
By these two mortal wounds, I gave myself,
With tears, to Him who pardons willingly.
My sins, in very truth, were horrible;
Yet Goodness Infinite hath arms so wide
That all who turn to it are gathered in.
But if Cosenza's pastor, who was set
To hunt me down by Clement, had read aright
That passage in the holy Book of God,
My bones would still be lying in repose
Beneath the shelter of the heavy cairn
Beside the bridgehead, hard by Benevento.
Now, drenched by rain and scattered by the wind,
They lie without the realm, on Verde's banks,
Where, with extinguished tapers, he removed
But by their curses one is not condemned ⌊them.
Beyond the refuge of the love of God,
Which can return, so long as hope stays green.
'Tis true, that whoso dieth in contempt
Of Holy Church, repentant though he be,
Must stay outside upon these rocky slopes
Full thirty times as long as he has dwelt
In his presumption, if by worthy prayers
The term of punishment be not reduced.
So, later, see if you can give me joy
By telling my good Constance where I am,

How you have seen me, and of this decree:
For here we reap much good from those below.»

CANTO
4

THE soul, whenever it is all absorbed
In pleasure or distress, experienced
Through one or other of our faculties,
Appears to give no heed to other thoughts:
And this disproves the error that avers
That one soul burns within us o'er another.
Therefore, when anything is heard or seen
That keeps the soul intently fixed upon it,
The time goes by, and man perceives it not.
For power to listen is one faculty
And power of concentration is another—
The latter fettered, and the former free.

  Of this I had a true experience
While listening in wonder to that soul.
Fifty degrees, indeed, the sun had risen
Without my knowing it; and we had come
Before a passage, where that crowd of shades
Cried out as one: «Here is the place you sought!»

  Often, when grapes are darkening on the vines,
The husbandman, his pitchfork full of thorns,
Will with a single forkful stop a gap
Far wider than that passageway through which
My leader mounted, with myself behind,
Alone, now that the throng had gone away.
One goes up to San Leo, down to Noli,
Or climbs Bismantova up to its peak,
With one's own feet. But here we had to fly:
I mean that on the pinions of desire
I followed on behind that noble leader
Who gave me hope, and lit the way for me.
We struggled upward through the cloven rock.
The mountain crags pressed close on either side;

Canto 4 : Dante follows Virgil up the Rugged Mountainside

Below, the ground required both feet and hands.

When we had come upon the open hillside
That crowned the summit of the lofty cliff,
I said: «My master, whither shall we go?»

He answered: «Do not take a backward step,
But clamber up the mountainside behind me
Until we meet some guide who knows the way.»

So lofty was the summit, that it soared
Beyond my sight; the mountain slope was steeper
Than line that joins a centre to mid-quadrant.
My strength was spent, and so I said to him:
«O gentle father, turn around and see
How I remain alone, unless you halt.»

«My son,» he said, «press on as far as that»—
And pointed out a terrace higher up
That winds around the mountain on that side.

Spurred onward by his words, I forced my
And struggled ever upward after him ⌊strength
Until the ledge was underneath my feet.
Then both of us sat down to rest upon it,
Facing the east, from where we had climbed up—
For looking backward often gives one courage.
My eyes first wandered to the shore below,
Then upward to the sun; I was amazed
To see that it was shining on our left.
The poet noticed that I seemed bewildered
As I gazed on the chariot of bright day,
Riding the sky 'twixt Aquila and us.
«If Castor,» he explained to me, «and Pollux
Were in the company of that great mirror
Which sheds its light both upward and below,
Then you would see the fiery zodiac
Reddening still closer to the Bears,
Unless it wandered from its ancient course.
If you would try to think how this can be,
Consider Zion: picture how it lies
On earth directly opposite this mount,
So that they share together one horizon
In different hemispheres. And so the path
Upon which Phaethon so badly drove
Must pass, perforce—as you can plainly see
If you but closely fix your mind upon it—
There to the left, and here upon the right.»

«Truly, my master, never have I grasped
So clearly what I now can understand,
But which my reason always failed to see:
How the third circle of the heavenly motion,
Which in a certain art is called equator,
And ever stands 'twixt winter and the sun,
Lies just as distant toward the north from here
As to the Hebrews it lay toward the south.
But, if it please you, I would gladly know
How far we have to go; the mountain soars
Much higher than my mortal eye can reach.»

And he replied: «This mountain is so made
That at the bottom it is much more toilsome;
But as a man ascends, it pains him less.
Therefore, when that time comes when it appears
To you that the ascent becomes as easy
As going down the current in a skiff,
Then you will have reached your journey's end,
And there you may expect to rest from toil.
No more I answer. This I know for truth.»

When my beloved master said these words,
A voice close by spoke out: «Perchance ere that
You will have reason to sit down and rest!»

When this was said, we both turned quickly
And saw upon our left a massive stone ⌊round
That neither of us had perceived before.
Thither we walked, and saw that there were people
Reclining in the shadow of the rock,
As men who rest themselves in idleness;
And one of them, who seemed to be fatigued,
Was sitting down and clasping both his knees,
Keeping his face concealed, bowed down between
  ⌊them.

«My goodly master,» said I, «cast your eyes
On that man there, who seems so indolent
That Sloth herself must surely be his sister!»
At this he turned toward us and gave heed,
But scarcely moved his face along his thigh,
Saying: «Go up then, you that are so brave!»

I now knew who it was; and my exertion,
Which still was somewhat quickening my breath,
Did not prevent my going up to him.
When I approached he barely raised his head

And said: «Have you discerned the reason why
The sun now drives his chariot on your left?»

His lazy movements and his frugal speech
Moved me to smile a little. I began:
«Belacqua, now no longer shall I grieve
About your lot! Why are you sitting here,
Pray tell me. Are you waiting for a guide?
Or are you merely governed by your habits?»

«My brother, what avails it to climb up?
The bird of God, who sits at yonder gateway,
Would never let me pass into the torments.
For first it is required that I remain
Outside the gate until the firmament
Revolves as much again as in my lifetime,
For I put off repentance till the last;
Unless, ere then, a prayer may chance to rise
From one whose heart lives in the grace of God.
A prayer from any other is unheeded.»

The poet had resumed the steep ascent,
And said: «Come on! Behold, the sun now touches
The high meridian; and on the shore
The foot of night is treading on Morocco.»

CANTO 5

I HAD already parted from those spirits—
Following the footsteps of my guide—
When from behind a shade stretched out his finger
And cried: «The sunlight does not seem to shine
Upon the left of that one lower down—
He looks and walks as if he were alive!»

At this, I turned around to look at them,
And saw that they were staring in amazement
At me, and at the shadow that I cast.
«Now wherefore are you so absorbed in
⌊thought,»

My master said, «that you have slowed your steps?

What meaning have these whisperings for you?
Come, follow me, and let these people talk.
Stand firmly as a tower whose pinnacle
Sways not for all the blowing of the wind.
For he whose mind is constantly in change
Will wander ever farther from his object,
Because his thoughts enfeeble one another.»

What else could I reply except, «I come!»
I said it, not without that flush of shame
Which sometimes makes one worthy of
⌊forgiveness.

Meanwhile there came across the mountain
Some folk, a little space in front of us,   ⌊slope
Chanting the *Miserere* verse by verse.
When they became aware that rays of light
Were stopped as they were passing through my
⌊body,

They changed their song into a strident «Oh!»
And two of them in guise of messengers
Ran from the crowd to meet us, and inquired:
«Pray tell us if you are alive or not.»

My master answered them: «You can go back
And tell those people who have sent you here
That this man's body is of flesh and blood.
If they have stopped because they saw his
As I imagine, this will answer them: ⌊shadow,
Let them do honor to him, for their good.»

Never did vapors of a meteor
So swiftly cleave the air at fall of night,
Nor lightning flash across an August sky,
As quickly as those two flew back above,
And turning with the others, rushed toward us
Like horsemen galloping with hanging rein.
«Many indeed are these who press upon us,»
The poet said. «They ask a boon of you;
So walk ahead, and listen as you go.»
«O soul,» they cried, «that on your road to bliss
Are passing through here with your mortal
Pray walk a trifle less impatiently,   ⌊limbs—
And look if one of us is known to you,
That you may carry news of him to earth.
Ah, why do you press on? Pray, why not stop?
All of us have died by violence,

Canto 5 : The Body of Buonconte da Montefeltro in the Arno

And dwelt in sin until our final hour;
But then the light of heaven smote upon us,
So that we were repentant and forgiving,
And issued forth from life at peace with God,
Who fills us with desire to look on Him.»

«However closely I may scan your faces,»
I answered, «none I recognize. But tell me,
Spirits wellborn, how I may do your will:
And by that very peace that I now seek
Following the steps of such a guide,
From world to world, I swear I will perform it!»

A shade began: «Each one of us relies
On your good will, without your swearing it,
Unless perchance it lies beyond your power.
So I, who speak alone before the others,
Beseech you, if you ever see that land
Between Romagna and the realm of Charles,
To speak of me with courtesy in Fano,
That prayers may be well made in my behalf,
And I may purge away my grave offences.
For I was of that place. But gaping wounds
Whence gushed the blood that once meant life to
Were given me in Antenor's domain,   ⌊me,
Where I believed that I should be most safe;
Este had it done, who injured me
A great deal more than was my just desert.
But had I taken flight toward La Mira
When they came on me at Oriaco,
I still should be alive where people breathe.
I ran into the marshes, where the reeds
And mire entangled me, so that I fell,
And watched my lifeblood form a crimson pool.»

Then said another: «Even as your desire
That draws you to the mount may be fulfilled,
So may you further mine with piety.
Once Montefeltro, I am now Buonconte.
Joanna and the others heed me not;
Therefore I move about with downcast brow.»

And I to him: «What violence or chance
Caused you to stray thus far from Campaldino,
So that your burial place was never known?»

«Below the Casentino,» he replied,
«There flows a stream—Archiano it is called—

Which springs from Apennine above the Arno.
There where its name is lost I had arrived,
Pierced through the throat and fleeing from the
                                              ⌊foe,
My heart's blood streaming red upon the plain.
Here sight failed me, and I fell to earth,
The blessed name of Mary on my lips.
My spirit fled, my flesh remained alone.
I'll speak the truth—go tell it to the living!
God's angel took me up; and he of hell
Cried out: 'O you of heaven, why do you rob me?
For one small tear that takes him from my grasp,
You bear away the immortal part of him;
But for the rest of him, I have my plans!'
You understand how in the atmosphere
There gathers humid vapor, soon condensed
To water when it rises toward the cold.
The devil joined his will malevolent—
Which works for naught but ill—unto his wit,
And by that power stirred up the fog and wind.
So, when the day was spent, he filled the vale
With mist, from Pratomagno to the mountains,
And made the sky above so overcast
That all the laden air was liquefied.
Down poured the rain, and to the watercourses
Ran such of it the earth could not endure.
And when the water gathered in great streams,
It rushed on headlong toward the royal river,
With such great force that nothing held it back.
Archiano's torrent found my frozen body
Close to its mouth, and swept it to the Arno,
Loosening upon my breast the cross
Formed by my arms in mortal agony.
Along its banks it rolled me, o'er its bottom,
And buried me beneath its floating booty.»

«Ah, when you have joined the world again
And rested from the rigors of your journey,»
A third soul added to the second's words,
«Pray, then remember me, whom men call Pia.
Siena gave me life, Maremma death—
As well he knows whose ring I used to wear
In wedlock, after he had plighted troth.»

CANTO 6

WHEN a game of dice is broken up,
The loser, saddened, will remain behind,
Making his throws again—a sorry student—
And all the others, leaving with the winner,
Will crowd him, one in front and one behind,
While yet another plucks him from the side;
Incessantly he heeds them all in turn,
And those whom he rewards, no longer press him—
Thus he defends himself from all the throng:
E'en so did I behave in that dense crowd,
Turning my face to them on every side;
With pledges, as I went, I freed myself.

Here was the Arretine who met his death
At Ghin di Tacco's unrelenting hands;
That other, who was drowned as he pursued;
Frederick of Novello, and the Pisan
Who made the brave Marzucco show his worth,
Were in that multitude, with hands outstretched.
I saw Count Orso, and a shade who said
He lost his life through envy and through spite,
And not because of any wrong committed—
Pierre de la Brosse I mean; and for this deed
Let Mary of Brabant beware in time,
Lest she be herded with the sinners' flock!

As soon as I was free from all those souls
Who only prayed that someone else should pray,
So that they might the quicker gain their bliss,
I said: «My light, I think that you deny
Expressly in your text, that any prayer
From earth can turn aside decrees of heaven:
Yet these are praying for that very thing.
Will, then, their hopes be utterly in vain?
Or were your words misunderstood by me?»
And he to me: «My writings are most clear.
The hopes of all those spirits are not vain,

If one looks close, and reasons carefully.
Judgment supreme in no wise is impaired,
Though ardent prayer accomplish in a moment
Penance incurred by spirits stationed here.
Down in that place where I affirmed this point,
Wickedness could not be purged by prayer,
For he who prayed had been disjoined from God.
In matters of such great uncertainty,
Reach no conclusion that is not made clear
By her whose light will show your mind the truth.
I will explain. I speak of Beatrice;
You will behold her smiling in her joy,
Above, upon the summit of this mountain.»

And I: «My lord, let us press on the faster,
For now I feel less wearied than before;
And see! The mount begins to cast a shadow!»

«We will go forward,» he replied, «as far
As we are able by this morning's sun;
But the ascent is harder than you think.
Before you reach the top, you will behold
The sun return, that now behind the mount
Lies hid, so that your shadow is not cast.
But see that spirit standing over yonder
Apart there by himself, who looks our way:
He will point out to us the speediest path.»

We now drew near to him. O Lombard soul,
What proud disdain was in your lofty mien,
How grave and slow the movement of your eyes!
No word he spoke to us, but let us pass,
And watched us silently as we moved by,
After the manner of a crouching lion.
But Virgil now drew close to him, and begged
That he point out the best ascent to us.
The spirit did not answer his request,
But questioned us about our life and country.
My gentle guide began: «Mantua—»
And on a sudden the self-centred shade
Rose to him from the place where he had stood
And said: «O Mantuan, I am Sordello,
Your countryman!» And then the two embraced.

Ah Italy! Enslaved, abode of grief!
Ship without pilot in a mighty storm,
Mistress not of states, but of a brothel!

Even here, that noble spirit was so prompt
To give glad welcome to his countryman
At the mere sound of his dear city's name;
While in thy land, thy living citizens
Are all at war, and rend each other's flesh,
Even those that dwell within one moated wall.
Search, wretched land, the states that line thy
Search in thy bosom, and attempt to find ⌊shores:
A single countryside that dwells in peace!
And what avails it that Justinian
Repaired thy bridle, if the saddle's empty?
Indeed, without him were thy shame the less.
And ye, who ought to be at your devotions
And let the emperor ride in the saddle—
Did ye but understand the word of God—
Behold how wild this beast has now become
From lack of stern correction with the spurs,
Since ye have laid your hand upon the reins!
O German Albert, you who have abandoned
This beast, become so savage and untamed,
You, who in the saddle should be seated—
May righteous judgment from the stars of heaven
Fall on your blood, and be so terrible
That your successor tremble at the thought:
Because your sire and you, held back by greed
Behind the Alps, have suffered Italy,
The garden of the empire, to run waste.
Come, see the Montagus and Capulets,
Monaldi, Filippeschi—heedless man!
See those bowed down by grief, and those in dread;
Come, cruel man, to see the oppressive rule
Of your own nobles; punish their misdeeds!
Come and see how safe is Santafiora!
Come, and look on Rome that lies in tears,
Widowed, forsaken, crying night and day:
« My Caesar, why art thou not here with me? »
Come, see how well the people love each other;
And if no pity for our lot will move you,
Then come if but to blush for your good name!
And if it be allowed that I may ask,
O Lord Supreme, that suffered on the cross
For us on earth—are Thine eyes elsewhere turned?
Or is this nothing but a plan divine

Which Thou art making, in Thy deepest counsel,
To work some good beyond man's understanding?
For each and every town in Italy
Is thronged with tyrants; every countryman
Who plays the partisan, becomes Marcellus.
My Florence! Surely thou may'st be content
With this digression that concerns thee not,
Thanks to thy people and their civic pride!
Many are just in heart, but slow to shoot,
From taking counsel ere they take the bow:
Thy folk have justice on their very lips!
Many refuse the burdens of the state;
Thy citizens respond with eagerness,
Although uncalled, and cry: « I'll take this load! »
Wherefore rejoice! Thou hast good cause for it:
Wealthy art thou, at peace, and worldly wise.
If I speak truth, the facts will bear me witness.
Athens and Lacadaemon, that ordained
The laws of old, and were so civilized,
Gave but a hint of proper ways of life
Compared to thee, who dost so formulate
Thy fragile rulings, that October's thread
Will not suffice as far as mid-November.
How often in the memory of man
Hast thou changed coinage, offices, and laws,
Thy customs even, and thy population?
And if thou can remember, and see clearly,
Thou'lt see that thou art like an ailing crone
Who finds no rest upon her bed of down,
But tosses to and fro to ease her pain.

CANTO 7

After the dignified and happy greetings
Had been repeated thrice, and once again,
Sordello drew away and said: « Who are you? »
    « Before the souls deemed fit to rise to God

Were sent upon this mount for penitence,
My bones were buried by Octavian.
Virgil am I: from heaven I am shut out
For want of faith, but for no other sin.»
Thus did my gentle leader make reply.

As one who sees before him suddenly
A sight that makes him wonder, and exclaim,
«It is! It cannot be!»—but half believing:
So seemed the other. Now he bowed his head,
And with humility returned to Virgil,
And, like a vassal, clasped him round the knees.
«O honor of the Latin race,» he said,
«Through whom our language showed its greatest
Eternal glory of my own dear city!   ⌐power!
How have I earned the grace that you come here?
If I deserve to listen to your words
Say if you come from hell – and from which circle.»

«The circles of the kingdom of despair
I crossed upon my way here,» he replied.
«I come by heavenly power that willed my
                              ⌐movements.

Not what I did, but what I failed to do
Lost me the right to see that Sun on high
Which you now seek, and which I knew too late.
There is a place below, sad—not from torments
But from its darkness, where the lamentations
Have not the sound of wailing, but of sighs.
There I abide, with little innocents
Bitten by death's fangs ere they had been
Baptized, to make them free of human sin.
There I abide with those who were not clothed
With the three sacred virtues, though they knew
The others, without vice, and practised all.
But if you have the knowledge and the power,
Give us your help, that we may sooner reach
The point where lies the gate of purgatory.»

«We need not stay in one fixed place,» he said,
«And we can wander up and round the mountain;
As far as I may go, I'll be your guide.
But see already how the day declines:
To climb the mount by night is not allowed,
Hence it is wise to choose a resting place.
Afar off on the right there are some spirits;

If you consent, I'll lead you to them now.
To know them will not be without delight.»
«But how is that?» he answered. «Should one
                              ⌐wish

To climb by night, would he be stopped by others,
Or would he lose the power to climb the mount?»
Sordello drew his finger o'er the ground
And said: «Behold! Not even beyond this line
Could you proceed, when once the sun has gone.
Nothing, however, but the shades of night
Would offer any hindrance to your climbing:
For they obstruct the will and sap its power.
By night one could, indeed, go down again
And wander round the mountain slope at will,
So long as the horizon hides the day.»
Thereat my lord, as if in wonderment:
«Lead on,» he said, «lead us to where, you say,
Delight is to be found for one who waits!»

When we had gone a little way beyond,
I noticed that the mountainside was hollow,
Just as in valleys here upon the earth.
«Yonder,» said the spirit, «let us go
To where the hillside shapes into a fold;
And there we will await the coming day.»

A sloping pathway, neither steep nor level,
Led us along the side of the depression,
To where the bank is only half as high.
Fine gold and silver, scarlet and pure white,
Blue of the brilliant wood of India,
An emerald's green, the moment it is split—
The colors of all these would be surpassed,
Just as a greater thing outshines a lesser,
By the bright shrubs and blossoms in that dell.
And not with hue alone had nature wrought,
But with the sweetness of a thousand perfumes
She made one blended fragrance, strange and rare.
Salve Regina now some spirits sang,
Seated upon the grass amid the flowers,
And hidden to the valley from without.
«Until the sun's last rays have disappeared,»
Began the Mantuan who was our guide,
«Pray do not ask that I should lead you there.
Here from this bank you better can discern

Canto 7 : The Poet Sordello kneels before Virgil

The actions and the faces of them all,
Than if you were among them there below.
He who sits highest, with the look of one
Who has neglected to perform his duty,
Whose lips are motionless while others sing,
Was Emperor Rudolph — he who had the power
To cure those wounds which murdered Italy;
But now, too late, another must revive her.
That other shade who seems to comfort him
Was ruler where the water takes its rise
That Elbe bears from Moldau to the sea.
His name was Ottocar; in swaddling clothes
He far excelled the bearded Wenceslaus
His son, who feeds on luxury and sloth.
And he, the small-nosed one, who seems to be
In earnest counsel with that shade benign,
Perished in flight, dishonoring the lily.
Look how violently he beats his breast!
And see that other shade who as he sighs
Has laid his cheek to rest upon his palm.
Those are the father and the father-in-law
Of France's curse. They know his evil life,
Whence springs the shame that causes them such
⌊grief.

«That stalwart shade who chants in unison
With him whose nose is large and masculine,
Was girded with the cord of every virtue.
And had that youth who sits behind him there
Ruled longer as a king upon his throne,
That virtue would have passed from sire to son —
But none can say this of the other heirs!
Though James and Frederick now possess the
⌊kingdoms,
The better heritage is held by neither.
Seldom indeed does human virtue rise
From trunk to branch: and thus it is ordained
By Him on high, that we may pray for it.
My words apply to him whose nose is large
And to the other Pedro singing with him,
Who makes Apulia and Provence to mourn.
So is the plant inferior to the seed
As Constance may her husband's virtues boast,
Louder than Beatrice and Margaret.

«See there the monarch of the simple life,
Harry of England, sitting by himself.
He has a better issue in his branches!
That shade who sits there lower than the rest,
Now looking upward, is the Marquis William,
For whom the war of Allesandria
Made Montferrat and Cavanese weep.»

CANTO 8

THE hour was come, that brings to those at sea
A longing to return, when they recall
The day on which they bade sweet friends
⌊farewell —
That hour which thrills the traveller with love
When from afar he hears the sound of bells
Seeming to mourn the dying of the day.
I ceased to listen to the song, and looked
In wonder at a shade who stood erect
And waved his hand, entreating us to hear.
He joined and lifted upward both his palms,
Fixing his steadfast gaze upon the east,
As if to say to God: «Aught else I scorn!»
Te lucis ante issued from his lips
With such devotion, and in tones so sweet,
That I was rapt in silent admiration.
And then the others joined to follow him,
And sweetly and devoutly sang it through,
Their eyes intent upon the heavenly spheres.
Here, reader, sharpen well your eyes to truth:
Now the veil is surely so transparent
That passing through it is an easy thing.
And then I saw that highborn company
In silence gazing upward, pale and meek,
As though in expectation of some portent.
Lo! Descending there from heaven's height,
I saw two angels, armed with flaming swords
Shorn of their tips, and broken at the ends.

As green as newly opened little leaves
Appeared their raiment, fluttering in the wind
Made by the beating of their pinions green.
One came to rest a little way above us;
The other on the bank across the vale,
So that the people were contained between them.
I now could plainly see their heads were blond,
But when I tried to look upon their faces,
My eyes were dazzled by excessive light.

«From Mary's bosom both of them are come,»
Sordello said, «as guardians of the valley
Against the serpent who will soon arrive.»
And I, not knowing whence he would appear,
Turned me around; and chilled with sudden fear,
Drew close against my master's trusty shoulders.

Sordello spoke again: «Let us go down
Among those mighty shades, and talk with them:
For seeing you will give them great delight.»

I think I only stepped three paces down;
And there below I marked a shade that gazed
On me alone, as if he sought to know me.
The air already was becoming dark,
But not so dark that I could fail to see
That which was hid between his eyes and mine.
Toward me he made, and I went nearer to him.
Noble Judge Nino! What a joy for me
To see that you were not among the damned!
We left no friendly word unsaid between us,
And then he asked: «How long since you have
⌊reached

The mountain, from across the distant waters?»

«Oh,» I replied, «from out the dismal realm
I came this morning, still in mortal life;
But I may gain the other by this journey.»

The moment that my answer had been heard,
Sordello and the other both drew back,
As people do when taken by surprise.

Sordello turned to Virgil, and the other
To one who sat beside him, crying out:
«Up, Conrad, see what God through grace hath
⌊willed!»

Then, turning toward me: «By that gratitude
You owe to Him whose ways are hidden deep,

Too deep by far for mortal understanding—
When you return across the waters wide,
Beseech my Joan to intercede for me
Where fervent prayers of innocents are answered.
I do not think her mother loves me now,
Seeing she has put off her widow's weeds,
Which she is doomed to wish for once again.
By her example one may understand
How long the fire of love endures in woman
If sight and touch no longer feed its flame.
The snake that leads the Milanese afield,
Will make less fair a sepulture for her
Than would my blazon of Gallura's cock.»
These were his words; and on his countenance
He bore the impress of that righteous zeal
Which glows—with proper measure—in the heart.

My eager eyes turned nowhere but to heaven,
To that point where the stars revolve more slowly,
Even as a wheel does nearest to the axle.
«What are you looking at?» my leader said.

And I replied to him: «At those three torches
With which the pole on this side seems aflame.»

And he to me: «The four so brilliant stars
You saw this morning, now are sunk below;
And these are risen up to where those were.»

While he still was speaking, lo, Sordello
Laid hold of him, pointing with his finger,
And said: «Behold! There is our adversary!»

On that side where the valley had no bound
There was a serpent—possibly the same
As that which gave the bitter food to Eve.
Through grass and flowers came the evil streak,
Turning its head around from time to time
To lick its back, as beasts will sleek themselves.
I did not see, and therefore cannot tell
How those celestial birds were set in motion,
But I could see that both of them were moving.
Hearing the air cleft by their emerald wings,
The serpent fled; the angels, flying back,
Wheeled upward to regain their sentry posts.

The spirit—that had moved beside the judge
When he exclaimed—throughout that whole
⌊assault

Canto 8 : The Angels putting the Serpent to Flight

Ne'er turned his eyes from gazing on my face.
«So may the light that leads you now on high
Find in your own free will sufficient worth
To raise you to the enamelled mountain peak,»
He said. «If you have any certain news
Of Val di Magra or its neighborhood,
Tell it to me—for there I once was great.
Corrado Malaspina I was called:
But not the elder, though from him I spring.
The love I bore mine own is here refined.»

«Oh,» I replied to him, «I ne'er have been
Within your lands: but where, in all of Europe,
Lies there a spot where they are not renowned?
The fame that honors your illustrious house
Proclaims its lords, proclaims their territory,
So that he knows it well, who ne'er has seen it.
I swear, as I may hope to reach that goal,
Your honored race does not despoil itself
Of praise for deeds of charity or valor.
By nature and tradition it is such,
That though the guilty head lead all awry,
It keeps the path and scorns the evil way.»
And he: «Now go! before the seventh time
The sun shall come unto that resting place
The ram bestrides and covers with his feet,
This courteous opinion of my house
Shall be more firmly fastened in your mind
Than e'er it could be by another's words—
Unless the course of justice be diverted.»

CANTO
9

THE concubine of ancient Tithonus
Gleamed white upon the terrace of the east,
Freed from the embrace of her sweet friend.
Her brow was glistening with shining gems
Set in the shape of that cold animal
Which strikes at people with its stinging tail;

The night upon those stairs which she ascends
Had mounted but two steps, and for the third
Was making ready, drooping both her wings,
While I, who still had Adam's flesh about me,
Conquered by sleep, was lying on the grass,
There where our company of five was sitting.

At that sweet hour of morning near the dawn
When the small swallow starts her plaintive songs,
Perchance in memory of her former griefs,
And when the mind, drawn outward from the flesh,
And hampered less by thoughts of earthly things,
Becomes as if inspired in its foresight,
I seemed to see an eagle, in a dream,
Hovering in the sky, with golden plumes,
Its wings outspread, and poising for a swoop.
It seemed to me that it was in that place
Where Ganymede, abandoning his people,
Was borne up to the high consistory.
I thought: «Perchance in this one spot alone
He strikes his prey; from any other place
He scorns to bear off booty in his clutches.»
And then it seemed that, having wheeled a little,
He swooped as if he were a thunderbolt,
And snatched me upward to the realm of fire.
There, I dreamed, both he and I were burning:
The fancied conflagration scorched me so,
That of necessity my sleep was broken.

Not otherwise Achilles shook himself,
Turning his awakened eyes about him,
Not knowing where he was; and then his mother
Took him away in secrecy, asleep,
Borne in her arms from Chiron unto Skyros,
Whence he was taken later by the Greeks:
'Twas even so I started up, when sleep
Was fleeing from my face, and I turned pale
As does a frightened man who turns to ice.
Beside me was my comforter alone;
More than two hours now the sun had climbed,
And I had turned my face toward the sea.
«Fear not,» my master said, «be reassured,
For we have reached a most propitious place;
Do not relax, but put forth all your strength.
For you are now arrived at purgatory:

See there the cliff that closes it around,
And see the entrance, where it seems divided.
A little while ago, ere break of day,
While your soul still slept within your body
Upon the flowers adorning yonder place,
A lady came, and said: 'I am Lucia.
Allow me, pray, to take this sleeping man
So that I may assist him on his way.'
Sordello and the others stayed behind;
She took you up, and as the day grew bright
She mounted, and I followed in her steps.
She laid you down here. First her lovely eyes
Showed to me that open entrance way:
Then she and slumber went away together.»

   Even as a man, whose doubt has been
                              ⌊dispelled,

So that his fear is changed to confidence,
As soon as truth has been revealed to him:
Even so I changed. Now when my leader saw
That I was freed from care, he took his way
Upward along the cliff, and I behind him.

   You can well see how I exalt my theme,
O reader: therefore do not be amazed
If I support it with still greater art!

   We now approached, and what had seemed a
Like to a fissure that divides a wall— ⌊breach—
We recognized to be an entrance gate,
And just below, and leading up to it,
Three steps of varied colors, and a guardian
Who till now had uttered not a word.
But as I gazed upon him more and more,
I saw him sitting on the topmost step,
His mien beyond my human power to bear;
And in his hand he held a naked sword
Which made such bright reflection of its rays
That many times I raised my eyes in vain.
«Speak forth, from where ye stand: what seek ye
                                ⌊here?»

He said to us. «Where has your escort gone?
Take heed ye go not upward for your ill!»

   «A heavenly lady, versed in all these things,»
My master answered, «but a short while since
Said to us: 'Thither go: there is the gate.' »

   «And may she speed your steps to further
The warder courteously replied to us.   ⌊good,»
«Come forward, and draw nigh unto our stairs.»

   When we had come before the first great step,
I saw that it was marble, smooth and white,
For I was mirrored in it as I stood;
The second, of a deeper hue than perse,
Was fashioned from a rough and calcined stone,
Riven with cracks, both lengthwise and athwart.
The third, which lay atop the other two,
Seemed to be porphyry, and of a color
As red as blood that spirts forth from a vein.
On this God's angel rested both his feet,
And sat upon the threshold, which to me
Appeared to be a rock of adamant.
With willing hand, my leader drew me up
The three steps of the stairway, as he said:
«Entreat him humbly to undo the lock.»

   Devoutly at the holy feet I fell,
Beseeching him to open unto me;
But first upon my breast I struck three times.
Upon my forehead seven _P_'s he traced
With his sword's point, and said: «See that thou
                                ⌊wash

These scars away, when thou hast entered in!»

   He wore a garment of a dusky hue
Like ashes, or dry earth when freshly dug;
And from beneath it he drew forth two keys.
One was of gold, the other one of silver.
First with the white, and later with the yellow
He turned the lock: so I was made content.
«Whenever one of these two keys may fail
So that it turns not rightly in the lock,»
He said to us, «this doorway will not open.
One is more precious; but the other one
Needs art and genius to turn back the bolt:
For 'tis the one that will untie the knot.
I hold them from St. Peter—who bade me err
Rather in opening, than in shutting out,
For all who should fall prostrate at my feet.»
The holy gateway's door he opened wide,
Saying: «Pass in: but I must give you warning
That he who looks behind returns outside.»

Canto 9 : Dante, in a Dream, carried off by an Eagle

And so the doors of that most sacred gate,
Fashioned of metal, resonant and strong,
Were swung around upon their mighty pivots;
Tarpeia echoed not more stridently
When good Metellus was removed from her,
Whereby she afterward remained despoiled.
At the first thundering sound, I turned aside:
I thought I heard *Te Deum laudamus*,
Sung in voices mingling their sweet sound.
That which I heard gave me the same impression
As we receive when people stand and sing
Accompanied by an organ, and the words
Are sometimes understood, and sometimes not.

CANTO
10

WHEN we had crossed the threshold of that
So little used, because man's evil love   ⌊door—
Makes the crooked path seem straight—I heard
A sound that told me it was closed again.
And had I turned mine eyes to look at it,
How could I ever have excused my fault?

We were ascending through a cloven rock
That alternately wound from side to side,
Even as a wave advances and recedes.
«Here we had better use a little cunning,»
My leader said, «and hug that rocky cliff
That lies on this hand now, and now on that.»

Thereby our footsteps were so much retarded
That ere we issued from this needle's eye,
The silver circle of the waning moon
Had reached its bed, and laid itself to rest;
And when we gained the open space above,
Where in a ledge the mountainside steps back,
We both had lost the way, and I was spent.
Twas so that we halted on a level place
More desolate than any trackless waste.

I think that from the edge which skirts the void,
The distance to the overhanging cliff
Would measure thrice a human body's length.
This ledgelike cornice seemed to be the same
Through its extent, as far as eye could see
On either side, alike to right and left.

Ere we had made a step upon the terrace,
I was aware that the great mountain wall,
So sheer and steep that it could not be climbed,
Was made of marble of the purest white,
Carved with an art unmatched by Polycletus;
Nay, even nature would have been outdone.

That angel, bearer of the great decree
Which brought the long-desired peace on earth,
Reopening heaven, closed by ancient ban,
Was carved before us there in very truth,
And shown in such a gentle attitude
It seemed he scarce could be a silent image.
One could have sworn that he was saying *Ave!*
For she was also pictured there who turned
The key that opened the exalted love;
And by her attitude she seemed to say,
Ecce ancilla Dei, as exactly
As one can see a figure stamped on wax.

«Keep not your mind fixed on one place alone,»
My gentle master said from where he stood
So that he had me on his left-hand side.

At this I turned my head around, and saw
Upon my right, where stood my noble guide,
Another story carved upon the rock,
A space beyond the sculpture showing Mary.
I therefore passed by Virgil, and drew near,
So that my eyes might better grasp its meaning.
There in the living marble were engraved
The cart and kine that drew the sacred ark
Which makes men fear to seize an office wrongly.
In front of it were sculptured seven choirs;
One sense insisted, «Yes, in truth, they sing,»
The while another gave the answer «No!»
'Twas likewise with the incense smoke I saw,
So wondrously depicted that my eyes
And nose were made in «Yes!» and «No!»
                                    ⌊discordant.

And there, before the holy vessel, danced
The humble psalmist, with his girded loins,
Who by that act was more, and less, than king;
And opposite Queen Michal was portrayed,
Looking on from out a palace window,
Like a lady scornful and depressed.

I moved from where I stood, to look upon
Another legend—next beyond to Michal—
That glistened white before me on the marble:
And here was chronicled the mighty pomp
Of that great prince of Rome whose excellence
Spurred Gregory to win his greatest triumph.
'Tis of imperial Trajan that I speak;
And at his bridle was a lowly widow
In attitude of sorrow and in tears.
Around about him pressed a throng of knights,
And o'er his head the eagles, all in gold,
Were moving, in appearance, in the wind.
The wretched woman who was in their midst
Seemed to cry out: «O lord, avenge my son—
For I am brokenhearted at his death!»

And he, to answer her: «Bide my return.»

Then she, like one obsessed by urgent grief:
«Yet how, my lord, if you should not return?»

«He who succeeds me, he will do it for you.»

And she: «How can the good deed of another
Take the place of those you fail to do?»

To which he made reply: «Console yourself:
For I must do my duty ere I go.
Justice so wills, and pity holds me back.»

For He Who never looked on aught that's new
Produced this form of speech that could be seen—
Novel to us because unknown on earth.
While in delight I stood and filled my eyes
With pictures of such great humilities,
Dear to behold, because of their Creator,
The poet murmured: «See, upon this side,
A crowd of souls who slowly come our way:
These will direct us to the lofty stairs.»

My eyes, which gazed intently at the sculpture,
Ever in eagerness to see new things,
Were now not slow, and straightway turned to
⌊him.

I would not, reader, have you be distraught
From holding to your worthy resolution,
Through hearing how God wills that debts be paid.
Heed not the form and manner of the torments;
Think on their consequences, and reflect
That, at the worst, the Judgment Day will end
⌊them!

«Master,» I said, «those now I see approaching
Do not appear to me like human forms:
I know not what they are, nor can I see.»

«The nature of their torment,» he replied,
«Makes them bend down so closely to the ground
That my own eyes, at first, were at a loss.
But look there fixedly, and ascertain
That which is coming underneath those stones;
Now you can see how every one is stricken.»

O proud Christians, weary and distressed,
Who in your poor diseased, distorted minds
Still put your confidence in backward steps!
Do ye not know that we are naught but worms,
Born to produce the heavenly butterfly
That wings to judgment lacking all defence?
Wherefore do your minds float up aloft,
Seeing ye are but crude, defective insects,
Like a worm whose form is incomplete?

As, to support a ceiling or a roof
One sometimes sees, like corbels, human figures
Whose knees are gathered upward to their chests.
So that their pictured suffering gives birth
To real distress in him who looks at them:
In such an attitude, I saw those souls.
In truth, each was distorted more or less
According to the load upon his back:
And even he who seemed to be most patient
Appeared to say: «I cannot suffer more!»

Canto 10 : The Marble Sculptures portraying Pride

CANTO
11

OUR FATHER, who art in heaven, uncircum-
⌊scribed,
Save by the greater love which Thou dost bear
For Thy first fruits created there on high—
Praised be Thy name and power by every creature,
For it is meet that all should render thanks
To the sweet emanation of Thy love.
Upon us may Thy kingdom's peace descend:
For by ourselves we cannot e'er attain it,
Strive how we will, for it must come to us.
And as Thine angel hosts make sacrifice,
Singing hosannas, of their will to Thee,
So may all men make sacrifice of theirs.
Give unto us this day the daily manna
Without which, in this desert where we dwell,
He must go backward who would most advance.
And as we should forgive all evildoers
The wrong that we have suffered, so do Thou
Forgive with grace; regard not our deserts.
Put not to proof our worth, that is subdued
In battle with the ancient adversary;
Deliver us from him that so assails it.
Dear Father, this last prayer is not for us
Who need it not; but it is made for those
Who have survived us, in the life on earth.» ⌈us,
Praying good speed, both for themselves and
Round about the cornice moved those shades,
Unequally tormented; but they each
Were wearied with a burden—such a load
As one might fancy in an evil dream—
To purge away the sullies of the world.
If yonder so much good is said for us,
What should be said and done on earth for them,
By those who have a firmly rooted will?
Indeed, we ought to help them wash away

The marks which they bore hence, that pure and
⌊light
They may go forth to reach the starry spheres.
«So may just mercy rid you of your burdens
That you may move your pinions and arise
Till you attain the heights of your desire:
Pray show to us which is the shortest way
To reach the stairs. If there be more than one,
Point out to us the path that slopes the least;
For he who comes with me is burdened down
With Adam's flesh, and therefore he is chary,
Against his will, of climbing up the mount.»
It was not manifest from whom now came
The words in answer to the ones just spoken
By him whom I was following, but this was said:
«Come with us to the right along the bank,
And you will find a passageway by which
A living man might possibly ascend.
And were I not prevented by this stone
That tames the arrogance of my proud neck
And forces me to keep my face cast down,
I would look upward at this living being—
Unnamed as yet—to see if I might know him,
And ask his pity for my heavy load.
From Italy am I, a Tuscan's son;
Guglielmo Aldobrandesco was my father;
I know not if you may have heard his name.
My forbears' ancient blood and gallant deeds
Made me so arrogant, that I despised
All of mankind, and held them in contempt,
And was forgetful of our common mother.
I died therefor, as any Sienese
Or child in Campagnatico knows well.
I am Omberto; and my pride does harm
Not to myself alone, for all my kin
Were dragged thereby down to calamity.
And 'tis for it that I must bear this burden
Here mid the dead, till God be satisfied:
For mid the living, I endured it not.»
Listening, I bent down, and one of them—
Not he who had just spoken—turned around
Twisting beneath the weight impeding him,
And recognized me. He called out my name,

Keeping his eyes laboriously upon me
Who walked beside them, stooping as I went.
«Oh,» I inquired, «are you not Oderisi,
Honor of Gubbio—honor of that art
Which they in Paris call illuminating?»

«Brother,» said he, «far fairer to behold
Are Franco of Bologna's pencilled leaves.
His is all honor now; and mine but little.
To tell the truth, while I was yet alive
I never should have been so courteous
When striving to excel, for which I yearned.
Here is made the payment for such pride;
And were it not that while I still could sin
I turned to God, I should not yet be here.»

O vanity of human eminence!
How short a time the verdure crowns the summit
Unless an age of dullness follows after!
Once Cimabue held the painter's field,
But now Giotto has the cry, and thus
The other's fame already is obscure.
Likewise one Guido snatches from the other
The glory of our tongue; and one is born
Who'll drive them both perchance from out the ⌊nest.
Worldly renown is but a breath of wind
Coming first from here and then from there,
And changes name because it changes quarter.
If one should cast away his flesh when old,
Instead of dying when a babbling infant,
What greater reputation will he have
After a thousand years—which to eternity
Are briefer than the twinkling of an eyelid
Beside the turning of the slowest sphere?

«He who so slowly plods the road before me
Was once renowned throughout all Tuscany;
But now his name's scarce whispered in Siena
Where he was ruler, when the raging mob
Of Florence was destroyed at Mont' Aperti.
Then she was proud as she is abject now.
A man's renown is like the hue of grass,
Which comes and goes: he fades and withers it
Who brought it forth in freshness from the earth.»

And I to him: «Your words have filled my
With true humility, and crushed my pride; ⌊heart

And who is he of whom you now were speaking?»
«That,» he replied, «is Provenzan Salvani;
And he is here because he once aspired
To subjugate Siena to his will.
Thus burdened, he has gone without repose
E'er since he died. With such coin all must pay
Who have been too presumptuous on earth.»

And I: «If every spirit who awaits
His dying day ere he repents, must stay
Below there, and cannot ascend thus far
Until his span of life has run again,
Except that he be helped by righteous prayer,
How is it he is suffered to come here?»

«While he was still alive, and in his glory,»
He said, «he, of his own free will, once stood
In Campo di Siena, shamelessly,
And there, to free a friend from sufferings
Inflicted in the prison house of Charles,
Abased himself and quivered in each vein.
This action let him pass the boundary.
No more I'll say. I know my words are dark:
But ere much time will pass, they'll be explained
By deeds of your own fellow citizens.»

CANTO
12

Wɪᴛʜ even pace, like oxen in a yoke,
That burdened soul and I went side by side,
As long as my good teacher would allow.
But when he said, «Pass onward now, and leave
For here 'tis well for each, as best he can, ⌊him.
To urge his bark along with sail and oars,»
I raised my body, standing up erect
That I might walk again conveniently,
Although my thoughts remained abased and
⌊stooping.

Canto 12 : The Souls of the Proud, bearing Heavy Stones

PURGATORIO: CANTO 12

I had moved on, and followed with good will
The footsteps of my master, and already
We both were showing we were light of pace,
When he admonished me: «Cast down your eyes:
In order to beguile your way, 'tis well
That you should see the pavement underfoot.»

As o'er the buried dead, their tombs display
The effigies of what they once have been,
So that their memory may be preserved—
And people go there to shed tears for them,
Caused often by the pricking of remembrance,
Which to the piteous alone gives spur—
Even so I saw that all that terraced pathway
Was carved with figures, rarer to behold
Because they were of better workmanship.

Upon one side I saw depicted him
Who once was fairer than all other creatures,
Falling like lightning downward from the skies.
Upon the other side I saw Briareus
Transfixed by the celestial bolt, and lying
Heavy upon the ground, in deathly chill.
I saw Thymbraeus; Pallas too, and Mars,
Bearing their arms, around their father, Jove,
And gazing on the giants' scattered limbs.
Nimrod I saw, below his mighty work
As if bewildered, looking at the people
That had been proud with him in Shinar's land.

O Niobe! With eyes how sadly weeping
I saw you represented on the pathway,
Between your seven and seven children slain!
And what a spectacle were you, O Saul!
Upon your own sword dying, on Gilboa,
Which felt thereafter neither rain nor dew.
Foolish Arachne! Thus I saw you there—
Already half a spider, prone in grief
Upon the shreds of your most baneful work.
O Rehoboam! Here your effigy
No longer threatens, but a chariot
Bears it away in terror-stricken flight.

And also there the stony pavement showed
How costly to his mother had Alcmaeon
Made her ill-fated ornament appear.
There too I saw Sennacherib portrayed,

Murdered within the temple by his sons,
Who there abandoned him when he was slain.
It showed the cruel slaughter and defeat
Tomyris wrought, when she declared to Cyrus:
«For blood you thirsted once: with blood I fill
⌊you!»

It showed how the Assyrians fled in rout
At Holophernes' death, and showed as well
The body of the slaughtered king himself.
Troy I beheld, in ashes and in ruins.
O Ilion! How abject and defiled
Did you appear upon the sculptured pavement!

What master of the brush or graving tool
Could reproduce those shadows and those features,
So to astonish all with eyes to judge!
Dead seemed the dead; the living seemed alive:
Who saw the scenes themselves, could see no more
Than I did, looking down upon that pavement.
Now be ye proud, and go with haughty mien,
Ye sons of Eve, and look not 'neath your feet,
Lest ye behold the evil path ye tread!

We now had farther passed around the moun-
More of his path the sun had left behind ⌊tain;
Than I in my distraction had perceived,
When he who, ever watchful, walked in front,
Began: «Lift up your head: no longer now
Must you go thus absorbed. Yonder behold
An angel, who prepares to come to us:
See how the sixth handmaiden of the day
Returns from service. With due reverence
Adorn your face and actions, that he may
Consent to guide us on our upward course.
Reflect, this day will never dawn again!»
I was well used to his admonishments
To lose no time, and so upon that theme
He could not speak but that I understood.

The glorious one approached us, clad in white;
His countenance was like the morning star,
And trembled with a heavenly radiance.
He opened wide his arms, and spread his wings.
«Come,» he said, «the stairway is hard by;
From this time onward you can mount with ease.
Not many come in answer to this call.

O human race! Born to ascend on wings,
Why do ye fall at such a little wind?»
He led us on to where the rock was cleft,
And smote me with his wings upon the brow,
Promising that my passage would be safe.

As on the right, when one goes up the hill
To reach that church which seems to overhang
That well-ruled town above the Rubaconte,
The steepness of the climb is interrupted
By stairways that were fashioned in an age
When measures, and the archives, were secure:
Just so the steep ascent is made more easy
That leads abruptly from the other cornice,
Grazing the lofty cliff on either side.
As we were turning to go up the stairs,
Beati pauperes spiritu was sung
In tones so sweet that speech could not describe it.

Ah me! How different are these passages
From those of hell! Here one comes in to song,
And there below, to savage lamentations.

Already we were on the holy stairs,
And it appeared to me that I was lighter
Than I had seemed before upon the plain.
«Master,» I inquired, «what heavy thing
Has been removed from me, so that I now
Scarce feel fatigue as I go on my way?»

He answered: «When the *P*'s that still remain
Upon your brow, though now almost extinct,
Shall, like the first, have been erased as well,
Then will your feet be governed by good will
So that no longer they will feel fatigue,
But rather will rejoice to be urged upward.»

Like those who go with something on their
                                        ⌊heads

But know it not, except that their suspicions
Are quickened by the signs of passers-by —
Wherefore the hand, to verify the fact,
Will seek and find, and thus perform an office
That cannot be accomplished by the sight —
Even so did I; and with my fingers spread,
I found six only of the *P*'s remaining
He of the keys had graven on my brow;
On seeing this, my noble leader smiled.

CANTO
13

WE now were at the summit of the stairway,
Where the mountain that is cure for ills
As one ascends it, is again cut back.
And here as well there runs around the mount
A cornice, similar to that below,
Save that it turns more sharply as it curves.
Here one can see no imagery or figures,
So that the mountain wall is bare and stark;
Bare too the pathway, all of livid stone.
«If we wait here, to ask our way of people,»
The poet said to me, «our choice, I fear,
May possibly involve too much delay.»
He now gazed steadfastly upon the sun,
And making his right foot into a pivot,
He turned his body round, toward the left.
«O blessed light,» he said, «in which I trust
To enter this new path, show us the way;
For surely we need guidance in this place.
Thou givest light and warmth unto the world:
And if no other reason may prevent,
Thy rays must ever serve as guides for us.»

As far as here on earth is called a mile,
So far we travelled onward in that place,
Urged to a swifter pace by our good will.
And flying now toward us, we could hear
Some kindly spirits, though we could not see them,
Who uttered biddings to the feast of love.
The voice that first flew by said loudly to us,
Vinum non habent, ringing clear and loud,
And passed on to our rear, repeating it.
But ere it had retired so far from us
That it could not be heard, another passed,
Shouting, «I am Orestes» — and was gone.

«What are those voices, father?» I inquired,

Canto 12 : Dante looking at the Spirit of Arachne

PURGATORIO: CANTO 13

And even as I asked, a third voice cried:
«Love, love ye those from whom ye have had
⌊evil!»

My master said: «This circle castigates
The sin of envy. Hence the scourge's lashes
Are drawn from love; but the restraining curb
Must surely have a different, harsher sound.
I believe, so far as I can judge,
You'll hear it ere we reach the pass of pardon.
But fix your sight intently through the air
And you will see some people, there in front;
I think each one is sitting 'gainst the cliff.»

Wider than before I strained my eyes,
Peering in front of me, where I perceived
Spirits in mantles colored like the stone.
And when we had advanced a little more,
I heard a cry, «O Mary, pray for us!»
Then, «Michael, Peter, all the blessed saints!»

I do not think that there exists on earth
Even at the present day, a man so hard
That he would not be moved by what I saw.
For when I had drawn near enough to them
So that their actions were made clear to me,
I grieved so, that the tears sprang from my eyes.
Their clothing seemed to be of coarsest haircloth;
One leaned upon the shoulder of another,
And all of them were leaning on the bank.
Thus do the blind who beg their daily bread
Take station in the churches of indulgence;
Thus one will lean his head upon another's,
The quicker thereby to excite one's pity,
Not by their words, but rather by their aspect,
Which begs for them as strongly as their speech.
And as the sun doth not avail the blind,
So to those spirits whom I have described,
The light of heaven hath here denied its blessing:
For through their eyelids runs an iron wire,
Sewing them shut—as it is often done
To a wild falconet, to keep him quiet.
It seemed to me that I was doing wrong
To stare at others, while unseen myself:
Wherefore to my counsellor I turned.
Full well he knew what I had mind to say,

And ere I asked him, he had made reply:
«Speak, if you wish: be brief, and to the point!»
Virgil was walking with me on that side
From which one might fall off, because the cornice
Is not encircled by a parapet.
Upon the other side of me, there sat
Those shades devout who through their dreadful
⌊sutures
Were pressing out their tears, which bathed their
⌊cheeks.

«O people sure to see the Light on high,»
I turned and said to them, «on which alone
Your whole desires are bent—may grace soon
All the defilement from your consciences, ⌊loosen
So that the stream of memory may flow clear!
Pray tell me—for I dearly wish to know—
If anyone amongst you be Italian.
Should this be so, it might be well for him
That I should know of it, and speak with him.»
«Brother, we all of us are citizens
Of one true city; but your meaning is,
'One who as pilgrim dwelt in Italy.' »
It seemed to me this answer had been made
Somewhere beyond the place where I now stood:
Therefore I threw my voice in that direction.
I saw that one among them looked alert;
And should you, reader, ask, «But how?» I'll say,
«The chin was lifted, as the blind will do.»
«O shade,» I said, «that stoop but to ascend,
If it was you who answered me just now,
Pray tell me what your name and what your city.»
«A Sienese was I,» she made reply,
«I cleanse my guilty life here with these others,
Praying, with tears, that God vouchsafe Himself.
Sapient I was not, though called Sapia;
And I rejoiced far more at others' ills
Than at my own good fortune. Lest you think
I would deceive you, listen to my words,
And learn how, as I tell you, I was foolish.
When I was going down the arch of life,
My fellow citizens had joined in battle,
Not far from Colle, with their adversaries.
I prayed to God for what He later willed:

Our men were routed there, and put to flight;
And seeing the pursuit, I felt a joy
Surpassing any I had felt before,
So that I turned my face to God, and cried:
'From this time onward, I shall fear Thee not!'
So does a blackbird, when the weather's fine.

«I longed for peace with God, as I lay dying;
And even then the burden of my sin
Would ne'er have been reduced by penitence,
Had it not been that good Pier Pettignano,
Who out of charity had grieved for me,
Remembered me in prayer. But who are you
That come here to inquire about our lot —
With eyelids yet unsealed, as I suppose —
And even seem to breathe while you are
⌊speaking?»

«For me, as well, my eyes will here be sealed,»
I said, «but not for long; for they have done
But small offence, through being turned with envy.
Far greater is the dread with which my soul
Anticipates the torments there below us,
So that even now the load weighs heavy on me.»

And she to me: «Who, then, has led you here,
If you expect e'er to return to earth?»

«He that is by my side, but says no word.
I am alive: and therefore ask of me,
Spirit elect, if you desire that I
Do aught for you, when I am back on earth.»

«Oh, this is such a novel thing to hear,»
She answered: «'tis a sign that God must love you:
Therefore at times assist me with your prayer.
For I beseech you, by your dearest hopes,
That if you tread again on Tuscan soil,
You will restore my name among my kin.
You'll see them there, among that boastful people
Whose hope is Talamone — who will lose
More hope there than in seeking the Diana:
The admirals will lose there even more.»

CANTO
14

Who is this, that circling round our mountain
Ere death has given flight unto his soul,
Opens and shuts his eyes to suit his will?»

«I know not; but he is not here alone.
Do you, who are the nearer, question him;
Accost him gently, so that he may speak.»

Thus two spirits, leaning toward each other,
Discoursed about us there, upon my right,
Then, to address me, lifted up their heads.
Now one began: «O soul that still are chained
Within your flesh, while going up to heaven,
In charity console us, and declare
The place from which you come, and who you are:
We marvel greatly at your privilege,
For such a thing has never come to pass!»

And I: «Down through the midst of Tuscany
There winds a stream that springs from Falterona
And runs its course a hundred miles and more.
I bring this body from that river's banks;
To tell you who I am, would be in vain,
Because my name has still but small renown.»

«If I can rightly penetrate your sense,»
He who had spoken first replied to me,
«It seems that you are speaking of the Arno.»

The other said to him: «Why did he strive
To hide that river's name, as if it were
A thing of horror that should not be mentioned?»

And then the shade to whom these words were
Replied: «I know not; but I think 'tis meet ⌊said
That valley's name should perish. From its source,
Where that great mountain chain from which
Is cut away, teems with so many waters ⌊Pelorus
That elsewhere scarcely they exceed that volume,
Down to where Arno renders to the sea

Canto 13 : The Souls of the Envious

That which the thieving sky had sucked away—
Whence every river draws its nourishment—
Virtue is shunned by all men as a foe,
Even as a serpent, either from ill luck
The region bears, or from perversity.
Hence all the dwellers in this wretched valley
So have changed their nature, that it seems
As if they had been fed by Circe's hand.

 «Among foul hogs, more fitted to eat acorns
Than other food, that human beings use,
The river first directs its paltry course.
As it comes lower down, it meets with curs
More snarling than their power would seem to
⌊warrant,

And turns itself away from them in scorn.
As it grows larger in its downward flow,
So much the more does that accursed ditch
Find that the dogs are turning into wolves.
Then, having dropped through many hollow
⌊depths,

It finds the foxes, so endowed with fraud
They have no fear of being caught by guile.
Nor will I cease because another hears me:
For 'twill be well, if on some future day
He may recall what is revealed to me.

 «I see your grandson, who has now begun
To hunt those wolves upon that river's banks.
He has become the terror of them all,
And sells their flesh while it is yet alive,
Slaying them afterward, like aged cattle.
He slaughters many, and his good name as well.
He comes forth gory from the dismal wood,
Leaving it in such a sorry state
A thousand years will not bring back the trees.»

 As when at tidings of distressing evil
The face of him who listens is perturbed,
From whatsoever side the ill may come:
'Twas even so I saw the other spirit
Who had turned round to listen, growing sad
As soon as he had understood those words.
 The speech of one shade, and the other's
⌊features

Instilled desire in me to learn their names,

And I combined the question with a prayer.
Thereupon the spirit who spoke first
Replied: «Though you would have me condescend
To do for you what you deny to me;
Because God hath vouchsafed you so much grace,
It is not meet that I should be a niggard.
Guido del Duca is the name I bore.
My blood was so consumed by envy's flame
That if I had beheld a man rejoicing,
You would have seen me turn a livid hue.
I reap the straw for which I sowed the seed.
Mankind, why do ye set your hearts on things
That, of necessity, may not be shared?
This is Rinieri, this the boast and honor
Of great Calboli's house; none other since
Has risen to inherit this man's worth.

 «From Po to Apennine, from Reno seaward,
'Tis not his race alone that has been stripped
Of character for truth, and happiness;
For all within these boundaries is full
Of roots so venomous, that 'twould be long
Before they could die out through cultivation.
Where are good Lizio, Arrigo Mainardi,
Pier Traversaro, Guido di Carpigna?
O people of Romagna, turned to bastards!
When will Bologna see another Fabbro,
Faenza see a Bernadin di Fosco,
That noble scion of a humble vine?
O Tuscan, do not marvel if I weep
When I recall to mind Guido da Prata
And Ugolino d'Azzo, living with us,
Federico Tignoso and his band,
The Traversari, Anastagi too—
Now both of these great houses lack an heir—
The knights and ladies, and the toils and pleasures
That love and courtesy made dear to us,
Where now men's hearts have all become so base.
O Brettinoro, why do you not flee,
Now that your kin and all of their retainers
Have fled from you, lest they should be befouled?
Bagnacavallo wisely breeds no sons;
Ill does Castrocaro, Conio worse,
To take the trouble to produce such counts!

89

Pagani's house will prosper when they lose
Their demon Maghinardo; even then
They will not boast a stainless reputation!
O Ugolin de Fantolin! Your name
Will stand secure: for no more will come
Who as degenerates could dim its lustre.
But, Tuscan, go upon your way—for now
I am inclined far more to tears than speech,
So greatly has our discourse wrung my mind.»

We knew that these kind souls could hear us
⌞leave;

And therefore they assured us by their silence
That we were going on the proper road.
When we had passed along, and were alone,
Like lightning flashing downward through the air
It seemed that we could hear a voice that said:
«Every one that finds me shall destroy me!»
It then passed on, as thunder rolls away
After a storm cloud has been rent asunder.

Scarce had our ears recovered from this sound,
When lo, another, with a crash so loud
It sounded like a sudden thunderclap:
«I am Aglauros, who became a stone!»
And thereupon I pressed close to the poet,
Making a backward step, instead of forward.

Now that the air was quiet round about,
He said: «That was the galling curb that ought
To hold a man in his allotted place.
But ye take in the bait, and then the hook
Will drag ye on toward the ancient foe:
Therefore of little use is curb or lure.
The heavens are calling you, and wheel about you
Displaying their eternal loveliness,
And yet your eyes look only on the earth!
Hence He that seeth all chastises you.»

CANTO
15

As much as is apparent of that sphere
Which, like a child at play, is ever restless,
Between the third hour's close and break of
⌞dawn—
So much there seemed remaining of his course
Toward evening. It was vespers there,
And midnight here in Italy; and now
The rays were striking us upon the nose,
For we had circled round the mount so far
That we were walking toward the setting sun.
The splendid radiance beat on my forehead,
Far more o'erpowering than it was at first;
And marvelling at these unaccustomed things,
I raised my hands and placed them on my brow
To form a visor—so to mitigate
The excess of brilliancy that shone before me.

Even as from water, or a mirror's surface,
A ray of sunlight will leap up again
In manner like to that in which it fell,
And will divide itself at equal distance
On either side the plummet, as is shown
By nature's laws, and by experiment:
Just so my face received that blinding light
Which was reflected from in front of me,
So that my sight was swift to fly away.
«O what is this, dear father,» I inquired,
«From which I cannot seem to screen my eyes,
That now appears to move in our direction?»

He answered: «Marvel not, if you are dazzled
By the celestial family: it is
A messenger, who bids us to ascend.
Soon it will be no longer hard for you
To gaze upon such sights, but 'twill become
As great a joy as you have ever felt!»

Canto 15: *Dante's Vision of the Stoning of St. Stephen*

As soon as we came near the blessed angel,
He said with a glad voice: «From here ye enter
A stairway far less toilsome than the others.»

And when we started thence to mount the
                                    ⌊stairs,
Some sang behind us, «Blessed are the merciful,»
And then, «Rejoice, O Thou that conquerest!»

My master and myself, we two alone,
Were going upward; as we went I thought
How I might gain some profit from his talk,
So that I turned to him, inquiring thus:
«What did that spirit from Romagna mean
By things that cannot possibly be shared?»

And he replied: «He knows the harm that
                                    ⌊comes
From his own greatest fault: so marvel not
That he rebuked you; 'twas to save your tears.
Because ye hope for worldly benefits
Whereof some part is lost by being shared,
Envy doth blow its bellows on your sighs.
But if your longing for the highest sphere
Turn your desires upward, then that dread
Of sharing benefits will leave your hearts.
For, up in heaven, the more there are to share,
So much the more of good doth each possess;
And charity burns brighter in that cloister.»

«Farther am I from being satisfied
Than if I had been silent from the first,»
Said I, «and doubts are gathering in my mind.
How can one good that is distributed,
Enrich a greater number with more good
Than if among a few it were divided?»

And he to me: «Because you fix your mind
On earthly things alone, you can reap naught
But unavailing darkness from true light.
That Good, ineffable and infinite,
Which reigneth there on high, doth speed to love
Even as a sunbeam seeks a lucid body.
It gives according to the warmth it finds:
Thus, in whatever measure love extends,
The greater the eternal value grows.
And hence, the more there are on high who love,
The more they love each other, perfectly;

And like a mirror one reflects the other.
Now if my arguments will not suffice you,
Inquire of Beatrice, who will respond
To all the longings that your soul may have.
But strive that those five wounds upon your brow
Which through contrition will heal up again,
May soon be gone—as two are gone already.»

I would have said, «Now am I satisfied!»
But at that point I reached the other cornice,
And so my eager eyes made me keep still.
For now, it seemed, I suddenly was rapt
Into an ecstasy, and I beheld
A crowd of many people, in a temple.
Upon the threshold stood a gentle Lady,
Most sweet and motherly, who seemed to say:
«My Son, why hast Thou dealt so ill with us?
Behold, Thy grieving father and myself
Were seeking Thee.» And as she ceased to speak
The vision faded, even as it had come.

Now there appeared to me another lady,
Whose cheeks were streaming with those tears
                                    ⌊that grief
Distills from indignation felt at others.
She said: «If you indeed are lord of Athens—
That city where all art and science shine,
About whose name the gods have fought so long—
Do you, Pisistratus, at once avenge
Those daring arms that have embraced our
                                    ⌊daughter!»

And then it seemed her kind and gentle lord
Replied to her, with an appeasing look:
«What shall we do to those who wish us ill,
If he who loves us, is by us condemned?»

Next I beheld some folk inflamed with anger,
Stoning a youth, and crying: «Kill him, kill him!»
And I saw him sinking down to earth,
For death weighed heavily upon him now,
Yet with his eyes he stormed the gates of heaven;
And in such cruel straits, he prayed aloud
To the good Lord of All, that He forgive
His persecutors; and he bore that look
Which doth unlock compassion in the soul.

Now when my mind turned outwardly again

To things that truly did exist outside it,
I knew these things were dreams, though they were
My leader, who could see that I behaved └true.
Like one who shakes himself from sleep, inquired:
«What ails you, that you can't support yourself?
Nay, you have gone for more than half a league
Veiling your eyes, and swaying on your legs
Like someone overcome by sleep or wine.»

«O gentle father, if you will but hear me,»
Said I, «I'll tell you what I thought I saw
A while ago, when legs were failing me.»

«Had you a hundred masks upon your face,»
Said he, «your thoughts, however insignificant,
Would never be concealed from me. Mark well:
What you have seen just now, was shown to you
To urge your heart to open and receive
The peaceful waters of the eternal fount.
I did not ask, 'What ails you?' like a man
Who sees but with the eye material,
And cannot see when sense hath left the body:
I asked but to give vigor to your foot—
For thus indeed must sluggards be spurred on,
That they may use their senses when they wake.»

Meanwhile, past vespertime, we moved along,
Peering ahead as far as eye could reach
Against the radiance of the setting sun.
And lo! A heavy smoke, as dark as night,
By slow degrees came rolling on toward us,
Nor was there any place of shelter from it;
And sight and breath from us were snatched away.

CANTO
16

No gloom of hell, nor blackness of the night
Bereft of stars beneath a barren sky,
Darkened with clouds as much as it can be,
E'er made before mine eyes a veil so dense,

Or yet so harsh a texture to my feeling,
As did that smoke which now invested us.

It suffered not my eye to stay unclosed;
And now my faithful and experienced leader
Drew to my side, and offered me his shoulder.
Even as a blind man walks behind his guide
So that he may not go astray or stumble
On aught that might do harm, or even kill him:
So I was moving through that bitter air,
Listening to my leader, who remarked:
«Take heed lest you should go astray from me.»

I now heard voices that appeared to pray
For peace and mercy, to the Lamb of God
That takes away the sins of all the world.
Here *Agnus Dei* was their litany—
Only one text and measure for them all,
So that they sang in perfect unison.
«Master,» said I, «do I hear spirits singing?»
And he replied to me: «You hear aright;
And they go loosening the knot of wrath.»

«Now who are you that cleaving through our
Seem to be speaking here of us as though └smoke,
You still were reckoning time by calendar?»
These words were spoken by a single voice.

Whereon my master said to me: «Reply,
And ask if it is there that we should mount.»

And I: «O being, cleansing yourself here,
So to return in beauty to your Maker,
If you will come, you'll hear a wondrous thing!»

«I'll follow you, as far as 'tis allowed;
And even though the smoke will blind our sight,»
He said, «our ears will take the place of eyes.»

I now addressed him: «With those swathing
Which death will loosen from me, I go up: └bands
I am come hither through eternal anguish.
Since God has so enfolded me with grace
As to ordain that I should see His court,
And in a manner so unprecedented,
Hide not the name men called you in your lifetime,
But tell it me. Say if I go aright
To reach the pass: your words shall be our guide.»

«I was a Lombard: Marco was my name.
I loved that virtue now no longer aimed at,

Canto 16 : Marco Lombardo follows the Poets through the Smoke

For everybody hath unbent his bow.
For the ascent, the path you tread is right.»
He answered thus, and added: «I beseech you
To pray for me, when you have reached the top.»
　　I said: «I pledge my faith to do for you
That which you ask; but with an inward doubt
I soon must burst, unless it be resolved.
At first 'twas but a single doubt; yet now
'Tis doubled, for 'tis strengthened and confirmed
By your opinions, coupled with another's.
The world, as you so truthfully have said,
Is utterly devoid of any virtue,
Pregnant with evil, and oppressed by it;
But I beseech you, show to me the reason,
That I may know, and tell of it to others—
Some say it lies in heaven, some on earth.»
　　The moan he made from grief became «Ah me!»
Then he began: «The world is blind, my brother,
And you in very truth have come from it!
Ye who are living seek for every cause
Up in the heavens alone—as if it were
A force that of necessity prevails.
If this were true, free will would be no more:
And then 'twould not be proper to rejoice
When things go well, or grieve when they go ill.
Heaven doth initiate your movements—
Not all, I say: but even if I said so,
Ye have the power to tell the right from wrong.
Free will, though it be hindered by fatigue
In the first struggles, will at last prevail,
If it be given proper nourishment.
Though free, ye bow before a mightier force
And better nature, that creates in you
Your mind, which is outside the care of heaven.
Hence, if this generation go astray,
The cause must lie within yourselves alone,
As I shall truthfully explain to you.
　　«Forth from the hand of Him who with delight,
Even as a maid who laughs in childish play,
Contemplates it ere it yet exists,
Issues the soul—so simple, it knows naught
Save that, proceeding from a blithe Creator,
It turns with eagerness to what allures it.

At first it likes the taste of trifling good,
And there deceives itself, in foolish quest,
Unless its way be guided or restrained.
Hence it was meet that laws should be established
As a restraining curb; that kings should rule
Who might discern at least the towers of truth.
The laws exist; but who enforces them?
No one—because the shepherd leading us
Can chew the cud, but has no cloven hoof.
Therefore the people, who perceive their guide
Seeking but earthly goods that they desire,
Feed on those goods themselves, and ask no more.
Well can you see that wicked government
Is the true cause of evil in the world;
'Tis not that nature is corrupt in you.
　　«Once Rome, which wrought such good upon
　　　　　　　　　　　　　　　　⌊the world,
Possessed two suns, to point the ways to her—
One the world's way, the other that of God.
Now one has dimmed the other, and the sword
Is welded to the crozier; and perforce
The two can never go along together.
When joined, the one no longer fears the other:
If you believe me not, think of the fruit—
'For by its own seed every plant is known.'
　　«There where the Adige and Po are flowing,
Valor and courtesy were wont to thrive
Ere Frederick brought war into the land.
Now it can be safely crossed by any
Who, from a sense of shame, would shun good
One thing is sure: he'll not find any there!　⌊folk.
But still three aged men remain, in whom
The older race seems to reprove the new.
They wait God's call to join a better life—
Conrado da Palazzo, good Gherardo,
And Guido da Castello, better named
The 'honest Lombard,' as the Frenchman called
　　　　　　　　　　　　　　　　⌊him.
Henceforward you must say: 'The church of Rome
Has fallen, with its charge, and both are mired,
Because in it two modes of rule conflict!'»
　　«O Marco,» I replied, «you reason well;
And now I understand just why it was

The sons of Levi lost the heritage.
But what Gherardo is it, who, you say,
Remains, a sample of that bygone breed,
As a reproach unto this barbarous age?»

«Either your words deceive me,» he replied,
«Or they are meant to prove me: for, 'twould seem,
You, speaking Tuscan, do not know Gherardo.
I know him not by any added name,
Save I should take it from his daughter Gaia.
May God be with you! I can go no farther.
Behold, that radiance which cleaves the smoke
Already brightens, and I must away,
Before the angel who is there can see me.»
Thus he turned back: nor would he hear me more.

CANTO
17

Reader, if ever on some lofty alp
A cloud closed round about you, so that you
Could only see as moles do, through their
⌞membranes,
Recall to mind how when the humid vapors
Begin at last to spread and fade away,
The sun's orb feebly will appear through them.
Then your imagination will be ripe
To understand how I again perceived
The sun, which was already at its setting.
Thus measuring my footsteps by my guide's,
Forth from that cloud I came into the sunbeams,
Which had already left the lower slopes.
Imagination, that dost so abstract us
That we are not aware, not even when
A thousand trumpets sound about our ears!
Who moves thee, if our senses show thee naught?
A light that is conceived in heaven moves thee,
Or by itself, or by a guiding will.
There now appeared in my imagination

The cruelty of her who changed her form
Into that bird whose singing most delights us;
And hereupon my mind was so pent up
Within itself, that whatsoever thing
Occurred to it, came from no outside source.
Then there came down into my phantasy
One crucified, contemptuous and haughty
In his look; and thus it was he died.
Around him stood the great Ahasuerus,
Esther his consort, and the just Mordecai,
Who was so worthy both in word and deed.
And as this image broke up of itself
Even as a bubble bursts, when comes the time
That water, under which 'twas formed, doth fail it,
There rose within my vision a young maiden
Weeping most bitterly, who said: «O queen,
Why, angry, have you chosen to be naught?
You have destroyed yourself to save Lavinia;
Now you have lost me—and I am the one
O mother mine, to mourn thee, more than others.»

As sleep is broken when, upon a sudden,
The new light strikes upon the sleeper's eyes,
And conquered, struggles ere it fades away:
Just so my vision faded, as there struck
Upon my face a light by far excelling
That sun to which we mortals are accustomed.
I turned around, to see where I might be,
When a voice murmured: «Here is the ascent!»

Now this withdrew me from all other thoughts,
And made my will so eager to behold
The speaker, that it was not satisfied
Until I stood before him face to face.
But as before the sun, which dims our sight
And by its radiance conceals its form,
So here my mortal powers were unavailing.
«This is a heavenly spirit, who unasked
Is showing us the way to scale the mount.
He doth conceal himself in his own light,
And deals with us as man deals for himself:
For he who waits the call, but sees the need,
Already sets his spirit to refuse it.
Now may our feet accept his gracious bidding;
And let us try to mount ere it grow dark,

PURGATORIO: CANTO 17

For afterward we cannot, till the dawn.»
Thus spoke my leader, and we turned our steps
Toward the stairway. When I placed my foot
Upon the lowest step, I felt close by me
A moving wing, it seemed, that fanned my face.
A voice said: «Blessed are the peacemakers,
For they have freed themselves from sinful wrath.»

So high above us were the sun's last rays,
Precursors of the night, that everywhere
The stairs already sparkled in the sky.
«Why do you melt away like this, my strength?»
I asked myself, for I began to feel
My legs were failing fast beneath my weight.

We now had reached the summit of the
⌊stairway

And stood there motionless, just like a ship
When it has reached the shore; and for a while
I hearkened, wondering if I might hear
Some sound that was peculiar to this circle.
I turned me to my master, and inquired:
«My gracious father, tell me what offence
Is purged in this new cornice where we stand?
Even though our feet are resting, you can speak.»

And he to me: «The love of what is good,
Defective in its duty, is here restored:
'Tis here the slackened oar is plied again.
But that you may more clearly understand,
Pray give me your attention: you will see
What good fruit you will gather by delay.

«Nor creature nor Creator,» he began,
«Was ever without love—or spiritual
Or elective. This, my son, you know.
Elective love is always free of error;
That other love can err in its objective,
Or from too little or too much intensity.
While it is turned upon the heavenly blessings,
And, for the lesser, keeps within its bounds,
It cannot be the source of wicked joys;
But when it turns to evil, or pursues
The good with too much or too little zeal,
'Tis then the creature thwarts its own Creator.
Hence you will see that love must be the seed
Within yourselves, whence every virtue springs

And also every punishable action.
Now since the face of love can never turn
Away from what promotes its object's good,
All things are thus immune from their own hatred.
And since no being e'er can be imagined
As independent of its own Creator,
It is impossible to hate one's God.
It follows then, unless I am in error,
That lust of evil is toward your neighbor,
And rises in three ways within your clay.

«First there are those who through their
⌊neighbor's fall

Themselves hope to excel, and therefore crave
To see him cast down from his high position;
Then, those who fear to lose, should others rise,
Their power or fortune, honor and renown,
With fear so great, they wish the opposite;
Then, those with such resentment for a wrong
That they become insatiate for revenge,
And these must needs work injury on others.
This threefold love is wept for down below.

«Now I would tell you of that other kind
Pursuing good, but not with proper judgment.
Each person, in a way that is confused,
Conceives a good wherein his mind may rest,
And longs for it: so all strive to attain it.
If dilatory love should lead you on
To see or to obtain that good, this cornice,
After due penitence, torments you.
There is another good, which doth not yield
True happiness: for 'tis not the good essence
That is the root and fruit of every good.
The love that yields itself too much to this
Is wept for in three circles here above us.
But wherefore it is spoken of as threefold,
I tell you not: that you must learn yourself.»

95

CANTO
18

My teacher, who had ended his discourse
Now looked attentively upon my face
To see if I appeared content. But I,
Already goaded by another thirst,
Was silent, and was thinking: «Now perchance
He is annoyed by too much questioning.»
But that true father, who had understood
My timid wish that still remained concealed,
By speaking first, emboldened me to say:
«I see so much more keenly in your light,
My master, that I clearly can discern
All that your reasoning described or means.
Therefore I pray that you expound to me
That love to which you, father, have ascribed
Every good action, and its opposite.»

«Direct on me,» he answered, «the keen eye
Of understanding: then will you perceive
The error of the blind who try to lead.
The mind, created well-disposed to love,
Is quickly moved toward everything that pleaseth,
So soon as pleasure rouses it to action.
Your apprehensive faculty will draw
An image from some object that exists,
And so display it, that your mind turns toward it.
And if, thus turned, the mind incline thereto,
That inclination is both love and nature,
Bound to you the more by pleasure's tie.
Then as a flame will move forever upward
By reason of its form, which is conceived
For rising to its proper element:
Just so the captivated mind aspires.
This yearning is a spiritual motion,
And rests not till it gains the thing it loves.
From this, it must be evident to you
How far the truth is hid from those who hold

That each love, in itself, is laudable
Because it may have matter that is good,
Yet every seal's impression is not good,
However good the wax itself may be.»
«Your words,» I answered him, «and my own
⌊mind,
Eager to follow them, have shown me love:
And yet my doubt is greater than before.
For if all love be sent us from without,
And if the soul proceeds not otherwise—
If it go right or wrong, 'tis not at fault.»
And he: «As far as reason can explain,
I'll tell you here. Beyond that, you must look
To Beatrice: for this now deals with faith.
Every substantial form that is distinct
From matter, or is united with it,
Doth hold a power specific in itself,
That is not felt as long as it is dormant,
But demonstrates itself in its effect,
Even as in plants green leaves betoken life.
Man does not know whence comes his under-
Of the existence of first principles,   ⌊standing
Or of the trend of primal appetites
Innate in you, like instinct in the bee
For making honey; and this primal will
Can never in itself be praised or censured.
But so that all may harmonize with it,
The faculty of reason is inborn,
And should defend the threshold of assent.
This is the source of all mankind's deserts,
According as it gathers in the good
Or winnows out the bad loves in its path.
Those who have sought this out in argument
Perceived this innate freedom, and bequeathed
Moral philosophy unto the world.
If, therefore, we assume that every love
Rises within you of necessity,
In you exists the power to restrain it.
To Beatrice, this noble faculty
Denotes free will; so bear this well in mind
If she proceeds to speak of it to you.»
The laggard moon—for it was nearly
⌊midnight—

Canto 18 : The Multitude of the Slothful

Stood like a flaming cresset in the sky,
Making the stars seem fewer than they were;
And counter to the heavens, it coursed along
Those paths the sun inflames, when seen from
Setting between Sardinia and Corsica. ⌊Rome,
And now that noble shade, through whose renown
Pietola has outshone Mantua,
Had freed his shoulders of my heavy weight;
And I, who had received his exposition
That gave such lucid answers to my questions,
Remained like one who rambles in a doze.
But I was wakened from this drowsiness
By a crowd of people that approached,
And had come round to us behind our backs.

　Even as of old Ismenus and Asopus
Beheld the crowds at night along their banks
Whene'er the Thebans felt the need of Bacchus:
Just so that endless company of spirits
Followed their course to curve around the cornice,
Urged onward by good will and righteous love.
And soon they were upon us—for the whole
Of that great throng was moving at a run.
Two weeping shades who ran in front, cried out,
«Mary ran in haste unto the mountain»—
«Caesar, when he wished to win Illerda,
Thrust at Marseilles, and pressed on into Spain!»

　«Haste, haste! So that our time may not be lost
Through lack of love,» cried those behind, «and ⌊that
Our zeal may cause His grace to be renewed!»

　«O spirits, in whom your present fervid zeal
Redeems, perchance, neglect and slothfulness
Or lukewarm eagerness for doing good,
This man who lives—indeed I do not lie—
Desires to climb, so soon the sun shines forth:
Pray show us where to find the nearest way.»
Thus spake my guide, and then a spirit answered:

　«Come after us, and you will find the pass.
So great is our desire to keep in motion,
We cannot rest: we beg you to excuse us,
If you should hold as want of courtesy
That which for us is righteous punishment.
As Abbot of San Zeno in Verona

I lived on earth in Barbarossa's reign,
Which Milan still recalls with bitter tears.
A certain man, with one foot in the grave,
Shall weep anon for that same monastery,
And shall lament that he did ever rule it:
Because, in place of its own rightful pastor,
He gave it to his miserable son,
Ill-formed in body, even worse in mind!»
I know not whether he said more or not,
For he had passed already far beyond us:
This much I heard, and took to mind with
⌊pleasure.

　Now he who was at every need my succor:
«Turn hither, and you shall see that two are
⌊coming
Who give a bite to sloth as they draw nigh.»

　And far behind the others, these were saying,
«That race for whom the sea was opened wide
Perished ere the Jordan saw their children!»
And also, «They who with Anchises' son
Could not endure the toil unto the end,
Forever lost the glory of their lives!»

　Now when those souls had passed so far away
That we no longer saw them, a new thought
Arose within me; then from it there sprang
Still other thoughts, profuse and varying.
Thus I went rambling on from thought to thought,
And closed my eyelids in my wandering,
So that my fancies changed into a dream.

CANTO
19

'TWAS at that hour at which the heat of day
When vanquished by the earth, or Saturn's power,
No longer warms the coldness of the moon—
When necromancers see, before the dawn,

THE DIVINE COMEDY

Fortuna Major rising in the east
Along its path that momently stays dark —
'Twas then there came to me in dream a woman,
Squinting and stammering, with crooked feet,
Her hands lopped off, and of a pallid color.
I gazed at her; and as the sun revives
Limbs that are deadened by the chill of night,
Just so my look gave freedom to her tongue,
Straightened her form, and in a little time
Constrained her pallid cheeks to glow with
⌊warmth,

And don the rosy hue that love requires.
There, when her speech had thus become unloosed,
She broke into a song, in tones so sweet
'Twas hard indeed to turn my ears away.
« I am, » she sang, « the siren who ensnares
The mariners upon the ocean deep.
So pleasant was my singing to the ear
That once I turned Ulysses from his path
By my sweet song; and he who stays with me,
Seldom departs — so wholly do I please! »
    She scarce had closed her mouth, when at my
A saintly lady suddenly appeared   ⌊side
And put her to confusion utterly.
« O Virgil, O my Virgil, who is this? »
She sternly said — and he meanwhile advanced,
His eyes fixed only on that modest face.
She seized the other woman, and tore back
Her drapery, and thus disclosed her belly;
The stench that issued woke me from my dream.
    « Thrice have I tried to wake you, » said my
⌊master,
« Arise now and press on, for we must seek
The opening through which you may pass in. »
    I rose and turned my eyes: the cornices
About the sacred mount were full of daylight.
We walked along, the sun behind our backs;
I followed him, and bore my head bowed down,
Like one whose mind is burdened by his thought,
Looking like half an archway of a bridge.
And now I heard: « Come ye, here is the passage! »
The words had such a sweet and gentle tone
As never can be heard in mortal regions.

With outspread pinions gleaming like a swan's,
He who had thus addressed us showed the way
And turned us upward through the walls of rock.
Moving his wings, he fanned us, and affirmed
That those who mourn on earth are blest in
⌊heaven:
Forevermore their souls will be in comfort.
    « What ails you, that you look but on the
⌊ground? »
My guide inquired, when we both had climbed
A little way above the gleaming angel.
    I answered him: « I walk in such mistrust
Because of a new vision, so compelling
That from it I can not withdraw my thoughts. »
    He said: « Have you perceived that ancient
⌊witch,
Who causes weeping in the rings above us?
And have you seen how man is saved from her?
Enough! Now strike the ground with swifter feet
And turn your eyes on high to see the lure
Whirled with the heavens by the Eternal King. »
    Just as a falcon first looks on his feet,
Turns to the call, and then outspreads his wings,
Because desire for food attracts him thither:
Even so did I; and thus I moved along
Through the cleft rock that forms a passageway
To where another circle rings the mount.
When I had issued forth onto the cornice
I saw some people on it who were weeping,
And all were lying prone upon the ground.
Adhaesit pavimento anima mia,
I heard them murmuring with such deep sighs
That one could hardly understand their words.
    « O ye elect of God, whose sufferings
Are mitigated both by hope and justice,
Direct us to the stair that leads above! »
    « If ye are come secure from doing penance,
And wish to find the path most speedily,
Let your right hands be always outermost! »
    The poet thus entreated; thus the answer
Came from in front of us, as I discerned,
Although the speaker had his face concealed.
    And now I turned my eyes unto my lord,

Canto 19 : Virgil reproves Dante for gazing downward

At which he nodded blithely in assent
To what the longing in my face expressed.
Permitted then to do as I had wished,
I moved along, and stood above that shade
Whose words had made me notice him, and said:
«O spirit, in whom tears are ripening
That fruit without which none can turn to God:
For my sake, lay your greater care aside.
Pray tell me who you were, and why these backs
Are all upturned, and whether you would have me
Seek aught for you, down in the living world.»

   And he to me: «Soon shall you learn why
Makes us turn our backs to it; but first, ⌊heaven
Know that I was successor unto Peter.
'Twixt Siestri and Chiaveri descends
A lovely stream, and from its name my race
Derives its proudest title and distinction.
A month and more, I proved how heavily
The mantle burdens him who keeps it clean,
So that all other loads seem like a feather.
Alas! I was converted late—too late;
But when I had become the Roman pastor,
I soon perceived the falseness of our life.
I saw that there the heart was not at rest,
And as it was not possible to rise
In that life, I began to long for this.
Up to that time I was a wretched soul,
Severed from God, and given up to greed;
Here, as you see, I now am punished for it.
What greed can do is here made manifest
In this purgation of converted souls:
The mount has no more bitter penalty.
And as our eyes, intent on earthly things,
Were never lifted up to heaven—so
Has justice sunk them here upon the ground.
Even as greed destroyed our love for good,
Whereby the labor of our lives was lost,
So justice holds us here in close restraint,
Captive, and fettered by the hands and feet;
And for so long as it shall please the Lord,
We must remain outstretched and motionless.»
I had knelt down, and was about to speak;
But as I started, he by listening

Became aware that I was doing reverence.
«What cause,» said he, «thus makes you bow
                 ⌊before me?»

   And I: «Because of your exalted rank,
My conscience rightly pricked me while I stood.»
   «Straighten your legs, my brother, and stand
He answered. «Do not err: a fellow servant ⌊up,»
Am I, with you and others, of One Power.
If ever you have rightly understood
Those words of holy Gospel, *Necque nubent,*
Well will you understand what I have said.
Now go your way: pray do not linger here,
Because your presence checks the flow of tears
With which ripen what your words have said.
Yonder on earth I have a niece, Alagia,
Good in herself, unless, indeed, our house
Has by its bad example made her wicked:
And she alone is left to me below.»

CANTO
20

ONE strives in vain against a stronger will;
And so unwillingly, to meet his wish,
I drew the sponge unfilled from out the water.
Onward I went, and onward moved my guide,
Over the vacant space along the cliff,
As on a wall one hugs the battlements—
Because those souls, who pour out, drop by drop,
The world pervading evil, through their eyes,
Crowded the margin of the precipice.
   O ancient she-wolf, be accursed forever—
Thou who dost seize more prey than other beasts,
Because of thy insatiable hunger!
O heaven, in whose wide spheres there seems to be
Someone who thinks conditions here are changed,
When will he come, from whom the wolf will flee?

We went along with slow and shortened steps,
And I was listening to the weeping shades
Whom I could hear lamenting piteously,
When now by chance I heard «O Blessed Mary!»
Cried out in front of us amid the wailing,
Just as a woman cries it, when in travail—
And then, «How poor thou wert, can well be seen
By reason of that lowly hostelry
Wherein thou didst lay down thy holy burden!»
I heard thereafter: «Good Fabricius,
You made the choice of poverty with goodness,
Rather than great wealth with wickedness!»
These words brought such delight unto my ears,
That I moved onward, seeking the acquaintance
Of that shade from whom they seemed to come.
He now proclaimed the liberality
Showed to the three young maids by Nicholas,
So as to guide their youth to ways of honor.
«O soul,» said I, «that speak so much of good,
Pray tell me who you were, and why, alone,
You now repeat these well-deserved laudations.
Your answer shall not be without reward,
If I return to live my span of life,
Which speeds so swiftly onward to its end.»

And he: «I'll tell you, not from any hope
Of comfort from below there, but because
Such grace shines forth in you, ere you are dead.
I was the root of that malignant tree
That overshadows all the Christian land,
So that good fruit is seldom plucked therefrom.
Yet if Douai and Lille, and Ghent and Bruges
But had the power, this soon would be avenged;
And this I pray from Him who judges all.

«Hugh Capet was I called upon the earth;
From me springs every Philip, every Louis
By whom in recent times the French are ruled;
My father kept a butcher shop in Paris.
And when the ancient kings had all died out,
Save one who'd taken orders, robed in gray,
I found that I held tightly in my grasp
The reins of government, and new-gained power,
And such a mighty company of friends,
That on my own son's head the widowed crown

Was placed: this son was the begetter
Of all that line of consecrated bones.
So long as the great dowry of Provence
Did not deprive my race of sense of shame,
They wrought no ill, although they wrought no
But then, by violence and fraud, began ⌞good;
Their rapine; and later—for amends—
They took Ponthieu, Normandy, and Gascony.
Charles came to Italy, and—for amends—
Made Conradin a victim, and thereafter
Drove Thomas back to heaven—for amends!
I see a time, not too remote from now,
When forth from France another Charles will go
In search of fame for him and all his race.
He leaves alone, unarmed, save for the lance
Of Judas; and he aims with it so well,
The paunch of Florence bursts from his assault.
Yet from this sally he will gain no lands,
But only sin and shame—as ill for him
As he doth deem they are of small account.
The other Charles, a prisoner in his ship,
I see disputing o'er his daughter's price,
As corsairs haggle over female slaves.

«O greed! How canst thou harm us any further,
Since thou hast so completely won my race
That they neglect their very flesh and blood?

«But now our other evil deeds will pale:
The fleur-de-lis will enter in Alagna
And capture Christ himself, seizing the person
Of His own vicar—thus a second time
I see Him mocked with vinegar and gall,
Slain once more between two living thieves.
I see this later Pilate so relentless
That this is not enough: but urged by greed,
He sails on farther, to the very Temple.

«O Lord of Hosts! When will my eyes rejoice
To see that vengeance, hidden in Thy counsels,
Which will burst forth to satisfy Thy wrath?

«Now, as to what I said about that bride
To whom alone the Holy Ghost came down,
Which made you turn to me for explanation:
That is the antiphon of all our prayers
So long as the day lasts; but, for the night

Canto 20 : The Souls of the Avaricious

We change, and make an opposite refrain.
Then we recall to mind Pygmalion,
Who from insatiable lust for gold
Became a traitor, thief, and parricide;
Also the misery of greedy Midas,
Who suffered from his covetous request,
At which 'tis always fitting one should laugh.
'Tis then that we proclaim the foolish Achan,
And how he stole the plunder, so that now
The wrath of Joshua seems to smite him here.
Then we accuse Sapphira and her mate,
And praise the hoof that kicked at Heliodorus;
In infamy the name of Polymnestor,
Who murdered Polydorus, echoes round;
And finally the cry rings through the cornice:
'Pray tell us, Crassus, what's the taste of gold?'

«At moments one speaks low, another loud,
According to the spur of our affection,
Now at a faster, now a slower pace.
Thus I was not alone when I recited
The good examples of the day just now:
But no one near me sought to raise his voice.»

We had already gone away from him,
And we were striving forward on our way
As fast as our shortcomings would allow,
When, like a thing that totters to its fall,
I felt the mountain tremble, and a chill
Seized on me, like chill of death itself:
Delos, in sooth, quaked not so violently
Before Latona built her nest thereon,
When she gave birth to those twin eyes of heaven.

Now all around, began a cry so great
That my good master drew up to my side
And said: «Fear not, while I am here to guide
All shouted, *Gloria in excelsis Deo*, ⌊you!»
So far as I could judge from those near by,
Whose cry 'twas possible to understand.

We stood there motionless and in suspense —
Even as those shepherds who first heard that
⌊song —
Until the earthquake and the chant had ceased.
Then we walked on along our hallowed path,
Watching the shades who, lying on the ground,

Already had resumed their wonted plaint.
And never, if my memory fail me not,
Did ignorance though striving with its might
Instill in me so great a wish for knowledge
As I now seemed to have within my thought.
I did not dare to ask, such was our haste;
Nor, of myself, could I make aught of it.
Timid and thoughtful, I went on my way.

CANTO
21

THAT inborn thirst which ne'er is satisfied
Save by that water which of old was asked
As bounty by the woman of Samaria,
Tormented me, and haste urged on my steps
Along the encumbered path behind my guide;
And I was grieving at that righteous vengeance,
When lo, as Luke described in Holy Writ
The Christ, appearing risen from His tomb,
Before two travellers upon the wayside,
Even so a shade who came up from behind,
Drew near, his eyes bent down upon the throng.
We knew not he was there, until he said:
«My brothers, may the Lord give peace to you!»

We turned to him. Virgilius at once
Gave back the proper answer to his greeting.
«In heaven's most blessed council,» he began,
«May you be granted peace by that just court
That relegates me to eternal exile!»

«Indeed,» the other said, while we went on,
«If you are shades unfit to rise on high,
Who then, has led you so far up His stairway?»

And now my teacher: «Look upon these marks,
Traced by the angel, that are on his brow,
And you will see that he will gain the kingdom.
But since that one who spins both day and night

101

Has not as yet drawn wholly bare the distaff
That Clotho winds and packs for every one,
His spirit, sister-soul of yours and mine,
In going upward, could not go alone,
Because it cannot see as our eyes see.
Wherefore, from out the ample throat of hell
I was withdrawn to show him. I shall do so,
As far as my instruction will permit.
But tell us, if you can, the reason why
The mountain heaved a little while ago,
And why those cries from all, even to its base.»
In asking thus, he found the needle's eye
Of my desire; and so it was that hope
Relieved the sharpness of my burning thirst.

 The shade replied: «Nothing beyond its wont
Nor unordained can sway the mountain's rule,
For it is free of every form of change.
No other influence can here be felt
Except those forces in the heavens contained
That work upon each other changelessly.
And therefore neither rain nor hail, nor snow,
Nor dew or hoarfrost ever fall above
That little stairway with the three short steps.
No dense nor fleecy clouds do e'er appear,
No lightning flash, nor Thaumas' lovely daughter,
Who down below so often changes place.
No arid vapor rises up beyond
The topmost step of those stairs that I mentioned,
Where St. Peter's vicar takes his stand.
Below, perchance, it trembles more or less;
But from the wind engendered in the earth—
I know not how—up here it never trembles.
It does so only when a soul feels pure,
So that it stands erect, or wills to move
To climb the mount; the cry then follows it.
The will alone gives proof of purity;
The spirit, wholly free to change its place,
Is taken by surprise, and given comfort.
It fain would rise ere then, but is prevented
By wish to expiate its sin through torment,
Instilled, like wish for sin, by heavenly justice.
And I, who in this woe confined have been
Five hundred years and more, felt only now

A free volition for a better seat.
Therefore you felt the shock, and heard the spirits,
Throughout the mount, give praise unto the
         ⌊Lord—
Who soon, I pray, will speed them upward too.»

 Thus spoke the shade; and since a man enjoys
His drink proportionately as he thirsts,
I cannot tell how great the good he did me.
My leader said: «Now I can see the net
That snares you here, and how it is unmeshed,
And why the earth shook, and the souls rejoiced.
If it may please you, let me know your name,
And in your answer may it be disclosed
Why you have lain here for so many years.»

 «In days when the good Titus, with the aid
Of the Almighty King, avenged the wounds
Whence issued forth that blood which Judas sold,
I bore on earth the honored name of poet
That will endure, beyond all other names,
With some renown—though lacking yet in faith.
So sweet I made my song,» the spirit said,
«Rome summoned me—for I was from Toulouse.
I earned the right to wear the myrtle wreath.
People still name me Statius in the world;
I sang of Thebes, and of the great Achilles;
But with my second burden, I fell down.
Sparks from the flame divine that has inspired
More than a thousand poets, were the seed
Whence sprang the ardor of my poesy.
I speak of the Aeneid: 'twas the mother
That nursed me in the noble art of song.
Without it, I would ne'er have weighed a drachm.
Ah! To have lived below when Virgil lived,
I willingly would stay another sun
Beyond my time ordained upon this mount!»

 These words made Virgil turn around to me;
His face, though silent, bade me hold my peace.
But man's will is sometimes powerless—
For tears and laughter follow all the sooner
Those feelings from which both of them arise,
According as one's truthfulness prevails.
I smiled, as one who signals with his eyelids;
At this the shade was silent, and stared hard

Into my eyes—where best the feelings show.
«As you may hope to finish your great task,»
Said he, «why did your face, a while before,
Display the flashing of a smile to me?»

Now am I caught upon both sides alike;
One bids me hold my peace, the other one
Urges me to speak. Therefore I sighed,
And my good master heard me, and began:
«Be not afraid, but speak and tell to him
What he is asking you so earnestly.»

Whereon I said to him: «O ancient shade,
It may be that you wonder at my smile;
But I would have you marvel even more.
This soul who guides my eyes to higher things,
Is that same Virgil, fountain of your fame,
Whence sprang your power to sing of gods and
If you believe I smiled for other reasons, ⌊men.
Reject them as untrue, and take as cause
Those words you just pronounced concerning

Already had he stooped to kiss the feet ⌊him.»
Of my good lord, who said to him: «My brother,
Not so: for we are both but empty shades!»

And he, as he arose: «Now can you see
How great a love for you burns deep within me;
For I had lost to mind our emptiness,
And thought a shadow was a thing of substance.»

CANTO
22

THE angel was already left behind—
He who had ushered us into the ring—
When he erased one mark from off my brow,
Proclaiming that all those who wish for justice
Beati are, and adding to these words,
Siliunt—but saying not the rest.
I, feeling lighter than at other passes,

Sped swiftly on behind those fleeting shades,
And followed upward freed of all fatigue,
When Virgil said: «Love, when it is enkindled
By virtue, always kindles other loves,
Provided that its flame shows outwardly.
Hence, from that hour when Juvenal came down
Among us in the limbo of inferno,
And I then learned from him of your esteem,
I bore you such good will, that never yet
Has anyone, unseen, held such regard;
Therefore to me these stairs will now seem short.
But tell me—and forgive me, as a friend,
If too great confidence should loose my rein—
And as a friend discuss with me this point:
Pray, how could avarice have found a place
In your great heart, which by your diligence
Was stored with such a quantity of wisdom?»

These words at first caused Statius to smile;
And then he answered: «Every word you say
Impresses me as proof of deep affection.
In truth, things often will appear to us
From which false reasons for our doubts arise,
Because the proper reason lies concealed.
Your question shows me it is your belief
That I was avaricious in my life—
Perchance because I dwelt in yonder circle.
Nay, avarice was much too far removed
From me: for that excess I dwelt
For many thousand months in punishment.
And were it not that I set right my thoughts
When I had grasped that passage where you say,
As if indignant with all human nature,
'O cursed greed for gold—to what extremes
Dost thou impel our mortal appetites,'
I now should suffer in the hateful jousts.
But when I saw our hands can spread too wide
In spending, it was then that I repented
Of these and of my other sins as well.
How many will arise with locks shorn off,
Because of ignorance, that obstacle
To true repentance, both in life and death!
Know then that every evil which rebuts
And forms the opposite of every sin,

Must dry its verdure here together with it.
Wherefore, if I have been among those shades
Who mourn their avarice, it is because
I suffered from the opposite extreme.»

　　«When you were singing of the cruel strife
That caused the double sadness of Jocasta,»
Said the great singer of bucolic songs,
«From what you've written there, with Clio's aid,
'Twould seem that you were still without that
　　　　　　　　　　　　　　　　⌊faith

Which must perforce accompany good works.
If this be so, what light from heaven or earth
Scattered your darkness, so that you have sailed
Thus close behind the Fisherman's true course?»

　　And he replied: «'Twas you who led me first
To slake my thirst in grottoes on Parnassus,
And, next to God, illuminated me.
For you were like a man who walks by night
And bears his lamp behind him to no purpose,
Yet shows the way to those who follow him,
When you said: 'The age renews itself;
Justice returns, and man's primeval state,
And a new progeny descends from heaven.'
Through you I was made Christian, and a poet.
That you may better see what I have drawn,
I'll stretch my hand to add the color to it.

　　«Already was the world, on every side,
Filled with the true belief, disseminated
By those who bore the eternal kingdom's message.
And those your words, on which I touched just
Agreed so well with what the preachers said ⌊now,
That I was wont to pay them frequent visits.
They became so holy in my sight,
That when Domitian persecuted them,
Their lamentations mingled with my own.
So long as I remained upon the earth,
I gave them succor; and their righteous living
Made me contemptuous of other sects.
I was baptized before I led the Greeks
To the Theban rivers in my song;
But, in my fear, I was a secret Christian,
And long professed the worship of the pagans.
For this lukewarmness, I was made to roam

Round the fourth cornice twice two hundred years.
Therefore do you who lifted, as I say,
The veil that had concealed the good from me,
Inform me, while we yet have steps to climb,
Where ancient Terence is, if you can do so,
And Plautus, Varro, and Caecilius:
Tell me if they are damned, and in what region.»

　　«They, Persius and myself, and many more,»
My leader said, «together with the Greek —
He whom the Muses suckled above all —
Are in the starless dungeon's first enclosure.
We often talk about that lofty mount
On which our nurses dwell eternally.
Euripides and Antiphon are with us,
Simonides and Agathon, and more
Whose brows were laurel-crowned of old in Greece.
There can be seen, of those whom you have sung,
Antigone, Deiphile, and Argia;
Ismene also, mournful as she lived.
There too is she who pointed out Langia;
The daughter of Tiresias, and Thetis,
Deidamia, and her sisters also.»

　　The poets both were silent. Eagerly
They looked about them at their new surround-
　　　　　　　　　　　　　　　　⌊ings,

For that close-walled ascent was now behind them.
Already four handmaidens of the day
Were gone behind; the fifth stood at the pole,
Its flaming tip thrust upward to the sky.
My leader now began: «I think it wise
To turn our right sides to the outer edge,
As is our custom when we climb the mount.»
Thus did our former habit serve as guide:
With less misgiving now we took our way
Because that worthy soul gave his assent.

　　They walked ahead, and I in solitude
Behind them, while I listened to their talk,
Which gave me knowledge of the art of song.
But soon their dialogue was interrupted
By a tree found midway in our path,
Laden with apples sweet and good to smell.
And as a fir tree tapers as it rises
From branch to branch, here it was otherwise —

I think this was that none might try to climb it.
And on the inner cliff that closed our way
A crystal waterfall gushed from the rock,
Splashing upon the foliage above us.
Both of the poets now approached the tree,
And from amid its leaves a voice cried out:
«Of this food ye shall have a scarcity!»
And then it said: «Much more did Mary wish
To make the wedding perfect and complete,
Than to feed her mouth, that speaks for you.
And ancient Roman women were content
With water for their drink; and Daniel
Disparaged food, and wisdom gained thereby.
The primal age, as beautiful as gold,
Made acorns savory with appetite,
And turned with thirst its rivulets to nectar.
Locusts and wild honey were the food
That fed the Baptist on the desert sands:
Wherefore he is in glory, and so great,
As by the Gospel is revealed to you.»

CANTO
23

WHILE on the leafage green I fixed my eyes,
After the fashion of a man whose life
Is lost pursuing little birds, he said
Who more than fathered me: «Come on, my son!
For now the time that is assigned to us
Must be more usefully distributed.»

   I turned my eyes, and also turned my steps
Toward the sages, who conversed so well
That verily my going cost me naught.
And lo! In lamentation and in song,
Labia mea, Domine was heard,
So that both grief and joy arose from it.
«Beloved father, what is this I hear?»

I asked, and he replied: «Spirits, perchance,
Who pass while loosening their knot of debt.»

   Even as a band of pilgrims, rapt in thought,
Who, passing unknown people on their way,
Will turn to look at them, but do not halt:
Just so a silent crowd of pious shades,
Moving behind us at a swifter pace,
Passed on, although they stared at us in wonder.
Each one was dark and hollow in the eyes,
And pale to look upon, and so shrunken,
The skin betrayed the lines of all the bones.
I doubt that Erisicthon e'er became
So thin and wasted to the very rind,
Even when he had most fear of being starved.
And therefore to myself I said: «Behold,
The people who lost Zion's citadel,
When Mary pierced her son's flesh with her teeth!»
   Their sockets seemed like rings without their
                            ⌊gems;

For those who in the face of men read *O M O*,
The *M* was here most plainly to be seen.
Who would believe the odor of an apple,
And of a spring could have sufficient power
To cause such longing, if he knew not how?
   While I still wondered what so famished
                              ⌊them—

Because as yet I did not know the cause
Of all their leanness and their sorry aspect—
A spirit turned his eyes, and gazed on me
From out the caverns that were in his head,
And cried aloud: «What grace to me is this?»
   I never could have recognized his face;
But in his voice was manifest to me
What in his present aspect was concealed.
This spark rekindled all my former knowledge
So that I knew the altered countenance
And recognized the features of Forese.
«Ah,» he entreated me, «Pray do not stare
At this dry leprosy that stains my skin,
Or at the lack of flesh that I may have;
But tell me, pray, the truth about yourself,
And who are those two spirits yonder there
Who bear you company: and speak at once.»

«Your countenance, which once I wept for
⌊dead,»

I answered him, «now makes me weep no less,
When I behold its great disfigurement.
Say, in God's name, why is your flesh so withered?
Make me not speak while I am marvelling,
For ill speaks he whose wish is unfulfilled.»

And he to me: «By will of God Eternal,
Into the water, into yonder tree,
Descends a power that makes me grow so lean.
All this great crowd, who sing as they lament,
Here must be purged by hunger and by thirst,
Because they have indulged their appetites.
The odor that is wafted from the fruit
And from the spray, distilled upon the verdure,
Enkindles our desire to eat and drink.
And as we tread the circle of this floor,
Our penalty is suffered more than once:
I should not say our penalty, but solace.
For that same will compels us to the tree
Which made Christ utter 'Eli!' even with joy,
When with His blood He ransomed all mankind.»

And I to him: «Forese, from that day
When you were carried to a better world,
Scarcely five years have rolled their courses by.
If, ere the hour of goodly sorrow came
That weds us once again to our Creator,
Your power for further sin was at an end,
How is it that already you are here?
I thought that I should find you there below,
Where time is paid for equally with time.»

«My Nella, with her overflowing tears,
Who has enabled me so soon to drink
Sweet wormwood in these torments,» he replied,
«By her prayers devout, and by her sighs,
Has thus withdrawn me from the lower hillside,
And freed me from the other cornices.
As much more precious in the sight of God
Is my poor widow, whom I loved so dear,
As she stands by herself in her good conduct.
For even the Barbagia of Sardinia
Is far more modest in its womenfolk
Than that Barbagia is, in which I left her.

«Dear brother mine, what would you have me
⌊say?
Already can I see a future time—
At which this hour will not be very old—
When from the pulpit it will be forbidden
To Florence's unblushing womankind
To go about with breasts and nipples bare.
What paynim women, even in Barbary,
Have ever needed holy discipline
To see that they go covered decently?
But if the shameless creatures only knew
That which swift heaven has in store for them,
Already would they stand agape and howl!
For if my foresight here deceive me not,
They will be sad before the beard can sprout
On him for whom they croon their lullaby.
And now, my brother, hide yourself no longer:
Not only I, but all this multitude
Are marvelling at how you veil the sun.»

And I to him: «If you recall to mind
The life we led together in the world,
To think of it even now will cause you grief.
From that same life, he who directs my steps
Turned me aside a little while ago,
When his fair sister»—pointing to the sun—
«Was at her full. He has conducted me
Through the deep blackness of the truly dead,
Clad in my mortal flesh, which follows him.
Thence his encouragements have drawn me
⌊upward,

Ascending as I circled round this mount
Which straightens you, distorted by the world.
He says that he will bear me company
Till I arrive where Beatrice will be;
There it behooves that I remain without him.
This is Virgilius, who tells me so»—
I pointed to him—«and this other one
That shade for whom a while ago your kingdom
Shook all its slopes, while sending him away.»

Canto 23 : Dante recognizes the Soul of Forese

CANTO
24

Nor speech nor walking hindered one the
For now, as we conversed, we moved apace Lother,
Even as a ship impelled by favoring wind.
The shades, that seemed things doubly dead to us,
Perceiving through the caverns of their eyes
That I had life, were struck with wonderment.
And I, continuing my discourse, said:
«Perchance, 'tis for the sake of someone else
That he climbs up more slowly than he could.
But tell me, if you can, where is Piccarda;
And tell me, are there any I should know
Among these people who so stare at me?»
    «My sister, who in goodness and in beauty
So excelled, 'twere hard to give the palm,
On high Olympus glories in her crown,»
He said, and added, «Here 'tis not proscribed
That every soul be named, because our faces
Are all milked dry and shrivelled by our fast.»
He pointed: «This shade here is Bonagiunta,
Bonagiunta, once of Lucca; next,
He, with face most withered of them all,
Once held the Holy Church in his embrace.
He was of Tours, and by his fasting purges
Bolsena eels, and good Vernaccia wine.»
He named me many others, one by one;
And at their naming all appeared content,
So that I did not see an angry gesture.
Gnashing their hungry teeth on emptiness
I saw both Ubaldino dalla Pila
And Boniface, whose crozier herded many.
I also saw Marchese, who of old
Had time to drink—with less thirst—at Forlì,
And even so was never satisfied.
    Like one who looks about, and notes one man
More than the others, even so did I,
And singled out that eager shade from Lucca.
He murmured—what, I know not—but I thought
I heard «Gentucca!» coming from that place
Where heavenly justice made him feel its sting.
«O shade,» said I, «who seem so well disposed
To talk with me, pray speak that I can hear you,
And by your speech make both of us content.»
    «A woman has been born, but not yet wed,»
He answered, «who will make my city please you,
However much all others give it blame.
With this prediction, go upon your way.
If you were led to error by my mumbling,
The truth will set you straight in time to come.
But tell me, do I see before my eyes
Him who evoked those novel rhymes beginning,
Donne ch'avete intelletto d'Amore»?
    «When Love inspires me,» I answered him,
«I take good note, and then give utterance
According to the dictate of his will.»
    «Brother, I now perceive the knot that held
Guittone and the notary and myself
From mastering that sweet new style,» he said.
«Clearly I see how closely do your pens
Follow on him who dictates from within you:
This certainly was not the case with ours!
He who would farther look, sees nothing more
To help him tell the one style from the other.»
As if content with this, he held his peace.
    Just as the birds that winter on the Nile
Will form into a flock, and then fly on
With greater haste, strung out into a line:
Even so did all those shades collected there,
Turning their faces round, increase their pace,
Their feet made light by leanness and good will.
And as a man, fatigued by running hard,
Will let himself be passed by his companions,
Walking until his panting is abated:
So did Forese let that throng pass on,
Remaining at my back. He said to me:
«When will it be that we may meet again?»
    «I know not,» I replied, «how long I'll live;
Yet my return will never be so soon

But that my heart will wish me here the sooner —
Because that place where I was set to dwell
Grows from day to day more stripped of good,
And seems foredoomed to woe and desolation!»

«Now go,» said he, «for I can see the culprit
Dragged at a beast's tail, off toward that vale
Where mortal sins can never be condoned.
The animal at every bound goes on
With e'er increasing speed until it strikes him,
And leaves his body hideously maimed.
Those wheels» — at this he raised his eyes to
⌊heaven —

«Will turn but little ere you will perceive
That which I here no further can explain.
Now do you stay behind: for in this realm
Time is so precious, that I lose too much
In walking thus at even pace with you.»

As from a troop of horse, a cavalier
Will sometimes gallop forth and seek to win
The signal honor of the first encounter:
So he departed, taking longer strides;
But with me in the path remained those two
Who were such mighty marshals of the world.

And when he had passed on so far before us
That I must needs pursue him with my eyes,
Even as my mind was following his words,
I saw the laden and luxuriant boughs
Of still another fruit tree, near at hand,
For only then it was I turned that way.
Under it were folk with hands upraised,
Shouting I know not what, toward the branches,
Like silly children crying eagerly
To one who will not give them what they want,
But who, to make their longing even keener,
Will dangle what they seek beyond their grasp.
Then they departed, as if undeceived;
And we forthwith approached the mighty tree
That sets at naught so many tears and prayers.
«Pass on your way, so that you draw not near:
The tree that nourished Eve is higher up,
And from its seed this plant was germinated.»
Thus from out the branches someone spoke,
Whereat Virgilius, Statius, and myself

Drew close, and walked along the inner side.
«Remember,» said the voice, «those direful
Begotten in the clouds, who, overgorged, ⌊beings
Strove against Theseus with their twofold breasts!
Think of those Israelites, who drank so much
That Gideon would not bear their company,
When he went down the hills to Midian!»
Thus, keeping close beside the inner rock,
We passed along, while hearing of the sins
Of gluttony, and of their sorry outcome.

When, walking free along the lonely road,
We had advanced a thousand steps or more,
Each of us wrapt in thought, without a word —
«What are your thoughts, you three who walk
⌊alone?»

A voice said suddenly, whereat I started,
Just as a frightened, timid beast will do.

I raised my head to see who it might be;
And never in a furnace was there seen
Metal or glass so glowing and so red
As him I saw, who said: «If you would mount,
Here you should turn aside: here is the way
For those in quest of everlasting peace.»

His aspect had bereft me of my sight,
Wherefore I moved and stood behind my mentors,
Like one who guides himself by sound alone.
And like the May breeze, herald of the dawn,
That gives out fragrance sweet with grass and
Suffusing, as it moves, the air about it — ⌊flowers
Such was a wind I felt upon my brow.
Distinctly I could sense the moving pinions,
And some ambrosial odor which they bore.
«Blessed are they whom grace has so illumined
That due to love of taste within their breasts
They burn not with an undue appetite,»
I heard, «but hunger only as is right.»

Canto 24 : The Souls of the Gluttonous

CANTO
25

THE hour brooked no delay in our ascent:
The sun had left meridian to the Bull,
While night had left it to the Scorpion.
And so—just as a man who, come what will,
Halts not, but goes relentless on his way
If he be goaded by necessity—
We entered through the gap that cleft the rock
And mounted one by one upon the stairs,
Which were too narrow for an easy passage.
And like a fledgling stork that lifts its wing,
Wanting to fly, yet dares not leave the nest,
And therefore lets its wing droop down again:
Even so was I. My wish to ask was kindled,
But quenched the moment that I moved my lips,
As one will do before he starts to speak.
My gentle teacher, though our pace was swift,
Did not forbear from saying: «Pray let loose
The bow of speech, which you have drawn so
⌞taut.»

Then I spoke forth with confidence, and said:
«How can one starve and waste his flesh away
Where need for nourishment does not prevail?»

«If you will call to mind,» he answered me,
«How Meleager's substance was consumed
The while a firebrand burned, 'twould seem less
⌞strange.

Think too how every movement of your own
Is followed by its image in a glass:
Then what seems obscure will be made clear.
But so that you may gain your heart's content,
I'll call on Statius here, and beg that he
Will speak and be the healer of your wounds.»

«If I disclose the everlasting secrets,»
The other said, «while you are present here,
It is because I cannot say you nay.»

And then to me: «My son, consider well
These words of mine, and they will be a light
To clarify the «how» that you have asked.
«The blood's own essence, which the thirsty
⌞veins
Can ne'er drink up, remains like scraps of food
Left on the table. In the heart of man
It first assimilates creative power
To make all human members—for 'tis blood
That, coursing through the veins, becomes these
⌞members.

Digested further, it runs to those parts
Of which one speaks not, and from these it drops,
Upon another's blood, within the vessel
Wherein one and the other meet together,
One passively, the other actively,
Because it flows from such a perfect place.
The junction made, its operation starts:
First it coagulates, and then gives life
To the material that it has made.
The active virtue now becomes a soul,
Even as a plant's, though it is different
In that it has not yet attained perfection.
Already it begins to move and feel
Like a sea fungus: thereon it proceeds
To organize the power implanted in it.
And now, my son, the virtue is displayed
That issues from the heart of the begetter,
Where nature on all members is intent.

«How, a mere animal, it learns to reason,
You cannot yet discern; and on this point
A wiser man than you has gone astray.
For in his teaching he has separated
The intellect potential, from the soul,
Because he could not find its proper seat.
Open your heart and grasp the following truth,
And know that when the brain's articulation
Has been perfected in the embryo,
The Primal Mover turns to it with joy
At sight of such a masterpiece of nature,
Breathing into it a spirit new
With power to absorb within its substance
Whatever it finds active there, to form

One integrated soul that lives and feels.
That you may marvel less at what I say,
Consider how the sun's heat turns to wine,
Combining with the essence of the grape.

«When Lachesis has no more thread to spin,
The soul, freed from its body, bears away
Its faculties, both human and divine.
All of the other faculties are mute;
But memory, and will, and understanding,
Are all more active than they were before.
Without a stop, and in a wondrous fashion,
It drops at once on one bank or the other;
And there it first has knowledge of its road.
As soon as it is settled in its place,
Around it beams its own creative power,
Like to its living form in shape and size.
And as the atmosphere, when filled with rain,
Will show itself adorned with divers colors
Resulting from the sun's reflected rays:
So in this place the circumambient air
Adopts the shape the soul imposes on it,
By virtue of its native power to form.
And like a little flame that follows close
Upon the fire, whichever way it turns,
So the new form assumes the spirit's semblance.
Since by its shape it now is visible,
'Tis called a shade; and, hence again, it shapes
Organs of all the senses, even sight.
This is the means by which we laugh and speak;
'Tis thus we can produce those tears and sighs
Which you have heard upon the mountain slope.
According as our desires and other passions
Affect us, so the spirit forms itself:
This is the origin of all your wonder.»

Now we had reached the final turning point,
And bent our course around upon our right.
We were intent upon another care:
For here a flame darts outward from the cliff,
And from the cornice comes an upward blast
That turns aside the flame, and leaves a pathway.
Hence we were forced to walk in single file
Along the open side. Upon one hand
I feared to fall; the fire was on the other.

My leader said to me: «Along this passage
One needs must keep a tight rein on the eyes,
Because one easily might miss the way.»
'*Summae Deus clementiae*' I heard
Within the bosom of that flaming mass,
Which made me care not less to turn to them.
I now saw spirits passing through the flame,
So that I looked at them and at my footsteps,
Dividing my attention 'twixt the two.
When the conclusion of that hymn was reached,
They shouted loudly, *Virum non cognosco*,
Then softly they began their chant again.
When that was finished, they cried out anew:
«Diana stayed, and drove forth from the wood
Helice, who had tasted Venus' poison!»
They then resumed their singing, and ⌐proclaimed

Husbands and wives who lived in chastity,
As is ordained by virtue and by wedlock.
And I believe this mode suffices them
Throughout the time they burn within the flame.
Such is the treatment, such the regimen,
Whereby their wound is ultimately healed.

CANTO
26

WHILE we were walking thus along the rim,
The one before the other, Virgil said:
«Take care, take care: enough that I should warn ⌐you!»

Striking our right shoulders was the sun,
Who darted forth his rays on all the west,
Changing its hue from azure into white.
My shadow made the flame appear more ruddy;
And I perceived that many of the shades
Gave heed to it, as they were passing me.

Canto 25 : The Sinners passing through the Fire

This furnished an occasion for them all
To speak about me, and I heard them say:
«He does not seem to be a shade like us!»

   Then certain of the spirits came toward me,
As near as they were able—taking care
Not to come forth where they could not be burned.
«O you that walk so far behind the others,
From reverence, but not from being slower,
Reply to one who burns in fire and thirst;
And 'tis not I alone who need reply,
For all these shades have greater thirst for it
Than Ethiop or Indian has for water.
Pray tell us how it is that you thus make
A wall against the sun: for it would seem
You have not passed within the net of death.»
Thus spoke a shade to me, and straightaway
I would have answered; but I turned my mind
Upon another sight that now appeared.

   For in the middle of the fiery path,
To meet those folk, there came a multitude,
Who made me stop and gaze at them in wonder.
Now on both sides I saw the shades advance,
And without stopping each one kissed another,
Seeming content with such a brief salute.
Even thus, amid their dusky regiments,
One ant upon another rubs its nose,
Perchance to ask the way, or learn its prospects.

   As soon as they had made their friendly
                                      ⌊greeting,
Ere they had moved a step to leave that spot,
Each shade attempted to outcry the rest—
The newcomers cried «Sodom and Gomorrah!»
The rest, «Pasiphaë got in the cow,
So that the bull might satisfy her lust!»

   Even as cranes will fly to different regions,
Some choosing sands, some the Riphaean hills,
In seeking to avoid the frost or sun,
So here some shades were going, others coming;
Weeping they returned to their first songs,
And to that cry which suited them the best.
Now those same spirits who had begged me speak
Pressed close to me, as they had done before,
Their faces showing eagerness to hear me.

And I, who twice had noted their desire,
Addressed them thus: «O souls who are assured
Of gaining peace—whenever it may be—
Know that my limbs have not remained on earth
In tenderness of youth, or ripe old age,
But with their flesh and blood are here with me,
And blind I climb this mountain seeking light.
On high a lady dwells who wins us grace
By which I bear my body through your world.
But now—so may your dearest wish come true,
That you may find a lodging in that heaven
Replete with love, and widest in extent—
Pray tell me, so that I may write it down,
Who you may be, and who that multitude
That walk upon their way, behind your backs.»

   Bewildered, like a rustic mountaineer
Staring about him speechless in a town
That he has entered in his country clothes:
'Twas thus each spirit now appeared to me.
But after they had conquered their amazement—
Which quickly is subdued in noble minds—
He who before had questioned me, spoke forth:
«Happy are you, who here within our borders
Have entered now, to die a better man!
Those shades who walk away from us have sinned
In that for which when at a triumph once
Caesar was mocked by being called *Regina*.
Hence they cry «Sodom!» as they walk away,
In self-vituperation. You have heard them:
Their glow of shame but aids the fire to burn.
Our transgression was hermaphrodite;
But since we did not keep the human law,
And like brute beasts indulged our appetites,
As we take leave of them, to our own shame
We cry the name of her who like a beast
Within a beast of carpentry was served.
Now you know our deeds, and how we sinned;
For you to know our names, and who we are,
The time does not suffice, nor could I do so.
But for myself, I'll tell you that my name
Is Guido Guinicelli. I am here
Because of true repentance ere I died.»

   As when Lycurgus' sons beheld once more

Their mother, while the father raged with grief,
So was I moved—but not so recklessly—
When he thus named himself. For he was father
In poesy to me and all my betters—
To all who used the graceful rhymes of love.
A while I walked along in silent thought,
And listened not, but gazed at him in wonder,
Yet drew not near him, for I feared the flames.
As soon as I had fed my eyes on him,
I offered myself wholly to his service,
Assuring him of my sincerity.
He said: «From what I hear you say, you leave
So deep an imprint of your love for me
That even Lethe never could efface it.
But if your vows were not pronounced in vain,
Pray tell me why, in speech and by your looks,
You show you hold me in such great esteem.»

    «The sweetness of your songs,» I answered him,
«Which will outlive the modern use of verse—
Their very ink will e'er be dear to me!»

    «Brother,» said he, «this shade I indicate»—
He pointed to a spirit farther on—
«Wrought better in his tongue than I in mine.
In tales of romance and in songs of love
He outshone all: and let the foolish talk
Who deem him bested by the Limousin!
They credit rumor rather than the truth;
Thus forming their opinions carelessly,
Ere they have given heed to art or reason.
In olden time, they judged Guittone thus:
Their clamor gave the prize to him alone,
Until the truth at last prevailed with others.
Now if such ample favor you possess
That you are free to enter in that cloister
Where Christ himself is abbot of the college,
Say Him a paternoster for my sake,
So far as may be necessary here
For us who have no power to sin again.»

    Perchance to yield his place to some one else
Who might be nigh, he vanished through the
                                                    ⌊flame,
Much as a fish darts downward through the water.
I now approached that shade he pointed out,

And told him I desired to prepare
An honored reputation for his name.
He answered me in Provençal, as follows:
«Your courteous request so pleases me,
I neither can nor will conceal myself.
I am Arnaut, who weep now as I sing;
Sadly I contemplate my bygone folly,
But see with joy the bliss that waits for me.
Now I entreat you, by that very power
That leads you to the highest of these stairs,
While there is time, be mindful of my pain!»
With that he hid himself beneath the fire.

CANTO
27

As when he first darts down his quivering rays
There where his Creator shed His blood,
While Ebro sinks beneath the lofty Scales,
And Ganges' waters boil in heat of noon,
So stood the sun. The day drew to its close.
When lo, God's joyous angel shone before us.
Outside the flame, upon the very edge
He stood, and sang *Beati mundo corde*
In far more vibrant tones than ours on earth.
«O hallowed souls, beyond here none can pass
Unless he first endure the flames' assault:
Enter the fire, and heed the chant beyond it!»
He said to us as we drew near to him.

    And when I heard these words, it made me feel
Like one placed in the pit for burial.
Clasping my hands, I stretched them up above me;
And gazing on the fire I called to mind
The sight of bodies burning at the stake.

    My kindly leaders turned around to me,
And Virgil said: «My son, here may be pain,
But never death. Remember, O remember!

If I could keep you safe on Geryon's back,
How much more safely will I guide you now,
When we are so much nearer to our God?
Believe me, were you even to remain
A thousand years within this flame's embrace,
You would not lose a solitary hair.
And if perchance you think that I deceive you,
Step forth, and make a trial of it yourself,
With your own hands, upon your garment's hem.
In truth, all fear must now be put aside;
Turn here, and come in all security.»

Yet I stood still, although my conscience
⌞pricked.

When he perceived that I stood fast and stubborn,
Somewhat disturbed he said: «Now look, my son—
This wall stands here 'twixt you and Beatrice!»

As dying Pyramus, at Thisbe's name
Opened his eyes and looked upon her face,
When the mulberry was turning red:
Even so did I, my stubbornness o'ercome,
Turn to my noble leader when I heard
That name which e'er comes surging to my mind.
Whereat he shook his head, and said, «Well, well!
So we stay here?» and smiled, as though I were
A child persuaded by a gift of fruit.

He went into the flame in front of me,
Requesting Statius to come behind,
For he had long been walking there between us.
As soon as I had entered in the fire,
I gladly would have jumped in molten glass
To cool me from that heat beyond all measure.
My loving father, to encourage me,
Spoke but of Beatrice as we walked along,
And said: «I seem to see her eyes already!»

A voice beyond the flame was leading us;
And we, who gave our thoughts to it alone,
Came forth to where the new ascent began.
Venite benedicti patris mei
Came from within a light before our eyes,
So brilliant that I could not look upon it.
«The sun is going, and the evening comes,»
The voice went on, «Wait not, but speed your
Before the west is darkened o'er by night!» ⌞steps

The road ascended straight between the rocks,
In such a fashion that my body screened
The rays that issued from the setting sun.
When we had mounted only some few steps,
We were aware the sun had set behind us,
Because my shadow now had disappeared.
And ere the whole expanse of the horizon
Had yet assumed the same unvaried hue,
Or night had won its privilege entirely,
Each one of us lay down upon a stair.
Indeed, the mountain's nature had deprived us
Of power or even desire to ascend.

Even as goats are quiet when they graze,
Though gay and lively on the mountain top
Before they have been fed, and in the shade
Rest still and silent while the sun is hot,
Kept by their shepherd, leaning on his staff,
And as he leans there, watching over them—
Or as the herdsman, living in the open,
Watches by night beside his quiet flock,
Seeing that no wild beast may scatter it:
'Twas even so with us—I like the goat,
The other two like shepherd guardians,
Walled in on either side by lofty rocks.

But little of the firmament appeared;
Yet in that space, I saw the stars shine forth
More brilliantly than usual, and larger.
Thus musing as I gazed upon this sight,
I fell into that sleep which oftentimes
Foresees a fact before it comes to be.

At the hour, I think, when Cytherea
Who ever seems to blaze with love's own fire,
First beamed upon our mountain from the east,
I thought I saw in dream a lovely lady
Who walked upon a plain, and gathered flowers;
And as she walked, she sang in accents sweet:
«Should anyone desire to ask my name,
Know I am Leah, and that I move my hands
To weave myself a garland of these blooms.
I deck myself to please me at the mirror;
And yet my sister Rachel never leaves
Her looking glass, but sits all day before it.
She is as eager to admire her eyes

As I to weave these garlands with my hands;
Work is my joy, and contemplation hers.»
   Now, through those splendors that precede
          ⌊the dawn,
Which, to all pilgrims, comes more gratefully
As they approach their home for which they long,
The darkness flew away on every side,
And with it went my slumber. I arose,
Seeing my masters were already risen.
«That luscious fruit which anxious mortals seek
With eagerness upon so many branches,
Shall ease your hungering this very day.»
These were the words that Virgil used to me,
And ne'er were tidings told that had in them
Such great capacity for bringing joy.
Within me more and more the longing grew
To be above: at every step thereafter,
I felt my pinions growing for the flight.

   When all the stairs had passed beneath our
And we were standing on the topmost step, ⌊feet,
Virgilius fixed his eyes on me, and said:
«My son, you now have seen the temporal fire,
And that which is eternal; you have reached
A place where I myself can see no farther.
Thus far I have conducted you with skill;
Henceforth your own good sense must be your
          ⌊guide.

The steep and narrow ways have all been passed.
Behold the sun, which shines upon your brow:
Behold the grass, the shrubs, and all the flowers
That grow so blithely in this region's soil.
Until you may behold those lovely eyes
Which, when they wept, brought me to succor you,
You may sit down, or walk upon the meadow.
Expect no further speech or sign from me.
Your will, upright and sound, is now released:
You'll do no wrong, if you but do its bidding;
Wherefore I crown you sovereign of yourself.»

CANTO 28

EAGER now to search within the forest
Whose foliage divine, thickset and living,
Tempered the brightness of the newborn day,
I waited not, but left the mountain's rim,
Slowly to take my way across the plain.
Its soil on every side breathed forth a fragrance;
A breeze, immutable within itself,
Smote me so delicately on the brow
That 'twas no heavier than a zephyr's stroke.
By this the boughs, in tremulous accord,
Were one and all deflected toward that point
Whereon the holy mount first casts its shadow.
But they were not sufficiently bent down
To stop the birds from setting forth their art:
For, singing with an uncontrolled delight,
They hailed the earliest breezes of the day
Amid the leaves, which, while they sang, sent forth
A soft accompaniment to their minstrelsy,
Such as is passed along from branch to branch
Through the pine forest on Chiassi's shore,
When Aeolus lets loose sirocco's blast.

   By now my laggard steps had carried me
So far within that ancient forest's shade
That I could see no more where I had entered.
When lo, across my path I saw a stream
Whose gentle ripples softly bent the grass
That sprouted on its banks toward the left.
All of the limpid waters here on earth
Would seem to me impure beside this stream,
So clear that it hides naught within its depths,
Albeit it rolls onward, black and dark,
Beneath that sempiternal shade so dense
That ray of sun or moon can never pierce it.

   My feet stood still, but with my eyes I passed
Beyond the rivulet, and gazed in wonder

Canto 28 : Dante, Virgil and Statius in the Ancient Forest

Upon a great variety of flowers;
And on the other bank there came to view —
As something will appear quite suddenly,
So wondrous as to drive all thoughts aside —
A lady walking all alone, and singing;
And as she went, she chose and plucked the
Enamelling the path beneath her feet.   ⌊flowers

    «O lady fair, who now appear to bask
In love's own rays — if I may trust your features,
Which oft in man bear witness for the heart —
Pray let your will be bent, and come this way,»
I said to her, «so far that I may hear
What you are singing in so sweet a strain.
For you remind me of Proserpine,
When her mother lost her, and when she
Forever lost enjoyment of the spring.»

    Even as a woman turns, when she is dancing,
Holding her feet together on the ground
So that she scarce puts one before the other:
Just so it was that she was turning toward me
Upon the saffron and vermilion flowers,
Her eyes downcast and modest, like a maid's.
And now she gave content to my entreaties
By drawing near, so that the sweet refrain
Of what she sang was clear, and its intent.
As soon as she had come before that spot
Where first the streamlet's waters bathe the grass,
She did me grace, and raised her eyes to mine.
I do not think so bright a radiance
Shone from the eyes of Venus, when her son
By accident transfixed her with his dart.
Smiling from the right bank opposite,
She gathered more and more of those bright colors
Which grow unsown in that exalted land.
Three paces wide, the stream kept us apart:
And Hellespont itself, where Xerxes crossed —
Even now a curb to human aspirations —
Did not endure more hatred from Leander
Because it parted Sestus from Abydos,
Than did this stream, for opening not, from me.

    «You are newcomers, and perchance some doubt
May make you marvel why I should be smiling
Here in this place, which once was set apart

To be the cradle of the human race.
But seek out *Delectasti* in the psalms,
And you will find the light to clear your minds.
And you in front, who made me a request —
If you would hear aught else from me, speak forth:
I will be prompt to answer all your questions.»

    «The water, and the murmuring in the forest,»
I answered, «undermine a new belief;
For what I heard was opposite to this.»

    «I'll show how that which made you ask and
                               ⌊wonder
Proceeds from causes deep within itself —
To clear away the mist enshrouding you.
The Good Supreme, rejoicing in itself,
Made man good, and for good, and gave to him
This place, to dwell here in eternal peace.
Through his default, man did not long remain
                                    ⌊here;
Through his default, his joy was changed to grief,
His gentle pastimes changed to lamentations.
So that disturbances — which may be due
To exhalations from the land or water
Rising with heat as far as possible —
Should not cause any trouble to mankind,
This mountain rises up so far toward heaven,
Hence 'tis free of them above the gate.
Now, seeing that the atmosphere rotates
Together with the primal revolution,
If not prevented by some obstacle,
The movement strikes this elevated spot
In purest air; and thus it makes the forest
Give forth a sound, because it is so dense.
And every tree thus smitten, has such power
That with its seeds it fills the moving air,
Which in its turn revolves, and scatters them.
According to their climate and their soil,
The other portions of the earth conceive
And bring forth plants with divers properties.
Therefore on earth it should not seem a marvel —
When this is understood — if, at some time,
A plant takes root without apparent seed.
Know that this holy place in which you stand
Is full of seeds of every form and kind,

And has such fruit as ne'er is plucked on earth.
　《That water which you see, arises not
From springs replenished by condensing vapors,
Like a stream that gains and loses strength,
But gushes forth from an unfailing source
That, by the will of God, receives again
So much as it pours forth in its two streams.
Upon this side it issues with the power
To take away all memory of evil;
There, to restore the memory of good.
Here it is Lethe called, and there Eunoe.
The wondrous properties are only valid
For him who tastes the water of both streams.
This water's savor overtops all others.
And though perchance your thirst has now been ⌊slaked
Without my making further revelations,
I'll add a corollary, as a boon:
Nor do I think my speech will be less prized
If it extend beyond what I have promised.
They who in ancient times proclaimed in song
The golden age, and its auspicious state,
Perchance dreamed on Parnassus of this spot.
Here mankind's parents dwelt in innocence:
Here is perpetual spring, here every fruit,
And here the nectar which they often name.''

　　Thereat I turned me round to face the poets,
And noted that they smiled at what she said
As she concluded; then I turned around
To look upon the beauty of my lady.

CANTO
29

WHEN she had finished, she resumed her song,
Much as a woman sings her song of love:
Beati quorum tecta sunt peccata.
And like the nymphs who wandered by themselves
Through sylvan glades, some looking for the sun

While others would avoid it: thus she moved,
Along the river's bank, and up the stream,
And I kept pace with her, with shortened steps,
As short as those which she herself was taking.
Not more than fifty paces had we walked
When both the river's banks curved equally,
In such wise that I faced the east once more.
And ere we had gone far on our new course,
The lady turned around and said to me:
《My brother, look—and give good heed as well.》

　　And lo, on every side a brilliant gleam
Suffused the wide expanse of that great wood—
So brilliant, that it seemed to me like lightning;
But lightning stops as quickly as it comes,
While this continued, brightening more and more.
Hence in my thoughts I said: 《What thing is
　　Now a sweet melody was borne along ⌊this?》
Upon the luminous air. There came to me
A righteous indignation against Eve,
Who, the sole woman, and but newly formed,
Could not endure the veil of ignorance,
Where heaven and earth were both obedient:
For had she but endured it with submission,
Sooner should I have tasted those delights,
And also for a longer time enjoyed them!

　　While mid those first fruits of eternal bliss
I walked, enthralled by wonder, on my way,
Eager to know still greater joys than these,
I saw beneath the foliage before me,
The very air was glowing like a flame;
And now the lovely sounds became a chant.

　　O virgins sacrosanct! If e'er for you
I may have suffered hunger, cold, or vigils,
My need now spurs me on to claim reward:
May Helicon pour forth for me its waters,
And may Urania with her choir aid me
To sing in verse of things incredible!

　　A little way beyond, the great expanse
That yet remained between them and ourselves
Made them appear like seven trees of gold;
But when I had sufficiently approached
That distance could no longer cheat my vision,
And I was able to distinguish clearly,

Canto 29 : The Elders in the Mystic Procession

That faculty which sets aside for reason
Materials for its judgment, now perceived
That they were candlesticks, and heard Hosanna!
Above were flaming many brilliant lamps,
Far more brilliant were they than the moon
When shining in a cloudless sky at midnight.

　　Filled with wonder, I now turned around
To my good Virgil: he replied to me
With look of wonder equal to my own.
I turned my eyes back to those things sublime
Which were approaching us, with pace so slow
That newly wedded brides would have outstripped
⌊them.

The lady said: «Why is your gaze thus fixed
Entirely on those living lights? And why
Do you not look upon what comes behind them?»

　　I saw that there were people, following
As though behind their leaders, clad in white—
Whiter than anything upon this earth.
The water on my left was glittering,
And when I gazed upon it, it reflected
The image of my side, just like a mirror.
When I had reached the point upon my bank
Where nothing but the stream kept us apart,
I halted where I stood, to see more clear.
I noticed that the flames were moving on,
Leaving the air behind them streaked with color,
So that it resembled streaming pennons.
Thus the air was striped with seven bands,
And all of them were of the selfsame hues
Of which the sun makes bows, and Delia girdles.
These flaming banners streamed toward the rear
Farther than I could see: they seemed to me
Ten paces wide, between the outer ones.
Beneath this sky so fair, as I describe it,
Came four-and-twenty elders, two by two.
Upon their brows were crowns of fleurs-de-lis,
And they were chanting: «Thou indeed art blest
Above all Adam's daughters. May henceforth
Thy loveliness be blest for evermore!»

　　And when the herbage and the tender flowers
Upon the other bank in front of me
Were cleared of that great band of the elect,

Just as in heaven star will rise on star,
Even so, four living beings came behind them.
Each one was crowned with verdant foliage,
And each was plumed with triple pairs of wings,
The feathers full of eyes: and such as these
Would Argus' eyes have been, had they been
I'll waste no verses to describe their form,　⌊living.
O reader, for another way to spend them
So urges me that I can spare them not.
But read Ezekiel, where he describes them
Just as he saw them come from icy lands
With wind and cloud and fire: such were they here
As you will find them in his hallowed pages,
Save for the matter of their wings—where John
Tallies with my description, not with his.

　　The space that lay between those four,
A chariot of triumph with two wheels, ⌊contained
And this was harnessed to a gryphon's neck.
He raised his wings through those six bands of
On either side the centre, in such wise　　⌊color
He harmed not one of them by piercing it;
So high they reached that they were lost to view.
Gold were the birdlike members that he had;
The others were of white, mixed with vermilion.
Surely, Rome never honored Africanus,
Or yet Augustus, with such car as this!
Even the sun's own chariot it outshone—
That chariot which, when driven off its course,
Was burned in answer to earth's fervent prayer
When Jove was just in his mysterious purpose.

　　Three ladies, who were dancing in a ring,
Came onward at the chariot's right wheel:
One, ruddier than the glow of living flame;
The second was as if her flesh and bones
Were fashioned out of gleaming emeralds;
The third was white as freshly fallen snow.
Now it seemed as if the white one led them,
And now the red; and to their leader's song
The others timed their movements, fast or slow.
Four others went rejoicing on the left,
In purple vestments, following the measure
Of one of them with three eyes in her head.

　　Behind the group that I have just described

117

There came two ancient men, in different garb,
But yet alike in dignity of bearing.
One showed himself to be a follower
Of great Hippocrates, whom nature made
To tend those creatures whom she holds most ⌊dear;
The other showed an opposite intent,
Bearing a sword so glittering and sharp
It frightened me — although across the stream.
I saw four others, humble in their aspect,
And last of all, a solitary sage
Of vision keen, but walking in a trance.
And all these seven were clad like those before,
Save that they bore no lilies on their heads,
But roses, and some other scarlet flowers.
The sight of them, a little distance off,
Might well have led a person to believe
That flames were burning bright above their brows.

When the chariot was abreast of me,
There came a thunderclap; and all that throng,
Seeming to find their progress stopped thereby,
Stood where they were, their ensigns in the van.

CANTO
30

WHEN that Septentrion of highest heaven
Which never has been known to rise or set
And has no clouds, except the veil of sin —
Which, there on high, was pointing out their duty
To all, just as the one below directs
The helmsmen seeking harbors here on earth —
Came to a halt, the saintly band of men
Who first had come between it and the gryphon,
Turned to the chariot, as to their peace.
And one of them, as if sent down from heaven,
Thrice shouted, *Veni, sponsa, de Libano!*
And all the rest did likewise after him.

Even as the blessed, at the final trump
Will rise up quickly from their sepulchres
With voice regained, and shout forth «Hallelujah»:
'Twas even thus, *ad vocem tanti senis,*
There rose before me on the heavenly car
A hundred messengers of life eternal.
Benedictus qui venis! was their chant
And while they scattered flowers round about,
Manibus O date lilia plenis!

As I have sometimes seen at break of day
The eastern regions all suffused with pink,
The rest bedecked with tranquil loveliness,
While the sun's face is rising, dimly veiled
So that the eye can gaze on it at length
Because its glare is tempered by the mists:
Even so, within a cloud of lovely blossoms
That rose and fell from the angelic fronds,
Some within the chariot, some without,
There now appeared a lady, garlanded
On her white veil, with crown of olive leaves,
And flame-hued vesture 'neath her mantle green.
And now my spirit — that for such long time
Had not been overcome and, struck with wonder,
Made to tremble at her very presence —
By influence of ancient love, upswelled —
Not from knowledge gathered through my eyes,
But through the mystic force that came from her.
And when that influence smote on my mind —
That influence sublime, which had transfixed me
Ere I had passed beyond my years of youth —
I turned me confidently to the left —
Just as a little child will seek its mother
When overcome by fear or in distress —
To say to Virgil: «Less than a drop of blood
Remains within me, that is not atremble:
I know the symptoms of that ancient flame!»

But Virgil had completely disappeared —
Virgil, beloved father of my song,
Virgil, to whom I turned for my salvation!
Not all the joys the ancient mother lost
Could keep my cheeks, but lately washed with ⌊dew,
From being soiled again with bitter tears.

«Dante, weep not at Virgil's leaving you!

Canto 30 : Beatrice appears among Angels

Weep not just yet: for you must later weep
For wounds inflicted by another sword.»

    Even as an admiral, on poop or prow
Inspects the crews that serve on other ships,
Instilling them with zeal to do their duty:
Just so, upon the chariot's left side—
For I had turned on hearing my own name,
Which of necessity is here recorded—
I saw that lady who had first appeared
Concealed beneath the angelic festival,
Direct her eyes at me across the stream,
Although the veil descending from her head,
On which Minerva's foliage was wreathed,
Did not allow her to be seen distinctly.
Royally, with anger in her mien,
She added—much like someone who in speaking
Keeps his most trenchant words until the last—
«Look well: for we indeed are Beatrice.
How have you deigned to clamber up this mount?
Did you not know that man is happy here?»

    My eyes dropped down upon the limpid
                              ⌊stream;
But when I saw my image, I withdrew them,
And looked upon the grass, for I was shamed.
As a mother may seem haughty to her son,
So she appeared to me—because the taste
Of scornful pity has a bitter flavor.
She held her peace. The choir of angels sang
In te, Domine, speravi, ceasing
When they reached *pedes meos* in the psalm.

    Just as the snow, that on Italia's back
Congeals beneath the branches of the pine trees,
Drifted and packed by the Sclavonian winds,
And later melts, and trickles through itself
When shadeless Africa breathes forth its blast,
As 'twere a flame that melts a candle down:
Even so was I, bereft of tears and sighs,
When I had listened to the song of those
Whose notes are with the eternal spheres attuned.
But when in their sweet melodies I heard
Their pity for me—just as if they said,
«O lady, why do you confound his spirit?»
That ice which was congealed around my heart

Melted to breath and water, and gushed forth
Through mouth and eyes in anguish from my
                                  ⌊breast.

    But she, who still was standing motionless
Beside the heavenly car, as I have said,
Addressed those pious beings with these words:
«Ye watch so closely in the eternal light
That neither sleep nor night can e'er prevent
Your knowledge of the happenings in the world.
Therefore my answer has a special aim—
That he who yonder weeps may understand,
So that his fault and grief will have one measure.

    «Not only through the working of the spheres,
Which guide each seed to some predestined end
According as the stars are its companions,
But through the bounteous gifts of Grace Divine,
Which fall from vapors in such lofty places
That human vision never can attain them,
This man was so disposed in his young life,
It seemed that every natural aptitude
Should have produced the worthiest results.
But soil is all the more unprofitable,
When sown with worthless seed or left untilled,
According as it has fertility.
For some short time, my countenance sustained
I led him, showing him my youthful eyes, ⌊him:
Along with me upon the proper path.
When on the threshold of my womanhood,
I changed my life for death, he took himself
Away from me, and gave himself to others.
When from flesh to spirit I was changed,
Beauty and virtue had increased in me;
And yet I seemed less dear, less pleasing to him.
He turned his steps upon an evil path,
And followed false appearances of good,
Which never pay a promise back in full.
So little did he care, that even the visions
With which in dreams I tried to call him back
Availed me not at all; he fell so low
That every means of working his salvation,
Save that of showing him the lost in hell,
Had proven that they were of no avail.

    «I then approached the gateway of the dead,

And there to him who now has brought him here,
My prayers and lamentations were directed.
The high decree of God would be transgressed,
Were Lethe passed and such sweet viand tasted
By him without some forfeit of contrition
Sufficient to bring forth repentant tears.»

CANTO
31

O YOU who are across the sacred river,»
She said—and now she turned to me the point
Of her discourse, that with its edge alone
Had seemed so trenchant—and went on forthwith:
«Say, say if this be true: to such a charge
Your own confession must be brought to answer.»

At this my faculties were so confused
That when I tried to speak, my voice died off
Ere it had been released to form my speech.
Waiting a while, she said: «What are your
Reply to me: your bitter memories   ⌊thoughts?
Are not as yet impaired by Lethe's waters.»

Now the commingling of my shame and fear
Forced such a feeble yes from out my mouth,
That eye alone could tell it had been said.
And as an arquebus, when it is shot
At too great tension, breaks both string and bow,
So that the shaft hits with a lessened force:
Thus did I break beneath that heavy burden,
So that both tears and sighs gushed forth from me;
And ere it passed my lips, my voice was choked.

«Within the love that I inspired in you
To lead you on to love the Good Supreme,
The pinnacle of all man's aspirations,
What trenches did you find across your path,
What chains to stop your course,» she said to me,
«So that you lost all hope of passing onward?

And what allurements, or what recompense
Did others' faces have to offer you,
To make you walk astray, and dally with them?»

After the heaving of a bitter sigh,
I scarce had voice to make reply to her,
And only with an effort gave it form.
Weeping I said: «Allurements of the moment,
With their false pleasures, turned my steps astray,
So soon as your sweet face was hid from me.»

And she: «Had you kept silence, or denied
What you have told me, not less manifest
Would be your fault—so mighty is the Judge.
But when the accusation of his error
Bursts from the sinner's mouth, then in our court
The grindstone is turned back, to dull the edge.
But nonetheless, so that you may feel shame
For your transgression, and another time
Be stronger if you hear the siren's song,
Hark to my words, and sow your tears no longer:
For you shall hear that even as buried flesh
I should have turned your steps the other way.
Never did art or nature set before you
Such sweet delight as my fair members were,
That now again are crumbled into dust.
And if the greatest of all man's delights
So failed you when I died, what mortal thing
Could afterward attract you to desire it?
You should, in truth, when wounded by the shaft
Of perishable things, have soared aloft,
In search of me, who was no longer such;
Nor should your pinions have been drooping down,
To wait for further strokes, from some young girl,
Or other vanity of brief duration.
Only a fledgling waits for second shots;
But for the watchful eyes of the full-grown bird
The net is spread, the arrow shot in vain.»

Even as children, silent and in shame,
Stand listening with eyes upon the ground,
Repentant, and acknowledging their fault,
So stood I then. And she admonished me:
«Since hearing makes you grieve, raise up your
                                          ⌊beard:

And when you see, you will but grieve the more!»

Canto 31 : Dante submerged in the River Lethë

With less resistance is a sturdy oak
Uprooted by a native thunderstorm,
Or tempest from the country of Iarbas,
Than I, at her command, raised up my chin.
And when by saying «beard» she meant my face,
I knew full well the venom of her speech.

When I had lifted up my head again,
I saw that those fair creatures in the car
No longer strewed their blossoms: and my eyes,
As yet but little reassured, perceived
That Beatrice now faced that animal
Which is one person in a twofold nature.
Even beneath the veil, across the stream,
Her loveliness surpassed her former self,
Just as on earth she had surpassed all others.
The nettle of remorse now pricked my heart,
So that whatever of all other things
Had most attracted me, I now abhorred.
And penitence so deeply stung me now
That I fell in a swoon; and only she
Who was the cause, knows what I then became.

When my heart restored my mind, I saw
Above me, her I first had found alone;
Twice I heard her say: «Hold fast to me!»
For she had carried me into the stream
Up to my throat, and dragging me behind,
Was speeding o'er the water like a shuttle.
When I was drawing nigh the blessed shore,
I heard, *Asperges me*—so sweetly sung
I call it not to mind, nor can I write it.
The lovely lady opened wide her arms,
Embraced my head, and pushed me 'neath the
So that perforce I swallowed some of it: ⌊wave
And then she drew me forth, presenting me
Thus bathed and wet, to those four lovely ones,
Who each in dancing o'er me passed her arm.

«Here we are nymphs: in heaven we are stars.
Ere Beatrice descended to the world,
We were ordained to be her handmaidens.
We'll lead you to her eyes: but ere you see
Their joyous light, your sight must first be
                                        ⌊sharpened
By yonder three, who can discern more deeply.»

This was their song; they led me with the others,
Until we came before the gryphon's breast,
Where Beatrice was standing, turned toward us.
«Take heed,» they said, «lest you should spare
                                        ⌊your gaze:
For you are now before those emeralds
Whence Love of old shot forth his darts against
                                        ⌊you.»

A myriad desires, that burned like flames,
Constrained my gaze upon those gleaming eyes;
But they were looking ever on the gryphon.
And like the sun reflected in a glass,
Within her eyes that twofold creature glowed,
Now with one nature's actions, now the other's.

Think, reader, how my soul was filled with awe
When I beheld a thing which did not move,
Yet in its image moved and was transformed!
And while my soul, in wonder and delight
Was feasting on that food which in itself
Can satisfy, but causes further longing,
The other three came forward; and their mien,
While they moved to their heavenly roundelay,
Showed them to be of more exalted order.

«Turn, Beatrice, O turn your holy eyes
Upon your faithful one, who to behold you
Has come so far,» they sang in unison,
«And of your grace, bestow on us the grace
To lift the veil that now conceals your mouth,
That he may see your second hidden beauty.»

O splendor of the living light eternal!
What man has paled beneath Parnassus' shade
Or drunk the limpid water of its fount,
Who would not seem to have a mind encumbered
Should he but endeavor to portray you
As there you stood, revealed in open air,
With heavenly harmony your only veil?

CANTO
32

So eager were my eyes, and so intent
To satisfy their ten long years of thirst,
That all my other senses were extinct.
On every side, a wall was round about them—
So greatly did that smile ineffable
Ensnare them in its long-remembered toils.
Perforce I turned my face toward the left,
For I had heard the goddesses reprove me,
Exclaiming: «You are gazing too intently!»

And that condition of the sense of sight
Which occurs on looking at the sun,
Bereft me of my vision for a while;
But when my sight conformed with lesser
⌊splendors—
Lesser, compared with that bright radiance
From which by force I had removed myself—
I saw the glorious army now had turned,
And wheeling to the right, was moving back,
Facing the sun, the sevenfold flame before them.

Even as a troop of soldiers, for protection,
Wheels with its standards, guarded by its shields,
Before it will completely face about:
Just so, that heavenly kingdom's soldiery
Which formed the van, had all passed on beyond
Before the pole had turned the chariot.   ⌊us
The ladies took their places by the wheels;
And then the gryphon moved his blessed load,
So that not a single feather quivered.
That fair one who had drawn me through the ford,
And Statius, and myself, were following
The right-hand wheel, upon the inner track.
And now, as we passed through the lofty wood—
Emptied by her who trusted in the serpent—
Our steps were measured by angelic strains.

Perchance an arrow loosened from the string
Would in three flights traverse as great a distance
As we had walked when Beatrice stepped down.
I now heard everybody murmur: «Adam!»
And soon they gathered round a lofty tree
That bore no leaf or blossom on its branches.
Its crowning boughs, which widened out the more
As they were higher, would be cause for wonder
Even to Indians—so tall were they.

«Blessed art thou, O gryphon, that thy beak
Does not break this tree whose fruit is sweet:
For afterward the belly writhes in anguish.»
Thus, round the sturdy tree, the others cried.

To this the twofold animal responded:
«Thus is the seed of righteousness preserved!»
Now he turned the pole that he had drawn,
Dragging it beneath the widowed tree trunk,
And to it tied the shaft made of its wood.

Even as our trees on earth begin to swell
At that time when, commingled with the rays
Of the celestial carp, the sun's great light
Beats down on them, and each breaks forth in
Of its own color, ere the sun has yoked   ⌊leaves
His steeds beneath another constellation:
Just so that tree, which had been stripped so bare,
Broke into leaf, disclosing lovely tints
That ranged between the violet's and the rose's.
I could not understand—nor mortals sing—
The hymn which then was sung by that assembly;
Nor could I bear to listen to the end.
Could I describe how those relentless eyes—
Those eyes whose wakefulness cost them so dear—
Sank into sleep, on hearing about Syrinx,
I would portray just how I fell asleep,
Even as an artist painting from a model;
Let him who can, attempt to picture sleep!
Therefore I pass on to when I woke.
My veil of sleep was rent by dazzling light,
And by a shout: «Arise! What dost thou here?»

As Peter, John, and James were led to view
The blossoms of that apple tree which makes
The angels greedy for its fruit, and heaven
Resplendent with perpetual marriage feasts,

Canto 32 : The Harlot and the Giant in the Chariot

PURGATORIO: CANTO 32

And from their trance were wakened by the
⌊Word—
By which far deeper slumbers had been broken—
Seeing their company diminishing
As Moses and Elias disappeared,
And seeing the raiment of their Master changed:
So came I to myself; and standing o'er me
I saw that lady most compassionate
Who led my steps along the river bank.
Distraught I asked her: «Where is Beatrice?»
   And she: «Behold her, 'neath the foliage
So newly grown, and seated on its root.
Behold the company that is about her;
The others, with the gryphon, are ascending,
With sweeter melody, and more profound.»
   I do not know if she said more to me:
For there before my very eyes was she
Who closed my mind to any other thought.
Alone upon the bare ground she was sitting,
Left there as guardian of the heavenly car
The two-formed beast had fastened to the tree.
The seven nymphs were gathered in a ring
Enclosing her; and in their hands they bore
The lamps, secure from Aquila and Auster.
   «Your stay within this forest will be brief;
But you will be with me, for evermore,
A citizen of Rome, as is the Christ.
So, for the evil-living world's advantage,
Keep now your eyes upon the chariot,
And write down later what you here have seen.»
Thus Beatrice; and I, who at her feet
Burned but to follow where she might command,
Now turned my mind and eyes where she had
   Never descended with so swift a flash ⌊willed.
Fire from thundercloud, when it is raining
From out that region which is most remote,
As now the bird of Jove came swooping down
Through that tree's branches, stripping off its
Its blossoms, and its leaves in his descent. ⌊bark,
He struck upon the car with all his might;
Whereat it reeled, like ships tossed by the waves
To windward or to leeward in a storm.
And then into the body of the car

There leaped a fox, that from her aspect lean
Seemed long deprived of any wholesome food.
After upbraiding her for ugly sins,
My lady put her to as swift a flight
As her fleshless body would permit.
Then from the place whence he had come before
I saw the eagle swoop a second time,
Leaving the chariot covered with his feathers.
From heaven came a saddened voice that said:
«My little bark, how evil is thy burden!»
   I thought the earth now opened 'twixt the
⌊wheels;
And from the crack there issued forth a dragon,
Who thrust his sharp tail upward through the car.
And like a wasp that will draw back its sting—
Just so, he now drew back his venomed tail,
Tearing away a portion of the bottom;
And wandering off, he went upon his way.
Now what remained there of the chariot,
Even as fertile soil grows thick with weeds,
Covered itself entirely with that plumage,
Offered perhaps with most benign intent:
And wheels and pole were feathered in less time
Than lips are parted by a single sigh.
When it was thus transformed, the holy car
Put forth heads upon its different parts—
Three on the pole, and one at every corner.
Like oxen three were horned; the other four
Had on the forehead each a single horn:
No monster such as this has e'er been seen.
   Safe as a citadel on some high mountain,
There now appeared upon the transformed car
A frowsy harlot, boldly leering round.
And then, as if to guard her for himself,
I saw a giant standing by her side;
And ever and anon they kissed each other.
Because she cast her wanton eye on me,
The savage man who was her paramour
Now scourged her from her head down to her heels.
Teeming with jealousy and fierce with rage,
He now untied the monster from the tree,
And dragged it far away into the wood:
Harlot and beast alike were lost to sight.

CANTO
33

D*EUS venerunt gentes* — this sweet psalm
The ladies, while they wept, began to sing
In choirs alternate, now three, now four;
Beatrice was listening to them
With sighs compassionate, and looks so sad
That scarce was Mary at the Cross more changed.
But when the other maids had given place
For her to speak, she rose upon her feet
And answered, with a countenance like fire:
Modicum, et non videbitis me.
Et iterum, my beloved sisters,
Modicum, et vos videbitis me.

    She now sent on before her all the seven;
And by a sign she motioned unto me,
The lady, and the sage, to follow her.
Then she moved on; and I do not believe
That she had walked ten paces on the ground,
Before her eyes had overpowered mine.
She said to me with tranquil mien: «Come on,
Come on more quickly — if I speak to you,
You will be readier to give me heed!»
When I was by her side, as duty bound,
She said to me: «Brother, why not take heart
To question me, since now we are together?»

    As it befalls those who attempt to speak
To their superiors with undue respect,
And fail to send their utterance through their ⌊teeth,
So it befell me — and in garbled language
I tried to say: «My lady, you well know
My need, and what is good for it.» And she:
«I wish from this time forth that you cast off
Timidity and shame, so that no more
You'll seem to speak like someone in a dream.
Know that the vessel which the serpent broke

Was, and is not; but let the culprit learn
That God's own vengeance fears no bullying.
Time will bring an heir to venge the eagle
That left its plumage in the car, and made
It first a monster, then the giant's prey.
For I discern — and that is why I tell you —
Some stars, which even now are close at hand,
Secure from hindrance or impediment,
Conjoining in *five hundred, one, and five,*
That, sent from God, will slay the thievish woman,
Together with the giant who sins with her.
Perchance my utterance may not persuade you,
For 'tis obscure, like Themis and the Sphinx,
And tends, like them, to cloud the intellect.
But soon the facts will be the Naiades,
Who will solve this difficult enigma:
Nor will the flocks and harvests be impaired.
Mark this, and even as I say these words,
Do you take care to teach them to all those
Who live that life which hastens unto death;
And bear in mind, while you are writing them,
Not to conceal that you have seen this tree
Which now has twice been pillaged in this place.
Whoever robs it, or tears off its boughs,
With blasphemy of deed offends his God,
Who made it holy, for His use alone.
Because he ate its fruit, the first-born soul
For full five thousand years of pain did yearn
For Him who venged this act upon himself.
Your intellect must sleep, unless it grasps
That for a special reason is the tree
So lofty, and so spreading at the top.
Had not vain thoughts so overwhelmed your mind,
Like Elsa's waters, and delight in them
Stained it, as Pyramus the mulberry,
You would in all that you have seen and heard,
Have recognized, within the moral sense,
God's justice in His ban upon the tree.

    «Because I see you with your intellect
Hardened to stone, and by this hardening
So darkened that my discourse dazzles you,
I ask that you will bear my words away:
Not written, but depicted in your mind,

Canto 33 : Dante drinks of the River Eunoë

As the pilgrim's staff is wreathed with palm.»
　«As it were wax, which cannot change the figure
Stamped on it by a seal, so is my brain
Imprinted now by you,» I answered her.
«But tell me why it is, your longed-for words
Soar so far above my comprehension,
That, seeking aid, it needs it all the more?»
　«That you may know,» she said, «your chosen
　　　　　　　　　　　　　　　　└school,

And see how ill its teaching parallels
The truths that I have uttered in my discourse—
And also, that the path which you now tread
Is just as distant from the way of God
As farthest heaven is remote from earth.»
　«I cannot recollect,» I answered her,
«That I have e'er estranged myself from you;
Nor does my conscience sting me with remorse.»
　«If you can not recall it, then take thought,»
She answered with a smile, «that you have drunk
Upon this very day of Lethe's waters.
And if from smoke a fire may be inferred,
Then your forgetfulness would seem to prove
Your will at fault, for elsewhere giving heed.
Truly, from this time forth my words shall be
Undraped—at least, as far as it is fitting
To lay them bare to your untutored sight.»
　　Both more resplendent, and with slower pace,
The sun was drawing near meridian,
Which passes here or there from different view-
Then, just as one who leads a company　└points.
Will stop if he encounter anything
Upon his path that causes him alarm,
The seven ladies halted by a shadow,
Such as a mountain casts on its cold streams,
Beneath green leaves and dark o'erhanging boughs.

And now in front of them I thought I saw
Tigris and Euphrates issue forth
From out one spring, then linger as they parted.
　«O light, O glory of the human race,
What stream is this, that gushes from one source,
Then seemingly divides itself in two?»
　　To this my question, this reply was made:
«Ask of Matilda, that she tell you of it.»
　　And then, like one who frees himself of blame,
The lovely lady said: «This, and some other
Were told to him by me; and I am sure　└things,
That Lethe's water has not hidden them.»
　　And Beatrice: «Perhaps some greater care—
Which oftentimes will rob the memory—
Has now obscured the vision of his mind.
But now look at Eunoe, that yonder flows:
Lead him there, and then, as you are wont,
Revive in him again his failing powers.»
　　Like a gentle soul that when a sign
Denotes another's will, makes no excuse,
But forthwith makes the other's will his own:
Thus, after she had taken hold of me,
The lovely one moved on; and courteously
She turned to Statius and said: «Come with him.»
　　If, reader, I had greater space for writing,
I now would sing, in part, of that sweet draught
Which never could have satiated me;
But inasmuch as I have filled the leaves
Allotted to this second canticle,
The curb of art now lets me go no farther.
From that most holy water, I returned
Made new—as trees are brought to life again
With their new foliage—purified,
And made fit for mounting to the stars.

DANTE ALIGHIERI

THE DIVINE COMEDY

PARADISO

Canto 21 : The Angels descending the Heavenly Ladder

DANTE ALIGHIERI
THE DIVINE COMEDY

PARADISO
Canto 1

THE glory of Him who moveth everything
Penetrates the universe, and shines
In one part more, and in another less.
Within that heaven which most receives His light
I have been, and seen things past the knowledge
Or power of any who comes back to tell—
Because, as it approaches its desire,
Our intellect so deepens as it seeks,
That memory has not the power to follow.
As much, however, of the holy realm
As I have treasured up within my mind,
Shall now become the subject of my song.

O good Apollo! For this final task
Make me such a vessel of thy power,
That I may merit the beloved laurel!
Thus far, one of the twinned Parnassan peaks
Has been enough for me: I now need both
To aid my struggle in this last arena.
Enter my breast, and breathe in me thy strength—
That strength by which thou drewest Marsyas
From out the sheath that covered o'er his limbs.

O power divine! If thou but lend thy aid
So that I may make manifest the shadow
Which that blest realm impressed upon my mind,
Thou'lt see me come unto thy chosen tree,
And crown my forehead with its leaves—whereof
My lofty theme, and thou, will make me worthy.

So rarely, father, have those leaves been culled
To grace a Caesar's triumph, or a poet's—
Owing to fault and shame in man's desire—
'Twould seem Peneus' leaf should bring delight
To Delphi's joyous shrine, whene'er it rouses
Longing for its crown in human breast.
A little spark ignites a mighty flame:
And after me perchance with worthier song
Prayer shall be made, that Cyrrha may respond.

Through divers passages, the world's great
Rises to mortal men; but from that place   ⌐lamp
Where crosses three are joined by circles four
It issues with a better augury,
Together with a more propitious star,
To mould and stamp the substance of the world.
Close to this pass for us the day had dawned,
While here the sun had set; thus, where we stood,
All that hemisphere was bathed in light,
The other dark—when I saw Beatrice
Turn to the left, and gaze upon the sun,
As never eagle fixed his eye upon it.
Just as a second ray will issue forth
Reflected from the first, to rise again,
Like a pilgrim wishing to return:
So by her action my own will was formed,
And I too fixed my gaze upon the sun,
Holding it there beyond our human wont.

129

For by virtue of that place designed
As man's abode, much is permitted there
Which here our faculties cannot attain.
Not long did I endure it—nor so little
But that I saw it sparkle round about
Like iron that comes glowing from the flame.
Then, on a sudden, light was heaped on light,
Just as if that One who has the power
Had with another sun adorned the sky.

 The eyes of Beatrice were wholly fixed
Upon the eternal spheres; and my own eyes,
No longer turned aloft, were fixed on her.
From that sweet contemplation I became
Like Glaucus, when he tasted of the grass
That made him consort of the ocean gods.
How I attained to this transhuman state,
No words can tell: let this example, then,
Suffice for him whom grace permits to feel it.
If I was but that part of me which Thou,
O Love that rulest heaven, didst last create,
Thou knowest, who didst lift me by Thy light.
That sphere which turns forever by Thy love,
Had focused my attention on itself
By means of Thy celestial harmony:
And kindled by the flaming of the sun,
Before me lay a reach of heavens far wider
Than lake e'er formed by river or by rain.

 The strangeness of the sounds and of the light
Enkindled a desire to know their cause,
Keener than any I had felt before.
And she—who saw me as I see myself—
Opening her mouth ere I had opened mine,
Addressed me thus, to soothe my troubled spirit:
«Thou seemst to make thyself so ignorant,
With false imagining, thou dost not see
What thou wouldst see if thou hadst cast it off.
For thou art not on earth, as thou believest;
But lightning, flying from its own true sphere,
Ne'er sped as now thou speedest up to thine!»

 If by these smiling words I was relieved
Of my first doubt, still more was I entangled
Within a new one, and I said to her:
«Already was I resting with content

From my amazement: but now I wonder
How I can e'er ascend through these light bodies.»
 When this was said, she sighed most piteously
And turned her eyes upon me, with that look
A mother turns on her delirious child.
«All things,» she said, «whatever they may be,
Have order in themselves: this is the plan
That makes the universe like unto God.
It is herein that these exalted creatures
Behold the imprint of the eternal power—
The end for which this order was established.
Within it, natural things are all disposed
According to their several destinies,
In varying nearness to their common source.
Thence they issue forth to different havens
Upon the mighty ocean of existence,
Endowed each one with instinct to proceed.
This instinct carries fire toward the moon;
It is the motive force in mortal hearts;
It binds together and unites the earth.

 «Now by the arrows of this bow are struck
Not only creatures unintelligent,
But also those with love and understanding.
Providence, which governs all these things,
Maintains in calm tranquility that heaven
In which the swiftest of the spheres revolves.
And thither now, as to a site decreed,
The virtue of that bowstring bears us on,
That always aims its shafts at joyous marks.
'Tis true, indeed, that oftentimes the form
Will fail to harmonize with the design,
When the material is deaf to answer.
Then from its course the creature deviates;
For though impelled toward the highest heaven,
It has the power to bend in other ways—
Just as when fire is seen to fall from clouds—
If the first impulse of its natural bent,
Turned by false pleasure, drives it to the earth.

 «No more, if I judge rightly, shouldst thou ⌊marvel
At thy ascent, than at a falling rill
That plunges from a mountain to the depths.
'Twould be as strange, hadst thou stayed down ⌊below

When freed from earth's impediment, as if
On earth a living flame were motionless.»
Then she turned her face again to heaven.

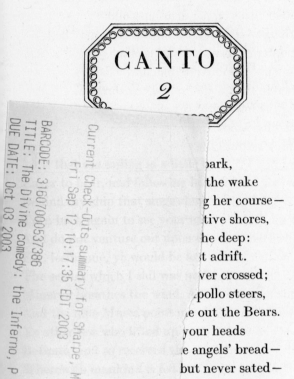

CANTO
2

. . . ark,
. . . the wake
. . . g her course—
. . . tive shores,
. . . he deep:
. . . st adrift.
. . . ver crossed;
. . . pollo steers,
. . . e out the Bears.
. . . your heads
. . . e angels' bread—
. . . but never sated—
. . . upon the deep
By keeping in my . . . at runs before you
Upon the water that turns smooth again.
Those glorious voyagers who sailed to Colchis
Were not more wonder-struck than ye shall be,
When they saw Jason harnessed to the plough.

That inborn and perpetual thirst for heaven
Created with mankind, bore us away
As swiftly as the movement of the skies.
Beatrice gazed aloft, and I on her;
And in the time, mayhap, it takes a shaft
To reach its mark, and fly, and leave the notch,
I saw I had arrived before a marvel
That drew my whole attention to itself.

She to whom my inmost thoughts were known,
As blithe as she was fair, now turned and said:
«Direct thy mind with gratitude to God
Who has united us with heaven's first star.»

It seemed as though a cloud were covering us,

Solid and smooth and dense, and sparkling forth
As 'twere a diamond the sun had struck.
Within itself that everlasting pearl
Received us, though remaining undivided,
As water can receive a ray of light.
If I was body—though here we cannot think
That one dimension could enclose another,
Which must be so, if body enter body—
Then should desire the more enkindle us
To stand before that essence where 'tis shown
How God and our own nature are united.
That will be seen there, which we hold by faith—
Not demonstrated, but self-evident,
Even as primal truth that man believes.

I answered: «As devoutly as I can,
My lady, I now render thanks to Him
Who has removed me from the mortal world.
But tell me, what are those dark spots I see?
Are they those which, seen by men on earth,
Give rise to all the fables about Cain?»

She smiled a little ere she made reply:
«If mortals err in forming their opinion
Even when the keys of sense do not unlock,
Surely no wonder should amaze thee now:
For thou canst see, I think, that reason flies
When following the senses on clipped wings.
But tell me, what is thy opinion of it?»

And I: «What here appears to be diverse
Is caused, I think, by bodies rare and dense.»

And she: «Thou wilt most certainly perceive
That thy belief is steeped in fallacy,
If thou but listen to my refutation.
The eighth sphere is ablaze with many lights
That both in quality and quantity
May be remarked to be of varied aspects.
If this were caused by bodies rare and dense,
Then there would be one single power in all,
Distributed in just degree among them.
It follows hence that powers diverse must be
The fruits of different formal principles,
Which, thou wouldst say, must perish, all but one.
Besides, did rarity cause that opaqueness
About which thou dost ask, this planet then

Would either lack its substance, through and
Or else, even as a body must apportion ⌊through,
Its fat and lean—in that same way—this sphere
Would interchange the pages of its book.
Were it the first, it would be manifest
During the sun's eclipse, when light would shine
Through the moon, as though it had no substance.
As this is not the case, we must discuss
The other theory. If it befall
That I refute it, I shall prove thee wrong.

«Now if this rarity hold not throughout
The body of the moon, there then must be
A point where dense will end, and rare begin.
And from this point another body's ray
Would be reflected backward, in such wise
As color is reflected from a mirror.
Now haply thou wilt argue that the ray
Will there appear much darker than the rest,
Being reflected from a greater distance.
From this contention, an experiment
—Which ever is the fountainhead of science—
Can set thee free, if thou but make the trial.
Take, then, three mirrors, and let two of them
Be set at equal distance from thyself,
The third set farther off, between the others.
Face toward them, and behind thy back install
A lamp which so illuminates all three
That thou canst see its image in them all.
Thou wilt perceive that the more distant one,
Reflecting least in quantity of light,
Will be as brilliant as the other two.

«Just as the soil, attacked by sun's warm rays,
When lying 'neath the snow, becomes denuded
Both of its former color and the cold:
So thee, denuded likewise of thine error,
I wish to animate with light so living
That it will scintillate when put before thee.

«Within that heaven where rules the peace
A body turns, that in its influence ⌊divine
Holds everything that is contained therein.
Next comes that heaven which has so many lights,
Distributing this influence among them
That are contained within it, yet distinct.

The other spheres, in varying degrees,
Dispose, to their own ends, their characters
And the creative seeds contained in them.
Thus do these organs of the universe
Function from grade to grade, as thou shouldst
They draw from up above, and act below. ⌊see;
Mark well how by this reasoning I advance
To reach the truth which thou desirest,
So thou mayest learn to hold the ford alone.
The movement and the influence of the spheres
Must be inspired by blessed agencies,
Just as a hammer works the blacksmith's will.
That heaven, embellished with so many stars,
Placed by the mind that causes it to turn,
Receives the image and becomes a seal.
And as the soul within your mortal dust
Permeating through your body's members,
Is conformed to suit its various needs:
Even so the governing intelligence
Spreads its excellence among the stars,
Though still revolving on its unity.

«Virtue diverse creates a different alloy
With that most precious body which it quickens,
In which 'tis fused as life is fused in you.
And from that blissful nature whence it flows,
This mingled virtue can shine through the body
As joy shines through the pupil of an eye.
From this virtue—not from dense and rare—
Proceeds that difference 'twixt light and light;
This is the formal principle which causes
The dark and light, according to its worth.»

CANTO
3

Tнат sun which first had warmed my heart
Had now, by argument and refutation ⌊with love,
Revealed to me the lovely face of truth:

And I, to own that I had been convinced,
Lifted my head, but only just so far
As was required to make my words come forth.
But now before my eyes appeared a sight
Which riveted my gaze on it alone,
So that I lost all thought of my confession.

    As through transparent panes of polished ⌊glass,
Or in water clear and undisturbed,
Yet shallow, so the bottom can be seen,
The outlines of our faces seem so faint,
That even a pearl upon a forehead white
Does not come back less quickly to our eyes:
Thus faintly, I saw faces prone to speak —
Whereat I erred in manner opposite
To that which made Narcissus love the fountain.
As soon as I became aware of them,
Thinking they were reflections in a glass,
I turned, to see whose images they were.
But I saw nothing; so I turned again
And gazed into the eyes of my sweet guide,
Which glowed with holy love as she was smiling.
«Be not astounded that I smile,» she said,
«At thy childish thought; because, as yet,
It rests not confidently on the truth,
But turns thee aimlessly as is its wont.
These are true substances which thou dost see,
Placed here for failure to fulfil their vows;
Speak with them and hear them and believe:
For that veracious light which satisfies them,
Permits them not to turn their feet from it.»

    Now to that shade who seemed to be most
I turned myself, and haltingly began, ⌊eager
Like one distracted by too great desire:
«O spirit, foreordained to heavenly bliss,
Who, in the rays diffused by grace divine
Art tasting sweetness inconceivable —
Much will it please me, if thou satisfy
My wish to know thy destiny and name.»

    Promptly with smiling eyes she answered me:
«Our charity may never lock its door
Upon a just request — no more than that
Which wills that all its court be like itself.
I was a virgin sister in the world,

And if thy memory look backward well,
My greater beauty will not hide me from thee,
But thou wilt recognize in me Piccarda —
Placed here with these other happy souls,
And blessed in this sphere that slowest turns.
Know then that our affections, which are fired
By naught except the Holy Spirit's bliss,
Rejoice at being formed as He ordains.
And this allotted place, which seems so lowly,
Is given us because we broke our vows,
Neglecting them in some particular.»

    And I: «In your transfigured countenances
There shines I know not what of the divine,
That changes all that we recall of you;
Therefore I was not quick to know thy face.
Yet what thou tellest me, is now an aid,
To recognizing you more easily.
But tell me: ye that here abide in bliss,
Do ye desire a more exalted place —
For wider view, — or state more intimate?»

    At first she smiled, as did the other shades,
And then she answered me with such delight
That love's first fire appeared to glow within her:
«The influence of love restrains our will
So that we yearn for naught but what we have,
And are not set athirst for other things.
Were we to wish for more exalted places,
'Twould be at variance with the will of Him
Who has assigned us this for our abode.
Such variance, thou canst see, would be amiss,
Since to exist in love is here required —
And if thou wilt take thought upon its nature.
Nay, 'tis essential to this blessed life
To hold itself within the will divine:
And hence our wills are made as one with it.
Thus, as we dwell within the various spheres,
This unity of will gives sweet content
To all the realm, and to its King as well.
His will, that binds our own, is peace to us:
It is the ocean to which all things flow
Created by the will, or formed by nature.»

    Then was it clear to me, how all the heavens
Are paradise; and yet the highest grace

Is not bestowed on all in like degree.
Just as one food perchance will satisfy,
While for another appetite remains,
So that we scorn the one and crave the other:
Thus did I plead, in act and by my words,
To learn from her what was the web in which
She had not drawn the shuttle to the end.

«A perfect life,» she said, «and special merit
Enshrine a lady in a higher heaven,
To follow whom the veil and robe are donned
By women, so that they may watch till death
And sleep beside that Bridegroom who accepts
All vows which love conforms unto His will.
To follow her, I fled from out the world,
And while I was a maiden, donned the habit
And pledged me to the pathway of her order.
Thereafter men more used to ill than good
Ravished me forth from her sweet nunnery:
And what my life was afterward, God knoweth!
This other splendor that appears to thee
Here upon my right, from whom shines forth
All of the brilliance that our sphere contains—
To her as well my story will apply.
She was a nun, and likewise from her head
The holy wimple's shade was snatched away.
But after she was to the world returned
Against her will, and contrary to custom,
Her heart continued faithful to her vows.
This is the glorious spirit of great Constance,
Who by the second stormy lord of Swabia
Conceived the third and last of all that house.»
After she had spoken, she began
Chanting *Ave Maria*; while she sang
She vanished, like a plummet dropped in water.

My eyes, which followed her as best they
On losing sight of her, now turned upon ⌊could,
That object which they longed still more to see.
To Beatrice their gaze again turned back;
But she flashed forth on me such radiant beams,
My sight was scarcely able to endure them:
This made me slower in my questioning.

CANTO
4

BETWEEN two viands, each in like degree
Ready and tempting, a man, though free, would
Before he would select one for his meal: ⌊starve
And so a lamb will stand between the ravenings
Of two fierce wolves, in equal dread of both;
Or dog stand wavering between two does.
Therefore I neither praise nor blame myself
If, urged in equal measure by my doubts,
I yet kept silence—since it had to be.
Mute I remained, however; my desire
Was painted in my eyes, which spoke my cause
More ardently than if set forth by speech.

Now Beatrice acted even as Daniel did
When he appeased Nebuchadnezzar's wrath,
Through which he had become unjustly cruel.
«I plainly see how each of two desires,»
She said, «attracts thee; thy anxiety
Is so constrained that it can not breathe forth.
Thou reasonest thus: 'If good will endures,
How can it be that violence of others
Lessen for me the measure of my worth?'
Moreover, still another doubt assails thee—
That souls, in harmony with Plato's thought,
Now seem to be returning to the stars.
These are the questions that within thy wish
Are striving equally to be explained:
I first shall treat of that which has most venom.

«Among the seraphim, not he who walks
Nearest to God, nor Samuel, nor Moses,
Nor either of the Johns, or even Mary
Has destined station in a heaven different
From that which holds the souls you just have
Nor is their blessed state of greater length; ⌊seen,
But all of them adorn the empyrean
In varying degrees of blessedness,

Canto 3 : Piccarda Donati, and Souls whose Vows had been broken

According as they feel the breath eternal.
And if thou saw'st them here, 'twas not because
They had been placed in this celestial sphere:
They were but showing thee this lowest heaven.
'Tis thus the human mind must be addressed;
For only through the senses can it grasp
What later it makes fit for intellect.
Therefore the Holy Scripture condescends
To meet your faculties, and speaks of God
As having hands and feet, but means it not;
The Holy Church portrays with human aspect
Michael and Gabriel, and that other one
By whom Tobias was made whole again.
Now what Timaeus says concerning souls,
Does not resemble what can here be seen,
Because he credits all that he recounts.
He says the soul returns to its own star,
Believing that it once was parted from it
When nature fused the body and the soul.
Perhaps his creed contains a different sense,
Divergent from the meaning of his words,
And so perchance is worthy of respect.
For if he means that to these spheres returns
The credit of their influence, or the blame,
It may be that his arrow hits some truth.
This principle, but little understood,
Once so misled the world, it went astray
In naming Jove, and Mercury, and Mars.

«Thy other doubt has less of venom in it,
Because the mischief that is hidden there
Can never lead thy soul astray from me.
That heavenly justice should appear unjust
In mortal eyes, is argument of faith,
Not of heretical iniquity.
But seeing that your human intellect
Is sound enough to penetrate this truth,
I will content thee, answering thy request.
If it be violence, although the victim
Contributes naught to him who uses force—
Upon that score, these souls were not excused.
For will can not be quenched against its will,
But rises, just as nature does in fire,
Though turned a thousand times by violence.

Because, when bends the will—or much, or little—
It yields but to some force, as did these souls;
For they were able to regain the cloister.
Now had their will been perfect—even as that
Which held St. Lawrence on the gridiron,
And Mucius to the burning of his hand—
It would, when they were free, have turned them
⌊back
Into that path from which they had been dragged.
But such a will as this is rare indeed.
And by my words, if thou hast heeded them
Even as thou shouldst, the argument is quashed
That yet would have disturbed thee many times.

«But now another pass confronts thine eyes,
And of thyself thou ne'er couldst issue from it—
Such is its nature—ere thy strength would fail.
I surely have instilled within thy mind
That souls who are in bliss can never lie,
Because the source of truth is ever near them.
And yet thou must have heard Piccarda say,
That Constance held affection for the veil—
So that she seems to contradict me here.
Often, my brother, to avoid some peril
An action has been done reluctantly
That ne'er, indeed, should have been done at all:
'Twas thus Alcmaeon, at his sire's behest
Murdered his mother—filial piety
Availing but to make him pitiless.
Upon this point I wish thee to reflect—
That force can be commingled with the will
To act so that they cannot be excused.
Will absolute does not consent to wrong
Save for the fear it has, should it resist,
Of falling into even greater trouble.
Hence when Piccarda uses that expression,
She means the absolute, and I the other;
So that, together, both of us speak truth.»
Such was the flowing of the holy stream
That issued from the source whence all truth
And thus were my desires set at rest.   ⌊springs;
«O thou beloved of the Primal Lover,»
I said, «thou whose discourse so flows o'er me,
Ever to warm and quicken me the more!

My own affection is not deep enough
To render thanks commensurate with thy grace:
But let Him honor thee who has the power.
I clearly see that human intellect
Can ne'er be sated till it gain the truth,
Beyond which naught of verity extends.
Like a beast within its lair, it rests
Within the truth divine, when once attained:
Attain it can, or else our hopes are void.
Hence at the very foot of truth will spring
Offshoots of doubt; but nature leads us on
From height to height until we reach the summit.
O lady, it is this that gives me strength,
And bids me ask you, with all reverence,
About another truth, obscure to me:
I wish to know if you who dwell in heaven
Can profit by good works performed by man
As satisfaction for your broken vows.»

　　The eyes of Beatrice now looked on me
Filled with the sparks of love, and so divine
That all my mortal powers were put to flight:
With eyes cast down, I all but lost myself.

CANTO
5

If in the heat of love I flame on thee
Beyond the measure that is seen on earth,
So that thine eyes are dazzled, marvel not.
The cause of this lies in my perfect vision,
Which, according as it apprehends, can move
Straight to that selfsame good it has perceived.
I clearly see how in thy consciousness,
The eternal light is shining forth already,
The very sight of which enkindles love.
And should aught else seduce this love of thine,
'Tis nothing but some vestige of that light—
Ill recognized—which there shines forth from it.

Thou didst ask if by another's prayer
A vow yet unfulfilled may be redeemed,
So that the soul be saved from controversy.»
Thus did Beatrice begin this canto;
And like a man who will not stay his speech,
She now maintained her sacred argument:
　「The greatest gift God's bounty has created,
The gift that most conforms to His own good,
That He himself of all most precious holds,
Is freedom of the will, wherewith are blest
All creatures that possess intelligence;
But they, and only they, are so endowed.
From this, to thee will now be evident
The exceeding value of a vow, if made
So God accept it when thou offerest it.
To close this compact between God and man,
That precious treasure must be sacrificed,
Though this is brought about by its own act.
What can be rendered, then, in recompense?
To use for other good what thou hast offered,
Would do good work, but with ill-gotten gain.
　「Upon the greater point, thou art assured;
But since our Holy Church gives dispensation
In this regard—which seems to void my truth—
Thou yet shalt sit at table for a while,
Because partaking of such heavy food
Requires some further aid for its digestion.
Open thy mind to what I now reveal,
And treasure it therein: for ill he learns
Who hearing, yet retains not what he hears.
　「This sacrifice is of two things combined:
The first, the very substance it is made of;
The other is the covenant itself.
The latter is ne'er cancelled if not kept—
Thou wilt remember that it was of this
I spoke a while ago with such precision.
And that is why the Hebrews were obliged
To make an offering only; 'twas allowed,
As thou shouldst know, to change the sacrifice.
The other—which is known to thee as substance—
May well be of such nature as permits
Exchange for other substance, without fault.
But let no person venture to exchange

Canto 5 : The Host of Myriad Glowing Souls

PARADISO: CANTO 5

His shoulder's burden at his own discretion,
Save that he turn both white and yellow key.
For every permutation is as naught,
If that which is put down, be not contained
In that assumed—even as four in six.
Hence anything of such intrinsic weight
That by itself it bears down every scale,
Is not redeemed by any other effort.

«A vow must never be considered lightly.
Be faithful—not unreasonably so,
Like Jepthah when he made his offering.
Better that he had said: 'I have done wrong,'
Than keeping faith to do a greater ill.
Insensate, too, that Grecian king, who made
Iphigenia mourn her beauty's loss,
Making both wise and foolish mourn for her,
When they were told of that strange sacrifice.

«O Christians, be more careful as ye move!
And be not like a feather to the wind,
Nor think that every water will absolve you!
Ye have the Testament, both New and Old,
The Shepherd of the Church to guide your steps:
Let these suffice to lead you to salvation!
If lust for evil cry to you aught else,
Be men, not silly sheep, so that the Jew
Who dwells among you, may not laugh in scorn;
And be not like the lamb that leaves its mother,
Foolish and wanton, fighting with itself
In useless frolics, for its own delight.»
Thus Beatrice to me, even as I write it;
Then, burning with desire, she turned again
Unto that region which is most alive.
Her silence and transfigured countenance
Held still my eager mind, which yet desired
To seek solution of some further doubts.

Just like an arrow that has struck its mark
Before the trembling bowstring is at rest:
So sped we on, and reached the second kingdom.
As she was entering in that heaven's light,
My lady beamed with such a radiant joy
That the very planet shone the brighter.
And if the star itself was changed and smiled,
What, then, did I become, by nature formed

Susceptible to change of every kind!

As in a fish pond that is still and clear,
The fish dart forward, if something is cast in,
Because they hope that they may get some food:
Just so, I saw a myriad glowing splendors
Drawing toward us, and by each was said:
«Lo, here is one who will increase our loves!»
And as each one came nearer, I could see
That it was full of happiness, which glowed
Brightly from its blessed radiance.

Consider, reader, if what here begins
Were to proceed no farther: thou wouldst yearn
And have a grievous craving to know more.
Then imagine how from these bright spirits
I longed to know their names and their estates,
As soon as they were manifest to me.

«O being born to good, whom grace permits
To see the thrones of everlasting triumph
Ere thou hast been released from earthly strife!
We are enkindled by that glorious flame
Extending through the heaven: then sate thyself,
If thou wouldst seek enlightenment from us.»
One of the pious spirits thus addressed me.

«Speak, speak with confidence,» said Beatrice,
«And trust them, as if each one were a god.»
«I see that thou art nested in thy light,
And that thou drawest it from out thine eyes,
Because they beam with radiance when thou
⌊smilest.

But yet I know not who thou art, or why,
O noble soul, thou hast been given rank
Within that sphere another's rays conceal.»
When I had done, I turned to face that flame
Which first had spoken to me—whereupon
It now grew far more radiant than before.

And as the sun, which by excess of light
Conceals itself, when heat has cleared away
The tempering influence of surrounding vapors:
So, by increasing joy, that holy shape
Concealed itself from me in its own radiance;
And thus enfolded, it replied to me
In such wise as the following canto sings.

137

CANTO
6

AFTER Constantine turned back the eagle
Against the heavens' course that it had followed
Behind the footsteps of Lavinia's spouse,
For full two hundred years the bird of God
Stood firm on Europe's utmost boundary,
Hard by those mountains whence it first set forth.
From there it governed all the world that lay
Beneath the shadow of its sacred wings;
From hand to hand its rule came down to mine.
Caesar I was: I am Justinian,
Who at the bidding of the Holy Spirit
Removed from law what was superfluous.

«Ere I assumed the burden of that task,
'Twas my belief Christ's nature was but one,
Not more; and with such faith I was content.
But blessed Agapetus, who was then
Pastor supreme, exhorted me, and thus
His words directed me to the pure Faith.
Him I believed; and what he taught to me
I now see clearly, even as thou canst see
That contradictories are false and true.
When I turned my footsteps to the church,
It pleased God of His grace to breathe upon me;
And to that mighty task I gave myself.
I gave my arms to Belisarius,
To whose right hand the heavens were so
                                        ⌊conjoined,
That 'twas a sign that I myself should rest.

«Though here my answer to the first inquiry
Comes to a stop, its character demands
I add a sequel to it, to the end
That thou mayst see with how much proper right
They move against that ensign sacrosanct —
Both he who has usurped it, and its foe.
Behold what virtue makes it venerable!»

And he began the story, from that hour
When Pallas died to give it sovereignty.
«Thou knowest that it dwelt in Alba Longa
Three centuries or more, till at the end
The three upheld its cause against the three.
Its deeds thou knowest: first, the Sabine wrong;
Lucretia's sorrow; then the seven kings,
And conquests of the nations round about it.
Thou knowest what that emblem once achieved,
'Gainst Brennus by the illustrious Romans borne,
And Pyrrhus too and his confederates.
And later came Torquatus; Quinctius,
Surnamed for his neglected locks; the Decii
And Fabii, whose fame I gladly sing.
It brought to dust the haughty Arabs' pride,
Who with the hosts of Hannibal once scaled
The Alpine rocks from which, O Po, thou comest.
Under that eagle, Scipio and Pompey
Won triumph in their youth; below that hill
Where thou wast born, it showed its cruelty.

«About that time when all of heaven decreed
To bring the world back to its calm estate,
Caesar, by will of Rome, assumed that ensign;
And now were known the imperial eagle's deeds
From Var to Rhine, on Iser, Seine, and Saône,
In every valley whence the Rhone is filled.
That deed, when it departed from Ravenna
And leaped the Rubicon, was done so swiftly
That neither tongue nor pen could follow it.
It turned its legions backward into Spain:
Then to Durazzo, and Pharsalia smote,
So that the blow was felt beyond the Nile.
Revisiting Antandros, Simois —
From whence it first set forth — and Hector's tomb,
It now marched on again, to Ptolemy's woe.
Thence, like a thunderbolt, it fell on Juba,
And afterward turned back upon your west
Where it had heard great Pompey's trumpet blast.
«And for the second standard-bearer's deeds
Brutus and Cassius now bewail in hell;
Perugia and Modena were raped;
Still weeping is the saddened Cleopatra,
Who, fleeing from the eagle's conquering hosts,

Sought from the asp a sudden frightful death.
With him the eagle reached the Red Sea's banks,
And through his government the world knew
⌊peace,
So that the shrine of Janus remained closed.

«But what the glorious standard that I sing
Attained before, and afterward achieved
Throughout the earthly realm beneath its sway,
Seems paltry, and its former lustre dims,
When our third Caesar's deeds are contemplated
With pure affection and unclouded eye.
For heavenly justice, which inspires me,
Vouchsafed to it, through him of whom I speak,
The glory of avenging wrath divine.
Now marvel here at what I shall unfold!
With Titus, it sped afterward to wreak
Vengeance for vengeance of the ancient sin.
And when the Lombard tooth bit Holy Church,
Beneath that eagle's wings came Charlemagne
With all his conquering hosts, to succor her.

«Now canst thou judge of those whom I accused,
And of their wicked deeds, which are the cause
Of all your tribulations and your ills.
The one sets up the fleur-de-lis of gold;
The other takes the eagle for his party,
So that 'tis hard to tell the greater fault.
Let Ghibelline intrigue be carried on
Beneath some other ensign: he goes ill
Who dares to part this sacred one from justice!
Let not this newer Charles and his Guelph hosts
Attempt to strike it: let him dread those talons
Which flayed a lion mightier than he!
Many a time ere now have sons bewailed
Their fathers' sins—and let him not believe
That for his lilies, God will change His arms!

«Know that this little planet is adorned
With spirits who have striven on earth to win
Honor and fame among their fellow men.
And when mankind's desires thus go astray,
It follows that the rays of love divine
Move upward—of necessity—less swiftly.
Our recompense according to our worth
Is part of our delight: for we perceive

That they are neither less nor more than right.
Hence living justice sweetens our affection,
So that it never can be turned aside
To any evil or iniquity.
Divers voices make sweet melodies:
So, in this life of ours, the various blessings
Produce soft harmony among the spheres.

«And here, within this present pearly sphere,
Shines forth the spirit that was Romeo,
Whose great and noble work was ill repaid.
The people of Provence, who strove against him,
Have not the laugh: he treads an evil road
Who uses others' deeds to their own ill!
Four daughters fair had Raymond Berenger,
And each was made a queen by Romeo,
A pilgrim and a man of low estate!
Yet Raymond by malignant words was moved
To ask a reckoning from this upright man—
Who paid him back with seven and five for ten.
And thereon he departed, poor and old;
And if the world but knew the heart he had
While begging crusts of bread from place to place,
Though much it praises him, 'twould praise
⌊him more.»

CANTO
7

HOSANNAH *sanctus Deus Sabaoth*
Superillustrans claritate tue
Felices ignes horum malachoth!
'Twas thus, revolving to its melody,
That spirit, upon whom now a twofold light
Shone with redoubled brilliance, sang to me.
He and the others trod the sacred dance,
And suddenly, like sparks exceeding swift,
Were lost to sight and sped into the distance.

I was in doubt, and said within myself:

«Tell her, tell her—O tell it to my lady
Who with sweet distillations slakes my thirst!»
But then that reverence which governs me,
Even by BE and ICE, bowed me down
Like one asleep; howbeit, not for long
Did Beatrice permit me to remain so.

     The radiant smile with which she spoke to me
Would gladden even one burning at the stake:
«I know, by my infallible advisement,
'How can a vengeance that itself is just,
Yet justly be avenged?' has set thee thinking.
But speedily I'll set thy mind at rest;
And listen to me, that thou mayst receive
The gift of a great doctrine from my words.

    «That man who ne'er was born, in not enduring
The curb set on his will for his own good,
By self-damnation damned posterity.
And hence upon the earth the human race
Lay sick for many centuries in error,
Until it pleased God's Word to go below
To join unto Himself in His own person—
By that sole act of His eternal love—
Nature, so remote from its Creator.

    «Now turn thy mind to that which I expound.
This nature, thus united with its Maker
Was pure and good, such as it was created,
But by itself was cast from paradise,
Because it turned aside, by its own act,
From its own life and from the path of truth.
Therefore the penalty the cross inflicted,
If measured by the nature thus assumed,
Was juster than all other penalties;
But ne'er was one of such iniquity,
If we regard the Person who did suffer,
In whom this nature had been so conjoined.
Hence from one action issued things diverse:
One single death pleased both the Jews and God.
Thereat the whole earth shook, the heavens
                             ⌊opened.

Henceforth thou readily shouldst understand
If it be said to thee that vengeance just
By just tribunal later was avenged.

    «But I perceive thy mind is now constrained,

Passing from thought to thought within a knot
From which it anxiously awaits release.
Thou sayest: 'What I hear, I understand;
But something else lies hidden: Why did God
Ordain this means alone for our redemption?'
This decree, my brother, lies concealed
From every person whose intelligence
Has not been ripened in the flame of love.
Howbeit, since man gazes at this mark
Full often, yet but little comprehends it,
I'll show thee why this was the worthiest means.

    «Goodness divine, which from itself drives off
All envy, burns forever in itself;
Sparkling, it reveals the eternal beauties.
Now what directly from it is distilled
Is everlasting; when it sets its seal,
The imprint of it ne'er can be removed.
And that which rains directly down from it
Is wholly free, because it is not subject
To influence of such more recent things.
It most conforms with good, hence gives most joy:
For holy love, which beams on everything,
Is most alive in what is like it most.

    «Of all these things mankind has benefit;
If even one be lacking, he perforce
Falls from the height of his nobility.
'Tis sin alone that takes away his franchise,
Making him unlike the good supreme,
So that he shines but little in its radiance;
And he can ne'er regain his former worth
Unless, with penalties for sin's delights,
He fills the voids created by his faults.
When, in its seed, your nature wholly sinned,
It was removed from all these dignities
Even as it was removed from paradise;
Nor could it of itself recover them—
If thou take thought—by any other way,
Unless it passed by one of these two fords—
Either that God, of His own clemency,
Remitted the debt; or that man himself
Made just atonement for his wickedness.

    «Fix now thine eyes within the deep abyss
Of the eternal counsel: concentrate

As closely as thou canst upon my words.
Never could man, within his limitations,
Have rendered satisfaction—lacking will
To stoop as low in subsequent obedience
As in his disobedience he aspired.
And hence was man excluded from the power
Of making reparation by himself;
Therefore 'twas meet that God, by his own
⎣methods,
Should re-establish man in perfect life—
Either by one means, or by both combined.
But as an action ever is more prized
In just proportion as it manifests
The goodness in the heart from which it springs:
So the truth divine, which sets its stamp
On all the world, was willing to proceed
By both its ways to lift you up again;
And 'twixt the primal day and final night
There ne'er has been, nor will there ever be,
Such an exalted act, by either way.
More bounteous was God, to give Himself
That man might lift himself by his own worth,
Than if direct forgiveness had been granted;
And all the other methods would have failed,
And justice have remained unsatisfied,
Had not the Son of God become incarnate.

«Now, that thy desires may be fulfilled,
I shall turn back, to clear a certain point
That thou mayst see it even as I myself.
Thou sayest: 'I see the water, see the fire,
The air, the earth, and all their combinations
Turn to corruption, lasting not for long.
These, however, are created things':
Therefore, if what I have said be true,
They ought to be secure against corruption.
The angels, brother, and this perfect place
In which thou art, were made, as one might say,
Just as they are, in their entire being;
But those same elements which thou hast named,
And substances which are produced from them,
Are all informed by a created virtue.
Created was the matter of their being;
Created was the informing influence

Within the stars that circle round about them.
The rays and motion of these holy lights
Draw out, from its potential elements,
The soul of every brute, and of the plants.
The good supreme inspires your life directly,
Instilling it with everlasting love,
So that for evermore ye long for it.
And hence an argument for resurrection
May be induced—if thou consider too
The manner in which human flesh was formed
When man's first progenitors were made.»

CANTO 8

THE world believed, when in its heathen peril,
That lovely Cypria sent down mad love
From the third epicycle, where she turns.
Hence not to her alone in times of old
Did antique nations in their fallacy
Give praise with sacrifice and votive cries:
They honored Cupid and Dione too,
One as her son, the other as her mother,
And told how Cupid sat on Dido's lap.
And after her from whom I take my prelude,
They named that star to which the sun pays court
Sometimes in front, and sometimes from behind.

I did not know that we had risen there;
But proof was furnished by my lady's aspect,
For now I saw her lovelier than before.
And as within a flame a spark is seen,
Or in a choir a single voice is heard
To come and go while others hold their song:
Even so within that light were other lights
Revolving in a circle fast or slowly,
According as they had eternal vision.
Never from icy cloud did any wind
Or lightning bolt descend so swift to earth,

141

THE DIVINE COMEDY

But that it would appear restrained and sluggish
To one who had beheld those lights divine
Approach us, as they ceased that circling dance
First started by the seraphim on high.
From out the midst of those who first appeared,
Hosannas sounded, in a strain so sweet
That ever afterward I longed for it.

    Now one of them drew near, and said to me:
«We all are ready here to do thy pleasure
In order that thou mayst have joy of us.
In one orbit, and with the selfsame thirst,
We course in circles with the heavenly princes
To whom thou once, when in the world, didst say:
'Ye whose wisdom moves the third high heaven.'
So filled with love are we, that for thy pleasure,
A little quiet will not be less sweet.»

    After my eyes had reverently turned
Toward my lady, and were made content
By sweet assurances of her approval,
They turned again unto that gleaming soul
That made so large a promise of itself.
«Say who ye are,» I said, with deep affection.

    How greatly did that spirit now increase
In size and brilliance, from that new delight
My words had added to its joy! It said:
«The world possessed me but a little while;
Had it been more, mankind would never know
Much of evil that will come to pass.
My gladness, radiating now about me,
Holds me concealed from thee, even as a creature
Shrouded in its covering of silk.
Much didst thou love me, and with ample cause:
Had I remained below, I could have shown thee
My love in fruit—thou knowest but the leaves.
    «That eastern bank, whose shores are laved by
                                  ⌊Rhone
After Sorgue's waters are with his combined,
Awaited me as lord, in course of time;
Ausonia's horn as well, that is begirt
By Bari and Gaeta and Catona,
From Tronto's estuary unto Verde's.
My brow already bore the shining crown
Of those dominions which the Danube waters

After it leaves behind its German banks;
And fair Trinacria, that's blackened o'er
Not by Typhoeus, but by sulphurous smoke
'Twixt Pachynus and Pelorus, on that gulf
Which most receives the brunt of Eurus' blasts,
Would even now be waiting for its kings,
Sprung in descent from me through Charles and
If evil rule—that scourge of all who live ⌊Rudolf,
Beneath its tyranny—had not enraged
Palemro's mob to cry: 'Death to the French!'
And if my brother had foreseen this truth,
He would cast off his Catalonian greed,
In order that it should not do him harm:
For verily 'tis needful he himself,
Or yet some other man, should take good care
No further load be added on his bark.
His niggard nature, sprung from lavish sire,
Sorely needs a bodyguard of knights
Who do not ever seek to line their coffers!»

    «Because, my lord, I know that thou dost see
There where all good begins and has its end
Even as I do myself—that lofty joy
Which is infused within me by thy words,
Is all the more acceptable to me—
And too, because thou seest it in God.
Glad thou hast made me; in like manner now
Explain to me this doubt sprung from thy words:
'How from sweet seed can issue bitterness?'»

    Thus I. And he: «If I can show thee truth,
Soon wilt thou see the answer plain before thee,
On which thy back is now completely turned.
The good supreme, which turns and satisfies
This realm entire, in which thou art ascending
Exerts its prescient force on these great spheres.
Within the true perfection of God's mind,
Are preconceived not only all these natures,
But also all that ministers to them.
Hence whatsoever from this bow is loosed,
Alights disposed to its predestined end,
Even as a shaft directed to its target.
Were this not so, the heaven in which thou walkest
Would so produce effects, that it would be
But ruins, never ordered works of art:

Canto 8 : Charles Martel addresses Dante and Beatrice

This could not be, if those intelligences
Who move these stars, were not themselves
⌊defective,

And he who made them so, imperfect too.
Now dost thou wish for more enlightenment?»

⠀⠀And I: «Not so; for now I see that nature
In doing needful things, can never tire.»

⠀⠀And he to me: «Would man be in worse plight
On earth, if he were not a citizen?»

⠀⠀«Yes,» I replied, «and here I ask no reason.»

⠀⠀«And can this be, if man lives not below
In different estates for tasks diverse?
No—not if your master writes correctly.»

Thus far that soul pursued his argument,
And then concluded: «Hence it is required
That man's endeavors spring from several roots.

Thus one is born a Solon, one a Xerxes,
Another a Melchisedech—or he
Who lost his son while flying through the air.

Revolving nature, seal of mortal wax,
Performs her functions perfectly, although
She acts alike on one and on another.

Hence Esau's seed is different from Jacob's;
Quirinus, though of meanest parentage,
Is whispered to be sprung from Mars himself.

If providence divine did not prevail,
One generation's nature would pass on
Unchanged, into the nature generated.

⠀⠀«Now that which was behind thee, lies in front;
But as a proof of my delight in thee,
Put on this corollary as a mantle:

Nature will fare ill, whene'er she finds
A destiny discordant with itself,
Like any seed without its proper climate.

And if the world below would fix its mind
Upon the true foundation nature laid,
Its population would be virtuous.

But ye will force into a cloistered life
A man predestined to gird on the sword,
And make a preacher wear a royal crown:
Thus do your footsteps leave the proper road.»

CANTO
9

AFTER thy Charles, O beautiful Clemenza,
Had cleared my doubts, he told me of the frauds
From which his seed would suffer later woe,

Saying: «Keep silence: let the years revolve!»
So I can only prophesy for thee
That bitter tears will follow all thy wrongs.

Already had that spirit's hallowed form
Turned back toward the sun which gave it light,
That good which is sufficient unto all.

O souls misguided, creatures impious,
Who turn aside your hearts from such a good,
And bend your foreheads down to vanity!

⠀⠀And lo, another of those radiant forms
Drew nigh, and by its outward brightening
Gave token of benevolence to me.

The eyes of Beatrice, that now were fixed
Upon me as before, again assured
That dear assent I ardently desired.

«O blessed soul,» said I, «pray grant my wish:
Afford me proof that what I think myself
I have the virtue to reflect on thee.»

⠀⠀Whereon the light, as yet unknown to me,
From out its depth whence came its earlier song,
Replied, as one whom doing good delights:

«In that part of Italia's sinful land
That lies between Rialto and those places
Where Brenta and Piave take their source,

Rises a hill, but to a modest height,
From which descended once a firebrand
To make assault upon the countryside.

From the same root we sprang, both he and I.
Cunizza was I named; and here I shine
Because the splendor of this star o'ercame me.

But I accept with perfect willingness
The reason for my lot, without remorse;

Though this seem strange unto the common herd.
  «Of this bright jewel, glistening in our heaven
Here at my side, great fame remains below;
And ere it fades, the centuries will pass:
This hundredth year shall be renewed five times.
See then, how man should strive for excellence,
So that his first life leave behind a second.
How different is the present multitude
Who dwell 'twixt Adige and Tagliamento,
For they repent not, though they feel the scourge.
But soon 'twill come to pass that Padua
Will stain the waters of Vicenza's stream,
Because her folk are stubborn against duty.
Where the river Sile joins Cagnano,
A certain lord now bears his head too high,
For whom the net already is prepared.
Feltro too will mourn that breach of faith
Her impious pastor made—so vile a deed,
That for a like, none entered Malta's gaol.
Exceeding large in truth would be the vat
To hold the life blood of the Ferrarese,
And weary he who would attempt to weigh
That vat this courteous priestling will bestow
To prove his party's faith! yet gifts like his
Will be the common usage of the land.
  «Above are mirrors—which you men call
                              ⌊thrones—
Wherefrom God judicant shines forth upon us,
And hence to us this utterance seems good.»
Here she was silent: and it seemed to me
That now she was turned elsewhere by the wheel
On which she took the place she held before.
    That other joyful spirit, whom I knew
To be illustrious, now came before me
Like a fine ruby glistening in the sun.
While they rejoice on high, their brightness grows,
As laughter comes on earth; but down in hell
A shade grows darker as the spirit saddens.
  «God seeth all,» said I, «and thine own sight,
O blessed spirit, is so deep in Him
That never can a wish escape from thee.
But wherefore does thy voice—which to the
Gives joy in never ending unison   ⌊heavens

With those blest seraphim, who veil their faces
With their six wings—not satisfy my wish?
Indeed, I should not wait for thy demand,
Could I see inwardly, as thou canst do.»
    The soul's discourse now opened with these
                                        ⌊words:
«The greatest valley that is filled with water—
Save for that sea which girdles round the earth—
Between discordant shores extends so far
Toward the west, that its meridian
Has served it formerly as a horizon.
Upon that valley's shore I used to dwell,
'Twixt Ebro and the Magra, whose short course
Divides the Tuscans from the Genoese.
The sun comes up, and sets, at selfsame time
Over Buggea and my native city,
Which made its harbor warm with its own blood.
They called me Folco, those who knew my name;
This heaven of Venus now bears my impression
Even as on the earth I bore its own.
For Belus' daughter, she who wronged Sichaeus
And Creusa, burned not more than I did,
So long as it was fitting to my locks;
Nor she of Rhodope, who was beguiled
By sly Demophoön; nor yet Alcides,
When Iole was shrined within his heart.
  «Here there's no repentance, only smiles—
Not for the fault, which slips our memory,
But for that Power prescient and ordaining.
We contemplate the art which here adorns
So great a work, and we discern the good
That turns the world below to that above.
  «But so that thou mayst carry to fulfillment
Desires that were born within this sphere,
I farther must proceed with my discourse.
Thou askest who is in this gleaming light
That like a ray of sun in limpid water,
Sparkles here so brilliant at my side.
Learn then that Rahab is at rest therein;
Because unto our order she is joined,
It bears her impress in supreme degree.
Within this heaven, where lies the very apex
Of that deep shadow cast here by your world,

She first arrived, of all those souls with Christ.
And it was meet to leave her in some heaven—
As a token of that mighty triumph
Won for mankind by His uplifted hands—
Because she lent her aid to Joshua
For his first glory in the Holy Land,
That little stirs the papal memory.

«Thy city, founded by that evil one
Who first did turn his back upon his Maker—
Whose envy has been cause of so much woe—
Makes and scatters that accursed flower
By which both sheep and lambs are led astray:
For of the shepherd it has made a wolf!
Gospel and doctors both alike for this
Are laid aside; but tattered margins show
The hours of study spent on the Decretals!
Upon these, pope and cardinals are bent;
Their thoughts are never turned to Nazareth,
Where Gabriel was borne upon his wings.
But Vatican, and other parts of Rome,
Chosen as burial places by that host
Of soldiery who followed Peter's steps,
Shall soon be freed of this adultery.»

CANTO 10

LOOKING upon His Son with that great love
Which both of them eternally breathe forth,
The Power Ineffable, the Primal Being,
So perfectly created all that moves
Through mind or space, that he who looks thereon
Can not exist, save that he taste of Him.

Now reader, elevate thy gaze with me
To look upon the lofty wheels of heaven,
Where the one motion strikes upon the other;
And there begin to contemplate with joy
The art of that great Master, who Himself

So loves it, that His eye is ever on it.
Behold how from that point there branches off
The ring oblique that all the planets bears,
To satisfy the world that calls on them.
Now if their pathway were not thus deflected,
Much virtue in the heavens would be in vain,
And potency on earth would be extinct;
And had that incidence been more, or less,
Much of this mundane order here below,
In north and south alike, would be annulled.
Remain now, reader, seated on thy bench,
And think upon the banquet spread before thee,
If ere thou be fatigued, thou wouldst rejoice.
The meat I set before thee: feed thyself,
Because the matter I shall now expound
Needs for itself the whole of my attention.

The greatest of all ministers of nature—
Who stamps the worth of heaven upon the world,
And by whose light our time is measured out—
In juncture with the region I have mentioned,
Was circling so, each day brought earlier dawn;
And I was with him, but was not aware
Of the ascent—even as a man
Does not perceive inception of a thought
Ere he is conscious of the thought itself.
Beatrice it is, so swiftly leading
From good to better, that this act of hers
Takes not a single moment out of time.

How brilliant must that inner fire have been—
Not manifest in color but in light—
There within the sun where I had come!
Genius, experience, and art combined
Could ne'er suffice to aid in my description,
So that the truth could ever be conceived.
And if our fancy is too weak for this,
'Tis not a marvel, for no mortal eye
Can gaze on light that far outshines the sun.
Of such as this was that fourth family
Of the Exalted Father, who contents them
Through His divine afflatus, and His Son.

Now Beatrice began: «Do thou give thanks,
Give thanks unto that Sun of all the angels,
Who by His grace has brought thee here alive.»

Never was heart of mortal so disposed
For prayer, so prone to give itself to God
With all good will, as I myself became
On hearing those sweet words which she
                              ⌞pronounced.

My love absorbed itself so much in Him,
That thoughts of Beatrice were all eclipsed.
She was not vexed, but smiled so joyfully
That by the splendor of her shining eyes
My fixity of mind was dissipated.

   I now saw many spirits passing bright,
Wreathing us with a chaplet of themselves,
Their voices sweeter than their looks were fair.
Thus oftentimes we see Latona's daughter
Encircled, when the saturated air
Retains the thread from which her belt is spun.
In that celestial court whence I return,
Jewels abound, so rare and beautiful,
That they can ne'er be taken from that realm:
Of these was that sweet song those spirits chanted.
Let him who has no wings to take him there
Wait tidings thence sent downward by the dumb!

   When, singing thus, those brightly blazing suns
Had gone three times around us in a ring,
Even as the stars revolving near the poles,
They seemed to me like ladies in a dance
Who pause awhile in silence, listening
To catch the cadence of a new refrain.
And now from one of them these words began:
«Since radiance of grace, whence springs true love,
Which afterward is multiplied by loving,
So shines on thee that it conducts thee upward
Upon that stair which no one can descend
Except that he ascend it once again,
None could refuse his wine to quench thy thirst,
No more than water ever could refuse
To seek its rest by going to the sea.
   «Thou wouldst know the blossoms of this
                              ⌞garland
Which, round about her, gazed with such delight
On that fair lady training thee for heaven.
One of the lambs was I of that good flock
Which Dominic has led upon the path

Where they will fatten, if they do not stray.
This spirit on my right was once my brother,
My master too, called Albert of Cologne;
And I myself am Thomas of Aquino.
If thou wouldst be informed of all the rest,
Come, follow my recital with thy gaze,
And let it circle round the blessed ring.
   «That other flaming splendor issues forth
From Gratian's smile; his work so helped both
That it gives pleasure here in paradise.   ⌞courts
And he who by his side adorns our choir
That Peter was, who, like the poor old woman,
Offered his treasure to the Holy Church.
The fifth light—the most beautiful of all—
Breathes forth such love that all the world below
Is eager to have knowledge of his state.
Reposing in it is a lofty mind
So full of wisdom that, if truth be told,
A second never rose to see so much.
And next behold the lustre of that torch
Who in the flesh beheld with keenest sight
The nature angelic, and its ministry.
Within the next, less radiant little light
There smiles that advocate of Christian times
Whose Latin was of use to St. Augustine.
   «If thou hast led the vision of thy mind
From light to light while following my praise,
Then must thou thirst to have the eighth one
Glorying in the vision of all good,   ⌞named.
Within its light that holy soul finds bliss
Who shows the world's deceit to all that heed.
The body whence this soul was hunted forth,
Reposes in Cieldauro, and it came
From martyrdom and exile to this peace.
Now farther on, behold the burning lights
Of Isidore, of Bede, and of that Richard
Whose contemplation stood above all men's.
This last, from whom thy look will pass to me,
Conceals a spirit deep in meditation—
So deep, that death for him came all too slowly.
It is the light eternal of Siger,
Who, when he lectured in the Street of Straw,
Could syllogize unpalatable truths.»

Then as a clock that calls us at the hour
When God's bride is wont to rise and sing
Matins to her Spouse, that He may love her—
That clock in which one portion drives another,
Sounding «ting, ting» with such a dulcet note
That every pious heart is filled with love:
Even so I now beheld that glorious wheel
Begin to move, rendering voice to voice
With harmony imcomprehensible
Save in that place where joy is everlasting.

CANTO
11

Insensate worldly cares of mortal man!
How inconclusive are those syllogisms
Which make thee beat thy wings in downward
⌊flight!

While some were at the law, or bent upon
The aphorisms, or following the priesthood,
Or seeking power by force or sophistry,
Or wearying themselves with plundering—
Some in affairs of state, and some fatigued
By pleasures of the flesh, and others yet
Wasting all their time in idleness—
Myself, emancipated from these things,
With Beatrice was now received in heaven.

When each one of the spirits had returned,
It stood upon the circle as before,
Still as a candle in a candlestick.
From out the bosom of that gleaming soul
Which first addressed me, and which now became
More radiant with smiles, I heard these words:
«Even as I am shining in its ray,
Just so, by looking in the eternal light
I knew thy very thoughts, and whence they came.
Thou art in doubt, and it is thy desire
That I explain my words in language clear
And comprehensible to thy perceptions,

The words where I just said, 'Where they will
⌊thrive,'
And also this: 'No second has been born.'
But here a clear distinction must be made.
«Providence—who so justly rules the world
That all created sight is overcome
Ere it penetrates within her depth—
So that the bride of Him who with loud cries
Had once espoused her with his sacred blood,
Might go to her beloved confident
In herself, and surer still in Him,
Ordained two princes for her own behoof,
To act as guides for her on either side:
The one, seraphic in his fervency;
The other, for his wisdom on the earth,
Became a splendor of cherubic light.
Of one alone I'll speak: in praising him,
My words will equally apply to both,
Because their works sought out one common end.
«Betwixt Topino and that stream which runs
Down from the hill that blessed Ubald chose,
There hangs a lofty mountain's fertile slope
From which Perugia feels the cold and heat
Through Porta Sole; and beneath her yoke
Gualdo and Nocera weep behind her.
From this slope, where breaks its steep ascent,
A sun arose to shine upon the world,
Even as the other dawns from out the Ganges.
Let him who speaks about that place not say
«Ascesi»—which is too inadequate—
But «Orient,» if he would say aright.
«Ere he had travelled far from where he rose,
He soon began to influence the earth
And make it feel some comfort from his virtue.
While still a youth, he roused his father's wrath
By following a certain dame—to whom,
As unto death, none willingly pays suit—
And in the presence of the bishop's court,
And *coram patre*, joined himself to her,
Loving her more and more forever after.
A widow for eleven hundred years,
She had remained unwooed until his time;
It was of no avail for her to hear

147

That he who fear imposed on all the world
Found her with Amyclas, undisturbed—
Nor yet to be so constant and undaunted,
She mounted on the very Cross with Christ,
While even Mary stood beneath its foot.

«But that my language should not be obscure,
Henceforth assume that Poverty and Francis
Are the two lovers in my narrative.
Their concord, and their aspects luminous,
Made their sweet love, their joyful contemplation,
Their wonder, to be cause of holy thoughts—
So much so, that the venerable Bernard
First bared his feet, then ran in quest of peace;
Yet as he ran, he seemed but slow of foot.
O rich, unknown rewards, O fertile good!
Egidius bares his feet, Sylvester also,
To follow the example of the bridegroom,
So pleasing now the bride appears to them.

«That father, that great master, went his way
Together with his bride and family
Who now had girded on the humble cord;
No cowardice of heart oppressed his brow,
That he was son to Pietro Bernardone,
Nor yet that he was wondrously despised;
But with a carriage worthy of a king,
He told his stern resolve to Innocent,
And gained from him approval for his order.

«Now after these poor folk had multiplied,
In following him, whose admirable life
Were best proclaimed amid the heavenly hosts,
The saintly purpose of this archimandrite
Was crowned with yet a second diadem,
Through Honorius, by the Holy Ghost.
And after that, through thirst for martyrdom,
And in the presence of the haughty sultan,
He preached the Christ, and those who followed
And then, because he found the Saracens ⌞Him.
Unripe for faith, he fled from idleness,
And sought to harvest the Italian crop.
Upon that rock 'twixt Tiber and the Arno,
He now received from Christ that final seal
Which two years long, appeared upon his limbs.

«When He who chose him for such goodly work

Was pleased to summon him to that reward
Which his humility had won for him,
Unto his order as his lawful heirs
He left in trust his well-beloved lady,
Commanding them to love her faithfully;
And from her bosom his illustrious soul
Willed to depart, returning to its realm,
And for his body sought no other bier.

«Reflect upon the merit of that man
Who was a worthy colleague to maintain
The bark of Peter on its proper course!
For this man was a patriarch to us:
Hence, whosoever follows his commands,
Will load himself with priceless merchandise.
But now his flock is greedy for strange food,
So that perforce it only can be found
Scattered in many pastures growing rank.
The farther that his sheep thus stray from him
And wander off afield, so much the more
Return they to the fold with empty udders.
Some sheep there are, indeed, who fear the harm
And follow close the shepherd—but so few
That little cloth is needed for their cowls!

«Now if my words have not been indistinct,
And if thou hast been giving them attention,
So that thou canst recall what I have said,
Part of thy wish will now be satisfied:
For thou wilt see the tree whence they are hewn,
And thou shalt learn why he that wore the thong
Once said: 'Unless they wander, they will thrive.'»

CANTO
12

THE very moment that the blessed flame
Had finished uttering his final word,
The saintly millstone started to revolve;
And ere it had turned once in its gyration,
Another garland closed it with a ring.

Canto 12 : The Rings of Glowing Souls

There motion matched with motion, song with
⌊song—
Song that surpassed in sweetness and delight
The singing of our Muses or our sirens,
Even as a ray surpasses its reflection.
And as sometimes across a tenuous cloud
Parallel bows appear, alike in hue,
When Juno gives the order to her handmaid,
The outer one made by the one within,
Even as the speech of that fair wanderer
Consumed by love as vapors by the sun—
Those bows which make mankind so prescient,
By reason of God's covenant with Noah
That nevermore shall floods submerge the earth:
So those two rings of sempiternal roses
Revolved around us, and in such a way,
The outer corresponded to the inner.

    Now when the dance and high festivity
Of singing luminaries flaming forth
Blitheness and tenderness, had come to rest—
At the same moment, and with one accord,
Even as our eyes, when so our pleasure wills,
Lower and raise themselves perforce together—
From out the heart of one of those new lights
There came a voice, that made me turn toward it
Just as a compass needle seeks the star.
It said: «That love which makes me beautiful
Urged me to speak about the other leader,
Even as his disciple spoke of mine.
'Tis meet, where one is named, the other too
Be mentioned: as they worked in unison,
In unison their glory should shine forth.

    «Christ's army, armed afresh at so great cost,
Was marching slowly on behind its standard,
With ranks depleted, weakened with mistrust,
When that great Emperor who reigns forever
Took steps to save His troops that were in peril—
Not as their due, but by His grace alone;
And to the succor of His bride He sent
Two champions, and at their words and deeds
The people rallied who had gone astray.

    «In that region where sweet Zephyr rises
To open budding leaves, wherewith Europa

Each year is seen to clothe herself anew—
Not distant from the beating of the waves
Behind which, when his course is long, the sun
Sometimes conceals himself from all mankind—
The happy town of Calaroga lies
'Neath the protection of that mighty shield
On which one lion mounts above another.
Therein was born the holy champion,
That ardent lover of the Christian faith,
Meek to his own, but ruthless to his foes.
His mind, the moment that it was created,
Was so replete with living virtue, that
Before his birth, his mother prophesied.

    «Now after his espousal with the faith
Was consecrated at the holy font
Where each endowed the other with salvation,
She who had given assent on his behalf
Beheld, while in a dream, the wondrous fruit
That was to issue from his heritage.
So that in syntax he might be expressed,
A spirit went from there, and christened him
With the possessive of his Master's name.
Dominic he was called. I speak of him
As of the husbandman whom Christ ordained
To aid Him as a laborer in His garden.
Both messenger and friend of Christ he proved:
The first love that was manifest in him
Was for that counsel which the Christ placed first.
Many a time his nurse discovered him
Silent and sleepless on the naked ground,
As though to say: 'Is this my destiny?'
«_Felix_ indeed was such a happy father;
Joanna—'Grace of God,' in truth—his mother,
If such may be the meaning of the name!

    «Not for the world, for love of which men toil
Following him of Ostia, and Taddo,
But only for the love of that true manna,
So great a teacher shortly he became
That he began to labor in that vineyard
Which whitens quickly if it be untilled.
And of the seat that was more bountiful
In earlier times toward the righteous poor—
Now a man unworthy sits thereon—

He asked not two or three as pay for six,
Nor for the favor of a benefice,
Nor yet the tithes belonging to God's poor,
But fought the errant world for that fair seed
Whose four-and-twenty plants are round about
⎣thee.

«Now, fortified by doctrine and firm will,
Together with the apostolic office,
Like mountain torrent from a lofty source
He started forward; and his onset struck
Among the sprouting shoots of heresy,
With greatest fury in those very places
Where resistance was most obstinate.
From him there sprang thereafter various rills
By which the garden of the church is watered,
So that its bushes grow with greater strength.

«If such was one wheel that upheld the chariot
In which the Holy Church made her defence
And vanquished in the field her civil strife,
It must indeed be evident to thee
How excellent must be that other wheel,
Which Thomas, ere I came, described to thee.
But the wheel's track, made by the highest point
Of its circumference, is now deserted:
Where stood good crust, the mould lies over all.
His family, which started out aright
And followed in his steps, are so turned round
That now their heels are where their toes should
It soon will be apparent from the harvest ⎣be.
How bad has been the tillage—when the tare
Complains the granary is taken from it!
Yet I affirm that whosoe'er should search
Our volume leaf by leaf, would find a page
Where 'I am what I used to be' is writ;
But 'twill not be a leaf from Acquasparta,
Nor from Casale: for of these two places,
One is too lax, the other one is too strict.

«I am the soul of him who once was called
Bonaventura of Bagnoregio,
Who always sacrificed the left-hand care;
Here are Illuminato, Agostino,
First to bare their feet in poverty
And wear the cord to win the love of God;

And here with them is Hugo of St. Victor;
Pietro Mangiadore, Spanish Pedro,
Whose twelve books shine upon the world below;
Nathan the prophet; and St. Chrysostom
The patriarch, with Anselm, and Donatus,
Who deigned to set his hand to grammar's art.
Here is Rabanus: at my side there shines
Joachim, the good Calabrian abbot,
Whose spirit was endowed with prophecy.

«The ardent courtesy of Brother Thomas,
And his respectful style, are reason why
I sing the praise of such a paladin:
And with me this company is moved.»

CANTO
13

LET him imagine, who would wish to grasp
What now I saw, and let him keep the image
Firm as a rock before him, while I speak—
First, fifteen stars that animate the heavens
In different quarters, with such brilliancy
That it o'ercomes all thickness in the air;
Now add the Wain, to which, both night and day,
The bosom of our heaven so suffices
That as it turns, it passes not from view.
Let him suppose the outlet of that horn,
Beginning at the very axle point
Round which the sky eternally revolves,
Had made two constellations of itself—
Like that which was produced by Minos' daughter
When she felt the frosty grip of death—
That one within the other has its rays,
And that they both revolve in manner such
That one goes first, the other after it:
Then will he have a shadow of the aspect
Of that true constellation, and the dance
That circled round the point at which I stood.

PARADISO: CANTO 13

Its glory was as far beyond our wont
As movement of that heaven which fastest turns
Is swifter than the movement of Chiana.
Not to Bacchus or Apollo did they sing,
But to those Three whose nature is divine,
Conjoined to human nature in the One.
The measure was complete, both dance and music;
And now those holy lights gave heed to us,
Happy in their change from care to care.

That luminary from within whose flame
The story of God's pauper had been told me,
First broke the silence 'mongst those souls divine,
And said to me: «Now since one straw is threshed,
And since its grain is safely stored away,
Sweet love impels that I thresh out the other.
Thou dost believe that in the breast of Adam,
From which the rib was torn to form the cheek
Of her whose tasting cost the world so dear,
And in that breast which, by the spear transfixed,
Made satisfaction, both before and after,
So great that every sin has been outweighed,
That light, so far as 'tis vouchsafed to man,
Was all infused—alike in Christ and Adam—
By that Creator who made both of them.
Hence thou dost marvel at my former words,
When I related that the excellence
Which in the fifth light flames, was never equalled.
Open thine eyes to that which I shall show:
My words and thy belief, as thou shalt see,
Lie in the centre of the ring of truth.

«Now both the mortal and immortal things
Are nothing but the splendor of the Word,
Which in His love our Father brings to birth.
That living light which so streams from its source
That nevermore is it detached therefrom,
Nor from that Love which, with the other two,
Forms the Trinity—that light, I say,
In nine subsistences combines its rays,
Itself eternally remaining one.
Thence unto the final elements
Downward from act to act it e'er descends,
Creating naught but brief contingencies.
And these contingencies I understand

To be things generated, which are made
With or without seed, by the moving heavens.
The wax of these, and that which shapes the wax,
Vary in essence; hence beneath the signet,
The living light shines through them, more or less;
And thus fruition of a single tree,
According to its kind, is good or bad,
And ye are born with different characters.
But if the wax were perfectly prepared,
And were the heavenly influence at its highest,
The seal perforce would shed its fullest light.
But nature such perfection never makes;
For like an artist she performs her work,
Skillful in art, but with a hand that trembles.

«Yet if that ardent love should e'er imprint
The perfect image of the Primal Power,
Complete perfection would result therefrom.
Thus was the earth made worthy to receive
Complete perfection of the living being;
And thus again, the Virgin could conceive.
It follows, I commend to thy opinion,
That human nature never yet has been,
Nor e'er can be, as pure as were those two.
And if I went no farther in discourse,
'How, then, was Solomon without a peer?'
Would be the question thou wouldst put to me.
But so thou mayst see clear what now is dark,
Consider who he was, and what impelled him
To make his just request, when God said: 'Ask!'
My words have been so clear that thou canst see
He was a king who asked for greater wisdom
In order to become a worthy king.
He sought no knowledge of these heavenly
If qualified *necesse* makes *necesse*;   ⌐spheres,
Nor if prime motion, by itself, exists;
He asked not if within a semicircle
A triangle can ever be inscribed
In which a right angle be not contained.
«Now therefore, if thou notest what I said,
A kingly prudence is that peerless vision
On which the shaft of my intention strikes.
And if to *surse* thou direct thine eyes,
Thou'lt see that it has reference to kings;

And they are many — though the good are rare.
Digest my words, and with them this distinction;
Thou'lt see that they concur with thy belief
Of our first sire, and our Beloved One.
And let this be as lead upon thy feet,
To make thy movements like a weary man's,
To every yea and nay thou seest not.
For low indeed is he among the fools
Who, without distinction, rashly says
Or yes or no: in either case he errs.
It happens oftentimes that one's opinion,
If formed in haste, will bend toward the false,
And then self-love will bind the intellect.

«He who would fish for truth, yet lacks the art,
Will leave the bank in vain — or even worse —
For he returns not such as he set out.
As proofs of this unto the world, there are
Melissus, Bryson, and Parmenides,
And many who went on, but knew not whither.
Thus did Arius and Sabellius,
And those who were as swords to Holy Writ,
Reflecting their true features in distortion.

«In judgment be ye not too confident,
Even as a man who will appraise his corn
When standing in a field, ere it is ripe.
For I have seen the briar show itself
Stiff and intractable all winter long,
Yet later bear the rose upon its stem.
And once I saw a vessel, staunch and swift,
Course o'er the sea for her entire voyage,
Only to perish at the harbor's mouth.
Let not Dame Bertha or old Martin think,
When they see one man steal, another pray,
That they perceive the heavenly counsels there:
The former one may rise, the latter fall.»

CANTO
14

FROM rim to centre, or the opposite,
Water will move, when in a round container,
If struck from the outside, or from within.
Into my mind this thought came suddenly,
Even as I say — as soon as silence fell
Upon that flaming spirit of St. Thomas —
From the similitude born of his speech
And that of Beatrice, who, when he closed,
Was pleased to speak to him, beginning thus:

«This man has need, although he tells it not —
Not with his voice, nor even in his thoughts —
To seek the root of still another truth.
Pray tell him if that light which decks your
Will be with you through all eternity, ⌊substance
Even as it clothes you now. If this be so,
Explain to him how it be possible
That when ye will be visible again,
The radiance will not impair your sight.»

Even as people dancing in a ring,
When urged and quickened by increasing joy
Will raise their voices, animate their movements:
So, at that ready and devout request,
The holy circles showed their new delight,
Both in their turning and their wondrous song.
Whoso laments that one must die below
To gain a heavenly life, has not seen here
The sweet refreshment of the eternal rain.

That One and Two and Three which ever lives,
And ever reigns in Three and Two and One,
Not circumscribed, yet all things circumscribing,
Three times was sung by all those blessed souls,
And with a song so sweet, that in itself
'Twould be a just reward for every merit.
And now I heard, in the divinest light
That graced the inner ring, a voice subdued,

Canto 14 : Dante and Beatrice translated to the Sphere of Mars

PARADISO: CANTO 14

Perchance as soft as that of Mary's angel:
«So long as will endure the festival
Of paradise, so long our love will flame
About us in a glorious panoply.
Its brilliancy depends upon our ardor;
Our ardor on our vision, which is great
As grace bestowed on it exceeds its worth.
When, sanctified and glorious, our flesh
Again will clothe us, we shall be complete,
And hence our persons more acceptable;
Wherefore that light which is vouchsafed to us,
And freely given us by the Lord Supreme,
That we may gaze on Him, will be increased.
Therefore our vision must increase as well;
The fervency from which it springs, increase;
The radiance increase, that flows from it.
But even as a coal will give forth flame
That yet is vanquished by its vivid glow,
So that its own appearance will show through:
Just so this light which now encircles us
Will be surpassed in visible effect
By our flesh, now covered by the earth.
Nor will so great a light fatigue our eyes,
Because our organs will be given strength
To cope with all that brings delight to us.»
So ready and alert to say amen
Did one and all appear, it seemed to me
That they evinced a longing for their flesh:
Not only for themselves, but for their mothers,
Their fathers, or for others dear to them
Before they had become eternal flames.

And lo, around about, of even brightness,
A lustre now arose beyond the first,
Like a horizon that is growing bright.
And as at early evening there appear
New objects in the heavens, so that they
Seem real at times, and then appear unreal:
Even so I thought I now began to see
New substances that seemed to form a ring
Outside the other two circumferences.

O wondrous radiance of the Holy Ghost!
How suddenly it glowed before my eyes,
Which, being overcome, endured it not!

But Beatrice appeared to me so fair,
So smiling, that it must be left untold
Among those sights my memory has lost.

After a while, my eyes regained their strength,
And I looked up—to find myself translated,
With my lady, to a higher joy.
That I was more uplifted, I perceived
When I beheld the planet's gleaming smile,
Which seemed to be more ruddy than its wont.
With all my heart, and with unspoken prayer
I made such offering of thanks to God
As was befitting His most recent grace.
And ere the ardor of the sacrifice
Was quenched within my breast, I was aware
My offering had been received with grace:
For now within two rays appeared to me
Such hosts of glowing, ruby-tinted lights,
That I cried out: «O Sun, that so adorns them!»

As, strewn with lesser and with greater stars,
The Milky Way so gleams between the poles
That even learned men are put to doubt:
Thus, constellated in the depth of Ares,
Those rays now formed the venerable sign
Of quadrants joined together in a circle.
Here memory transcends my faculties:
For there upon that cross flashed forth the Christ—
So gloriously, that similies are vain.
But he who takes his cross and follows Christ
Will pardon me for what I leave untold,
When he beholds, within that brightness, Christ.

From arm to arm, from summit to the base,
Were moving brilliant flames, which sparkled bright
When'er they came to meet, or as they passed—
Even as particles of dust on earth,
Rapid and slow, their aspect ever changing,
Will seem to dance within a ray of sunlight
Streaming perhaps in streaks across the blinds
That people, making use of skill and art,
Have managed to contrive against the glare.
And as the harp and viol, with their strings
In sweet accord, make sounds that please the ear
Of one who cannot understand the tune:

So, from out the lights that shone before me,
A melody flowed round about that cross
Which ravished me, although the hymn was
I knew it was a hymn of lofty praise,   ⌊strange.
For I made out the words, « Arise and conquer, »
Like one who hears, yet cannot understand.
So much was I enamored with this sound,
That ne'er on earth had I heard anything
That had so bound me with such gentle fetters.
    Perchance my language may appear too bold,
In that it seems to lessen my delight
From those fair eyes which satisfied my thirst;
But he who knows how all those seals of beauty
Increase in power as they are higher placed,
And that as yet I had not turned me round
Toward those eyes, perchance may grant reprieve,
From my own accusation. I speak truth:
That holy pleasure is not here debarred,
For it becomes the purer as it mounts.

CANTO
15

A WILL benign—wherein is manifest
That love which righteously inspires us,
As evil love is shown in will to sin—
Now ordered silence on that wondrous lyre,
And quieted those sweetly vibrant chords
Which heaven's right hand e'er slackens and
                          ⌊draws tight.
Indeed, how can those substances be deaf
To righteous supplication, who were mute
Of one accord, to give me will to pray?
'Tis meet that he should sorrow endlessly,
Who, seeking things that never will endure,
Divests himself forever of this love.
    As through the clear and tranquil skies at even
Startling the eyes from their accustomed calm,

A meteor will flash out suddenly,
Seeming to be a star that changes place,
Save that where it flashed no star is missed,
And that it lasts but for a single instant:
So, from the rightward arm down to the foot,
Of that cross of light, a star shot forth
From out the constellation gleaming there.
It did not pass outside its band of light,
But ran its course along that radial strip,
Even as a flame that shines through alabaster.
    With like affection did Anchises' shade
Stretch forward—if our greatest Muse speak
When, in Elysium, he perceived his son.   ⌊true—
O sanguis meus, o superinfusa
Gratia Dei! sicut tibi, cui
Bis unquam coeli ianua reclusa?
Thus spoke that light: whereat I gave him heed,
And then looked back again toward my lady.
    Upon both sides, my eyes were wonderstruck:
Because in hers was glowing such a smile
That mine, I thought, had glimpsed the final
Of grace vouchsafed to me in paradise.   ⌊depths
    Thereafter, pleasing both to eye and ear,
The spirit added to his earlier speech
In language so profound, I grasped it not.
Nor did he hide himself from me by choice,
But by necessity, because his thoughts
Were far above the range of mortal mind.
But later, when the bow of his affection
Had been so far relaxed that what he said
Was at the level of our comprehension,
The first thing that I understood was this:
« Blessed be Thou, in triune unity,
Who art so courteous toward my seed! »
And he went on: « My son, thou hast appeased,
Within this light in which I speak to thee,
A hunger—pleasant and of long duration—
Derived from reading in that mighty book
Wherein nor black nor white is ever changed,
By grace of her who plumed thee for thy flight.
Thou dost believe thy thoughts stream forth to me
From Him, the First Source, as from unity,
If that be known, both five and six derive;

Hence thou dost not ask me who I am,
Or why I seem to thee to be more joyful
Than any other in this happy throng.
Thy thought is true; for in our life above
Greater and lesser gaze upon that Mirror
In which thy thought appears ere it has formed.
But that the holy love in which I watch
With ceaseless vision, and which makes me thirst
With sweet desire, may now be satisfied,
Pray let thy voice, in confidence and joy,
Sound forth thy will, sound forth to me thy wish,
To which my answer is even now decreed.»

Ere I replied, I turned to Beatrice,
Who heard before I spoke, and gave a sign—
Which made the wings of my desire grow.
So I began: «For every one of you,
Love and intelligence became alike,
As soon as the prime equality appeared:
Because that very Sun which lights and warms
With heat and fire, has such equipoise ⌊you
That all similitudes are meaningless.
But in the case of mortals, will and speech
Have pinions feathered in a different way,
For reasons that are manifest to you.
Hence I, who am but mortal, and imperfect
Because of this disparity, give no thanks—
Save with my heart—for thy paternal welcome.
O living topaz, studded in this gem,
I beg thee earnestly to grant my plea,
And satisfy my wish to hear thy name.»

«O leaf of my own branch, and my delight
Ere thou didst come—I was thy parent root!»
Thus he began his answer, and continued:
«That man from whom thy family is named—
Who for a century has circled round
Upon the lowest cornice of this mountain—
Was son to me, and thy great-grandfather.
Truly it is meet that thou shouldst strive
To shorten by thy prayer his long fatigue.

«Florence, within the circuit of those walls
From which she still hears tolled both tierce and ⌊nones,
Abode in temperate and modest peace.
She had no necklace, and no diadems,

No fine-shod dames, nor girdle set with gems
That caught the eye far more than he who wore
Not yet did fathers worry over daughters: ⌊them.
For then the time to wed, and marriage portions,
Did not, as now, exceed both bounds of reason.
She had no houses without families;
And Sardanapalus had not yet come
To show what can be done within a chamber.
Not yet was Montemalo far outstripped
By your Ucellatoio, which in falling,
Will be most swift—even as in its rise.
Bellincion' Berti have I seen attired
In bone and leather; I have seen his lady
With face unsmeared by painting at the glass,
And those who led the Nerli, the Vecchietti,
Content to walk about in unlined pelts,
Their dames content with spindle and with thread.

«O happy women! Every one was sure
Of her own burial place; and none as yet
For France's sake lay in her bed forlorn.
One o'er the cradle kept her careful watch,
And in her lullaby, spoke that sweet tongue
Which yields the first delight to happy parents.
Another, drawing tresses from her distaff,
Told to her family the ancient tales
Of Troy, of Rome, and of Fiesole;
And Lapo Salterello or Cianghella
Would have been held as great a wonder then
As Cincinnatus or Cornelia now.

«To such a tranquil and a happy life
Among such patriotic citizens,
In such a house, in such a loyal city,
Mary bestowed me, as she was invoked
By wailings of my mother in her travail;
And in your baptistery I soon became
At once a Christian and a Cacciaguida.
My brothers were Moronto, Eliseo;
My wife came from the valley of the Po;
The name thou bearest was derived from there.
I later joined imperial Conrad's host;
He made me knight among his chivalry,
So greatly were my feats of arms esteemed.
With him, I strove against that evil faith

Whose followers usurp your jurisdiction
Through fault of pastors. 'Twas by that foul race
I was released from the deceitful world,
The love of which debases many a man,
And came from martyrdom to this repose. »

CANTO
16

How petty our nobility of blood!
If here on earth thou makest people boast,
Where our affection has but feeble strength,
To me it ne'er will seem a wondrous thing;
For there, where appetite is not perverted—
In heaven, I say—I made a boast of thee.
Thou art indeed a cloak that shortens quickly;
Unless we patch thee out from day to day,
Time goes round about thee with his shears.

With « you »—a usage first allowed in Rome,
In which her people now least persevere—
I now resumed the thread of my discourse.
Beatrice, who stood upon one side.
Withdrawn and smiling, seemed like her who
⌊coughed

When Guinevere was first surprised in fault.
I said: « You are my forefather, and give me
Full confidence to speak; and you uplift me so,
That I am greater than I really am.
My mind is filled with joy from many sources;
Therefore it felicitates itself
That it can now endure this and not burst.
Now tell me, pray, beloved forefather:
Who were your ancestors, and what the years
That in your early youth were chronicled?
And tell me of the sheepfold of St. John:
How large it was, and what the families
Within it worthy of the highest rank. »

As at the breathing of the winds, a coal

Is quickened into flame, even so I saw
That light glow warmly at my blandishments.
And as it grew more lovely to my eyes,
So, with a softer and a gentler voice,
But not in modern idiom, it said:
« Between that day when *Ave* was pronounced,
And that on which my mother, now a saint,
Gave birth to me with whom she had been
⌊burdened,

This planet had returned beneath the Lion
Five hundred times, and eighty times again,
To be rekindled there beneath its paw.
My forefathers and I myself were born
Where the last city ward is first attained
By him who races in your yearly sport.
As to my ancestors, let this suffice:
About their names, and whence they thither came,
'Twere better to be silent than to speak.

« All those who at that time were domiciled
Between Mars and the Baptist, bearing arms,
Were but a fifth of those who live there now.
But the community, which now is mixed
With Campi, with Certaldi, and Fighine,
Was pure, even to its meanest artisan.
O how much better, if those men I name
Were neighbors, rather than within your walls—
Your boundaries at Galuzzo, Trespiano!
Then were no need that you endure the stench
Of Aguglione, and that man of Signa
Who even now has eyes sharp set for loot!

« If they who were the most degenerate
Had not been like a stepdame unto Caesar,
But like a mother kind unto her son,
A trader, who is now a Florentine,
Would have been turned back to Simifonti,
Where once his grandsire as a beggar roamed;
Its counts would still hold sway o'er Montemurlo,
The Cerchi would be in Acone's ward,
The Buondelmonti in the Val di Greve.
The intermingling of her populations
Was e'er the cause of her adversity,
As gorging food will make the body ill.
A blind bull falls more headlong than a lamb;

Canto 16 : The Soul of Cacciaguida speaks of Florence

And oftentimes a single sword will cut
More deeply and more surely than will five.
  «Consider Luni, think of Urbisaglia,
How they have passed away; and after them,
Chiusi, Sinigaglia too, are going;
Then 'twill not seem so difficult or strange
To hear how families become extinct,
Since even cities have their term of life!
All your things on earth will end in death,
Even as you yourselves; but some endure,
Hiding their weakness from brief human lives.
And as the turning of the lunar sphere
Covers and bares the shores unceasingly,
So does fortune with the Florentines.
Hence thou shouldst not seem to be amazed
At what I tell thee of her citizens
Whose fame is hidden in the mists of time.
  «I saw the Ughi, Catellini, Greci,
Filippi, Alberichi, and Ormanni,
Illustrious citizens in their decline;
And, mighty as their lineage was old,
Him of La Sannella, him of L'Arca,
Ardinghi, Soldanieri, and Bostichi.
Above that gate—which at the present time
Is laden with a novel treachery,
So heavy that 'twill soon be jettisoned—
The Ravignani dwelt, from whom has sprung
Count Guido, and whoever has assumed
The surname of the great Bellincione.
He of La Pressa had already learned
How governing is done; and Galigaio
Had his hilt and pommel bright with gold.
Mighty by then had grown the stripe of vair,
Sacchetti, Giuochi, Fifanti, and Barucci,
Galli, and those who blush for the false bushel.
That parent stock whence the Calfucci spring
Had come to power; and the Sizii
And Arrigucci held the curule chairs.
  «How glorious I saw those families,
Now fallen through their pride! The golden balls
Embellished Florence with their valiant deeds;
And likewise did the ancestor of those
Who, every time your papal chair is vacant,

In the consistory now glut themselves.
That haughty race which rages like a dragon
Behind a man that flees, but acts the lamb
To him that shows his teeth or even his purse,
Was rising, but from humble origins.
Thus Umbertin Donati was not pleased
When his wife's father made him of their kin.
Already Caponsacco had descended
From Fiesole unto your market place;
And worthy were the Giudi, Infangati.
I'll tell a thing incredible, yet true:
One used to enter in the smaller circuit
Under a gate that bore the Pera's arms.
And everyone who bears the noble crest
Of that great baron to whose house and fame
The feast day of St. Thomas still does honor,
Knighthood received from him, and privilege;
Though he who puts a border round the shield
In these days mingles with the populace.
  «The Gualterotti, Importuni throve;
And even now the Borgo would be quieter
Had they been spared the coming of new
                              ⌊neighbors.
That house whence comes your own adversity—
Through its just wrath, which has cost you dear
And has prevented happy living there—
Was honored even in its kindred lines.
O Buondelmonte, wrongly didst thou flee
Its nuptials, at another's instigation!
For many who now sorrow would rejoice
Had God consigned thee to the Ema's flood
When first thou camest to the city's gates!
'Twas meet that Florence, in her last calm hour,
Should make a sacrificial offering
To that battered stone which guards the bridge.
  «With these families, and many others,
Florence I saw abiding in repose,
So that she had no reason to lament.
And with these then I saw her citizens
So glorious and just, that never once
The lily was reversed upon the staff,
Nor to vermilion changed by bitter strife.»

157

CANTO
17

LIKE him who sought out Clymene of yore,
To ascertain the truth about his birth,
And still makes fathers chary of their sons:
Even so was I, and so was seen to be
By Beatrice, and by that saintly light
That previously had changed its place to meet me.
My lady said to me: «Send forth the flame
Of thy desire, so that it may come forth
With good impression of the seal within;
Not that our knowledge may increase thereby,
But so thou may'st habituate thyself
To tell thy thirst, that thou be given drink.»
   «O my beloved root,—so high upraised,
That just as we see that a triangle
Of its three angles, has but one obtuse,
So you, while gazing on that utmost Point
To whom all periods of time are present,
Can see contingent things ere they exist!
While I was yet in Virgil's company,
Upon the mountain where our sins are cured,
And while descending to the realms of death,
Words of grave import were pronounced to me
About my future life—although I stand
Foursquare indeed against the blows of fate.
Hence my will would be content to know
What fortune may be drawing nigh to me,
Because a shaft foreseen will come the slower.»
'Twas thus that I addressed the selfsame light
That spoke to me before; and my desire,
As Beatrice had willed, was now confessed.
   Not in words obscure, with which the foolish
Were deceived, before the Lamb of God,
That takes away our sins, was sacrificed,
But in clear words and simple Latin speech
That loving forefather replied to me,

Enshrined within his glorious radiance:
«Contingencies that do not pass beyond
The bounds of your material life on earth,
Are all depicted in the eternal sight,
Yet do not take their destined course from it—
Even as a vessel going down a stream
Takes nothing from the eye in which 'tis mirrored.
Thence, as an organ's dulcet harmony
Comes to the ear, there comes before my eye
The future that is now in store for thee.
   «Even as Hippolytus went forth from Athens
Falsely by his stepmother accused,
Just so from Florence must thou take thy way.
This is decreed; the scheme is brewing now,
And soon will be accomplished by that man
Who plots where Christ is daily bought and sold.
As usual, the blame will lie upon
The injured party, in the common cry;
But vengeance will bear witness to the truth.
All things which thou dost love most tenderly
Thou wilt abandon; this becomes the shaft
Which first the bow of exile will let fly.
Next thou wilt learn how bitter is the taste
Of others' bread, how weary is the road
Of going up and down another's stairs.
But what will weigh the most upon thy shoulders,
Will be the senseless, evil company
Among whom thou wilt fall in that sad vale,
Who all ungrateful, full of maddened fury,
Will turn on thee—but shortly afterward
Their brows, not thine, will blush in shame for it!
Their conduct will show forth their brutishness,
So that it will be well to stand aloof,
And make thyself a party for thyself.
   «Thy first asylum and abiding place
Will be the favor of that Lombard knight
Who bears the holy bird upon the ladder.
And he will have such kind regard for thee,
That 'twixt you both, in asking and in giving,
That will be first which others take as last.
Now in his company thou shalt perceive
One stamped at birth with valor by the stars,
So that his goodly deeds will be renowned.

The nations are not yet aware of him,
Because his age is tender; for nine years
These spheres have wheeled about him, and no
⌊more.

But ere the Gascon cheats the noble Henry,
Some sparkle of his virtue will appear,
For he will spurn both money and intrigue.
So widely will his great magnificence
Be known, that even his enemies
Will be unable to hold still their tongues.
Look thou to him, and to his benefits;
By him will many people be transformed,
And rich and poor put in each other's places.
Within thy memory thou shalt bear off
Some news of him—which thou must not reveal!»
    Then he told me things incredible,
And added: «Son, this is the explanation
Of what was told to thee; these are the snares
That lie in wait for thee a few years hence.
And yet I will not have thee hate thy neighbors;
Thy life shall have a future far beyond
The just chastisement of their perfidies.»
    As soon as by his silence that blest shade
Had shown to me that he had put the woof
Into the ready web I laid before him,
I said, like one who in perplexity
Seeks counsel from a person who discerns,
And wills uprightly, with benevolence:
«My Father, I perceive how time speeds on
To deal me such a blow as is felt most
By him who yields his spirit to despair;
And thus 'tis well to arm myself with foresight,
That if I lose the place I hold most dear,
I may not lose the others by my songs.
In passing down through realms of bitterness,
And o'er that mountain from whose pinnacle
The eyes of my fair lady raised me here,
And afterward from light to light in heaven,
Things I have learned which, if I tell of them,
Will have a bitter taste to many men;
Yet, should I be a timid friend to truth,
I fear to lose renown among those men
To whom the present will be ancient times.»

That light in which the precious treasure
⌊smiled
That I had found there, flashed its rays at first,
As does a golden mirror in the sun,
And then replied: «A conscience overcast
Or with its own or with another's shame,
Will well perceive the harshness of thy words.
But nonetheless—all falsehood laid aside—
Do thou make manifest all thou hast seen,
And let them scratch where'er the itch may be!
For though thy voice be bitter to the taste,
Yet will it leave behind good nourishment,
When in the future it shall be digested.
This cry of thine will act even as the wind,
Which smites most fiercely at the highest peaks—
And that, for thee, is no small proof of honor!
Hence have been made manifest to thee
Here, on the mount, and in the woeful valley,
Only those souls whom fame has singled out:
The mind of him who hears will never rest,
Nor have its faith confirmed, with an example
That has its root unknown and undisclosed,
Nor yet with other obscure argument.»

CANTO 18

That glass of blessedness had now returned
To his own thoughts, while I was tasting mine—
Tempering the bitter with the sweet—
When she who was conducting me to God,
Said: «Change thy thoughts: remember I am near
To Him who lightens every human burden!»
    At her sweet voice, I turned myself around;
And of the love that filled those saintly eyes
Of my consoler, I shall say no more:
Not only can I not rely on words;
'Tis also that unaided memory

Can ne'er return so far upon itself.
This much I can relate about that moment:
That when I looked upon her once again,
My spirit's longing was for nothing else.
And while that joy eternal, shining full
On Beatrice, was shedding joy on me
With its reflected glory from her eyes,
She said to me, even as she vanquished me
With radiant smile: «Now turn thee round, and ⌊hear
That heaven is not within my eyes alone!»

Even as here on earth, one sometimes sees
Affection in the eyes, when strong enough
So that the soul is wholly rapt by it:
Thus, by the flaming of that saintly light
To whom I turned, I recognized in him
Desire to speak with me a little longer.
He said to me: «In this fifth resting place
Of our fair tree—that draws life from its summit,
And sheds no leaves, but always bears its fruit—
Dwell blessed souls who in the world below
Were of such great renown that any poet
Would find in them abundant theme for verse.
Gaze therefore on the twin horns of the cross:
And he whom I shall name, will come to us
Swift as the fire of lightning from a cloud.»

When Joshua was named, I saw a light
Drawn through the cross, so soon as he was called;
Nor had I heard his name ere it appeared.
And at the name of the great Maccabee
I saw another moving and revolving;
The lash that set it spinning was delight.
When I heard Charlemagne and Roland called,
My eager gaze was fixed upon two more,
As hunter watches falcon in its flight;
And then my eyes saw passing on that cross,
William of Orange, and stout Renoart,
Duke Godfrey de Bouillon, and Robert Guiscard.
Then, as he left to mingle with the throng
Of other lights, that soul who talked with me
Proved where he ranked among that heavenly ⌊choir.
Now to the right I turned, to ascertain
From Beatrice, by gesture or command,
What next I was to do; and I beheld

Her eyes so clear, so full of happiness,
That her fair countenance surpassed itself—
Even the recent beauty it had shown.
And as by doing good from day to day,
A man perceives his virtue gaining strength
By reason of the greater joy he feels:
Just so I felt—while I was circling round
Together with that heaven—my arc was wider,
From seeing that her loveliness increased.
And as a pale young girl will quickly change,
So soon the blush has faded from her cheek
And once again her face resumes its pallor:
Such was the transformation in my eye
When I had turned, caused by the dazzling light
Of Jupiter, the sixth star to receive me.

I saw within that Jovian radiance now
The sparkling of the love pervading it,
Forming in letters, there before my eyes.
As birds, when rising from a river's bank,
As though rejoicing o'er their feeding ground,
Will form in circles, or in other ways:
Even so, within their lights, those holy saints
Were flying round about while they were singing,
And formed a D, an I, and then an L.
At first they moved in cadence with their song;
But afterward, when they had formed a letter,
They paused, and stayed in silence for a while.

Thou Pegasean goddess, who dost raise
Our talents, making them to be long-lived
Through building realms and cities with thine
Illume me, so that I may set forth ⌊aid—
Those words, so far as I could comprehend!
Display thy power for me in these brief verses!

In five times seven vowels and consonants
Those characters appeared, and I took note
Of them, as they seemed formed to me.
Diligite Justitiam were the first
Of verbs and nouns that were depicted there;
Qui judicatis terram were the last.
And then the *M* of that last word remained,
But so arranged, that Jupiter shone forth
Like shining silver overlaid with gold.
And I saw other lights descend and rest

Canto 18 : The Blessed Souls circling to form Letters

CANTO
19

Atop the *M*, and there, it seemed to me,
They sang the Good that draws them to Itself.
Even as, when burning logs are struck together,
Innumerable sparks fly up, from which
Fools will attempt to read an augury:
Just so from there a thousand lights or more
Seemed to ascend in varying degrees
Allotted by their Sun which kindles them.
When each was quiet in his destined place,
I saw an eagle's head and neck displayed
And patterned in those living points of flame.
He who is painter there, has none to guide Him,
But guides Himself; and from Him is derived
The essence of the instinct to build nests.
Those other blessed souls, who seemed content
To form a lily on the letter's summit,
With movement slight completed the design.

O gentle star! What and how many jewels
Showed to me that justice here on earth
Comes from the heaven of which thou art a gem!
Wherefore I pray that Mind, whence spring thy
And motion, that He look down and see ⌊power
Whence comes the smoke that vitiates thy rays,
So that His wrath will rise a second time
Against the trafficking within the temple
Whose walls were built with blood and
⌊martyrdom.

O soldiery of heaven, on whom I gaze,
Offer your prayers for those who here on earth,
Following bad example, go astray!

In former times we used to fight with swords:
But now 'tis done by taking, here and there,
That bread the pitying Father keeps from none.
But thou who writest only to erase,
Mark well that Paul and Peter still are living,
Who died to save the vineyard thou despoilest.
Well canst thou say: «I long so avidly
For him whose will it was to live alone,
Who for a dance was dragged to martyrdom,
That I know neither Fisherman nor Paul.»

BEFORE me now appeared with pinions spread
The lovely image that the souls displayed,
Entwined and joyful in their sweet fruition.
Each one of them was like a ruby small
From which a ray of sunlight, glowing bright,
Reflected backward till it struck my eyes.
And what it now behooves me to relate
Was never told by voice nor writ in ink,
Nor even grasped by man's imagination.
The beak spoke forth, for I both saw and heard it;
And with its voice it uttered «I» and «my»,
When in conception it was *we* and *our*.

Thus it began: «Through being just and good
I am exalted to this heavenly glory
Which cannot be surpassed by our desire.
The memory I left on earth is such
That evil men are giving it their praise,
But still do not pursue its good example.»
And as from many embers one sole heat
Makes itself felt, e'en so, among those souls
Inflamed with love, there came one sound alone.

Now I spoke again to them as follows:
«Eternal flowers of everlasting joy,
Who make your perfumes seem as one to me,
Pray satisfy, by speaking, that great fast
Which for so long has kept me hungering,
For I could find no nourishment on earth.
Full well I know, if there be other realm
In heaven wherein God's justice may be mirrored,
Its unveiled glory is revealed to yours.
Ye know how eagerly I wait to listen;
Ye also know that doubt which troubles me—
The fast of such long standing I endure.»

Even as a falcon, issuing from the hood,
Will move its head and clap its wings with joy,

Pluming itself, and show its eagerness:
'Twas even so that symbol now became,
Woven by the praise of heavenly grace
With songs they sing on high. The eagle said:
«He who turns his compasses divine
To the world's edge, and has therein devised
So many things occult and manifest,
Could not impress His power in such a way
On the whole universe, but that His Word
Must remain in infinite excess.
And this makes certain that the first proud being
Who was the paragon of all creation,
Through not awaiting Light, did fall unripe.
Hence every nature that has less perfection,
Is but a scanty vessel for that good
Which has no end, nor measure save itself.

«Therefore the vision of our intellect,
Which must perforce be one of many rays
Of that great Mind suffusing everything,
Can never, by itself, attain such power
But that it must discern its source to be
Greatly beyond what it can see alone.
Therefore that vision granted to your world
Can see within the sempiternal justice,
Even as the eye can look into the sea:
Though it perceive the bottom from the shore,
It cannot penetrate the ocean's deep
To see that which is hidden there below.
Unless it comes from out that light serene—
Which ne'er is clouded—light does not exist:
'Tis darkness, shadow of the flesh, or poison.

«Now is revealed to thee the hiding place
Where living justice was concealed from thee,
About which thou didst ask so frequently.
Thou saidst: 'A man is born on Indus' banks
Where no men live to speak to him of Christ,
Nor even any who can write or read;
His wishes and his actions all are good,
So far as human reason can discern;
Devoid of sin in action or in speech,
He dies without the faith, and unbaptized:
Where, then, is the justice that condemns him,
And where his fault, if he does not believe?'

«Who art thou, that wouldst pretend to judge
With thy short vision of a single span,
Of things that are a thousand miles away?
For one debating subtleties with me,
Indeed there would be wondrous cause for doubt,
If there were not the Scripture to direct you.
O earthly animals! O stupid minds!
The primal will—which of itself is good—
Has ne'er moved from itself, the good supreme.
Only so much is just, as matches it;
Created good cannot encompass it;
Radiant primal good remains the cause.»

As when the stork will wheel above her nest
After she has given her young their food,
The nourished brood look back again at her:
In much this way I lifted up my brow,
And so, as well, became that blessed image
Which moved its wings impelled by many wills.
And while it wheeled about, it sang these words:
«As are my notes to thee, who know'st them not,
Such, to you mortals, is the eternal judgment.»

When the Holy Spirit's shining flames
Were quieted, the voice within that sign
Which caused the world to venerate the Romans,
Began again: «No one has e'er attained
This kingdom, who did not believe in Christ,
Before or after He was crucified.
But mark you, there are many crying 'Christ!'
Who at the Judgment Day will be less near Him
Than one may be who ne'er has known the Christ.
Such Christians will the Ethiop condemn,
When the two companies will be divided,
One rich forever, and the other poor.
What will the Persians say unto your kings,
When they will see that volume opened wide
In which their evil deeds are written down?

«There will be seen, among the works of Albert,
The act which soon will set that pen in motion,
By which the realm of Prague will be laid waste;
There will be seen, as well, that misery
Which he who will be killed by a wild boar
Brings on the Seine, by counterfeiting coin;
There will be seen the pride that quickens thirst,

Canto 19 : The Blessed Souls forming an Eagle in the Sky

And so inflames both Englishman and Scot
That neither can remain within his borders.
There will be seen the luxury and sins
Of him of Spain; his of Bohemia too,
Who knew not valor, nor desired it!
And there too will be seen the reckoning
Cast for the cripple of Jerusalem—
A single virtue 'gainst a thousand vices!
The greed and cowardice will there be shown
Of him who guards the island of the fire,
Whereon Anchises ended his long life.
To demonstrate his utter paltriness
His record will be in abbreviations,
That much may be expressed in little space.
The foul deeds of his uncle and his brother—
Bringers of shame upon their noble house
And on two crowns—will be made known to all:
And he of Portugal, and he of Norway
Will there be known; and he of Rascia,
Who, to his harm, has seen the coins of Venice.
   «O blessed Hungary, if she can save
Herself from further wrongs; likewise Navarre,
If she can fight behind her mountain wall!
Now all men must perceive, as proof of this,
How sadly Famagosta, Nicosia
Bewail themselves, and cry their woes aloud,
Because their beast runs headlong with the rest.»

CANTO 20

WHEN he who sheds his light on all the world
Has sunk so far below our hemisphere
That daylight fades away on every side,
The heavens erewhile illumined by his beams
Are set ablaze again with many lights,
That shine by virtue of the sun alone.
This act of heaven came now to my recall,

When that fair emblem of the world's great men
Became all silent in its sacred beak,
Because those living splendors, every one
More brilliant than before, commenced to sing;
Their songs have fallen from my memory.
Sweet Love, enmantled in a glorious smile!
How ardent didst thou seem in those soft flutes,
Inspired by naught but breath of holy thoughts!
   And now, as soon as those effulgent jewels
With which the sixth bright planet was bedecked,
Had hushed the music of their saintly chimes,
I seemed to hear the murmur of a stream
That falls down crystal-clear from rock to rock,
Showing the wealth of waters at its source.
As sound is modulated on a lute
By fingering the strings upon its neck—
Or at the vent, in playing on a bagpipe—
'Twas even thus, without delay or pause,
The eagle's murmuring rose through its neck,
As though resounding in a hollow space.
There it was transformed into a voice,
And thence it issued through the beak, to form
The words my heart was waiting to receive.
   It now began: «That part of me which sees,
And which, in mortal eagles, braves the sun,
Must now command thy undistracted gaze,
Because, of all the lights composing me,
Those flames wherewith my eye gleams in my ⌊head
Are loftiest, in all of their degrees.
For he who as the pupil shines therein,
Was that great singer of the Holy Spirit
Who moved the ark about from town to town;
And now he knows the merit of his song,
So far as it proceeded from his heart,
By his reward, which is proportionate.
And of those five who form my eyelid's circle,
That one who glistens nearest to my beak
Gave comfort to the widow for her son.
And now he knows, forsooth, how dear it costs
To turn from Christ—from his experience
Of this sweet life, and of its opposite.
   «He who follows on the upper arc
Of that circumference of which I speak,

Delayed his death by his true penitence.
Now he perceives that God's eternal judgment
Is altered not when on the earth below
A worthy prayer postpones it for a day.
The next—with good intent that bore bad fruit—
Gave place unto the pastor, having made
Himself, with me and all the laws, a Greek.
He knows now that the evil which has sprung
From his good work, to him has not been hurtful,
Although thereby the world might be destroyed.
He whom thou seest on the downward arc
Was William, whom that verdant land bewails
Which weeps so long as Charles and Frederick live.
And here he knows how highly heaven prizes
A ruler who is just; he shows it forth
Even now, by aspect of his radiance bright.
But who would credit, in the erring world,
That fifth among this saintly arc of lights
Is Ripheus, the knight who fought for Troy?
He now knows much about the grace divine
That worldly intellect can ne'er discern;
Though even he can never plumb its depths.»

    As seems the lark, that soars upon the air
First singing, and then silent and content
With the last sweetness of her own glad song,
That image of the Eternal Pleasure's imprint
Whose will ordains that everything shall be
That which it is, did then appear to me.
Although my doubt and I were just as close
As colored coating to a piece of glass,
It would not suffer me to wait in silence.
«What things are these?» came rushing from my
                                ⌊lips
As though impelled by force of its own weight.

    Then I beheld a festival of lights;
And now, with even more enkindled eye,
The blessed emblem made reply to me,
To keep me from bewildering suspense:
«I see that thou believest in these things
Because I say them, seeing not the *how*:
Although believed in, still they lie concealed.
Thou art like one who knows a thing by name,
But is unable to conceive its essence,

If some one else reveal it not to him.
Regnum cœlorum suffers violence
From burning love, as well as living hope,
Which overcomes the will divine itself:
Not in the way that man prevails o'er man,
It lets itself be conquered willingly,
And being conquered, conquers by its goodness.
    «The first and fifth who flame upon my brow
Cause thee to wonder, when thou dost perceive
That they adorn the region of the angels.
They did not leave their bodies—as thou
                                ⌊thinkest—
As gentiles, but as Christians firm of faith
In Christ that died, or Christ that was to die.
For one of them returned to flesh from hell—
Whence none comes back through thirst for
                                ⌊righteousness—
And this was recompense for living hope
That placed its strength in orisons to God
For his resuscitation, that his will
Might be employed for good upon the earth.
That glorious spirit—his of whom I speak—
Returning for a while into the flesh,
Had faith in Him who has the power to help;
And in believing, burned with such true love
Than when the spirit died a second time,
'Twas worthy of this joyful state of bliss.
    «The other spirit—through the grace that
                                ⌊springs
From well so deep that never mortal creature
Has gazed within the sources whence it flows,
Set all his love on justice in the world;
Wherefore, from grace to grace, Almighty God
Opened his eye to see salvation's way.
Thus he believed in it, and from that time
No longer could endure the pagan stench,
But e'er reproved the heathen for their folly.
And those three ladies by the right-hand wheel
For him were sanction of baptismal rite
A thousand years before its institution.
    «Presdestination! O how far removed
Thy root lies from the cognizance of those
Who do not see the first cause as a whole!

Ye mortals, have a care in how ye judge;
For even we ourselves, who look on God,
Do not as yet know all of the elect.
This lack of knowledge is the sweeter for us,
Because our good is fashioned in this good:
Thus what God wills, we also will ourselves.»

    In such a manner, by that holy image,
To clarify my faulty human sight,
Sweet medicine was given unto me.
And as a skillful player upon the lute
Accompanies a singer on its strings,
Whereby the singing gives still more delight:
Even so, while it was speaking, I recall
That I perceived the pair of radiant souls
Moving their flames in concord with their words,
Just as the eyes are moved in unison.

CANTO
21

ALREADY were my eyes again directed
Upon my lady's face — so too my mind,
That was removed from every other thought.
She was not smiling; but she said to me:
«Were I to smile, thou wouldst become, I think,
Even as Semele, when she was burned to ash;
Because my beauty, which is more enkindled,
As thou hast seen, the higher one ascends
The stairway to the everlasting halls,
Would blaze so bright that its untempered rays
Might blast thy mortal vision, as a bough
Is shattered by a mighty thunderbolt.
We now are lifted to that seventh glory
Which underneath the burning Lion's breast
Shines on the earth, though tempered by his rays.
Now let thy mind keep pace behind thine eyes;
And let them be a mirror to receive
That image which will here be manifest.»

He who can understand with what delight
I gazed upon that saintly countenance
When to another care I now was turned,
Will know, by weighing one side with the other,
How pleasing then it could become to me
To do the bidding of my heavenly guide.

    Within the crystal circling round the earth
That bears the name of its illustrious lord,
During whose reign all wickedness lay dead,
I now beheld — its color like to gold
In the sun's rays — a ladder raised so high
That it was lost beyond my mortal vision.
I saw, however, coming down its steps,
Such multitude of splendors, that it seemed
As if each star in heaven were shed from it.
And as the daws, according to their wont,
Assembling at the dawn, bestir themselves
To warm the chilly feathers of their wings —
When some will go away without returning,
And others still remain and wheel about,
Or circle back to gain their starting point:
Just so, it seemed to me, that company
Glittering on the ladder, now behaved
When they arrived upon a certain step.

    That spirit who had kept the closest to us
Became so bright that in my thought I said:
«Well I perceive the love thou showest me;
But she who signals me the how and when
Of speech or silence, now keeps still; thus I,
Against my wish, must hold my peace.» And she,
Who in the sight of God's omniscience
Discerned full well my unexpressed desire,
Now said to me: «Let loose thine ardent wish!»

    Then I began: «No merit of my own
Can make me worthy of response from thee;
But for the sake of her who lets me speak —
O blessed soul, that now remains concealed
Within thine own delight — pray let me know
The reason that has placed thee near to me;
And tell me why the sound is silenced here
Of that sweet symphony of paradise
Which in the other spheres vibrates with love.»

    «Thou hast the sight and hearing of a mortal,»

He answered me. «There is no singing here,
Even as Beatrice no longer smiles.
By the stairway of these hallowed steps
I have descended here to give thee greeting,
With speech and with the light that mantles me.
It was not greater love that urged me on;
For love surpassing mine up yonder glows,
As manifested by the greater light.
Exalted love, that makes us ministers
To serve the counsel governing the world,
Assigns to each his task, as thou dost see.»

«Full well I grasp,» said I, «O radiant spirit,
How love, left free, suffices in this court
To execute decrees of Providence.
But this is what seems hard to understand:
Why thou alone, amongst these other souls,
Art foreordained to carry out this office.»
Now barely had I uttered these last words,
Before the light turned swiftly round and round,
Just as a millstone whirls about its hub.

Then, from within, the loving spirit said:
«The light divine is focused here on me,
And pierces through this flame with which I burn;
Its potency, conjoined with my own vision,
Exalts me here so far above myself
That I can see the essence whence it flows.
From it proceeds the joy with which I burn.
In just proportion, as my sight is clear,
Do I increase the clearness of my flame.
Neither that soul which has most light from God,
Nor yet that seraph who most fixedly
Gazes on Him, could answer thy demand:
For what thou askest is so deeply sunk
Within the depth of the eternal statute
That 'tis cut off from all created sight.
When thou returnest to the mortal world,
Take back this truth with thee, so that no more
Will it presume this mystery to solve.
The mind that here glows bright, on earth is ⌊smoky;
Consider then, how can it do below
What here it cannot do, though raised to heaven?»
Thus did that soul's discourse prescribe to me;
I drew me back, abandoning my question,

And merely asked him humbly who he was.

«Between the two Italian shores there rise,
Near to thy fatherland, two mountain crags,
So high that thunder far below them rolls.
They form a ridge that men call Catria,
'Neath which a hermitage is consecrated,
Devoted once to praise of God alone.»
In this wise he again commenced to speak;
And then continuing, he added: «There
I was so steadfast in the work of God
That, nourishing myself with olive juice,
I comfortably lived through frost and heat,
Happy with my thoughts in contemplation.
The cloister used to yield abundant harvest
For these heavens, but now it is so bare
As shortly must perforce be brought to light.
Within those walls, I was Pier Damiano;
Pier Peccatore was I in the house
Of Blessed Mary, on the Adriatic.

«Not much of mortal life remained to me
When I was summoned forth to don the hat
Which ever is passed on from bad to worse.
For Cephas, and the Vessel of the Lord
Walked lean and barefoot on their sainted way,
Taking their food from any house that chanced;
But modern pastors need on every side
Some folk to prop them up, and some to lead them
And lift their trains—so fat are they become!
And now they spread their mantles on their
⌊palfreys,
So that two beasts are covered with one hide.
O Patience! How canst thou endure so much?»

When this was said, I saw some other lights
Descend from step to step, and whirl about;
And every turn made them more glorious.
They gathered round that spirit, and stood still,
Uttering a cry of such intensity
That here on earth its like could not be found:
Its crashing thunder robbed me of all sense.

166

CANTO
22

BEWILDERED, I now turned me to my guide,
Like a small child that always seeks a refuge
Wherever it may have most confidence.
And she, much as a mother who will soothe
Her pale and breathless boy with her sweet voice,
The sound of which brings back his courage, said:
«Knowest thou not that thou art now in heaven?
And knowest thou not that all of heaven is holy—
That what is done here comes from righteous zeal?
What change in thee the singing would have
⌊wrought—

And I, if I had smiled—thou now canst judge,
Because the cry has troubled thee so greatly;
And hadst thou understood that shout of prayer,
That vengeance would already be revealed
Which thou wilt surely see before thou diest.
The sword flashed from on high cuts not in haste,
Nor tardily, save in the mind of him
Who yearns for it, or waits for it in fear.
But turn thyself to look on other sights:
For thou wilt see some souls of great renown,
If thou turn back thine eyes as I desire.»

As was her pleasure, so I turned my gaze,
And saw a multitude of flaming spheres,
Each enhancing others by its radiance.
I stood like one repressing in himself
The point of his desire, who dares not ask
For fear lest his presumption be too great.

The largest and most lustrous of those pearls
Came forward from the throng, to satisfy
My inner longing for enlightenment.
From out its depths I heard: «Wert thou to see
The love that burns here, as I do myself,
Thy thoughts would soon express themselves in
⌊words;

But that by waiting thou mayst not retard
Thy high endeavor, I will make reply
To satisfy thy thought which is concealed.
«The mountain on whose slope Cassino lies,
In times of old was peopled on its summit
By a deluded and an evil race;
And I am he who to that spot first bore
The name of Him who introduced on earth
That truth which has exalted us so high.
Such abundant grace shone forth upon me
That I persuaded all the neighboring towns
To leave their impious and misleading ways.
These souls were men of lives contemplative,
Enkindled by that ardor which incites
Holy fruits and flowers to germinate.
Here is Macarius, and Romualdus;
Here are my brethren who with steadfast hearts
Forever in the cloister kept their feet.»

And I to him: «The love which thou dost show
In speaking with me, and the kindliness
That I can see and note in all your ardors,
Have made my confidence expand itself—
Just as the sun so acts upon the rose
That it will open to its full extent.
Hence I entreat thee, father, to assure me
If I may hope to be allowed such joy,
That I may see thee with uncovered face.»

He answered: «Brother, thy exalted wish
Will be fulfilled above in that last sphere
Where all desires, both thine and mine, are
There all desire is perfect and mature, ⌊granted.
There every wish is whole, and there alone
Each part remains where it has always been;
'Tis not in space, nor turns on any pole.
This our ladder reaches up to it;
Therefore it fades away beyond thy view.
To those great heights, even to its topmost part,
Jacob the Patriarch saw it extend,
When, bright with angels, it appeared to him.
But to ascend it, none now lifts his feet
From off the earth; for in these times, my Rule
A worthless scrap of paper oft is held.
«The walls that once enclosed a holy abbey

167

Now shelter robbers' dens; the saintly cowls
Are now but sacks filled with corrupted meal!
Foul usury does not so rear its head
Against whatever pleases God the most,
As does that fruit which so has turned monks'
⌊hearts.

For whatsoe'er the church holds in its keeping,
Belongs to those who ask it in God's name,
Not to the families, or worse, of monks.
The flesh of mortals is so delicate,
'Tis not enough to make a good beginning
That will not last till oaks their acorns yield.

«Peter began with neither gold nor silver,
And I myself, with fasting and with prayers;
Francis with humility, to found
His convent; if thou seek the start of each,
And look again where it has gone astray,
Thou soon wilt see how white is changed to black!
But Jordan running backward in its course,
Or even the sea in flight before God's will,
Were marvels greater than a rescue here!»

When he had spoken thus, he drew away
To join his company, which closed its ranks;
Then, like a whirlwind, all were rapt on high.
Now my sweet lady, by the merest sign,
Urged me to go behind them up that ladder—
So did her virtue influence my will.
Never on earth, where one goes up and down
By natural laws, was motion of such speed
As that with which I took my upward flight.

O reader—as I hope I may return
To see that holy triumph, to which end
I oft bewail my sins and beat my breast—
I saw that sign which follows after Taurus,
And found myself within it, quicker far
Than thou wouldst draw thy finger from the fire.

O glorious stars! O light of mighty power,
The source whence all my genius is derived,
As I acknowledge—whatsoe'er it be!
He who is sire of every mortal life,
With you was rising, and with you was setting,
When first I felt and breathed the Tuscan air;
And now again, when I was given grace

To enter into your exalted sphere,
Your region was the place allotted me.
To you my spirit now devoutly prays
That it be given power to carry out
The mighty enterprise which lies before it.

«Thou art so near to ultimate salvation,»
Said Beatrice to me, «it now behooves thee
To see thou keep thine eyes both clear and sharp.
And therefore ere thou farther enter in,
Look down again upon the mighty world
Which I have here set out beneath thy feet,
So that thy heart, in all its utmost joy,
May show itself to the triumphant throng
Exulting here in this ethereal round.»

Through all those seven spheres that I had
⌊crossed

I gazed again, and saw our earthly globe—
So paltry that I smiled at its expanse.
For I appraise that counsel best of all
Which holds our earth to be of least account;
And he who elsewhere looks is right indeed.
I saw the shining daughter of Latona
Without that shadow which had made me think,
A while ago, that she was rare and dense.
The aspect of thy son, Hyperion,
I here sustained; and round about him moved,
As I could see, both Maia and Dione.
The tempering influence of Jupiter
Appeared to me, betwixt his sire and son;
Their different motions I could understand.

The seven spheres were all displayed to me—
How vast is their extent, how great their speed,
How far apart they are in their abodes.
As I revolved with those immortal twins,
I saw entire, with hills and river mouths,
That trivial threshing floor which maddens us;
And then my eyes sought those of Beatrice.

CANTO
23

Just as a bird, among the cherished branches,
Will sit upon the nest to watch her brood
The whole night long, when darkness hides all
⌊things,
And then, in search of food to nourish them—
A task whose heavy toil seems her delight—
Flies forth betimes to perch upon a twig,
There to await the sun with eagerness,
Her wistful gaze intent upon the dawn,
That she may see the objects of her love:
So my lady stood, erect and watchful,
Turned to where the sun makes slowest course.
And I, who saw her rapt expectancy,
Became as one who in his longing heart
Obscurely pines, and yet becomes appeased
By the mere hope of gaining his desire.
But short indeed, for me, the interval
Between the period of my suspense,
And when I saw the heavens growing lighter.

Said Beatrice to me: «Look on the hosts
Of Christ's great triumph, and the many fruits
Harvested by the turning of these spheres!»
It seemed to me as if her countenance
Were all aflame; her eyes brimmed with such joy
That I must pass it by without description.

As, when the moon is full in sky serene,
Trivia shines among the eternal nymphs
That everywhere adorn the firmament,
I saw, above a myriad of lustres,
A sun that seemed to fill them all with light,
Just as our sun illumines all the stars;
And through that living light the radiant
⌊substance

Beamed so transparently upon my face
That I could not endure the sight of it.

O Beatrice, thou gentle, blessed guide!
She turned and said: «That which o'erpowers
⌊thee

Is might against which naught can shield itself;
For therein is the wisdom and the power
That cleared for men the path 'twixt heaven and
⌊earth—
That path for which mankind had yearned so
⌊long.»

Just as lightning leaps from out a cloud
Because, expanding, it can not remain there,
And contrary to nature, falls to earth:
Even thus my mind, so suddenly enlarged
Amid those heavenly viands, burst its bonds;
Nor can it now recall what it became.

«Open thine eyes, behold me as I am;
For thou hast seen such things, that thou art able
Now to withstand the brightness of my smile.»

Like a man who still has memory
Of a forgotten vision, and will strive
To bring it back again into his thoughts:
Just so was I, on hearing her command,
So welcome, that it ne'er can be erased
From out that book which chronicles the past.
If I had now to aid me all those tongues
Polymnia and her sisters have enriched
With their sweet milk, I never could attain
A thousandth part of truth about that smile;
Nor could I e'er in song describe the splendor
It cast upon her saintly countenance.
And therefore, in depicting paradise,
The sacred poem here must make a leap,
As a man will who finds his way cut off;
But whoso thinks upon the weighty theme,
And of the mortal shoulders that support it,
Will find no fault if they should prove too frail.
This is no voyage for a little bark—
This ocean which my venturous prow now
⌊cleaves—

Nor for a pilot who would spare himself.
«Why is it that my face enamors thee
So that thou turnest not to that fair garden
Blossoming underneath the rays of Christ?

Here is the Rose, in which the Word Divine
Became incarnate; here the Lilies too
Whose fragrance sweet denoted the good way.»
Thus Beatrice: and I, for her commands
Now wholly ready, then applied myself
Again to battle with my feeble eyesight.

    As, in a sunbeam streaming through a cloud,
My eyes, themselves protected by a shade,
Have looked upon a meadow full of flowers:
Just so, I now beheld a shining host
Illumined from above by burning rays,
Although I could not see the source of light.
O Power Benignant, that dost so imprint them—
Thou didst vouchsafe to raise Thyself on high
To grant my feeble vision greater scope!

    The very mention of that lovely flower
To which I offer prayers both morn and eve,
Constrained me to behold the brightest Light.
And while on both my eyes were now depicted
The glory and the measure of that star
Which there excels, as she excelled on earth,
Athwart the heavens there floated down a flame,
Formed in a ring, as 'twere a diadem,
That circled her, and then revolved around her.
Whate'er on earth is sweetest melody,
And has the greatest power to draw the soul,
Would seem as thunder from a riven cloud
Beside the resonance of that sweet Lute
By which that lovely Sapphire was adorned,
Whose azure permeates the brightest heaven.
«I am Angelic Love, that circles round
The Joy Sublime that issues from that womb
Which is the resting place of our Desire;
I shall encircle thee, O Heavenly Lady,
Till thou wilt join thy Son, to make His sphere
Yet more divine, because thou art within it.»
Thus did the melody come to an end
While it still was circling; all the rest
Took up the strain and praised the name of Mary.

    The royal mantle of the universe
That covers all the spheres, and glows most bright,
And is most quickened in the breath of God,
So far above us had its inner margin

That from the place where now I chanced to be
I was as yet unable to discern it;
Hence my eyes had not sufficient power
To follow that bright flame incoronate
Which rose on high, after her glorious Seed.
Much as an infant, after it has sucked,
Will stretch its arm toward its mother's breast,
Because its love will flame up outwardly:
Just so did every gleaming radiance
Stretch upward with its flame, so that their love
For Mary was made manifest to me.
They afterward remained there in my sight,
Singing *Regina coeli* with such joy,
That its delight has never parted from me.

    How great is the abundance garnered up
In those rich coffers, that upon the earth
Were such good fields made ready for the seed!
Here they abide, and glory in the treasure
Gained while they wept at Babylon in exile,
Leaving behind their gold and earthly goods.
And there, beneath the most exalted Son
Of God and Mary, sits enthroned in triumph,
Together with the councils old and new,
He who holds the keys of such great glory.

CANTO
24

O FELLOWSHIP elected to the feast
Of that most Blessed Lamb, who gives you food
So that your hunger e'er is satisfied!
Since by the grace of God this man foretastes
The heavenly manna falling from your table,
Ere death prescribes for him his destined time,
Pray give heed to his intense desire,
And shed some dew upon him; for ye drink
Forever from that fount for which he thirsts.»
Thus Beatrice; whereat those joyous spirits
Assumed the shapes of spheres upon fixed poles,

And brightly flamed like comets in the sky.
　　As wheels in the machinery of clocks
Revolve, so that to him who looks at them
The first seems quiet, and the last to fly:
Just so, those whirling singers, as they danced
In different measures, made me judge their worth
According as their speed was fast or slow.
Then from one—the loveliest of all—
I saw a flame shoot forth, so luminous
That none it left behind was near so bright.
Three times round Beatrice it now revolved,
Singing a song, of music so divine
That memory repeats it not to me.
Therefore my pen omits it with intent;
For to depict the depths within such folds,
Our thought and speech are of too vivid color.
　　«O blessed sister who dost pray to us
With such devotion! By thine ardent love
Thou hast withdrawn me from that glorious
　　　　　　　　　　　　　　　　⌊sphere.»
The blessed radiance had ceased to whirl,
And to my lady had addressed its voice,
Which spoke to her as I have just related.
　　And she: «Eternal light of that great man
To whom our Lord bequeathed the glorious keys
Of these delights, for him to hold on earth,
Prove thou this man, on points both light and
As it may please thee, in regard to faith, ⌊grave,
Through which thou once didst walk upon the sea.
If he loves righteously and rightly hopes,
And has true faith, it is not hid from thee,
Whose vision sees where all is manifest.
But since this realm has won its citizens
By means of faith, 'tis well, to do it honor,
That he should be allowed to speak of it.»
　　Much as a bachelor will arm himself,
And speak not till the master sets the thesis,
With proofs to argue it, and not decide:
Just so I armed myself with reasonings
The while she spoke, in order to prepare
For such a questioner, and such profession.
　　«Speak forth, good Christian, and declare
　　　　　　　　　　　　　　　　⌊thyself:

Tell, what is faith?» Whereat I raised my brow
Toward that light whence this had issued forth.
　　I turned to Beatrice, and she forthwith
Made signs to me that I should now pour out
The water from that fount which in me welled.
I said: «O may that grace which now permits
That I be shriven by the great commander,
Grant to me clear expression of my thoughts!»
And then: «O Father, just as on that theme
The truthful pen of thy dear brother wrote
Who led, with thee, the Romans to the light—
Faith is substance of the things we hope for,
The evidence of things invisible:
And this to me its very essence seems.»
　　He answered me: «Indeed, thou thinkest right,
If thou dost understand why he has placed it
First as a substance, then as evidence.»
　　And I to him: «Those mysteries profound
Whose secrets here are manifest to me,
Are all so hidden from the eyes of men
That their existence is in faith alone,
Upon which our exalted hope is based.
Hence as a substance it may be conceived.
But from this faith, a man must syllogize,
Having no other sight; and that is why
It can be designated evidence.»
　　I heard: «If all that is received on earth
As doctrine, were thus clearly understood,
Sophistry would surely find no place!»
This was breathed forth from that enkindled love,
And then he added: «Well have we examined
The weight and alloy of this precious coin;
But tell me if thou hast it in thy purse?»
　　And I: «Indeed I have it—bright and round,
So that I have no doubt about its mintage!»
　　The light profound that shone there in such
　　　　　　　　　　　　　　　　⌊glory,
Now asked: «This precious gem, on which all good
Is founded—tell me, whence came it to thee?»
　　«The copious outflow of the Holy Spirit
That is poured forth on parchments old and new,
Forms a syllogism most conclusive,
Which has so keenly proven it to me,

That every demonstration now appears
Obtuse and inconclusive by its side.»

«The ancient premise and the new as well
That so convince thee,» he went on to ask,
«Why dost thou hold them for the word divine?»

I said: «The proof that showed the truth to me
Is in the miracles that followed them,
Since nature ne'er struck iron on the anvil.»

And then he asked: «But how art thou assured
That they took place? Naught but that very thing
Which so cries out demand for proof, affirms it!»

«If Christianity could win the world
Without the aid of miracles, this fact
Surpasses miracles a hundred times.
For poor and fasting thou didst enter in
To sow the goodly plant throughout the field.
'Twas once a vine, but now 'tis but a nettle.»

When I had done, that high and holy court
Resounded a *Te Deum* through the spheres,
With melody according to their wont;
And that great lord who in his questioning
Had led me up so far from bough to bough
That we were drawing near the topmost leaves,
Began again: «That grace which holds communion
With thy own mind, has up to now made thee
Open thy mouth as far as it is right;
Thus I approve of all that thou hast said.
But now 'tis needful that thou put in words
Thy faith itself, and whence it was obtained.»

«O holy saint, of such discerning faith
That at the sepulchre thou didst outrun
Feet that were swifter than thine own, and
⌊younger,»

I answered him, «thou askest me to show
The form of my unhesitating faith,
And likewise dost thou ask the cause of it.
I now reply: 'In one God I believe,
Sole and eternal, who moveth all the heavens,
With love and with desire, Himself unmoved.'
And for this faith not only have I proofs
Both physical and metaphysical,
But also in that truth rained down from here
Through Moses and the prophets and the psalms,

Through the Gospels, and through you, who wrote
After the Holy Spirit made you blest.
And I believe Three Persons in one Essence:
But these I hold to be so one, so trine,
That they admit at once of *sunt* and *est*.
The nature holy and mysterious
On which I touch, is stamped upon my mind
By many a passage in the holy Gospel.
That is indeed the fundamental source—
The spark that grows into a vivid flame
And shines within me like a star in heaven.»

Much as a lord who when he hears good news
Clasps his servant to him in his joy
As soon as he has ceased to tell the tale:
Thus, pouring blessings on me in his song,
When I had done, the apostolic light
At whose command I spoke, thrice circled round
So greatly did I please him in my speech.   ⌊me,

CANTO
25

IF e'er it happen that this sacred poem,
To which both heaven and earth so set their hand
That it has made me lean for many years,
Should overcome the cruelty which bars me
From that fair sheepfold where, a lamb, I slept—
Foe to the wolves that e'er make war on it—
Then with another voice, and fleece renewed,
Will I return a poet, to be crowned
At that same font in which I was baptized.
For there it was I entered in the faith
By which our souls are manifest to God,
And for whose sake here Peter circled round me.

Toward us now there moved another light
Out of that sphere from which had issued forth
The first fruit of the vicars left by Christ;
Whereat my lady, filled with happiness,

Exclaimed to me: «Look, look, there is that lord
Whose shrine men visit in Galicia!»

   As when a dove alights beside his mate,
And each displays affection for the other
By wheeling round, and cooing in soft tones:
Just so I saw one great and glorious prince
Greeting the other, as they sang the praise
Of food that satisfies them there on high.
But after their laudations had been made,
Each one of them stood motionless before me,
So blazing, that my sight was overcome.

   Said Beatrice, with smiling countenance:
«O blessed soul, by whom the bounteousness
Of this our court on high has been described!
Do thou make hope resound upon this height:
Thou showest hope, as many times as Jesus
Shed His greatest brightness on the three.»

   «Lift up thy head and reassure thyself;
For whatsoe'er comes up here from the world
Must soon be ripened in our heavenly rays.»
These joyful words came from the second radiance;
Whereat I raised my eyes up to those heights
Whose awe had kept them weighted down before.

   «Because our Emperor wills of His grace
That thou shouldst be confronted with His counts,
In His most secret hall, before thou diest,
That, having seen the truth of this high court,
Thou mayst encourage, in thyself and others
Hope begetting righteous love on earth,
Say what it is, and whence it came to thee,
And how thy mind now blossoms with its flowers!»
Thus further did the second light discourse.

   That woman of compassion, who was guiding
My untried wings on such a lofty flight,
Anticipated me with this reply:
«No child within the whole church militant
Has greater hope than he; and this is written
Within that Sun whose rays illumine us.
Hence it is granted him that he may come
From Egypt to behold Jerusalem,
Before his term of strife is yet fulfilled.
The two remaining points I leave to him—
Because they were not asked for information,

But so that he may tell, when he returns,
How much delight this virtue gives to thee.
'Twill not be hard for him, nor will he boast:
Let him reply, and may God's grace accord it!»

   Much as a pupil, willing and prepared,
Discourses on his lessons to his master,
So that his learning may be thus disclosed,
I answered: «Hope is sure expectancy
Of future glory, which is but effect
Of grace divine, and of preceding worth.
From many a star this light comes down to me;
But in my heart 'twas first instilled by him
Who was the Greatest Leader's greatest singer.
For in his lofty psalmody he says:
'Let those take hope in Thee who know Thy
                    ⌊name—'

And who could know it not, with faith like mine?
But later, thou as well didst plant it in me,
With thy Epistle—so that I am filled,
And thus on others shower down your rain.»

   And as I spoke, there gleamed a flash of light
Within the bosom of that living flame—
Sudden and frequent, just as lightning will.
«The love with which I burn for that great virtue
Which followed me until I gained the palm
And issued from the battlefield,» he said,
«Desires that I should speak again to thee,
Who takest such delight in it: pray tell,
What is it that is promised thee by hope?»

   «The Scriptures old and new set up the mark,»
I said, «that mark which points it out to me:
For of the souls that God has made His friends,
Isaiah says that every one of them
Shall, in his land, be clothed with double raiment;
And by his land he means this blessed life.
Thy brother even more explicitly
Makes manifest to us this revelation,
There when he speaks about the robes of white.»

   First, when these words were ended, we could ⌊hear
Sperent in te above us sweetly sung.
To this the heavenly choirs all rejoined:
And afterward among them shone a light,
So brilliant, were there such a gem in Cancer,

Winter would have a month of but one day.
And as a joyful maiden will arise
To join the dance—in honor of the bride,
And not for any purpose that is wrong—
So did I see that brightly glowing splendor
Draw near the two, who circled in a wheel,
As was most fitting to their ardent love.
It joined them in their measure and their song;
And my fair lady kept her eyes on them,
Silent and motionless, as 'twere a bride.

«This one is he who lay upon the breast
Of Christ, our Pelican, and for this office
Was designated from the Cross itself.»
This came from my lady: none the more,
Either before or after she had spoken,
Did these her words disturb her fixity.

As one who strains his eyes and tries to see
The sun when it is partially eclipsed,
But yet, from looking, cannot see at all:
So I became before that latest flame,
Till it was said: «Now wherefore dost thou try
To see a thing that has no reason here?
On earth my body is but dust of earth;
And there it will remain with all the rest,
Until our destined number is complete.
With both their vestments in the blessed cloister
Are those two lights alone who rose on high:
And this shalt thou report to those below.»

Now at this word, the flaming band of lights
Desisted from their mingled harmony
Made by the murmuring of the triune breath—
Even as when, to shun fatigue or danger,
Oars that erewhile have plied the sea amain,
Are at a whistle's blast all brought to rest.
Ah me, how greatly was my mind disturbed
When I turned round to look on Beatrice,
Because I could not see her—though I was
Close by her side, and in the world of bliss!

CANTO 26

WHILE I stood troubled by my loss of vision,
From out that radiance which extinguished it
There came a voice that caught my ear and said:
«Until thou wilt regain the sense of sight,
Which thou hast lost by gazing here on me,
'Tis well to win some recompense by speech.
Therefore begin: speak forth thy soul's true aim,
And count upon it that thine eyesight's power
Is but bewildered, and is not destroyed;
For that fair lady who is guiding thee
Through this blest region, treasures in her look
The power that was in Ananias' hand.»

«As it may please her, late or soon,» I said,
«Let healing cure my eyes—those gates through which,
A fire ever burning me, she entered.
The selfsame Good which makes this court content,
Is alpha and omega of each precept
Which, soft or loud, is read to me by love.»
That very voice which took away from me
The fear my swift bedazzlement had caused,
Now incited me to speak, and said:
«Assuredly this matter must be sifted,
And with a finer sieve: thou must declare
Who made thee aim thy bow at such a target.»

And I: «By philosophic arguments,
And by authority revealed from here,
Such love was bound to be impressed on me;
For good, when apprehended by the mind,
Straightway enkindles love, in just proportion
As it may harbor goodness in itself.
Hence to that Essence—so replete a source
Of every good, that good outside of It
Is but an emanation of Its light—
The mind of everyone who clearly sees

Canto 26 : St. John examines Dante concerning Love

PARADISO: CANTO 26

The truth on which this test is surely based,
Must turn in love—more than to any other.
This truth was shown to my intelligence
By him who demonstrates the primal love
Of all the sempiternal substances.
The voice of that true Author makes it plain,
Who, speaking of Himself to Moses, said:
'All of my goodness I will make thee see.'
And thou didst make it plain to me as well,
In that sublime announcement, which on earth
Clearest expounds this heavenly mystery.»

    I heard: «Because of human intellect,
And of authorities concordant with it,
Thou dost direct thy highest love to God;
But say again if any other cords
Draw thee to Him—that thou mayst declare
With just how many teeth this love may bite.»

    The holy purpose of Christ's glorious eagle
Was not concealed from me, for I perceived
To what point he was leading my profession.
And therefore I began: «All of those teeth
That urge the human heart to turn to God
Have prompted with my love concurrently—
Because the world's existence, and my own,
The death which He endured that I may live,
And that which all the faithful hope as I do,
Together with that living consciousness,
Have drawn me from the sea of evil love
And landed me upon the righteous shore.
Those leaves of the Eternal Gardener
I love full well, and in the same proportion
As goodness is conveyed to them from Him.»

    As soon as I was silent, a sweet song
Resounded through the heavens, and my lady
Said, «Holy, Holy, Holy!» with the rest.

    As a man wakes before a brilliant light,
Because the sense of sight receives the flash
That spreads about from membrane into
                    ⌊membrane,
And when he is awakened, will shrink back—
So mindless is his sudden wakening—
Until his judgment comes to give him aid:
'Twas thus that Beatrice, with those her eyes

That cast their brightness for a thousand miles,
Dispelled the motes that had been blinding me,
So that I saw still better than before;
And in astonishment I questioned her
About a new, fourth light that now appeared.
My lady answered me: «Within those beams
The soul that was created first of all
Is gazing with delight upon its Maker.»

    Much as a bough that, having bent its top
Before the blast, will then uplift itself
By its innate power, and stand erect,
So did I in wonder while she spoke.
And then desire for speech, with which I burned,
Restored my confidence, and I began:
«O fruit that wast alone produced mature,
O ancient father, to whom every bride
Is daughter and a daughter-in-law as well:
With all devotion that is in my power
I beg that thou wilt speak. Thou seest my wish;
I say it not, that I may hear the sooner.»

    Sometimes an animal within a sack
Will stir, so that its impulse is revealed
By movement of the cover, that betrays it:
'Twas thus that primal soul made evident
Through his bright covering, how joyously
He came to the fulfillment of my wish.
He said: «Even if thou tell it not to me,
I can discern thy wish, with greater ease
Than thou canst know what seems to be most sure.
For I can see it in the Glass of Truth,
Which is Itself reflector of all things,
But which Itself can never be reflected.
Thou now wouldst hear how long it is since God
Installed me in that lofty garden, where
This lady made thee fit for such steep stairs;
How long the garden gave my eyes delight;
The truthful reason for the wrath divine,
And what the language that I made and used.

    «My son, 'twas not the tasting of the fruit
Which was the cause of that great banishment,
But only the transgression of the bound.
In limbo, whence thy lady summoned Virgil,
I yearned for heaven while the sun revolved

Four thousand times, three hundred, and two
⌊more;

And while I was on earth I saw him pass
Through all the constellations on his course
Nine hundred times, and thirty times again.
The language that I spoke there was extinct
For many years before the race of Nimrod
Began the unaccomplishable task;
For no production of the intellect,
Which changes in obedience to the heavens
And human tastes, is ever permanent.
It is but natural that man should speak;
But how he speaks—in this way or in that—
Is left by nature to his own desire.
Ere I descended to the woe of hell,
The Good Supreme was known on earth as Jah,
From whom comes all the gladness that surrounds
It later was called El; and that must be,　⌊me.
For usages of men are like a leaf
That drops from off its bough, and others come.

Upon that mount which towers above the wave
I dwelt, in innocence and guilt as well,
But from the first hour to the one that follows
After the sun shifts quarter at the sixth.»

CANTO
27

Unto the Father, Son, and Holy Ghost,»
All paradise began to sing, «be glory»–
So that the strains inebriated me.
And what I saw before my eyes now seemed
To be a smile of all the universe:
For I was drunk with joy of sight and sound.
O bliss, O happiness ineffable!
O life, made whole with perfect love and peace!
O riches, leaving nothing for desire!
Those four bright torches blazed before my eyes;

And now the one that first came out to us,
Shone with a brightness greater than before.
It soon took on an aspect that was such
As Jupiter's might be if he and Mars
Were birds, and each changed plumage with the
⌊other.

When Providence, which in that place assigns
Appointed turn and office to them all,
Had ordered silence on that blessed choir,
I heard a voice say: «If my color changes
Be not amazed; for while I speak to thee
These others, thou shalt see, will change as well.
He that on earth has now usurped my place—
My place, my place that now lies vacant there
Before the presence of the Son of God—
Has made a sewer of my sepulchre
With blood and filth, whereat the evil one
Who fell from here, is greatly pleased below!»

With that same hue with which a cloud is
When opposite the sun at morn or eve,　⌊tinged
Now I saw the entire heaven suffused.
And like a modest lady, who abides
In full reliance on herself, yet pales
If she but hear about another's faults,
So Beatrice was changed in her appearance;
And such eclipse, I think, took place in heaven
While the Power Supreme was suffering.

Thereupon his words again came forth,
His voice so different from what it was,
That scarcely was his countenance more changed:
«My son, the bride of Christ was never nurtured
With blood of Linus, Cletus, and my own,
In order to be used for gain of gold.
But for the acquisition of this state,
Sixtus, Pius, Urban, and Calixtus
Shed their lifeblood after many tears.
'Twas not our purpose that the Christian people
By our successors be divided thus,
Some on the right hand, some upon the left;
Nor that the keys entrusted to my hands
Should e'er become an emblem on a standard
Borne to make war on those who are baptized;
Nor yet that I should figure on a seal

Canto 27 : *The Heavenly Host singing Gloria in Excelsis*

Affixed to bargained-for indulgences—
Whereat I often blush, feeling hot shame.
In garb of shepherds, those rapacious wolves
Are seen from here on high throughout the
⌊pastures.

«Defending arm of God! Why liest thou still?
In Gascony and in Cahors they wait
To drink our blood. O happy enterprise,
To what a worthless ending must thou fall!
But, as I think, that mighty Providence
Which fought at Rome with Scipio to save
The glory of the world, will soon bring aid.
And thou, my son—who with thy mortal weight
Art destined to return again—speak forth:
Do not conceal what I do not conceal!»

Much as our atmosphere will send down flakes
Of frozen vapors, when the sun has touched
The horn of heaven's goat: just so it was
I saw the ether now adorn itself
By sending up, like flakes, those glorious vapors
That had made sojourn with us there awhile.
My sight pursued their shining semblances
Until the space between us was so great,
It lost its power of penetrating farther.
Whereat my lady, seeing I had ceased
From looking upward, said to me: «Look down,
And see how far it is thou hast revolved.»

I saw that since the hour when first I looked,
I had moved through the sector that extends
From end of the first climate to the mid;—
So that past Cadiz I could now discern
Ulysses' foolish course; nearer, the shore,
On which Europa was a pleasing burden.
And even more of this our threshing floor
Would I have seen, had not the sun been placed
Beneath my feet—a sign, and more, removed.

My captivated mind,—that ever takes
Such sweet delight in thinking of my lady,
Now urged my willing eyes to turn to her.
If nature or if art has e'er made lures
Of human flesh, or human likenesses,
To catch the eye and thus ensnare the mind,
All these together would appear as naught,

Compared with that sweet joy which shone on me
When I had turned to see her smiling face.
And now that power vouchsafed me by her glance,
Withdrawing me from Leda's fair abode,
Impelled me upward to the swiftest heaven.
So uniform its parts, instinct with life,
And so exalted, that I cannot tell
The place that Beatrice selected for me.
But she, who saw my wish, began to smile,
With so much gladness in her countenance
It seemed that God himself rejoiced therein:

«The order of the universe, which holds
The centre quiet, while the rest revolves,
Here begins, as from its starting point.
Now in this heaven there is no other *where*
Except Divine Intelligence, where burns
The love that turns it, and the power it sheds;
Light and love enclose it with one circle,
Even as it engirdles all the rest,
And He controls it who enhances all.
Nor is its motion by another's shaped
But all the rest are measured by its rule,
As ten is by its half, or by its fifth.
How time can root in such a flowerpot,
And yet can have its blossoms in the others,
Will shortly be made manifest to thee.

«O greed, that so o'erwhelmest mortal men
Beneath thy flood, that no one has the power
Even to lift his eyes from out thy waters!
Well indeed in men the will blooms forth;
But long-continued rain will turn true plums
Into abortioned forms and blighted fruit!

«Faith and innocence are only found
In little children, and in later years
Both fly away before the beard has grown:
One, as a prattler, may observe the fasts
Who afterward, when he has ruled his tongue,
Will eat all kinds of food in any season;
Another loves his mother, gives her heed,
While yet he prattles, but when afterward
His speech is perfect, wants to see her buried.
And even so, the skin of that fair daughter
Of him who comes at morn and goes at eve,

Is darkened, though at first of aspect white.
Do thou reflect, so that thou may'st not marvel,
That there is no one now on earth who rules,
And hence the human race has gone astray.
Ere January will occur in spring—
By reason of that fraction men neglect—
These supernal rings will roar so loud
That the storm so long awaited there
Will turn the sterns to where the prows now head;
Then the fleet will run a proper course,
And fair, ripe fruit will follow from the flower.»

CANTO
28

WHEN she who holds my mind imparadised
Had thus unfolded and exposed the truth
About the present life of wretched mortals—
Then, as in a glass a man can see
A flaming waxen torch alight behind him,
Before he has it in his sight or thought,
And turns around to verify the image
Perceiving it in just accord with truth,
As music is attuned to its own measure:
'Twas even so, my memory recalls,
That I saw, gazing in her shining eyes,
Those snares which love had set to capture me.
And when I turned, whereon my eyes were struck
By all which is apparent in that heaven
To one who looks intently on its motion,
I saw a point of radiating light,
So piercing, that the eye on which it smites
Must close perforce by reason of its glow.
And whatsoever star seems small on earth,
Would seem to be a moon if placed beside it,
As star beside a star is sometimes seen.

Now at a distance that appeared to be
The space between a halo and its centre

When it is painted by the densest mist—
Thus distant from the point, a ring of fire
Was whirling with such speed that it surpassed
The motion which most swiftly girds the world.
Now this ring was circled by another,
And that one by a third, and then a fourth,
And then again a fifth one, and a sixth;
Thereon the seventh followed, spread so wide
That even were Juno's messenger complete,
It still would be too narrow to contain it.
So too the eighth and ninth; and each of these
Turned with a slower motion, as its number
Was the more removed from unity.
The more translucent flame was in that ring
Which was the nearest to the pure scintilla—
I think because it shares its truth the most.

My lady, seeing I was sore distressed
And anxious, now said: «From that single point
Depend the heavens, and all that nature holds.
Look on that circle which is nearest it,
And know it turns so rapidly because
It is spurred onward by its ardent love.»

And I to her: «If only were the world
Disposed as I perceive these wheels to be,
What thou hast told me now would be enough.
But in the sensate world one can discern
That revolutions are the more divine
As they are farther distant from the centre.
And therefore—that I may be satisfied
Within this wondrous and angelic temple,
Whose utmost boundaries are light and love—
I must hear further why the selfsame method
Does not obtain in model and in copy:
For by myself I cannot understand.»

«If thine own fingers cannot loose this knot,
In truth it is no marvel—for the cord
Has grown so hard for want of being tried.»
Thus spoke my lady, adding: «Hence accept
What I now say, if thou wouldst be content,
And sharpen thy intelligence upon it.

«These corporeal rings are wide and narrow
In just proportion to the quantity
Of virtue that is latent in their parts.

Canto 28 : The Sparkling Circles of the Heavenly Host

The greater virtue must work greater good.
A greater body holds the greater good
If all its parts are equally perfected;
Therefore this ring, which carries with itself
The universe entire, corresponds
With that one which knows most and has most ⌊love.
It follows that if thou apply the test
Of excellence, ignoring the appearance
Of these existences disposed in rings,
Thou wilt discern the marvellous accord
Of every heaven with its intelligence—
Of more with greater, and of less with less.»

    And even as the hemisphere of air
Appears to us resplendent and serene,
When Boreas blows from out his gentler cheek,
Because impurities that troubled it
Have been dissolved and swept away, to let
The heavens smile forth from all their various ⌊quarters:
So I became, as soon as my sweet lady
Had satisfied me with her clear response,
And like a star in heaven, the truth was seen.

    When she had ceased from speaking, all the ⌊rings
Emitted brilliant sparks, not otherwise
Than iron does when molten in the pot.
The sparks all stayed within the flaming rounds;
More numerous were they than chessboard squares
Reduplicated into countless thousands.
Hosannas I could hear re-echoing
From choir to choir, in praise of that fixed point
Which holds them in their sempiternal *ubi*.
Then she, who saw how much my mind was filled
With doubtful thoughts, assured me: «These first ⌊circles
Have shown thee seraphim and cherubim:
Thus rapidly they follow in their bonds,
And strive to emulate the point of Good,
Succeeding in proportion as they see.
These other angels who revolve about them
Are designated thrones of God's own aspect:
With them the primal triad was complete.
And thou shouldst know that each one has delight
Proportionately as his vision pierces
Within that truth where every mind finds peace.
And hence it may be seen how blessedness

Has its foundation on the act which sees
And not on that which loves, that follows it.
Now of this seeing, merit is the measure
To which good will and grace have given birth—
And thus, from step to step, is progress made.

    «The triad next beyond, that in like manner
Puts forth its leaves in sempiternal spring,
Safe from nocturnal ravages of Aries,
Forever sings hosanna in three songs,
Re-echoed by three orders of delight
Of which the triad is itself composed.
Within it are the three divinities:
First are the dominations, then the virtues,
And after them, the order of the powers.
In the two penultimate delights
Archangels turn, and principalities;
The last is wholly of rejoicing angels.
These various orders fix their gaze on high,
And downward so prevail, that unto God
All are attracted, while they all attract.
Now Dionysius set himself of old
To contemplate these orders with such zeal,
That he assigned to them the names I gave.
But Gregory dissented afterward;
Hence, when his eyes were opened in this realm,
He smiled, when thinking of his former error.
And even if a mortal man on earth
Declared this secret truth, be not amazed:
It was revealed to him by one who saw it,
With much other truth about these spheres.»

CANTO
29

Wʜᴇɴ the twinborn children of Latona,
Surmounted by the Ram and by the Scales,
Share the horizon as a common belt,
As long as from the time the zenith holds

The two in perfect balance, till they break
The equipoise by changing hemispheres:
So long stood Beatrice without a word,
A smile illumining her countenance,
Her gaze upon that point which mastered me.
She said: «I'll tell what thou dost wish to hear;
I ask it not, for I already see it
Where every *when* and every *where* are centred.

«'Twas not that we might gain still greater
⌞good —

Which is not possible — but so that He
Might in His radiance declare, 'I am,'
That in eternity, outside of time,
Outside of every other comprehension,
Eternal Love unfolded in new loves.
Nor e'er this was He in idleness:
Neither *before* nor *after* yet existed
When God Himself upon the waters moved.
Now form and matter, simple and combined,
Took on existence that had no defect,
Like triple arrows from a three-stringed bow.
And as in glass, in amber, or in crystal
A ray so shines that from its first small glint
No time elapses till it is complete:
Just so the threefold action of its Lord
Shot forth and took on being all at once:
No part had any separate beginning.
Concurrently with the existences
Was order made, and these two were the summit
In the world, when pure act was produced.
Pure potency was in the lowest place;
Between was potency conjoined with act;
Nor can the bond between them e'er be loosed.

«Jerome has written for you of the angels
That were created many centuries
Before the other portions of the world;
But truth is told in many passages
By those inspired by the Holy Ghost,
As thou wilt see, if thou but watch for it.
And in some measure it is shown by reason,
Which scarce could brook that those who move
⌞the spheres

Could long exist save in their perfect state.

Now dost thou know both when and where, and
⌞how,

These beings of God's love were made: and so
Three flames of thy desire are now extinguished.

«But one could not count twenty in the time
It took for one division of the angels
To reach the lowest of your elements.
The rest remained, and started to revolve
As thou canst see them, and with such delight
That nevermore they cease from circling round.
Now the true cause that brought about the Fall
Was the accursed arrogance of him
Thou sawest crushed by weight of all the world.
Those whom thou seest here, in humbleness,
Acknowledged that they sprang from that great
⌞Good,

Which made them fit for such intelligence.
And that is why their vision was exalted
By merit and illuminating grace,
So that they have a full and steadfast will.
I will not have thee doubt: so be assured
That merit in receiving grace will grow
According as the heart is open to it.

«Hence, if my words are rightly harvested,
Thou now canst contemplate without my aid
Much in regard to this consistory.
But since throughout your schools upon the earth
Men teach that this angelic nature wills
And understands, and even can remember,
I will say more, that thou canst see the truth
Which these upon the earth do now obscure
By such false teaching and equivocation.
These substances, since they rejoiced to see
The face of God, have never turned their eyes
Away from it, where nothing is concealed.
Their vision therefore is not intercepted
By other things; no memory they need,
Retaining all in undivided thought.

«On earth men dream when they are not asleep,
Believing they speak truth, or otherwise;
But in the latter is more fault and shame.
By other paths than one, do ye proceed
In your philosophy, so much do lust

And lure of outward show bear you away.
And even this is suffered here on high
With less offence, than when God's holy word
Is set aside, or in its sense perverted.
None there considers how much blood it costs
To sow it in the world, nor with what joy
God looks on him who humbly follows it.
Each one now strives to make an outward show
Offering inventions of his own
For preachers' themes; but silent is the Gospel!
One says the moon turned backward in its course
During Christ's passion, and was interposed,
So that the sun's light did not reach to earth;
While others say the light concealed itself,
And therefore the eclipse took place alike
For Indians and for Spaniards, and for Jews.
Florence has fewer Lapi, fewer Bindi,
Than fables that from pulpits now are shrieked
In every year, on every side alike.
And thus the flocks, who do not understand,
Come from their pasture fed with wind alone;
And yet their blindness frees them not of blame.
«Christ did not say to His first company:
'Go forth, to preach vain stories to the world,'
But for sure foundation gave them truth.
So mighty did this truth sound from their mouths
That in their battle to enkindle faith
They made their shields and lances of the Gospel.
Now men go forth to preach with quips and jests;
And if perchance the congregation laughs,
The cowl puffs up—they ask for nothing more.
But such a bird is nesting in the hood,
That could the vulgar see it, they would know
What sort of absolution they obtain!
From this, such folly has increased on earth
That without proof of any testimony,
To any kind of promise men now flock.
The pig of Anthony grows fat thereon,
And others too—far more like pigs are these—
Who pay in money that is counterfeit.
«But we digress enough. Now turn thine eyes
Once more to that straight path which we have
⌊left:

Thus may our way be shortened with the time.
The angels grow to such a mighty throng
That never yet had mortal thought or speech
Sufficient compass for describing it.
If thou but think on that which is revealed
By Daniel, thou wilt see that in his «thousands»
A multiple determinate lies hid.
The Primal Light irradiating all
Is thus received in just as many ways
As there are splendors which to it are joined.
Affection follows action that conceives,
Hence it is, the sweetness of their love
Will glow with heat of varying amount.
«Behold the vastness of the eternal good,
Since it has made itself so many mirrors
By which its virtue is distributed—
One in itself, remaining as before!»

CANTO
30

Perchance six thousand miles away from us
The sixth bright hour is glowing, while our world
Inclines its shadow almost to the level;
And now midheaven changes, far above,
So that a star fades out of earthly sight.
And as the brightest handmaid of the sun
Advances nearer us, in like proportion
The whitening sky shuts out each star in turn,
Until the fairest one has disappeared.
Not otherwise did that triumphant choir,
Which e'er disports itself around the point
That overcame me, and appears enclosed
By that which it encloses, melt away.
Therefore, to turn my eyes on Beatrice,
Love and the empty sky alike constrained me.
If all that hitherto was said of her
Were concentrated in one eulogy,

'Twould not suffice to tell about that instant.
The beauty I beheld was far beyond
All human measure; thus I am convinced
That God alone can know its full degree.
I know that I am vanquished on this score:
No comic poet, or a tragic one,
Was e'er so fully mastered by his theme.
For as the sun will most affect the eye
That trembles most before it, even so
Remembrance of that smile affects my spirit.

From that day I saw her first on earth
Until the moment when I saw her now,
The sequence of my song has run its course:
Now must my effort cease from all attempt
Of following her beauty in my verse—
Like any artist pushed beyond his powers!

Now she who merits worthier heralding
Than that of my poor trumpet, which must now
Bring to a close its arduous theme, spoke forth
With voice and gesture like a ready leader's:
«We now have issued from the largest sphere
Into that heaven of purest light composed—
Light intellectual, with love transfused;
Love of true good, transfused throughout with
Joy that surpasses every sweet delight.   ⌐joy;
Here wilt thou behold two mighty armies
Of paradise; and one in that same form
Which it will have upon the Judgment Day.»
Much as a sudden lightning flash darts forth
Which overcomes our sight, so that the eye
Loses its power to see the clearest objects:
Just so a vivid light shone round about,
And left me veiled in such a dazzling glare
That nothing else was visible to me.

«The love that gives its quiet to this heaven
E'er flashes forth a welcome such as this,
To make the candle worthy of the flame.»
No sooner had these brief words come to me,
Than I perceived that I was raised above
The limits of my own intelligence.
So great was my new vision's added strength
That any light which ever was conceived
Were not too bright for me to bear its fire.

The light I saw was like a blazing river—
A streaming radiance set between two banks
Enamelled with the wonders of the spring.
And from that stream proceeded living sparks
Which set themselves in flowers on every side,
And glowed like rubies in a golden setting—
Until, as if o'ercome by that sweet scent,
They plunged again into the gleaming flood,
Whence others issued forth to take their place.

«That high desire that now enkindles thee
So that thou seekest knowledge of this sight,
Pleases the more, the more it is intense.
But ere so great a thirst in thee be slaked,
Thou first must drink the water of this stream.»
Thus spoke to me that sun which gives me light.
And then: «The river, and the topazes
That enter in and issue forth from it—
The smiling flowers—are shadows of the truth.
They are not difficult to comprehend:
Defect of this inheres in thee alone,—
For thou hast not as yet sufficient vision.»

No babe, awakening later than its wont,
E'er turned its face to take its mother's milk
With greater eagerness than now I strove
To make even better mirrors of my eyes,
Stooping toward that flood which flows its course
In order that therein we may be bettered.
And even as my eyelids drank of it,
It seemed at once to change its very form,
Becoming circular instead of oblong.
Much as a crowd of people who are masked,
And then appear again in aspect new
When they have doffed their borrowed semblances:
Just so the flowers and those sparkling jewels
Were changed into a greater jubilee,
So that both courts of heaven were manifest.

Splendor of God, by whose immortal light
I saw that triumph of the realm of truth,
Vouchsafe to me the power to tell of it!

On high there shines a brilliance that displays
The sight of God to whatsoever creature
Finds its peace in sight of Him alone.
It spreads into a circle of such width,

That its circumference would be too large
To form a girdle round the sun itself.
Its whole appearance issues from a beam
Reflected from the primum mobile,
From which it takes its life and potency.
And as a hillside decked with leaves and flowers
Is mirrored in the water at its base,
As though to see itself thus glorified:
Just so, above that light on every hand,
Were mirrored, in a multitude of thrones,
All those of us who have returned on high.
And if the lowest grade reflects such light,
How vast indeed must be the amplitude
Of this great rose, in its remotest petals!
My sight embraced its fullest height and breadth,
So that the quality and quantity
Of all that joy to me was manifest.
For *near* or *far* means nothing in that region;
And where God's power is thus immediate,
The laws of nature are of no avail.

Into the yellow of th' eternal rose—
Which opens outward, rising tier on tier,
And breathes a breath of everlasting spring—
Did Beatrice—like one who holds his peace
And yet would speak—conduct me, as she said:
«Behold, the countless hosts arrayed in white,
Behold how great the circuit of our city!
Behold our seats, so peopled with the blest
That few henceforward are awaited here!

«On that great seat whereon thine eyes are fixed,
By reason of the crown placed over it,
Ere thou thyself wilt join this marriage feast,
Will sit the soul, erstwhile imperial,
Of Henry, who to straighten Italy
Will come ere she be reconciled to good.
For blind cupidity, bewitching you,
Has made you even as a little child
Who drives away his nurse, and dies of hunger.
Then one will rule as Prefect in the church
Who openly and secretly refuses
To take the road beside him and advance.
But God will not endure him there for long:
For he will be thrust downward to that place

Where Simon Magus writhes for his deserts;
He of Anaga will be lower yet.»

CANTO
31

THUS, in the semblance of a snow-white rose,
There was displayed to me the saintly throng
That Christ, with His own blood, had made his
⌊bride.

That other host—who, as they fly, behold
And sing His glory, which enamors them,
His goodness, which has given them such glory
Just like a swarm of bees, which at one time
Alight upon the flowers, and then again
Return to where their savory toil is stored,
Descended to the heart of that vast flower,
So bright with leaves, thence rising up again
To where their love eternally abides.

Their countenances were of living flame,
Their wings of finest gold; the rest of them
Was whiter than the whiteness of the snow.
When they went to the flower, from rank to rank,
They left there something of the peace and love
Which they had gathered while they fanned their
Nor did the presence of this flying host   ⌊sides.
Between the flower and all the thrones above,
Obstruct the vision, or impair its splendor—
Because the Light Divine strikes through all
According to their merit, so that naught   ⌊things
Can ever be impediment to it,
This kingdom so secure, so filled with joy,
Peopled with ancient and with modern folk,
Centres its love and vision on one mark.

O Trinal Light, which in a single star
Givest them all such rapture, seeing Thee,
Look down in pity on our strife below!
If barbarians, coming from a land

That every day is covered by Callisto
As she revolves beside her cherished son,
Looking at Rome and her great monuments,
While Lateran still ruled all mortal things,
Were wonder-struck at such a spectacle,
Imagine with what wonder I was filled,
Who came from earthly things to things divine,
From time unto eternity itself —
From Florence, to a people just and sane!
In truth, between my wonder and my joy,
I felt no wish to listen or to speak.

Like a pilgrim, who will find refreshment
In gazing round the temple of his vows,
Hoping some day to tell about its wonders:
Just so, as I walked through that living light
I led my eyes to look upon the ranks
That were above, below, and round about.
Faces I saw, conducive unto love,
Lit by Another's radiance and their own,
And actions graced with every dignity.

Till then, my contemplation had embraced
Only the general form of paradise,
Without regarding any single part.
Now with rekindled zeal I turned around
To ask some information of my lady,
On things regarding which I stood in doubt.
I purposed one thing, and another answered:
I saw not Beatrice, but an aged man,
Clad in the raiment of those glorious saints.
His eyes and cheeks betokened love benign;
His kindly mien was full of tenderness
That would be fitting to a tender father.
«Where, where is she?» I hastily cried out.

And he: «To put an end to thy desire,
I here am sent by Beatrice to thee.
Look up — there on the third array of seats
Below the highest rank — and thou wilt see her
Upon that throne allotted by her worth.»

Without response I lifted up my eyes,
And saw her as she made herself a crown,
Reflecting on herself the eternal rays.

From that highest region of the thunder,
An eye upon the bottom of the sea,

Down in the ocean's nethermost recess,
Is not so far as I was then from her.
Howbeit, this was naught to me: her image,
Unblurred by aught between, was shining clear.

«O lady in whose aid my hope is strong,
And who to save my erring soul didst deign
To leave thy footprints in the soil of hell!
I now can recognize the grace and virtue
Of all the many things that I have seen
By reason of thy goodness and thy power.
From servitude to freedom thou hast led me,
By every path that lay within thy means
For the accomplishment of such a task.
Preserve in me thy own magnificence,
So that my spirit, which thou hast made whole,
May, pleasing thee, be loosened from the body.»
Such was my prayer; and she, though far away,
Appeared to smile, and look again on me:
Then she turned back to that Eternal Fount.

Now spoke the saint: «So that thou mayst
⌊complete

Thy journey to perfection, — to which end
Prayer and holy love have sent me here,
Fly with thine eyes around this lovely garden:
The sight of it will make thy vision fit
To rise still higher through God's radiant light.
The Queen of Heaven, for whom I burn with love,
Will grant us every grace within her power,
Because I am her faithful servant Bernard.»

Even as one who from Croatia comes,
Perchance, to look on our Veronica,
And who is never sated by the sight,
But says in thought, the while it is exposed,
«Lord Jesus, Verigod of Verigod,
Was this the aspect of thy countenance?»
E'en so was I, while I was marvelling
At that great love of him who in the world
By contemplation tasted of that peace.

«O Son of grace,» he said, «this blessedness
Will ne'er be known to thee, if thou retain
Thy gaze below here, on the lower places:
Seek out the most remote of all the rings
Till thou behold, upon her throne, the Queen

Canto 31 : The Saintly Throng in the Form of a Rose

To whom this realm is subject and devoted. »
⠀⠀I lifted up my eyes. Even as at dawn,
That portion of the sky toward the east
Surpasses that in which the sun declines,
Just so, as mountain overtops a vale,
I saw a portion of the distant circles
Surpassing in its brilliance all the rest.
And as the region whence there will emerge
That pole which Phaethon once drove so ill,
Flames most, while either side is not so bright:
'Twas even so, that oriflamme of peace
Seemed brighter in the centre; in like manner,
Its flame grew less pronounced to right and left.
At its heart, with pinions far outstretched,
Were countless thousands of rejoicing angels;
Differing each in movement and in light.
I saw there, beaming with a happy smile
Upon their sports and songs, a shining beauty
That was a joy to all the other saints.
But even if I had such wealth in speech
As in imagination, I would shrink
From trying to describe its loveliness.
And Bernard, seeing that mine eyes were fixed
Attentive on its glowing warmth, now turned
His own with such affection to it, that I flamed,
With ardor new, to gaze on it once more.

CANTO
32

INTENT upon the source of his delight,
The contemplator willingly assumed
The office of a teacher, and began:
«That wound anointed and closed up by Mary,
Was opened when inflicted on mankind
By that fair woman who is at her feet.
Beneath her, in the circle which is formed
By that third row of seats, is Beatrice,
With Rachel by her side, as thou canst see.

Rebecca, Sarah, Judith, also her
Honored as great-grandmother to the singer
Who once cried *Miserere* for his guilt,
Thou canst also see, if thou but look
From rank to rank in gradual descent,
The while I name the petals, one by one.
⠀⠀«Downward from the seventh tier of seats,
And upward, sits a band of Hebrew women,
Dividing all the tresses of the flower.
Thereby they form a wall that thus divides
The holy stair, according to the view
Of Christ that those of either faith professed.
Upon this side, where all the petals blossom,
Are seated those who held as their belief
That Christ was yet to come to save the world;
Upon the other side, where thou canst see
Those empty spaces in the semicircles,
Sit those whose faith knew Christ already come.
Even as on this side, the glorious throne
Of Her who reigns in heaven, and the rest
Seated below Her, form a line of severance:
There, opposite, behold the great John's seat —
That martyr who endured the wilderness
And hell itself for two years afterward —
Augustine, Francis, Benedict, and others,
Below him, are allotted to those seats
From rank to rank as far as where we stand.
⠀⠀«Behold God's foresight, wondrous and
⠀⠀⠀⠀⠀⠀⠀⠀⠀⠀⌊supreme!
This garden will be filled in equal measure
By those two aspects of the faith divine.
And further know that downward from that tier,
Crossing the middle of the two arrays,
The thrones are filled by those who earn their
By reason not of merit of their own,⠀⠀⠀⌊seats
But that of others, in a certain manner:
For these are souls that were released by death
Ere they had power to exercise their wills.
This thou canst see if thou their features scan,
And hear the childish accents of their speech.
⠀⠀«Thou art in doubt, and yet thou keepest
⠀⠀⠀⠀⠀⠀⠀⠀⠀⠀⌊silence!
But I will loose from thee those mighty bonds

In which thou art by faulty reason held.
Within the ample confines of this realm,
No particle of chance can find a place:
No more, indeed, can sorrow, hunger, thirst.
Whatever thou beholdest has been set
By the eternal order; so that here
The ring conforms exactly to the finger.
Therefore it is, that all this multitude
Who have been swiftly garnered to true life,
Are not thus graduated *sine causa*.
The King through whom this kingdom is at rest
In such great love, and in such great delight
That man can never dare to hope for more,
Creating all our minds in His glad aspect,
Gives them grace according to His will,
In varying measure: let the fact suffice.
Now this is clearly manifest to you
By those twin brothers in the Holy Writ,
Who in their mother's womb in anger stirred.
Hence the Light on high must crown us fitly,
Awarding grace in different degrees,
Even as the different hair that crowned their
Therefore they sit in graduated tiers,   ⌊heads.
Not in accordance with their earthly ways,
But following the keenness of their vision.

 «Moreover, in the early centuries,
The parents' faith alone in Christ to come,
Combined with innocence, insured salvation.
But after those first ages were complete,
It was required that males be circumcised,
To make more powerful their feeble wings.
But later, when the time of grace had come,
This innocence of children unbaptized,
And therefore lacking Christ, was held below.

 «Upon that face most like to that of Christ,
Do thou now gaze: for its supernal radiance
Alone can make thee fit to look on Christ.»

 I saw such gladness raining down on Her,
Carried by those fair Intelligences
Created but to fly across that height,
That whatsoever I had seen e'er this
Held me not suspended in such wonder,
Nor showed to me such likeness unto God.

That love who had come down to Her before,
Spread out his shining wings in front of Her,
And sang: *Ave Maria, gratia plena!*
In answer to this canticle divine
The blessed court responded on all sides,
And every countenance was more serene.

 «O sainted father, who for my sole sake
Deigning to come to me, hast left
The eternal bliss of thy allotted place!
Who is that angel gazing in the eyes
Of Heaven's bright Queen, with look of so much
                                          ⌊love
That he appears as though he were aflame?»
Thus again I sought the blessed words
Of him who drew his beauty forth from Mary,
As from the sun the morning star draws light.

 And he to me: «All confidence and grace
Existing in an angel or a soul,
Exist in him, and we would have it so;
For he it is who bore the palm to Mary,
At that great moment when the Son of God
Vouchsafed to weight Himself with our great load.

 «But now do thou come onward with thine eye,
Even as I go forward with my speech
To name the great patricians of this court.
Those two who yonder sit in greater bliss,
Through being closest to the Heavenly Empress,
Are, as it were, the two roots of this rose.
In him who sits beside her on the left
Behold that ancient sire from whose rash tasting
Mankind has tasted so much bitterness.
See on the right the venerable father
Of Holy Church, to whom below on earth
Christ gave in trust the keys of this fair rose.
And he who ere he died beheld the grief
Of that fair bride—the bride who had been won
By virtue of the nails and of the spear—
Sits on one side; upon the other rests
That leader in whose time was sent the manna
To feed his thankless, fickle, stubborn folk.
And there, across from Peter, Anna sits—
So well content to look upon her daughter,
Who as she sings hosanna, holds her gaze.

And opposite the father of mankind
Lucia sits, who unto thee sent down
Thy lady, when thy brow was bent to fall.

 «But since thy vision's time is nearly spent,
We now will stop—much as a skillful tailor,
Who cuts the gown according to his cloth;
And we will gaze upon the Primal Love,
That, looking toward Him, thou mayst penetrate
As far as possible through His effulgence.
And yet, lest thou perchance shouldst backward
⌊slip,
When thinking to advance by thine own wings,
'Tis needful that thou gather grace by prayer—
Sweet grace from her who has the power to aid.
Do thou here follow me with thy affection
So that thy heart depart not from my speech.»
Then he began his holy orison.

CANTO
33

O VIRGIN Mother, daughter of thy Son,
Humbler and more exalted than all others,
Predestined object of the eternal will!
Thou gavest such nobility to man
That He who made mankind did not disdain
To make Himself a creature of His making.
Within thy womb, that love was re-enkindled
Whose heat has germinated this fair flower,
To blossom thus in everlasting peace.
Thou art our noonday torch of charity;
And down below thou art for mortal men
The living fount of hope. Thou art so great,
O Lady, and thou art of so much worth,
That whoso hopes for grace, not knowing thee,
Asks that his wish should fly without its wings.
And thy benignity not only gives
Its succor to the suppliant, but oftentimes

Will lavishly anticipate his plea.
In thee is mercy, and magnificence,
And pity, for in thee is concentrate
Whatever good there be in any creature.

 «This man, who from the nethermost abyss
Of all the universe, as far as here,
Has seen the spiritual existences,   ⌈strength
Now asks thy grace, so thou wilt grant him
That he may with his eyes uplift himself
Still higher toward the ultimate salvation.
And I, who ne'er for my own vision burned
As I now burn for his, proffer to thee
All my prayers—and pray they may suffice—
That thou wilt scatter from him every cloud
Of his mortality, with thine own prayers,
So that the bliss supreme may be revealed.
And furthermore I beg of thee, O Queen
That hast the power to do whate'er thou wilt,
After his vision to keep his love still pure.
May thy protection quell his human passions!
Lo, Beatrice and many a blessed soul
Entreat thee, with clasped hands, to grant my
⌊wish!»

 Those eyes so loved and reverenced by God,
Were fixed upon the suppliant, and showed
How greatly She is pleased by earnest prayers.
Then they were turned to that eternal light
Whose depth, one must believe, no other eye
Has vision clear enough to penetrate.

 And I—who now was drawing near the end
Of all desires—ended, as was meet,
Within myself the ardor of my longing.
Here Bernard smiled and made a sign to me
That I should look on high; but I indeed
Was doing what he wished, of my own will,
Because my vision, being purified,
Was piercing more and more within the rays
Of light sublime, which in itself is true.
Thenceforward, no mere human speech could tell
My vision's added power: for memory
And speech are both o'ercome by such excess.

 Just as a man who sees things in a dream,
Will still retain impression of his feelings

THE DIVINE COMEDY

Although the rest return not to his mind,
So now am I: for though my vision fades,
The sweetness growing from it yet distills
Its essence in the wellsprings of my heart.
Thus the snow is melted in the sun;
And thus the Sibyl's oracle was lost,
Written on leaves so light upon the wind.

    O Light Supreme, that art so far exalted
Above our mortal ken! Lend to my mind
A little part of what Thou didst appear,
And grant sufficient power unto my tongue
That it may leave for races yet unborn,
A single spark of Thy almighty flame!
For if Thou wilt come back to my remembrance,
That I may sing Thy glory in these lines,
The more Thy victory will be explained.

    I think the keenness of the living ray
That I withstood would have bewildered me,
If once my eyes had turned aside from it.
And I recall that for that very reason
I was emboldened to endure so much,
Until my gaze was joined unto His good.

    Abundant grace, by which I could presume
To fix my eyes upon the Eternal Light
Sufficiently to see the whole of it!

    I saw that in its depths there are enclosed,
Bound up with love in one eternal book,
The scattered leaves of all the universe—
Substance, and accidents, and their relations,
As though together fused in such a way
That what I speak of is a single light.
The universal form of this commingling
I think I saw, for when I tell of it
I feel that I rejoice so much the more.
One moment brought me more oblivion
Than five-and-twenty centuries could cast
Upon those Argonauts whose shadow once
Made Neptune wonder. Even thus my mind,
Enraptured, gazed attentive, motionless,
And grew the more enkindled as it gazed.

    For in the presence of those radiant beams
One is so changed, that 'tis impossible
To turn from it to any other sight—

Because the good, the object of the will,
Is all collected there. Outside of it
That is defective which is perfect there.
Henceforth my speech will fall still further short
Of what I recollect, as 'twere a babe's,
Wetting his tongue upon his mother's breast.

    There was no other than a single semblance
Within that Living Light on which I gazed,
For that remains forever what it was;
And yet by reason of my vision's power,
Which waxed the stronger in me as I looked,
That semblance seemed to change, and I as well.

    For within the substance, deep and radiant,
Of that Exalted Light, I saw three rings
Of one dimension, yet of triple hue.
One seemed to be reflected by the next,
As Iris is by Iris; and the third
Seemed fire, shed forth equally by both.
How powerless is speech—how weak, compared
To my conception, which itself is trifling
Beside the mighty vision that I saw!

    O Light Eternal, in Thyself contained!
Thou only know'st Thyself, and in Thyself
Both known and knowing, smilest on Thyself!

    That very circle which appeared in Thee,
Conceived as but reflection of a light,
When I had gazed on it awhile, now seemed
To bear the image of a human face
Within itself, of its own coloring—
Wherefore my sight was wholly fixed on it.
Like a geometer, who will attempt
With all his power and mind to square the circle,
Yet cannot find the principle he needs:
Just so was I, at that phenomenon.
I wished to see how image joined to ring,
And how the one found place within the other.
Too feeble for such flights were my own wings;
But by a lightning flash my mind was struck—
And thus came the fulfilment of my wish.

    My power now failed that phantasy sublime:
My will and my desire were both revolved,
As is a wheel in even motion driven,
By Love, which moves the sun and other stars.